THE
ROAD
REMEMBERED

A NOVEL

*To Camille,
Thanks for
your support. I
hope you enjoy
my story. All the best,
Kaye D. Schmitz
Kaye D. Schmitz*

KAYE D. SCHMITZ

THE ROAD REMEMBERED BY KAYE D. SCHMITZ
Kensington Studios Press is a division of Kensington Media
St. Augustine, FL 32092

ISBN: 978-0-57886-488-4
Copyright © 2021 by Kaye D. Schmitz
Cover design and interior formatting by *Hannah Linder Designs*

Available in print from your local bookstore, online,
or from www.kayedschmitzauthor.com

For more information on this book and the author, visit:
www.kayedschmitzauthor.com

Library of Congress Cataloging-in-Publication Data
Schmitz, Kaye D. The Road Remembered / Kaye D. Schmitz 1st. ed.

Printed in the United States of America

To my wonderful father, the late Herman Dykes, whose account of his time in the Army during World War II served as my primary inspiration for this novel.

To the World War II veterans I interviewed, all of whom allowed me to use their names and actual experiences as characters and plot points in my story. These heroic veterans include Erwin Davis and his late twin brother, Ervin, Army, who fought in the 89th Infantry Division, European Theater Operation; the late Cecil Reese, Army, who served in the battle of Pearl Harbor; Gloria Porter Bowie, the fifth class of WAVES, stationed in Hawaii; Mabel Toth, Canadian Women's Army Corps, who served all of her time in Canada; Joe D'Aloia, Marine, who served in the Pacific; and the late Mike Spencer, Army Air Corps, who fought in the European Theater Operation, and protected the 89th Infantry Division from the air.

And, as always, to my darling husband, Michael, my best friend, my first reader, my sounding board, the one who encourages me when I get frustrated and declare my words "garbage," and my co-collaborator through the giggles of life.

LETTER TO
MY READERS

Dear Friends,

This novel was inspired by not one, but nine true stories, as well as actual battles during the European Theater Operation of World War II. Those of you who know the history may notice I took a few liberties with both battles and timelines during the telling of this story so I hope you will read the "Note from the Author" at the end of the book to find out why.

The story first came to me not long after my father died at age ninety-three. At his funeral we displayed a map he had received when he left the service in 1945 that traced his steps with the 89th Infantry Division across Europe from LeHavre, France, to Zwickau, Germany. (See map at the end of this section.)

Later, I found the transcript of an oral history he had done with one of my cousins who interviewed him about his war experiences for a class she was taking. When they talked, they referred to the map, so as I read Dad's words with the map open in front of me, it was as if he were sitting beside me, telling me about his journey. His story inspired my character, Sam Ryan.

What struck me most about the transcript was Dad's attitude about the war. He was a nonviolent person with a soft heart, so to read about his horror when he knew that a bullet he fired had cost another person his life was gut-wrenching. I had heard some of his stories through the years, but in the transcript, they took on a life of their own and swirled around in my head until I had no choice but to write them down. I researched World War II, the 89th Infantry Division, and Patton's Third Army. The treasure trove of information cascaded down around me like gold dust and before long, I discovered

Erwin Davis in Austin, TX, who, with his twin brother, Ervin, had been bazooka gunners with the old "Rolling W," as the 89th Infantry was called. I was thrilled to find someone who had trod the same ground as my father—and who was still alive! After several Google attempts to find an email address, I stumbled on a phone number and called it. Imagine my surprise when he actually picked up. And what did I do? I started to cry. Sobbed, in fact. When I could finally speak again, I explained that I felt as if I had contacted my father from the grave. I flew to Texas and spent a marvelous afternoon with Mr. Davis and his family, where he presented me with a copy of the diary he kept during his time in Europe.

Once I started writing this story, it became my passion project. But something was missing. The novel began as a study about humanity in the midst of war, but my research continued to portray worse and worse atrocities, especially for children and the Jewish people. So I dug into war resistance efforts and discovered Irena Sendler, a Polish Social-Worker and nurse, who saved more than 2,500 children, mostly Jewish, from extinction at the hands of the Nazis. A number of stories were written about her life, the most famous of which is *Life in a Jar* by Jack Mayer. She was such a remarkable woman that a movie is being made about her life and will star Gal Gadot. Irena's life was the inspiration for my character, Gerda Zeigler.

I hope you enjoy my story and that you will also read the first chapter of the follow-on story, located after the conclusion of this one.

Kaye D. Schmitz

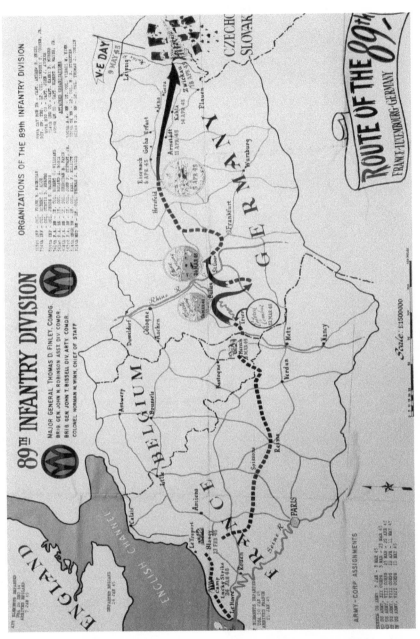

Route of the 89th Infantry Division, across Europe from its January 7, 1945, arrival in England through V-E Day just outside Zwickau, Germany, on May 9, 1945. This map was reprinted courtesy of National Archives and Records Administration, Cartographic Branch, College Park, MD.

THE
ROAD
REMEMBERED

Kensington
STUDIOS PRESS

CHAPTER ONE

SUZANNE

My father's name was Sam Ryan and I had adored him my whole life.

On the day of our trip, I trudged up his driveway in the semi-blackness of pre-dawn, my calves screaming in protest at the steep climb in spite of the number of hours I spent weekly in spin and Pilates classes.

Dad had insisted I be there at "zero-dark-thirty." Yeah, Army-speak spilled from his lips regularly, even though seventy years had passed since his drill sergeant—somebody named Miller, I think—had barked that phrase at him. I got an "As you were" occasionally too.

The driveway leveled off, but even before I saw him, the comfortable fragrance of Old Spice reached me from where he stood on the front porch and caressed me like a warm hug. He walked slowly toward me, his appearance still impressive. Despite his years, he held himself proudly erect, having lost only half an inch or so of his former six-foot-two height.

He reached the edge of the top step and if I hadn't known better, I would have sworn he posed there, waiting as the early morning sun crept over the fence that lined his driveway and peeped through the new leaves of the crape myrtles. In seconds, the rays strengthened and found his thick white hair, brushing it with soft gold and transforming it into a halo around his still-handsome face.

His Tyrone Power face, according to Mother. I saw it, too, from the old movies I watched with her. Dad's eyes glowed with the same warm brown, and in the pictures I saw of him as a young man, his hair gleamed coal black in the sun. For my money, however, his gorgeous face looked more like George Clooney, especially as they both aged.

He paused on the top step after refusing my offer to help him down. Regardless of the minor stroke he'd suffered ten years earlier, his fierce independence continued to dominate his spirit. Damned stubbornness, I called it. Funny. Even though I'd been adopted, he used those same words to describe me too.

The one bit of help he'd accepted was for driving. Oh, he hadn't wanted to. He fought it kicking and screaming. But after the second time in six months old Elmer Henderson hauled him out of the ditch —during a snowstorm, for goodness sake, when he'd shivered alone for hours because he forgot to charge the cell phone I'd given him— his good friend, Judge Tom Bennett, convinced him to hand over his keys. He did it. But he wasn't happy about it.

Fortunately, I lived close by, and after Mother died, Dad lived independently with my help and a few services from the community. Meals on Wheels did most of the cooking, but I became Dad's primary caretaker, his shopper, chauffeur, property manager, and friend, with the help of my grown son, Stephen, who also lived on our street. Steve excelled in the "friend" category and he loved taking his own sons to spend time with their great-granddad.

I watched Dad descend the stairs, leaning on his cane, one slow step at a time. Excitement filled his face. He tried to hide it, but he couldn't fool me. He loved adventures. And we were headed for a doozy.

He'd received the invitation close to a year earlier, four months before Mother died, and to her delight, made up his mind to attend right away. She knew she couldn't go with him. Her cancer was too advanced by then. So she convinced me to put the trip on my calendar and to cajole him into attending if he waffled at the last minute.

But he hadn't. So there we were, the day of the trip, preparing to fly overseas to attend the seventieth anniversary celebration of V-E Day—the end of World War II in Europe. We'd join several of his former Army buddies from K Company in the 353rd Regiment of the

89th Infantry Division at Le Havre, France, where the former soldiers first touched the European mainland on their way to join the war. From there, the old "Rolling W," as the 89th Infantry was called, would reprise its trek across Europe—France, Luxembourg, and Germany, all the way to Zwickau, close to the Czech border—and culminate with a huge party on May 9, 2015. Other Divisions planned celebrations too, Dad told me, so the gathering included all military who helped defeat Hitler. And, surprising to me, even German citizens.

At precisely half past six in the morning on May 1, 2015, I backed Dad's Buick Park Avenue onto Frederick Street in Lock Haven, Pennsylvania, where we had lived since the early fifties, and we were on our way. A union man all his adult life, "Buy American" governed his purchases, so I drove the 2005 model, the last year of the Park Avenue in the United States before its manufacturing moved to Shanghai.

Commuter traffic was light so early in the day, and we reached Paul Mack Boulevard in record time. Our route wound through the base of the Appalachian Mountains and, for a while, he stared in silence. Then he tapped the window with the crook of his cane. "Those hills," he said, "remind me of the ones we crossed in Germany. We scaled the first range just north of the Black Forest and the second, the Erzgebirge, after we crossed the Rhine River. Close to Zwickau."

"Tell me about it, Dad," I said. He'd always been reluctant to talk about his stint in combat, although I'd asked him countless times. True to form, he let my request hang and continued to stare at the landscape. I waited. His chin sank into his chest and a faint "harrumph" reached me from the second button on his freshly laundered shirt. Even with Mother gone, he remained fastidious about his appearance—shaved every day, selected a clean shirt from the top of the stack placed in his middle drawer twice a week by Emma, the housekeeper, and had his shoes shined and his hair cut every Wednesday two blocks from his house. Like clockwork.

Silence followed and I wondered if he'd fallen asleep.

But after a long pause the words began, slowly at first, trickling out in snatched thoughts and broken phrases before gaining momentum. His narrative bloomed in rich detail and his voice grew stronger. He sat straighter in his seat and I swear, when I glanced at him, his face looked more youthful, as if his body had retreated in time to match his younger-man recollections. His descriptions painted vivid pictures of a brutal time in our world's history.

And I hung on every word, fascinated.

CHAPTER
TWO

SAM

I've always been reluctant to talk about the war. Especially to Suzanne. When she asked me again en route to the sites of those battles, however, I decided it was time.

I didn't share my initial thoughts, which had centered on memories from seventy years earlier for days now, during my preparation for our trip. I relished the thought of a reunion with the guys from my Army unit, the old "Rolling W." We'd rarely gathered during the intervening years. I'd only seen them at occasional celebrations and lately, at the more frequent funerals.

They had popped into my head, one by one, the previous afternoon, along with the German baker's daughter, Gerda. Memories of them and our time together brought a smile to my face and a skip to my step. Oh, I didn't really skip. I was almost ninety, so everybody, even Suzanne, wanted to tell me what I could do. Mostly what I *couldn't* do. Like skipping. So I was forced to give up a lot of things that made me happy in favor of things that kept me safe.

And I was damned sick and tired of it. None of the young people in my life—not one—understood that I still felt young too. Nineteen or twenty. Twenty-six, tops.

But those guys from my unit would.

Which is why, when the reunion invitation reached me more than a year ago, I made up my mind, then and there, to attend. To test myself one more time and to remember myself as a young man through the eyes of those who were young right along with me.

My wife, Betty, applauded my decision. But then she up and died on me four months later. On my eighty-ninth birthday, of all horrible times.

With my buddies still in my head the previous afternoon, I rose from my recliner to retrieve my passport in Betty's memory box on the top shelf of her closet. To reach it, I balanced on the decrepit kitchen stool and stretched on my tiptoes until my fingers brushed against the container. Suzanne would have had a fit if she knew, so I didn't plan to tell her.

I pulled the decorative tin toward me. Words on the top read "Berghmann's *Bäckerie,*" from a lovely little shop tucked behind Hauptmarkt Straβe, off the main square at the center of Zwickau, around the corner from the site of our anniversary celebration.

Back in the den, my "Zen Zone" as Suzanne called it, with the box cradled in my lap, Betty's presence leaped out at me, flowed through my fingers as small vibrations that pulsed with her spirit and throbbed with her love. Still palpable on its surface months after her death.

Betty's Beautiful Box. That's what she called it from the moment I placed it in her hands after my return from the war. The family-owned bakery specialized in *Lebkuchen,* baked daily for generations from an ancient family recipe. My Betty delighted in the earthy flavor of the spicy cookies, her first taste of anything German. But the rectangular box that held them tickled the whimsy in her soul. Every surface of the tooled tin bloomed in raised flowers, woven into intricate vines that climbed exotic trees and populated a fanciful forest, perfect for the likes of Hansel and Gretel to explore.

Exactly as Betty did. I remember seeing her massage its embossed exterior with her delicate fingers, her fascination with the craftsman-ship glowing on her face. After she ate all the cookies, she couldn't bring herself to throw the box away. So she layered it with memories, decade after decade.

I watched her hold it from time to time and reminisce through its contents, more often in the months before she died. She'd show me items, whatever memory held special meaning for her that particular day, and I'd laugh or cry along with her. More tears than smiles after her cancer snarled aggressive. The helplessness I felt overwhelmed me.

Which I found ironic. She'd always considered *me* the strong one. Stable Sam. Sturdy Sam. Solid Sam. But I couldn't make her cancer go away. I couldn't fix it as I had fixed a thousand things during our lives together.

She was my constant companion for almost seventy years and before she died, I couldn't imagine facing even one day without her beside me. Neither could I imagine getting out of bed and having the focus to put one foot in front of the other. When she left me, she took the joy, the very color of the universe with her and for the first few months, my days drifted by in gray shadow, smoky wisps of life that passed me by and left me cold.

Suzanne saved me. "It's no good burying your grief, Dad," she said. "You have to go through it, to embrace it. To learn who you were *with* Mom so you can discover who you'll become *without* her." It took months, but I finally understood she was right.

So my gratitude for Suzanne's help, coupled with the anticipation of seeing my old friends again, released the floodgates of my war memories.

I began my story in July of 1944.

CHAPTER
THREE

M y nineteenth birthday, July 5, 1944, fell almost a month to the day after the battle on the beaches of Normandy. Most birthdays are memorable, but that one especially so.

Even now, I clearly remember how everyone in our small town of Prospect Park, Pennsylvania, waited anxiously for word of casualties from across the ocean. To find out if our loved ones had survived the slaughter of Operation Overlord, now known as D-Day.

The newspapers weren't any help. They didn't report deaths until families were notified so the rumor mill filled the empty spaces. The buzz of half-truths and outright lies careened through the streets scattering gossip with the speed of flying leaves in a hurricane. Thousands of our boys, the busybodies whispered, fell during that battle, victims of German mortars and machine guns. Of course none of us wanted to believe any of those boys had belonged to us.

So for the month after the battle, we waited. And experienced the war in our small-town way, always on the periphery of our awareness, but mostly as an inconvenience. Like blackout curtains, for instance. Which, by the way, enhanced our view of the stars from the front porch swing. Or the sugar shortage, which forced the mother of my friend, Billy Wainwright, to sweeten her chocolate cake with Karo syrup. Funny thing was, once she switched to Karo, she won top prize at the county fair. So despite the few hardships, if you could call them that, and the worry about our boys in the thick of the fighting, our lives drifted along in everyday sameness on the fifteen-acre family farm my mother had inherited from her father just outside Prospect Park.

My nineteenth birthday changed all that. It still remains as one of those "moments in time" when I understood, as it happened, my life would never be the same again.

My mother had added my favorite cupcake to my lunch bag. Vanilla with butter cream frosting. I savored every bite of it at my station on the Driscoll Bearings manufacturing line where my friend, Billy, who worked at the local selective service office, found me licking my fingers clean.

"I have news, Sam," he said. "And I thought I should tell you in person."

I waited.

He shifted from foot to foot and refused to meet my eyes. "Your draft classification changed," he said, "with Driscoll's loss of the military contract. You're classified as One-A now."

Billy referred to the government contract Driscoll held to supply thrust bearings for Liberty Ships. The cancellation notice came through a week earlier, effective at the end of the month.

Which meant no more job and no more military deferment for a bunch of us welders.

I shrugged. I'd expected it.

That part didn't bother me. The thought of following my older brother, Walter, into the war, in fact, pumped pride into my chest. I did worry about Mother, though, with one fewer pair of hands to help with the younger kids in the family.

So I'd expected to get my letter in the mail any day. Instead, Billy came to tell me in person. That was weird. Something was up.

"That's not all you came to tell me, is it, Billy?" Fear ran a cold finger down my spine.

"No." His voice barely made it past a croak, but he stopped fidgeting and squared his shoulders. His eyes found mine. "Walter was killed on Omaha Beach, Sam. He died a hero."

The manufacturing din of metal clanging against metal and the buzz and pop from acetylene torches faded away with Billy's words.

"The battle was a bloodbath," he added quietly. "Six of the eighteen crafts on Omaha beach were lost. Along with thousands of soldiers."

Billy continued to talk. I saw his mouth moving and I caught most of his words before a fuzzy roar seized my ears as if I'd suddenly been dunked in the pond behind our house.

My mother's favorite picture floated into my head, the one taken the night before Walter left for basic training. She'd insisted we stand in birth order with Walter beside her, me on his other side. Richard, the next oldest, stood by me, with his arm around his twin, Kathleen. Then Sarah and Winnie with our little brother, Freddie, last.

My mother's smile sent sparkles to her eyes with all of her children beside her.

For the last time, as it turned out.

Walter had assumed the role of man of the house after our dad took off the night little Freddie, his seventh child, made his appearance in the world. On my fifteenth birthday. Until then, Dad's drinking binges normally kept him away for a week or two, not more than a month, usually. But that night Walter and I agreed, if Dad ever showed up again, bringing the stench of stale beer and vomit to our front porch, we'd send him packing, back the way he came. We'd all had enough.

Even all these years later, I still can't understand how a man could justify leaving his wife and family after fathering seven children. Too many mouths to feed for a man with too little ambition, perhaps? Who's to say? Regardless, the reason didn't change the facts. He was gone. And Walter, at seventeen, picked up the slack the best he could while the rest of us rallied around him with part-time jobs to keep the family together.

Our Dad had never been into farming—didn't have time for it with all his drinking, I guess—so after my grandfather died when Walter and I were toddlers, my mother rented out most of the tillable acreage to our neighbor, Robert Reynolds, who kept the land planted in soybeans and corn. His land butted up to ours and he raised the same crops on his own farm, except he had an acre or so planted with the best strawberries I ever tasted. My family was invited over to sample them whenever we pleased.

On the remaining three acres that surrounded the house and included the small patch of woods that led to the family cemetery, we raised a few animals and had a garden.

As second oldest, I dropped out of school, and Walter and I worked at whatever jobs we could to help our mother feed and clothe the younger ones. I got a job with Elmer Henderson's father at the auto shop where he taught me to weld and then helped me get the job at Driscoll Bearings at quite an increase over what he paid me.

Richard picked up a few part-time hours at the sawmill after school and Kathleen helped Billy Wainwright's mother fill her cake orders. The younger girls, Sarah and Winnie, planted and tended the Victory Garden and cared for our animals—chickens and pigs, our little black sheep, Inky, and our cows, Bonnie and Belle. We all pitched in to take care of Freddie.

With our combined earnings, the rent from the farm, and Mother's wages at the shirt factory, we made do.

Oh sure, we were poor. Everybody was. But most times we didn't know it. In fact, right after the family picture was taken, we butchered "Pig-malion"—over Winnie's anguished protests since she had raised and named him—and had ourselves a good old-fashioned pig roast. We invited everybody for miles around and ate great for the next week.

Billy's mouth kept moving, but his words never registered past the roaring in my ears.

He shook my arm. Gently. "Sam," he said, "you still with me?"

The roaring calmed. "I saw a newsreel," I blurted. "American warships, planes. To protect the soldiers. What...?"

"At Omaha," he interrupted, "the clouds rolled in so thick that morning, the Navy and air crews worried they would hit their own boys. So the shells they did fire didn't even come close to the Germans." His voice was low. "I'm sorry, Sam, but the first few boats didn't stand a chance."

"Ryan. Sam Ryan." Butch Cantwell, my supervisor, shouted my

name down the line and all the industrial noise from the factory floor crashed back into my head. "You're holding things up, Ryan. What gives?"

"Sorry, sir. I got bad news." My voice faltered. "I need to take the rest of the day off."

I had to be with my mother when Western Union arrived. Hearing about Walter would be really hard for her. And finding out I was One-A would only make it worse.

Butch nodded. During the war, many Driscoll employees had lost family members and took time away from the line. For him, it was no big deal. He'd get my station covered, then business as usual.

But for me, everything had changed.

Walter was dead.

I was One-A. Next in line to take his place at the front.

That's when the cold reality of war left the periphery of my mind and shot into my brain, clawing its way into every cell.

I took the long route home, jouncing over rutted roads in Walter's old jalopy, a makeshift vehicle with an ancient Oldsmobile chassis and engine surrounded by multicolored Ford body parts. We built it ourselves with whatever we could scavenge. And did without the stuff we couldn't. Like floorboards. The ground whizzed by under our feet at fifteen miles per hour or so, although most days we didn't come close to getting that kind of speed.

I eased past the shirt factory where Mother worked but didn't stop since I knew she planned to hitch a ride home with the Gibbons girls. I swung by the sawmill, instead, to get Richard.

"What are you doing here?" he asked.

Normally I loved going to the mill where the earthy smell of newly cut lumber filled me with visions of fresh forests and new beginnings. But that day, Walter's loss drove everything else from my head.

"See if Mr. Harding will let you go early today," I said.

"Why would I do that?" Richard puffed himself up and his hostility rose. "Mr. Harding said I could work eight..." He stopped short and his face paled. "Oh my God." His words barely made any sound. "It's Walter, isn't it?"

"See if you can leave and let's go."

"Sam. My God, Sam. You have to tell me." His face twisted in fear.

Several bouts with rheumatic fever during his childhood had affected his frame, left his body small for his age, his face almost delicate. His work boots sported thick heels, but they didn't help. Not enough, anyway. He remained almost three inches shorter than I was and even the heavy work at the sawmill hadn't filled out his muscles to match Walter's or mine. Worse, he'd inherited our father's quick temper and walked around with a chip on his shoulder.

He'd waited impatiently to turn eighteen and dreamed of fighting beside Walter in France and Germany. On his birthday—two days before Freddie's and mine—he marched proudly into the selective service office and registered for the draft, then reported for his physical right away.

"Yes, Richie, it's Walter. And it *is* bad news. The worst. We need to be with Mother when Western Union comes."

Despite my devastation at losing my older brother, I had managed to control my tears but the primal sound of Richard's grief was more than I could stand. He fell to his knees, raw emotion consuming his body, and I leaped from the car, rocking him in my arms, the way I'd seen Mother do. And I cried with him.

We sat in the mud for a long time, the cool dampness of it seeping into my hips and numbing my knees. Mr. Harding came over and I managed to tell him about Walter. He helped Richard into the jalopy, and my brother sobbed the few remaining miles from town to our small farm. We reached the house shortly before the Gibbons girls' car cleared our long lane.

But the Western Union boy's bicycle was already visible, resting on a juniper bush by the front porch. When Mother and the girls drove up, I watched Mother's face. She saw the bicycle right away and I could tell from her expression she assumed it brought bad news.

She stumbled out of the car and I rushed over to keep her from falling. But one look at my face—and Richard's—confirmed her fears. Still, she forced me to read the telegram's message out loud.

"'The Secretary of War desires me to express his deepest regret that your son, Private First Class Walter James Ryan—'"

I couldn't finish. And despite my best efforts, Mother fell to her knees anyway. My sisters ran out of the house and hung on her. We all cried. All of us, even the Gibbons girls. Deep, racking sobs that drove the birds from the trees and the poor little Western Union boy back down the lane as fast as his legs could pedal.

I don't remember how long we huddled in a pile on the grass but eventually the Gibbons girls rose and went home. Then Billy and his mother rumbled up our lane in Billy's big blue Packard and brought us a chicken casserole and chocolate cake. Mrs. Wainwright's famous award-winning chocolate cake. She hugged my mother and they cried together. Billy and my sisters took the food in the house and found Freddie asleep on the floor of Walter's closet, his face filthy and tear-stained.

The military memo declaring Walter a war hero arrived the following day along with a letter from a Private Jerry Chambers, one of Walter's friends lucky enough to survive the D-Day slaughter. I'd hoped to read it alone to spare Mother any gory details, but she saw it and insisted we read it together.

Dear Ryan Family,

Walter and I became friends the first day of basic training and remained so until he breathed his last breath. I don't mean to make his death harder on you but wanted you to know about his final moments.

The operation was different from our expectations right from the start. As you can imagine, the reality of the approaching H-Hour pierced our hearts aboard the Empire Javelin *as each second in the steely gray of pre-dawn ticked us closer to combat.*

The weather was much worse than anyone had anticipated with angry clouds that obliterated the sky, then raced across the English Channel and plunged into a north wind that thrashed the water into whitecaps.

Churning through them, our ship's bow smacked every wave—rearing and then diving—before shooting plumes of spray straight up as we huddled together on the top deck.

Standing behind Walter, I clutched his rucksack as shoulder to shoulder and helmet to helmet we stepped from the pitching ship into our waiting landing crafts, dangling in the air above the rough seas. We sandwiched together and strained to remain upright while the winches, screeching with each jolt, jerked us downward and allowed icy swells to tower over us and drench us to our very souls.

Our commanding officer, Lieutenant Harold May, although young and green, had gained our confidence when he described the German fortifications awaiting us on Omaha Beach. The Atlantic Wall, *he called it, almost two thousand miles of mines, barricades, and barbed wire obstacles, stretching from the tip of Norway to Spain.*

To counter this threat, the lieutenant explained, the Allies planned to bomb the area from both air and sea before our squads landed, so we anticipated weak German resistance and a cratered beach for cover on our way to the sea wall, our first objective.

As we expected, the dawn crept in quietly, a whistling wind the only sound that reached us. No gunfire broke the stillness. Our confidence soared and we were ready to get back on solid ground and do what we'd been trained to do. When our landing craft slammed the sandy beach bottom, the ramp lowered and slapped the water. The lieutenant, in front of Walter, told us to move out and I felt Walter tense.

But machine gun fire erupted before we could surge forward and Walter crashed backward into me. I was afraid he'd been hit. We righted ourselves and I heard the lieutenant's helmet clatter to the bottom of the boat, then saw his head fall forward as he slumped against Walter. Walter pushed the lieutenant's shoulders away to reveal the front of his own uniform soaked with the lieutenant's blood. We both gagged.

Machine gun fire was steady and beside us, others fell. We staggered down the ramp together, searching for the bunkers we'd been told awaited us.

But the beach was smooth. Unmarked. No craters where we could hunker down.

We splashed into the water, swirling red from the floating bodies of our friends. Mortars whistled overhead and machine gun bullets kicked up sand, dancing it in front of us. We picked our way around dead and dying soldiers, some of whom cradled exposed bones from severed limbs and cried out for their mothers.

My eyes teared and my brain clouded but I was vaguely aware that Walter staggered ahead. Dazed, I followed him as fireworks from tracer ammunition exploded, illuminating the dark clouds to daylight. A mortar shell whizzed past us and shrapnel claimed a hunk of his upper arm, sending a whiff of almonds from the plasticine straight into my nostrils. Seeing him get hit cleared my brain. Restored clarity.

Walter zigzagged across the beach toward a triangular anti-tank obstruction rising from the sand, then threw himself behind it. In seconds, I joined him, but tracers flared again, a yard over our heads. Bullets thwacked the obstacle above us.

"There's an anti-tank mine strapped to this obstacle," he said and pointed up with his good arm. He tied a handkerchief around the other one, to stem the blood flow, I assumed. His face twisted in pain, but he continued. "If that gunner hits it, anything close to it will be blown all to hell. We have to get to that sea wall." The bullets slowed and Walter said, "Go! I'll be right behind you." So I took off running and thought I heard Walter follow me. But the machine gunner started again, that anti-tank mine as his main target. I reached the sea wall at the same second his bullets connected with the mine. I turned and saw Walter fall, *halfway between the obstruction and me. He died immediately and didn't have time to suffer.*

Walter saved my life that day and is a hero. But I have wished every second since that we had left that obstacle together so he'd still be here.

Sincerely and with deep-felt emotion,
Private Jerry Chambers

I found the letter from Private Chambers both heartbreaking and oddly comforting at the same time. I'm not certain how my mother felt about it, but I appreciated the fact that he took the time to give us details about Walter's death we would never have gotten any other way.

Walter's body arrived the day after we received those letters and was sent straight to Carruthers Funeral Home. Mother and Richard and I went to identify him, but Mr. Carruthers stopped me in the hall.

"I did the best I could, Sam, but you probably don't want your mother to see him."

She heard what he said and hesitated, but Richard bulldozed into the room where Walter's body lay. I followed. The unmistakable odor of formaldehyde, overlaid with lilac, slammed into our senses but the flowery fragrance did nothing to mask the stench of death.

Mr. Carruthers had spoken the truth. His repair work couldn't conceal the fact that chunks of Walter's head must have been missing. His whole body rested under a red, white and blue covering that sank in spots, as if other pieces of him might be gone too.

I was glad Mother hadn't seen him.

Richard took one look and backed into the wall. His emotions spilled over again, and he stood there and cried. Then screamed, "Those damned, dirty Germans. I'll kill every last one of them." His fists beat the wall and he ran from the room, knocking Mother off-balance. She grabbed for the door jamb to keep from falling.

"I hate having to ask this, Sam," Mr. Carruthers said, "but I need you to tell me definitely whether this is your brother, Walter." His voice fell to a whisper. "I'm so sorry. It's a formality."

Walter's face was waxy and held none of the devilish humor for which he'd been known in the family. I saw a resemblance, but I wasn't absolutely certain. "He has a birthmark," I said, "a dark diamond shape just below his Adam's apple." Mr. Carruthers lifted the covering and moved Walter's tie to the side. I kept my eyes steady on his uniform shirt, forcing myself to avoid looking for parts of him that might be absent. I undid the buttons, hands shaking and mind clutching desperately at the last little bit of hope that the Army was wrong and I wouldn't see the dark diamond birthmark.

But it was there. My heart sank. "It's him," I said. Despite the difference in his face, I was certain beyond a doubt the ravaged body in front of me had once been my older brother.

I returned to the hallway and avoided Mother's eyes. In a few minutes, Mr. Carruthers led us to a small conference room to discuss details of the funeral.

"We will not want an open casket," I said and covered Mother's hand with mine. "We will bring a picture of Walter in his uniform. People should remember him that way."

Methodically, Mother and I answered the final arrangements questions and had almost finished when Billy burst into the room, his eyes huge, his hair wild.

"Sam, it's Richard." Urgency laced Billy's voice. "I had to tell you right away."

Mother half rose beside me. "What's happened?" she asked.

"He told me you were here and I guess he had just seen his... Walter," Billy said. "He stormed into our office and demanded to know the results of his physical. Said he wanted to enlist right then. On the spot. Wanted to be overseas, killing Germans before the week was over."

Mother covered her face with her hands and her shoulders shook.

"Well," Billy hesitated, "you know we normally mail the results out." He shifted from one foot to the other. "But Richard insisted on knowing. He was loud, disruptive. So, I took him in the back room and told him his childhood fevers had affected his heart. His paper-work came back Four-F. I'm so sorry. I had to tell him the truth. I know there's no reconsideration—no negotiation—for heart issues. I didn't—"

"Then what?" I asked. "What did he do?" Fear gripped me.

"He ran out. Like a crazy man. Jumped into Walter's jalopy, took the road out of town."

I rose and started for the door.

"My car's right outside," Billy said. "I'll drive you."

"We'll find him, Mother," I called back to her. "Please finish with Mr. Carruthers."

We hopped into Billy's Packard. "Where do you want to start?" he asked.

"At the house," I said. He drove out of town and at the intersection with our dirt lane, found the tire marks where Richard turned too sharply, obviously causing the jalopy to spin out and stir up a dust cloud. We followed it and Billy braked at the porch. I ran in and startled the girls but a quick glance told me what I needed to know.

"Which way did Richard go?"

"I thought he was with you and Mother," Kathleen said from the kitchen sink with the other girls crowded around her. Freddie perched on the countertop. "We all walked over to the Reynolds Farm to pick strawberries. You know how much Freddie loves that. We just got back and never saw—"

"Stay in here," I interrupted. "Whatever happens, do not come outside."

I ran out the back door and Billy met me at the side of the house. We rushed to the barn and I called Richard's name. No answer.

The barn door wouldn't open so Billy and I threw our whole bodies into pushing until we heard a loud snap. Then the door moved easily.

I jerked it open at the same instant the gunshot blasted.

It exploded in my ears and ripped a hole in my heart.

Billy stepped back, and I entered alone. The odor of gunpowder attacked my nose and settled in my throat, a caustic smoky taste in the back of my mouth.

Richard's body lay draped over a bale of hay. Our father's shotgun, missing from the hooks over the fireplace, rested at a weird angle on top of him. Traces of black powder circled his lips and bloody bits of his skull covered the distance between him and the far wall.

I didn't recognize the anguished wail piercing the air around me. To my knowledge, I'd never made that sound before.

I was furious with him. Still am all these years later. How could he have been so stupid? So selfish? Didn't he know our mother had enough to deal with? That with Walter gone, the family needed him more than ever?

Through the years, he'd exhibited our father's tendency to raise hell first and fix things later. But what he did that day couldn't be fixed. One squeeze from his finger on the trigger, and there was no turning back.

The fury left me, and grief flooded in. Overwhelming, all-consuming grief. With no tears left to cry, I choked out dry sobs. I sat with Richard for a while, but didn't touch him, and left him lying exactly the way I'd found him. I figured the sheriff would prefer it that way.

Kathleen and Sarah had run outside at the sound of the shot, but Billy stopped them from opening the barn door. They swarmed around me when I stepped back out and I told them what had happened. I also told them to stay in the house with the younger ones and that none of them should set foot in the barn. Under any circumstances.

Billy led the way back to town and I followed in Walter's jalopy. I saw the sheriff first, then dragged myself back to the funeral home to rejoin my mother.

She had already guessed what happened. We hugged hard and she collapsed in my arms.

I arranged for a double funeral instead of the one we'd discussed and assured Mr. Carruthers the second casket needed to be closed too.

During the days that followed, we all drifted in a daze, numb to the outside world, other than our neighbors streaming into our house with enough food, I remember thinking, to feed an Army regiment. Of course, given what I learned later about the scant contents in C-

Rations, the mountain of food would easily have fed several regiments.

The double funeral for my brothers took place at our church, where the choir sang without Mother's soprano to support them. We buried them both in the family plot at the edge of the farm rather than sending Walter to Arlington National Cemetery because Mother wanted to keep him close.

Not one person suggested we try to find my father to let him know what had happened.

We reached the gravesite through a cold rain that set in for the day. Mother could barely stand, so we sat her in a kitchen chair and surrounded her with umbrellas. Despite the weather, soldiers in dress uniforms completed the military rituals—folding the flag covering Walter's coffin, solemnly handing it to Mother, and then firing three volleys into the air in an age-old battlefield custom. Funny. I had always assumed gunfire at a soldier's grave was considered a twenty-one gun salute. But I learned, during my own Army training, that the volleys stemmed from a much older custom to let everyone know the dead soldiers had been properly cared for. A nice tradition, I thought, but it did nothing to ease my pain.

After the mournful notes of *Taps*, Reverend Perdue struggled to be heard above Mother's sobs, but he cut the service short, so she could be put to bed. Her church ladies busied themselves in our kitchen and organized the donated dishes into a feast for those who had gathered to pay their final respects.

At the end of the month, I finished my job at Driscoll Bearings and passed my military physical with flying colors. I tried to keep the news of my status change from Mother, who had caught a cold at my brothers' funeral service. She was sick at home the day my letter arrived with notice to report to Fort Meade, Maryland, the following week. My face betrayed me, and she collapsed again.

My last night at home, Mother's fever shot up and her church ladies joined us in taking turns to sit beside her. The next morning her improvement amazed us all. She even joined the family for breakfast and my heart lifted.

"How's your mother doing?" Mrs. Wainwright asked from the front porch when she arrived for her turn with my mother.

"She's much better," I said. "In fact, we're all better. I think the worst is over."

How naïve of me.

The world clashed in a global conflict that had already devastated my family and turned my life upside down.

I should have known the worst was yet to come.

I STOPPED TALKING AND TOOK A SMALL BREAK TO COMPOSE myself after the still painful memories of my brothers' deaths.

I stole a quick glance at my daughter, who wiped tears from her cheeks with one hand and drove with the other. She had turned seventy months earlier, and to me, she was still beautiful.

We'd adopted her as a toddler, so our DNA wasn't part of her genes. But we'd always been told we looked alike. Her hair had been dark when she was younger—not as black as mine—but curly, like Betty's. And with her brown eyes and five-foot-eight height, most people didn't know she'd been adopted. Not that we cared what people knew or didn't know. Or thought. Suzanne was ours the same as if Betty and I had gone through pregnancy and labor.

I remembered the picture I had found of her college graduation in Betty's Beautiful Box the day before—right on top of my Engineering Diploma from Drexel University in Philadelphia, courtesy of the GI Bill. Without conscious thought, after replacing the picture and my diploma, I let my fingers trace the raised letters of the shop's name on the decorative tin. Berghmann's.

As had happened yesterday, my mind shot back seventy years and drifted through the ornate bakery door, with its little bell tinkling the first notes of *Edelweiss*, and into the spicy smells swirling around me from all directions. My car's interior faded and I was surrounded by the enticing bouquets of honey, ginger, and citrus mingled with the fragrances of baking bread and hot strudel that formed an unmistakable scent not found anywhere else on Earth.

Except on Gerda, I remembered. The baker's daughter. Savory aromas from the ovens wafted from her hair and clung to her apron. Even floated on her smile. Or so it seemed.

Gerda. What an extraordinary woman.

I wondered if she were still alive.

Chapter Four

"Bekah," Gerda pleaded, "please stop crying."

They sat on the roof outside Gerda's bedroom window, their honey-colored braids touching as Gerda hugged the younger girl's thin shoulders and tried to calm her.

Their friendship began on Rebekah's first birthday when the two families closed their shops early to celebrate. Not once during the fifteen years since had Gerda looked at Rebekah differently because of her religion. Not once.

Maintaining the appearance of a normal life, however, complete with long-time friendships, grew increasingly difficult all over Germany with each new law passed by Hitler's Nazi regime. Everyone felt the sting of it, including the two girls huddled together.

"But they're sending us away. Making us leave our home. Only a few hours from now. That's why I woke you. To let you know," Rebekah whispered, tears tightening her throat. "How will I see you? How can we still be friends?"

"We'll always be friends," Gerda said. "Like our parents and grandparents."

Their families' friendship had begun two generations earlier, when the first Rosenbaums, Rebekah's grandparents, started the butcher shop and helped Gerda's grandparents, the Berghmanns, open the bakery right next door. For years, the families worked together to help each other's businesses. When customers at Berghmann's outside café ordered a sandwich, Gerda's mother, Karla, ran over to Rosenbaum's for freshly cut meat while her father, Otto, prepared the bread, hot from the oven. Likewise, when people bought meat from Rosenbaum's, Rebecca's parents, Ruth and Hiram, always recommended Berghmann's for bread and dessert.

The families' easy camaraderie through the years and the birth of their children—Gerda and Ernst to Otto and Karla, and Jakob and Rebekah to Ruth and Hiram—hit its first bump when the *Führer* declared a national boycott of Jewish businesses in 1933. Nazi party members made a point of visiting Berghmann's after that and refused sandwiches made with meat from Rosenbaum's, so nine-year-old Gerda ran to the butcher shop through the back yard, instead, and her father lied to his customers about where the meat came from.

"Times are different now," Rebekah said through her tears. "Your family could get in trouble for being friends with us."

Gerda knew she was right.

After the fervor of the 1933 boycott died down, the butcher shop continued to do a good business since their long-term customers trusted Rosenbaum's to carry the freshest meat at a good value. But in the years that followed, the Nazis increasingly denied the family access to markets and advertising in local newspapers. With Zwickau so far from Berlin, Jewish harassment remained light, so the two families made the best of things and lived as normal a life as possible.

Once the Nuremberg Laws passed in 1935, however, Jewish people were stripped of their citizenship and declared "enemies of the race-based state." Officials warned Otto and Karla that prison loomed if they maintained their friendship with the Rosenbaums. After the 1936 Olympics in Berlin, while the world busied itself with other things, Nazi leaders assumed an aggressive stance and more violently enforced Anti-Semitic Laws. But in 1938, *Kristallnacht*, or the November pogroms, began a more sinister surge in anti-Semitic abuse, with businesses and synagogues destroyed and shards of glass from their shattered windows littering the street. The Rosenbaum's had been lucky. Their butcher shop had been spared. Until now.

Luck no longer protected them and they faced forced evacuation in mere hours.

"I don't think we'll be in trouble, Bekah," Gerda lied. "We'll find a way to stay friends."

"You don't understand. Have you seen our front door? And our shop windows?" Without waiting for an answer, she rushed on. "The SS painted the word *Jude* all over them. And they dragged Jakob out of the house this morning. On his eighteenth birthday. They didn't even tell us where they were taking him. My father thinks he'll go to a forced labor camp. My mother couldn't..." Sobs overtook her and drowned out her words.

"You're right, Bekah," Gerda said. "That's not good. It's really bad, in fact. But Jakob's strong. I'm sure he'll be fine. And maybe you can go see him after he's—"

"No!" Gerda had never heard her friend scream before. "No, we can't. I already told you, we're being evacuated in a couple of hours. The SS gave my father a long list of instructions about what we can take and what we must leave. For them." She spat out the last words through clenched teeth and fresh tears traced new tracks on her already-wet cheeks.

As the bakery's delivery person, Gerda had seen the horror Rebekah described. In every sector of the city, she witnessed Jewish families forced to leave their homes, thrown out by the SS and allowed to take very few possessions.

"I don't know where they'll send us," Rebekah continued. She drew a deep breath and held out her hand, her fist clenched. "And we'll be forced to wear this." Her fingers parted to reveal a patch of yellow fabric, a six-pointed star outlined in black with the word *Jude* printed in its center. "As if we were cattle requiring a brand."

Gerda had seen that too. People she knew and liked, forced to wear the Jewish Star of David as a badge of shame. She had also seen the Jewish-only sector's cramped conditions and its filth. The thought of her friend living there sent shudders through her body.

She closed her eyes against her memories of Jewish people singled out by roaming SS soldiers, who delighted in inflicting pain on them by yanking gold-filled teeth from gums and severing ring-laden fingers from hands.

Her worst shocks stemmed from seeing old or disabled people shot in the streets as if those conditions were crimes against the state.

Rebekah hung her head and then looked up into the eyes of her friend, returning to her initial fear. "Once we're gone, we can no longer be friends. It will be too dangerous for you."

Gerda struggled to find words of comfort. "Of course we'll still be friends," she said. "I know we can figure it out. Look," she continued, "here's what we'll do. I'll follow you in the morning with my bread wagon. The SS, and even the *Gestapo,* let me take it all over the city for deliveries. So I'll see where you go and then it will be easier for me to find you again. To come and see you. To help you. And your family." She hugged her friend one more time. "It will be okay, Bekah. We'll make it work. Please stop crying."

⸻⸺⸻

GERDA SLEPT FITFULLY FOR THE NEXT COUPLE OF HOURS, then woke to shouts followed by screams. She eased her curtains away from the window and looked down to the sidewalk, horrified at the scene. Two uniformed men dragged Rebekah's mother out the front door of the butcher shop and down the three steps to the street while a third forced a silver menorah from her fingers.

Gerda flung her clothes on and sped down the stairs.

"*Mutti,*" she whispered when she stepped into the bakery's back room, "the SS have evicted Rebekah's family. They're dragging *Frau* Rosenbaum out her front door. We have to help."

"*Nein, Liebchen,*" her mother whispered back, hugging her close. "We're being watched. If we do anything to help, we could be taken too."

"But...but..."

"I know, *Liebling.* It is terrible." Gerda's mother swiped tears from her own cheeks. "The world is crazy right now. But Mr. Rosenbaum knew it was coming. And your father and I have talked about it. There is nothing we can do." At Gerda's stricken face, her mother continued, "We've been warned, *mein Schatz.* And we must protect you and Ernst.

And our business." Tears flowed freely down her face. "I'm sorry," she whispered.

Without another word, Gerda loaded her bread wagon for the day's deliveries, one of which was close to the Flossenbürg sub-camp near the Auto Union plant, now known as the "Jewish-only" sector of the city. She figured that's where Rebekah and her family would be taken. Without her mother's knowledge, she added several pieces of strudel and left by the bakery's front door.

Rebekah's mother sat on the curb in front of her shop with Rebekah's arm around her shoulders. The uniformed men guarded their door and wicked grins stretched their faces as they watched Mr. Rosenbaum struggle to get his two-wheeled cart, piled high with the family's belongings, down the stairs. With only one step to go, a guard pushed him and he tripped, falling to the sidewalk with his right leg twisted under him. Another of the men turned the cart over, spilling its contents to the ground.

The sound of their laughter filled Gerda with disgust but she didn't allow it to show on her face.

"*Hallo,*" Gerda called, her voice pleasant. The uniformed men turned to her and their faces transformed from mocking sneers to obscene leers. "Would you gentlemen care for some fresh-baked strudel?" Her face was a mask of innocence. She couldn't ask them to leave her friends alone, but she could give the Rosenbaums time to pull themselves together.

Right away, the men surrounded her wagon, but she managed to stay out of their reach as she handed out the confections. While Gerda had the SS men occupied, Rebekah straightened the cart and secured their belongings. Her parents rose slowly from the sidewalk, her father wincing with pain. The yellow Star of David adorned their breast pockets.

Gerda was embarrassed for them, but worse, for the monster her German government had become.

"*Danke, Fräulein,*" one of the uniformed men told her. He touched her arm and she pulled away, pretending to reach for napkins. When they finished eating, the men rounded up Rebekah's family and herded them into the street.

Gerda waited a few minutes, then followed behind. She wasn't sure what she would do if the men continued to abuse her friends, but she kept them within her sight, regardless. They stopped at more houses along the way, wielding the same kind of rough treatment on the new families, swelling the crowd of Jewish people and marching them through the streets. Non-Jewish children taunted the group and threw stones and rotten fruit at them.

Her tears streaming, Gerda grabbed several children by their shoulders and sent them away but stopped and hung back again when the soldiers fixed her with icy stares.

Her friends reached their destination and were forced to stop in front of a table with two men in Nazi uniforms at the entrance to the Jewish-only sector. More SS soldiers waited beside them and, along with the original three, blew whistles, shouted, and shoved the Jewish people to the registration table. In the confusion of too many bodies pressing through too small a space, an elderly man fell and was trampled. When he couldn't rise, a guard shot him in the head.

Which prompted anguished shrieks from his wife.

They shot her too.

Gerda's hand flew to her mouth and she sank her teeth into its flesh to keep from crying out. She swallowed several times and took deep breaths but the bile rose and found her throat anyway. Fresh tears flooded her face as she pushed away thoughts of the dead couple's family and how devastated their children and grandchildren must be. She looked around, helpless, wishing she could do something, anything.

A sickening silence hung over the throng after that, but the remainder of the relocation finished without further incident.

She watched the families file through and was astounded at the number of small children who entered, many only babies. Her heart ached. She had heard rumors that Jewish children too small to work were often killed on the spot. She hadn't seen that while she watched, but she feared it was only a matter of time.

Rebekah turned before disappearing into the crowd. Neither of them dared wave, but their eyes locked.

Reluctantly, she turned her wagon to the street of her first delivery, wiping her tears, and forcing her face into a pleasant expression, while inside, her stomach burned and her mind seethed.

Something had to be done. If her parents were too afraid, then she'd do it.

Whatever "it" turned out to be.

CHAPTER
FIVE

GERDA
1942

E
very day for the following six months, Gerda wheeled her wicker bread wagon to the Jewish-only sector of the city in addition to her regular stops.

Every single day. Rain or shine, hot or cold, it didn't matter.

Strudel, she had found, worked better to get her past the SS checkpoint at the Jewish-only sector than bread or even the famous *Lebkuchen*. For which she was grateful. The *Lebkuchen* would have been harder to sneak out without her parents' knowledge. She suspected her *mutti*, Karla, saw most of the extras she took, but believed they went to the Rosenbaums. They never discussed it. Her family was safer that way.

The German guards paid little attention to her once they devoured the buttery-rich strudel. But there was one exception. Meeting him the day after Rebekah's family arrived had been a stroke of good luck.

Gerda showed up at the chain-link fence and asked to see her friend, but an older guard refused and shouted at her to be on her way. She turned to leave when a younger soldier caught her eye, his curly blond hair barely contained under his military cap. His bright blue eyes focused intently on hers.

At her smile, he held up his hand in the "Heil Hitler" greeting and she returned it.

He moved closer to the fence separating the area from the rest of the city. "*Guten Tag, Fräulein,*" he said. She liked his voice, deep and rich. And free from the guttural resonance she heard in many of the other soldiers' speech patterns. His body language was different too. Less aggressive. Kinder, somehow.

She wedged her hand through the small holes in the fence, her eyes still locked with his. *"Hallo,"* she said. He shook her hand as much as the fence allowed and again, she smiled.

"Kann ich dir helfen?" he asked. "May I help you?"

"Ja, bitte," she responded. "I would really like to see my friend, Rebekah Rosenbaum. She came here yesterday. And," she added, reaching into the top of her wagon, "I hope you will accept this strudel from our bakery, for your trouble." She handed him the still-steaming pastry, made fresh that morning from cherries her mother had canned during the past growing season. "My name is Gerda, by the way. Gerda Berghmann."

"Aldrik Ziegler," he told her, his fingers still imprisoning hers. "Stay here," he added. "I think I know where your friend is. I'll get her." He released her hand and devoured the pastry in two bites, wiping his lips with his sleeve. Moments later he was back, Rebekah trailing along behind him, her head down.

"Bekah," Gerda called softly. Her friend raised her head and a smile lit her eyes. She ran to the fence. The older guard who sent Gerda away rushed over when Rebekah's fingers wrapped through the holes in the metal fence, and he hit them with his club. Rebekah pulled her hand back and screamed. Her fingers immediately reddened and swelled, then cramped up like a claw. The older guard pulled his arm back to strike again.

"Stop," Gerda screamed. She threw herself against the fence, but Aldrik caught the older man's arm and forcefully lowered it.

"I'll take care of this, Konrad," he said. The authority in his voice was unmistakable.

For a moment, Konrad stood his ground, his presence intimidating, menacing. Rebekah shrank back, fear plain on her face. Konrad glowered—first at Aldrik, then at Rebekah, and finally at Gerda, causing her to shudder at the intense hatred in his eyes. Several long moments passed before he backed away. He turned toward the guard station and a small boy crossed his path. He hit the child in the shoulder with his club and then kicked him when he fell. Gerda lunged for the fence again, but Aldrik motioned her to stay back. "I will talk to him, *Fräulein*. Please do not do anything more to upset him."

"For *me* to upset *him*? Are you kidding? He—"

Aldrik held up his hand again. "Please, *Fräulein*, visit with your friend." He snapped to attention, clicked his heels together and held up his arm. "*Heil* Hitler." He turned sharply and joined Konrad at the guard station.

"Bekah," Gerda said. "I'm so sorry he hurt you, but look, I brought bread and pastries for your family." Rebekah hung her head and cried quietly, her shawl wrapped around her fingers. "Bekah," Gerda tried again. "I know your hand hurts, but are you okay here? And your parents? How are they doing?"

"How do you think they're doing?" Rebekah asked. "We're sharing a small apartment with three other families. There aren't enough beds, or bathroom facilities. And not nearly enough food. Fifteen of us in three rooms! Why are they treating us like this? What did we do to them?" She collapsed into sobs again.

Gerda just stood. Helpless.

After several minutes, Rebekah wiped her eyes and moved closer to the fence. "Here's the worst part," she whispered. "The guards came through yesterday to inspect us. They took the few things of value we had left—*Mutti's* wedding ring, my father's "Best Merchant" medal, and valuables from the other families. Then," she took a deep breath before she could continue, "they spent a long time examining one of the babies. He's only nine months old and has a birthmark that fills one side of his face." Rebekah's tears flowed freely. "Gerda, I'm so afraid for them. You've heard the rumors about what they do to babies." She swiped at her tears. "Especially when they think one is less than perfect. We watch the door every minute, afraid they will come and take him away."

"No, surely they wouldn't..." Gerda didn't finish. She knew better. She had already seen too much of what "they" were capable of. "Is there any way to help?"

Rebekah was silent, her head bent. "I don't see—"

Gerda heard a deep gasp and Rebekah's head snapped up then locked eyes with her friend. "Gerda, *you* have to take him away. To keep him safe."

"What? No. I couldn't. How do you think—"

"Your wagon," Rebekah said. "You can hide him in your wagon."

"Bekah, they'll shoot us. All of us. I couldn't."

"Gerda, I really believe they're going to kill him anyway. You could save his life." Her voice caught in a sob. "You're the only one who can."

Gerda stole a quick glance at the soldiers and her mind spun. Konrad berated an old man with only one arm and clubbed him until he fell to the ground. Aldrik stood by and let it happen.

Gerda made a quick decision. "Okay," she said. "You take the bread and pastries to your apartment. Tell his parents what we have in mind. Have them give him something to keep him from crying. Aspirin or whiskey. Maybe schnapps. See what they say. And then come back. I'll figure out how we can get him in the wagon. Hurry. They're not watching us right now."

Rebekah ran and Gerda showed her bread and pastries to others quarantined within the sector. With little or no money available to them, they gave her small trinkets or traded clothes for their purchases. The guards remained focused on the old man.

Rebekah returned, a pile of clothes in her arms. Mostly expensive coats—thick and heavy. "Here you are, Gerda," Rebekah said clearly. "The families put these together to pay you for your bread."

Gerda stared at her friend. "It wouldn't take all this to pay for—" But she stopped talking at the intense look in Rebekah's eyes. "Yes," Gerda said after a moment. "This will work fine." She rearranged several loaves and cleared out the bottom of her wagon, piling the still-warm bread and pastries along the sides.

"*Herr* Ziegler," Gerda called. "Can you open the gate wide enough for me to receive this payment?"

The guard named Ziegler joined them at the fence and unlocked the gate. He avoided touching Rebekah but watched as she transferred the pile of clothes to Gerda, who tucked it carefully into her cart. A small grunt reached her ears, but she ignored it and handed Rebekah more bread. A long look passed between them and tears filled their eyes.

"Thank you," Rebekah said. "All the families will be happy about this."

The friends touched fingers through the metal links of the fence. "Good luck," Rebekah mouthed.

Gerda nodded. "I'll come and see you again," she said. "Maybe tomorrow."

She turned her wagon back in the direction of her route.

"*Fräulein*. Halt." Konrad's voice.

Gerda stopped and the hair on the back of her neck rose. She arranged her face in pleasant innocence and turned. "*Ja?*" she asked. "*Kann ich dir helfen?*"

"I would like strudel," he said. "Is cherry the only kind you have?"

She dared to take a quick breath. "*Nein*," she answered. "I have apple and peach also. Which would you like?"

"Apple," he told her and held out his hand.

Panic hit her. She had piled bread on top of the strudel to make room for the pile of clothes with the baby inside. She smiled at the guard. "Certainly," she said. "Let me get it for you." She opened the top of her wagon only far enough to see inside and moved some of the loaves. The pile of clothes stirred with another small grunt. She cleared her throat. "Excuse me," she said to the soldier. "My allergies are active."

"Probably the smell from these filthy Jews," he said, contempt dripping from his voice.

Gerda rummaged quickly through her wagon and pulled out an apple strudel. "Here you go." She handed him the confection and forced a smile. "No need to pay," she told him. "Please enjoy. I will come back tomorrow with more."

She turned before he could answer and strode purposefully down the intersecting street. Once he could no longer see her, she collapsed into a chair at an outside café and let her head fall to her hands.

Treason. An executable crime. Death to her and her family. And Rebekah's family. And the baby's family.

The baby. She didn't know if he could breathe. She opened the top of her wagon and gently moved the clothes and coats, exposing the perfect little features partially covered with the dark birthmark. Thick lashes lined his closed eyes but he lay still. Her heart constricted and her whole body trembled. She reached in and shook him. Nothing. A sob formed in her throat and she shook harder.

One tiny fist emerged from the garments and then the other in a full body stretch, accompanied by a deep breath. His eyes opened and grew wider with his smile. She thought her heart might explode. He was so beautiful. How could anyone think of killing him?

She refrained from picking him up but saw a note and a baby bottle on his chest. His name was Kurtiss Liebermann and she had no clue what to do with him. She sat for a moment, trying to decide where to go next, but continued her regular delivery schedule. She needed time to think.

She finished her rounds and by the time she returned to the bakery she had a plan.

"Papa," she said, "you mentioned we need more brandy. I'll be glad to take the truck and go to the family farm to get more. I'd like to see Ulrich and Ilyse again. May I have the keys?"

"That's a fine idea," he said. "But it will be dark once you get there. You should spend the night and come home in the morning."

"Of course," she said. "You're right. That will be safer."

"I'll put together some things for you to take them," *Mutti* said.

Gerda unloaded the few remaining loaves from her wagon and busied herself in the kitchen, making a sandwich and getting milk. When she was alone, she filled the baby's bottle and stashed it back in her wagon. She saw movement but couldn't pick the baby up yet.

"Here," her father said. He reached for her wagon. "I'll store this back by the ovens."

She jumped up. *"Nein,"* she told her father. "I can't carry much of the brandy at one time by myself, so I thought I would load it up in my wagon to make it easier."

He shrugged and left but her mother fixed her with a stern look. "Gerda," she said when they were alone, "did something happen this morning? Did you see Rebekah?"

"*Ja, Mutti,*" she answered. "She's miserable there. Her family is sharing cramped quarters with too many other people and a guard hit her hand and probably broke her fingers." She avoided her mother's eyes and rushed on. "I told her I would go and see her again tomorrow. I think it will help her to have her friends around. It's a horrible place." She continued making her sandwich and closed her wagon. She sensed her mother's stare boring into her.

"Did anything else happen?"

"Well, I met a young guard who seemed nice. I think he'll be a good contact when I go there. His name is Aldrik." Still no eye contact.

"Gerda. Look at me."

She turned and faced her mother. "*Ja?*"

Without warning, a loud yelp sounded from her wagon. Her mother gasped and Gerda opened the top and looked at the baby. His face screwed into a thundercloud, on the verge of a loud wail. She reached down and grabbed him, cuddling him to her chest.

Her mother gaped. "What on earth—?"

Gerda's eyes filled and she rocked the baby back and forth. "Oh, *Mutti,*" she said, "he has a birthmark on his face. A large one. The German soldiers were going to kill him. I had to save him." She nuzzled the baby's neck. "I had to," she whispered.

"And now," her mother said, "you're going to involve the rest of the family at the farm."

"Yes," she whispered. "Somehow, I will find somebody to take him through the Black Forest to France. Maybe to Vichy. There aren't as many Germans in that part of France, so he should be safe there. I'll find someone who knows a member of the Resistance. They'll help." She looked deeply into her mother's eyes. "Please don't try to stop me, *Mutti.* I'm sure this baby's family is as good as Rebekah's. And they haven't done anything wrong. I don't know why the Nazis are being so cruel, but it's not right."

Her mother pressed her lips together and closed her eyes. She nodded, a slight movement, but enough to ease Gerda's heart. "I'll be careful," Gerda said. "I'll figure out a way to keep our family safe." Again, she nuzzled the baby's head. "And this little fellow too."

"May I hold him?"

Gerda handed the baby to her mother who held him away from her. "Whew! He needs a diaper change. Did they send any with you?"

Gerda remembered helping change her younger brother, Ernst, when he was a baby, but until that moment, hadn't thought about all the care a baby needs. "I don't know," she said. She rummaged through the clothes and coats in her wagon and found two diapers at the very bottom. Triumphantly, she held them up for her mother to see.

"Okay, give them to me," her mother said. "I'll change him while you get your things ready. The sooner you're on your way, the better."

An awareness jolted through Gerda with such force, the diapers almost fell from her outstretched arm.

This child is only the first.

She would save the children. As many as she could. She would find a way.

She *had* to.

CHAPTER
SIX

SAM
1944

Basic training came on the heels of burying my brothers. My mother hadn't fully recovered on that early morning in August when Billy picked me up and took me to the bus station in Prospect Park. I didn't want to leave the rest of my family right then, with Walter and Richard's deaths hanging so fresh in everyone's hearts. But the choice hadn't been mine to make. During the ride, I almost strangled in the depth of my grief, but I put on a brave front and tried to convince myself that things were looking up. It didn't work. My emotions were a mess and all through the bus ride to Philadelphia and in the boarding house that night, I struggled to breathe.

The following morning, I boarded the Western Maryland Railway, headed for Catonsville, outside of Baltimore. Normally, the line's loads consisted of coal and freight and only occasionally included passenger cars, so regardless of the scant number of people who filed into them, the seats featured cramped, elbow-to-elbow discomfort. I purposely avoided eye contact on my way down the aisle and slumped into a window seat, praying no one would bother me. I simply didn't feel like talking.

But a jiggle from the seat next to me, along with a wave of sweaty heat, accompanied by body odor, told me my prayer went unanswered. Moisture fell from the disturbance beside me and formed blurry blotches on the newspaper resting in my lap.

Dammit it all to hell. Irritation consumed me. I didn't turn.

So he nudged my shoulder.

"Hey buddy," he said, in a slow, deep voice, "you headed for Fort Meade?"

My mother hadn't raised me to be rude, so no matter my irritation and the fact that I longed to avoid interaction with another human being, I raised my eyes and focused on sharp green ones in a pleasant, freckle-filled face. Which dripped with sweat from the August heat, brown bangs plastered to his forehead.

"Yes," I said and held out my hand. "The name's Ryan...Sam Ryan."

"Eugene Dickinson," he answered. He wiped his enormous palm on an already-soaked handkerchief before it engulfed mine. "But," he added, his grin quick and endearing, "everybody calls me Dickie."

I was not a small man, but the one beside me was huge, and I liked him right away. If my destiny included time in a foxhole, I decided, Eugene "Dickie" Dickinson would be a good companion. "I'm from Saratoga Springs," he continued. "New York. You?"

"Prospect Park, Pennsylvania."

"We'll be good friends." He said it as if it were a done deal. And that was that. We were.

He must have sensed my reluctance for conversation because once he pronounced our relationship status, we talked little. The train pulled into Catonsville and he stood and handed me my suitcase, then moved aside and let me enter the aisle first. We disembarked to find the station a chaos of men—some in uniform striding along with purpose and others in civilian clothes looking around with hesitation. Dickie and I fell into the latter group.

A lump formed in my throat. I was away from home for the first time in my life. And homesickness filled my heart. Truth was, even at my age, I wanted my mother's hug.

I didn't have time to dwell on it, however, because right away the loudspeaker boomed out the annoying, staccato voice of the man we would come to know and despise as our sergeant. The sound erupting from Bernard Miller's sneering lips informed us of, and confirmed, the hell we would endure for the next few weeks.

I drew my last civilian breath and followed Dickie to the rendezvous point.

A bunch of rag-tag guys, all shapes, sizes, and ages, loitered on an empty platform beside a putrid-green—Army green, I came to learn—bus. Sergeant Miller, a short man in sharply pressed khakis, his creased garrison cap at a rakish angle that almost covered one eye, stood in front of it with a clipboard and barked orders as if he had expected us to arrive already trained to fall in and form ranks.

But we weren't. So we didn't.

Which, judging from his behavior, angered him even more. His voice rose by several decibels.

I stood beside Dickie, and a shorter man than I filled the space on my other side. I knew enough to face forward, but my peripheral vision revealed a white tee shirt with thick black hair bursting from above its crew neck. Its short, rolled sleeves revealed the outline of a pack of cigarettes, secure in the side I could see. Camels, I would learn later. With Sergeant Miller at the other end of the line, I stole a quick glimpse of the man's face and saw hollow cheeks under heavy, dark brows that all but met over his nose. Curly black hair tumbled down his forehead and his jaw muscles moved double-time on the wad of chewing gum he worked between his teeth.

"Simon Levy," he said from the side of his mouth. "Brooklyn."

Sergeant Miller materialized in front of him, nose to nose. "So you think your words are more important than mine, soldier?" Levy stood motionless. "Well, soldier? Do you?" Miller screamed in his face.

"No, of course n—"

"You will answer 'Sir, no sir,' when I speak to you, scumbag." Miller's nose almost brushed the one of the man beside me. My armpits swam in sweat.

"Sir, no sir!" Levy answered.

Miller's nose moved to me. "You think this is funny, mister?" he said to my chest.

"Sir, no sir," I shouted.

"I can't hear you," he screamed, his lips snarling at my neck.

"Sir, no sir!" I repeated. Louder. Much louder.

His nose lingered a few seconds longer, then moved farther down the line to harass other hapless souls. My sweat ran so freely, the soaked waistband of my pants allowed drips to slide down my legs all the way to my ankles.

After several more encounters along the line of men-about-to-become-soldiers, the banty rooster of a sergeant instructed us to board the bus. Which we did at a swift trot.

Torrential rain from the previous two days had transformed the roads at Fort Meade to muddy, rutted paths. We tramped through them to reach the supply tent and pick up our Army-issued clothes. All putrid green. Even down to our socks.

I told the clerk who issued shoes I wore a size twelve-and-a-half regular. He handed me black boots in size thirteen wide. "Don't worry," he said, cutting off my objection. "You'll grow into them."

No protests, no questions, no explanations. "Follow the rules" was the order of the day. Of *every* day, as it turned out. Regulations provided us with everything we needed to know. And everything, I found, was regulated. Everything.

Instructions accompanied every second of every day, every step, and every breath. Clothes hanger hooks always pointed toward the wall and the clothes on them always pointed left. We weren't told why. We weren't allowed to ask why. We were expected to simply do as we were told. I drove myself crazy wondering why anybody cared so much about such trivial things. Until I figured out the idea was to strip us of our individuality and force us to be the same, a single unit working as a team.

Not until I reached combat did I fully appreciate that thought process.

I entered the door of my barracks, juggling my pack and rifle, and chose a bunk about halfway down on the right. The bottom. Walter and I had shared bunk beds as children, and he made me sleep on top, even though I was too small to reach it without a stool. So I decided to give the bottom bunk a try.

Fresh pain hammered my heart with the thought of Walter. Followed right away by the knowledge that hot-headed Richard would have already boiled over at this point. I couldn't imagine him facing Sergeant Miller for long without landing in the guardhouse for insubordination.

I arranged my supplies in the locker at the foot of my bed and heard soft voices beside me. I glanced at the men on the bunk next to mine and did a double take. The two men looked exactly alike. I mean *exactly*. They stopped talking when they saw me staring and one of them stood to extend his hand. When I shook it I felt a large ring that seemed too heavy for his fingers. The other man wore a similar ring.

But the face and build of the men in front of me hit me hardest. The boyish faces were so young, I was certain they had never seen a razor, and the slender torsos couldn't possibly have weighed more than one hundred thirty pounds, soaking wet. They didn't even look old enough to be in the service.

"The name's Davis," the standing one said. "I'm Erwin and this is my brother, Ervin. We're from Pearl, Texas. Almost two hundred miles from Houston," he added. "That's always the first question we get."

The brother identified as Ervin stood and I looked from face to face in search of differences. There were none. They topped out at around five feet, ten inches with well-groomed brown hair. My mother would have termed their faces "angelic," although I was sure they wouldn't have wanted to hear that. They wore matching plaid summer shirts and dark pants, and both sets of shoes appeared to have been spit-polished. They radiated serenity, and I worried for their gentle souls when they faced the atrocities of war.

"Really?" I said. "That's the first question you get? How about why there are two of you who look exactly alike?" I had never seen identical twins in my small universe. The only other twins I had seen were my brother, Richard, and sister, Kathleen, who looked nothing alike. So I openly gaped. "How did your mother know who was who?" I asked.

The man who called himself Erwin smiled, and his soft brown eyes crinkled at the corners. "Oh, that was the fun part," he said. "She didn't always know. We were good boys, growing up, but we still put her through a few fits when we got into trouble."

"It will be interesting to see how many fits you put our sergeant through," I said. "Has he seen you yet?"

"Yes," the other brother said. "Although I'm not sure he understands there are two of us."

We all grinned. It should be interesting, I thought, the first time the sergeant saw them together. Really interesting.

The barracks door flew open and slammed against the wall. A tangle of arms and legs fell into the empty space and rolled, end over end, all the way down the open aisle between bunks and stopped at my feet.

Dickie Dickinson appeared at my side and we watched the scuffle for a few minutes. When it showed no sign of stopping, he reached into the mass of human flesh and hauled Simon Levy out by the scruff of his neck. Bright red welts shone under each eye and his arms continued to windmill even though his blows no longer landed on their target. A steady stream of colorful expletives exploded from his swollen lips.

I bent to retrieve the poor guy lying prone on the floor. Another skinny kid. I remember wondering what the heck Uncle Sam was thinking to entrust the safety of our great country to all those youngsters.

"You want to talk about it, son?" Dickie asked.

"That jackass insulted me and my heritage," Levy shouted.

The man in my arms shook his head. "Did not," he croaked. "... only said..." He slumped against me and I held him tighter to keep him from falling. Beside us, Simon Levy caught a second wind and lunged at the two of us, but Dickie pulled him up short.

"Enough of this," Dickie said. He shook the man he held and the arms stopped thrashing. "We're all in this together," he continued. "Our only enemies now are the Germans. We don't have time to fight each other."

Dickie was right. From that moment until the end of the war, our lives depended on each other and we needed to operate as a team. Petty squabbles had no place in our unit.

The new man, we all learned, was Eddie Simmonds, fresh in from Queens, New York.

Which meant nothing to me. I'd never been outside Pennsylvania before. But the rough language spewing from Simon Levy helped me understand that Queens, the borough where Eddie Simmonds lived, bordered Brooklyn, the borough where Simon Levy lived. Apparently that proximity had spawned a long-term feud among the neighboring residents, much like the one between the Hatfields and McCoys. Nobody remembered when it started or what it was about; it simply existed. And many of the borough residents, especially the young ones, acted on it without understanding or caring why. That knowledge actually made me feel sorry for Sergeant Miller. Whipping us into a cohesive unit would take every ounce of energy the small man possessed.

The six of us bunked side by side. Eddie Simmonds settled in above me, then the Davis brothers next to us, and Dickie Dickinson on the other side of them with fiery Simon Levy in the top bunk. We stashed our supplies, made our beds and found the mess hall to have lunch, or "chow," in Army-speak. Every meal, we learned, was called "chow."

I walked beside Eddie, not quite my height, with dark blond hair and watery blue eyes. He had recently turned eighteen, like the Davis twins. Simon Levy was twenty, a year older than I was, and Dickie Dickinson was the oldest of our group, at twenty-four. Except for Dickie and me, they were all wiry with bone-thin limbs and gaunt features.

I stood behind Eddie in line and marveled at the amount of food he added to his tray. The six of us shared a table, with the boys from Brooklyn and Queens positioned at opposite ends. A few days of training, I figured, would beat their differences out of them.

"Listen up, scumbags." Sergeant Miller's annoying voice commanded our attention from the door. "Full march at fifteen hundred hours. With field packs and rifles." He stormed out and I couldn't help but wonder how he sustained his apparent rage for such long periods.

I had yet to learn Army time, but a corporal visited each table and let us know we needed to meet at the parade grounds, dressed in fatigues and ready to march, at three o'clock. Sharp.

In August. In the afternoon heat. With thirty-pound packs and a rifle.

We quickly learned how to fall in and took off at a fast jog. Twenty minutes later, Eddie stopped beside me and threw up every bit of food he had consumed at lunch. And then some. All around me, fledgling soldiers followed suit, creating havoc with the ranks and incurring the wrath of hell from Sergeant Miller.

Of which we were all recipients.

It got worse. The mingled odors of greasy vomit and marsh-gas mud caused more and more of us to empty our guts. I thought poor Sergeant Miller might burst a blood vessel as he ranted and raved into one green face after another. When he reached the Davis twins, if my stomach hadn't also been on the brink of emptying again, I might have laughed. One of the twins bent double and dry heaved. Sergeant Miller confronted him, nose to nose, and chewed him out, ridiculing his weak stomach and insinuating his mother hadn't been married when he was born. Then he approached the other twin and after two words, stopped short and whipped his head back and forth between them. Much as I had done when I first saw them. I don't know if he thought the afternoon heat caused him to see double, but it stemmed his tirade. At least temporarily.

Sick or not, we all suffered equally from the sergeant's anger and were not allowed to march back to camp until each man in the unit completed fifty jumping jacks in a row with full field packs.

We staggered through the gates of Fort Meade at dusk, filthy and exhausted. And angry enough to go AWOL.

CHAPTER
SEVEN

SAM

Each day dawned more difficult than the last until we settled into the swing of things, only to be transferred to Fort McClellan in Anniston, Alabama, for a new in-depth routine and rifle training. Once there, we received the M-1 Garand rifles and our target scores improved significantly over those from shooting the old Enfields at Fort Meade.

We had only been there about a week when we received our "Rolling W" shoulder patches that identified us as part of the 89th Infantry Division. Once trained, our unit would join General George Patton's Third Army. Right in the heart of the fighting.

I lay in the swampy Alabama mud amid the heat and marsh gas that steamed around me, stinging my nose and eyes, but I banished those thoughts and focused on the target in front of me on our first day of live ammunition training. Sweat threatened to cloud my vision, but I fired off a full round of cartridges, almost choking on the sharp, sickly sweet smell. My target shredded and I later received an "Expert" medal, as did all the soldiers in my little band. It gave me a sense of comfort to know the people I counted on to keep me alive could shoot well enough to do so.

I was amazed that, regardless of the weather, our training always took place in mud. We ran in the mud, stretched out in the mud to shoot at targets, and later, bellied our way under yards of stretched barbed wire in the mud. For weeks during that training, the machine guns they fired over our heads contained blanks, but on our first day of muddy slogging with real bullets zinging above us, I couldn't believe how difficult it was to keep my head down. The whine of live ammunition sounded different overhead and with my nose only an inch above the mire, I experienced such acute claustrophobia, all I could think about was hightailing it out of there. But the knowledge that a bullet could connect with my brain at any second kept my panic at bay and forced me to finish the exercise.

I wriggled under the final obstacle in my barbed wire path when I heard a weird thwack beside me and turned in time to see the head of the soldier in the next row burst in a bloody explosion of red. Sergeant Miller shouted the order to cease fire. The soldier lay still, facedown, and medics ran to his side, but it was too late. They turned him over and found a copperhead trapped beneath him from the dead weight of his body. Once freed, the snake slithered away.

The soldier's name was Hanson, we found out. Our regiment's first casualty of war. From a different barracks, fresh in from Chicago. Only eighteen. The poor guy had probably never seen a snake before, so his natural instinct was to stand and flee. We felt horrible for him.

At the Enlisted Men's Club later that evening, Dickie bought us all beers, since he was the only one old enough in Alabama where the drinking age was twenty-one. The New York boys could buy beer at eighteen, but only in New York. For the rest of us, the drinking age in our states was twenty-one, same as Alabama. Which brought the usual round of griping about being old enough to die for our country, but not old enough to buy beer.

I didn't normally drink, but Hanson's death had so rattled me, I swallowed the brew in two gulps. The bitter cold liquid constricted my throat and I struggled to breathe. The six of us huddled quietly at a table in the corner and kept to ourselves.

After half an hour or so, soldiers from a different company, their shoulder patches sporting the lightning bolt of the 25th Infantry Division, burst into the room in a noisy cluster and appeared to be several drinks ahead of us. Eddie Simmonds stood at the bar to refill our peanut bowl and one of the newcomers bumped into him.

"Watch where yer goin'," the newcomer slurred. He staggered, then assumed a fighting stance. His buddies formed a half-circle behind him, their fists clenching and unclenching.

"Look fellas," Eddie said. "I don't want no trouble—I'm here for a beer with my buddies." He turned and headed back to our table. But the drunken fool grabbed Eddie's arm and spun him around, sending peanuts flying in a spectacular arc.

We all rose, but Simon reached the soldiers in two steps, with Dickie a heartbeat behind him. The rest of us formed a wall as backup, ready to defend our pals if it became necessary. The drunken man drew his fist back and Dickie held Simon with one hand and placed his other on the forehead of the troublemaker. Both men's fists flailed the air, but Dickie held fast and towered over them by almost a foot. I stepped beside Simon and put a hand on his shoulder. He stopped swinging.

"Go about your business, boys," Dickie said quietly, "and leave us be."

The men from the other group remained tense for several long seconds. Then, one by one, they backed off and ushered their mouthy friend to a spot in the opposite corner. Simon put his arm around Eddie and we all returned to our table.

To the casual observer, it was nothing—a few soldiers getting in the faces of a few other soldiers. But to me, that confrontation cemented a significant step on our path to brotherhood, especially given the way Simon and Eddie scrapped on the day they met.

Like family, regardless of how we acted or reacted to each other in private, we would always present a unified front to the rest of the world.

And we could always count on each other. Always.

Which, I figured, would be critical once we made it to the battlefield.

CHAPTER EIGHT

GERDA

In the six months after Rebecca's family entered the Jewish-only sector, Gerda had spirited close to one hundred children from harm's way, most of them babies.

The guard, Aldrik, greeted her when she arrived and always accepted the treats she brought. On the rare occasions he greeted her with suspicion, she agreed to meet him on the other side of the fence where they exchanged kisses. After a while, kissing Aldrik became part of her routine. While she still didn't understand why the Nazis hated Jews, she found she enjoyed her time with Aldrik. She wished she didn't have to be dishonest, but saving the children outweighed everything else.

Rebekah worked with the Jewish families to choose the children Gerda helped. Taking a child through the forest to a safe house and then arranging for its keep was expensive, so Rebekah and the families worked together to find funds among their meager possessions to help pay for the children's trips. Gerda insisted, however, the new families accepted the children with the understanding they would be returned to a blood relative after the war was over, and she kept careful records with the child's name and the name of the family to whom the child was entrusted. Duplicate sets of names, inscribed on small pieces of paper, filled glass jars buried in the bakery's back yard with another set buried at the farm. Gerda's mother had proven herself a willing helper to get the children to safety.

Neither Gerda's father nor Ernst knew anything of the operation.

Within months, all the children small enough to leave the Jewish ghetto in Gerda's bread wagon were gone. Larger children presented too much risk.

Impressed with Gerda's efforts, the Resistance approached her about saving children in the Buchenwald concentration camp, an hour and a half from Zwickau. In that facility, they told her, a strategy to save youth was already under way, led by Antonin Kalina, from Czechoslovakia, and Gustav Schiller, from Poland.

Hundreds of children, the Resistance fighters said, had been concentrated in a windowless barracks, known as "Block 66," and were kept hidden and relatively safe. An SS officer accepted bribes to conduct the daily *appells*, or roll call, within the barracks and away from the eyes of the other SS guards, rather than outside for all to see. On most days, the Resistance told Gerda, the guard skipped roll call altogether and turned in the same numbers.

But after the Wannsee Conference near Berlin at the beginning of 1942, Resistance leaders worried that even bribing the guard might no longer work because of the new strategy adopted by the top Nazi leaders who attended the conference. A strategy, Gerda learned, labeled the "Final Solution to the Jewish Question."

Which called for exterminating the entire Jewish population.

Worse, after the strategy was adopted, four thousand children were executed immediately and in Auschwitz, where two hundred thousand Jewish people were sent, the Nazis murdered seventy percent of them as soon as they arrived.

So the Resistance pleaded with Gerda to intensify her efforts, to help more children escape before it was too late.

"*Mutti*," Gerda whispered to her mother one night in early May, "what should we do? We can't let those children die. *Bitte*, help me figure this out."

They talked until dawn and created the beginning of a plan. That same morning, Gerda loaded the bakery truck with fresh bread and pastries and drove the hour and a half to the Buchenwald camp to get the lay of the land and see for herself what might work before reporting to her Resistance friends.

At the gate, she bribed her way in with strudel and *Lebkuchen* and told the guard she had fresh bread and pastries for Kommandant Krueger and his wife. Dressed in her Sunday finest, Gerda was invited into the Krueger's parlor with a basket of the most sought after items from the bakery. She sat on the expensive couch and noticed the table lamps, the shades of which sported unusual designs. "I've never seen anything like these lamp shades," Gerda told *Frau* Krueger. "Did you have them made special?"

Frau Krueger laughed as she poured coffee. "Oh *ja*," she answered. "They were made right here on the premises." She stopped pouring and studied Gerda's eyes. "From the tattooed skin of some of our filthy Jewish prisoners."

Gerda stifled her gasp and tried to maintain a steady gaze. "Well, they're very interesting," she said. "Please, won't you have a pastry to go with your coffee?" Gerda swallowed hard to keep from throwing up while *Frau* Krueger picked over the items in her basket, touching each one. "In fact," Gerda said, hiding a shudder, "please keep the whole basket. As a gift."

She couldn't imagine the thought process that went into killing a person and then skinning him to make a decoration for her parlor. But once the woman who had ordered that to be done had handled Gerda's pastry, she considered it tainted.

"Would you like a tour of the facility?" Kommandant Krueger asked.

Gerda agreed. At least it would get her out in the fresh air. She closed her mind to what she might see and planted a bland expression on her face. "*Gut.* Come with me." Gerda followed the kommandant to the main area of the camp. "*Leutnant* Ziegler will show you around. Thank you for coming. My wife and I will look forward to your fresh goods every week." With a "*Heil* Hitler," the senior officer left.

"I didn't know you were here, Aldrik," Gerda said. His eyes smoldered, his desire for her evident.

"*Ja*," he said. "What are you doing here?"

"Expanding my family's business. The kommandant has agreed to let me come here each week to sell my bread and pastries." She looked up at him and smiled. "It's a bonus that I will also get to see you." He moved closer and hugged her. In his embrace, she could see over his shoulder. At the chain link fence, a young prisoner stared at her—a filthy, emaciated man in a dirty striped uniform. She stared back and gasped when she recognized him.

Jakob. Rebekah's brother.

Aldrik pulled away from her. *"Was? Was is es?* What is it?"

"Oh," she said. "I was startled you would hug me out here in the open. Couldn't you get in trouble?"

He laughed and released her and they walked toward the fence. Jakob gave her a slight shake of his head and she pretended not to know him. Aldrik showed her various parts of the camp, but she cut it short, saying she had to get to the family farm by nightfall.

She met with her cousins, Ulrich and Ilyse, along with three members of the Resistance and agreed to help smuggle children out of Buchenwald. But instead of transporting them all the way to Baden-Baden, more than three hours away and then through the Black Forest to Vichy, she outlined a plan to get them to Walpersberg, less than an hour's walk, and have them escape through tunnels in an old mine that eventually emptied into France. She thought it was the perfect plan, she told them, with Jakob on the inside to select the children and Aldrik on the outside who would trade her kisses for ignorance of her whereabouts.

They all agreed. Resistance members would wait in the woods behind Buchenwald on the days Gerda made deliveries there. She had also decided she would take plenty of the family's pear brandy, *Birnen-Brand*, made on the family farm in Baden-Baden, to dull the reflexes of the German guards. Then she would lead the children out of Block 66 to the trees beyond, where the Resistance would spirit them out of camp to the tunnels. Other Resistance members would meet them there and escort them through the tunnels, into France or Luxembourg, to families waiting for them.

It would work, Gerda assured them. It *had* to work.

The Germans' "Final Solution" had already escalated, claiming more Jewish lives daily.

Gerda had to save as many of them as possible. She had no other choice.

CHAPTER NINE

SAM

We boarded transport trucks for Fort Butner, North Carolina, and the final leg of combat training prior to our transfer to Fort Shanks, New York, and the journey overseas. We considered ourselves lucky that our training location included the mild climate of North Carolina rather than the thin cold air in Camp Carson, Colorado, or the heavy icy air in Fort Dix, New Jersey. Regardless, more rigorous training than we had yet encountered awaited us. Fortunately, our little band of brothers remained intact, although some of us received instruction in different areas.

The Davis twins, for example, were chosen for bazooka training. Which, I must admit, struck me as ironic. They were not large men and I worried about them lugging the weight of such a weapon across the battlefield. Or crossing rivers with it. Or climbing mountains. All of which we'd been told we would have to do. The M1-Garand rifles we carried weighed about nine and a half pounds and stretched to more than three and a half feet long—not an insignificant size to haul into battle. Even for large men like Dickie and me, they took some getting used to. But the bazooka weighed almost fourteen and a half pounds with a length of more than five feet. And the rockets, at a foot and a half long and a hefty three and a half pounds each, on top of a full field pack, had to be a burden for Erwin, who shouldered them.

The twins also told me the bazooka's range was held to around thirty yards, which meant their bodies were visible to the enemy when they tried to secure a clear field of fire. And according to other bazooka gunners I spoke with, the backblast was supposed to be horrendous, and often exposed the gunners' positions even further.

But the brothers looked forward to it, especially since they'd been guaranteed they could serve together. Unusual, I learned, for any branch of the Armed Forces to allow brothers to fight side by side after all five boys in a family named Sullivan died together when their Navy ship went down in 1942.

The rest of us engaged in the most intense, strenuous physical activity we'd seen to date. Our daily maneuvers consisted of forced marches, proficiency tests, and combat readiness. We were replacement troops with less training than the soldiers who engaged in battle before us, so our physical fitness was monitored via "burp-up" exercises that tested our endurance and strength. Those of us who passed earned the "Expert Infantryman's Badge." And even more important, an extra five dollars in our monthly paychecks. Those who didn't pass were transferred to a non-combat unit. The passing qualifications included the ability to run a hundred yards in twelve seconds in Army boots and uniform, do thirty-five push-ups and ten chin-ups, navigate an obstacle course at a sprint, and then demonstrate accuracy with a Colt .45, the Garand M-1 rifle, and the Browning M2 standard issue submachine gun. We all passed easily.

The hills and rolling forest land around Camp Butner simulated conditions we expected to encounter in Europe and provided opportunities for us to practice river crossings. We also worked on our camouflage in the trees, but most of the time we were covered in mud, probably the best camouflage of all.

The worst exercise, in my opinion, included rehearsal for the dreaded gas attacks. Our new drill sergeant, Sherwood "Woody" Williams, informed us the Treaty of Versailles, signed after the First World War, prohibited gas warfare. But he also told us Hitler paid no attention to such agreements. So we prepared. Just in case.

The training I found most helpful came a few days after we arrived.

Hand-to-hand combat.

Having grown up with my brother Richard's temper, I'd engaged in many fistfights and out-and-out roll-around-in-the-mud brawls, much to our mother's displeasure. And the New York City boys, Simon and Eddie, well versed in street fighting, gladly anticipated the opportunity to punch somebody. But our gentle giant, Dickie, shied away from brawls. I wasn't sure why and wondered if he'd hurt someone unintentionally in his former life and simply chose to avoid fights.

We heard from Lieutenant Colonel James Grier, who introduced the training, that it was designed to overcome the fear of the unknown for soldiers who'd never engaged in physical combat. So he set up regular boxing training as a contest every night, with Divisional Championships on Friday nights.

Simon and Eddie loved his rules.

Rule, actually. There was only one.

Anything goes.

In fact, fifty percent of the points awarded the winner came from sheer aggressiveness. Simon Levy excelled in that one.

The second combat training device pitted entire platoons against each other, armed in heavy boxing gear, with the directive to "fight until you drop." Our boys made up for a lack of height and weight in wiry scrappiness, so we often won those contests too.

Our gritty little band didn't fare quite as well in the third part of the training, since it required stealth and finesse. But it approximated real battle conditions as closely as possible, so we worked extra hard to master the proper techniques.

By the end of our time there, we could hold our own with any of them. We were in perfect physical condition and had gained muscle mass. Which also improved our mental conditioning and confidence levels.

We considered ourselves ready to face Hitler's best.

How cocky was that? And incredibly naïve.

CHAPTER
TEN

SAM

The Friday before our final week of training, the six of us received forty-eight hour passes. We couldn't believe our luck. We hitched rides into nearby Durham and spent a huge portion of our hard-earned pay on a steak dinner with the works. After we ate, Simon and Eddie left us in search of women. Dickie shook his head in mock disgust. "Eddie, I thought you were engaged," he said. "What would your fiancé think about you catting around with other women?"

"Lay off, man," Eddie said. "I love my Sylvie, but I seen her a hunnert times. Just looking for a new view. Don't mean nothing."

They strutted out and the rest of us retired to a local bar. Our time stateside waned, so we hoped for a quiet evening.

We found a table close to the jukebox and ordered beers. In North Carolina, the drinking age was eighteen, so we were all able to buy our own. Gradually I became aware of the song filling the air, "A Fellow on a Furlough," by Jack Hanna, a slow dirge that made me wish I'd stayed in bed. I went to the jukebox to pick out something livelier.

"The song playing makes you want to slit your wrists, doesn't it?" A tall, lanky soldier studied song titles beside me and spoke without turning his head. "How about this one?" His finger rested on "G. I. Jive" by Johnny Mercer.

"That should work," I said. He turned my way and I held out my hand. "Sam Ryan, 89th Infantry."

"Cecil Reese. 9th Infantry. Fresh in from Guam."

"How long you been in?"

"Since January 1940. First stop after basic was Pearl Harbor."

"Oh," I said, "you were there during ..."

"Yes." He hung his head. "What a god-awful day. People don't understand how bad it was."

"Will you join us?" I asked. "I'd like to buy you a beer."

I introduced Cecil around the table and he took a seat between Dickie and me.

"Pearl Harbor, huh?" Dickie asked. "We haven't faced combat yet. What did it feel like to be in the middle of it?" Talking to a seasoned veteran on his way home from the war, even a different part of the war, could give us valuable insight into what we might expect.

Cecil took a long sip of his beer. We waited, giving him as much time as he needed.

"I'll never understand it," he said. "We received an alert around five o'clock on the evening of December fourth that an attack from Japan was imminent. I was a gunnery sergeant and our unit consisted of anti-aircraft gunners and radar trackers. So we should have been prepared for an attack like that. And with the mortars and equipment we had, we could easily have defended ourselves."

I watched his hands clench and unclench, and his breathing quickened. His glass shook and Dickie signaled the waitress for another round.

"We took up our positions," he continued, "in the hills above the base. Our ammunition was loaded and we sat, ready and waiting. Prepared."

We were mesmerized, trying to imagine how he must have felt, knowing the enemy was almost upon you, but also knowing you had everything you needed to defend yourself and your fellow soldiers.

"But early on the morning of December fifth, President Roosevelt canceled the alert. So we returned all the ammo to the munitions dump and went about our other duties for the next day and a half. I remember having a wonderful time that Saturday night. We crowded the Enlisted Club and everything was free. Food, drinks. A lot of my friends got sloppy drunk. For some reason, we never saw an officer anywhere. They wouldn't have been in the Enlisted Club, of course, but as far as I could tell, they were nowhere on base. We never even saw MPs. It was crazy. The next day, Sunday, very few of us had duty."

He took a deep breath. "And then a few minutes before eight o'clock on Sunday morning, December seventh, all hell broke loose. Most of my unit still slept, many of them hung over. But we heard the planes. I ran outside and saw them. Flying low. So low, I made eye contact with one of the Japanese pilots. It made my blood run cold. They flew in over the island, out to the harbor, then turned around and circled back." He took a long drink and then continued. "That's when they dropped the first bombs. Torpedo bombs. On the battleships berthed in the harbor." He stopped talking, then after a minute, said quietly, "Eleven minutes was all it took to devastate the fleet."

He lowered his head and his hands covered his eyes. It looked to us like he relived the horror. When he continued, his eyes shone with unshed tears. "We still couldn't find our officers, so we mustered ourselves to our combat position in the hills."

"I was going to ask you that," Erwin said. "If your unit was anti-aircraft, you were shooting at them, right?"

"That's the worst part," Cecil told us. "We did a great job of getting everything into position on our own. And our anti-aircraft guns should have been able to make short work of those planes. But we didn't have any ammunition. We couldn't get it without permission. And there was no one around to give it."

"For how long?" I asked. My throat was dry.

"Three hours."

"But the attack only lasted..." Dickie said.

"Right," Cecil answered. "Less than two."

We didn't know what to say.

"At one point," Cecil continued, "I suggested going to the ammo dump and getting what we needed so we could join the fight. But we had a clear view of the roads below us. Once the shelling started, civilians got scared and abandoned their vehicles, then ran in every direction. The roads were useless, snarled in a knot of traffic. No one could get through. We would never have made it to the ammo dump and back again in time to do any good."

"So you had to sit there and watch?" Ervin asked.

"Yes." Cecil's voice was no more than a whisper. "We sat there. Helpless. While our fellow soldiers died horrible deaths." He swallowed hard. "Shells tore through *The Arizona's* armored decks and hit her magazine below. She exploded in a mushroom cloud of flames, her sides ripped open like a tin can. The water around her burned with fire and sailors who didn't immediately die from the blast fought their way through the flames, trying to stay afloat until one of the smaller ships could get to them. Or until they could swim to shore. Many of them didn't get that far.

"Even as high as we were in the hills, shrapnel from the bombs flew past us. But worse," he stopped talking and closed his eyes before continuing, "the screams reached us. We watched in disbelief as charred bodies pitched over the sides of the huge battleship on its way to the bottom, the stench reaching us on the morning breeze. It struck our nostrils and turned our stomachs."

We remained silent. Not one of us had experienced that magnitude of horror.

"*The Arizona* sank completely in minutes," Cecil said. "With more than eleven hundred souls still aboard her."

He took another sip and his hand shook before the beer reached his lips.

"That same wave of bombers," he continued after a moment, "reached the airfield. With our planes lined up for them in an open field, row after row of fighter planes parked so close their wings almost touched. Can you imagine?"

"Why?" I asked.

"To prevent sabotage, we were told later. But from whom?" His voice rose and his tortured eyes held mine. He shook his head. "I can't figure out why anyone thought more planes could be destroyed by a few saboteurs sneaking around inside a hangar than out there in an open field as sitting ducks for the Japanese. It only took seconds for them to wipe out one hundred eighty-eight of them. By eight o'clock in the morning, it was done."

"They really accomplished all that in only eleven minutes?" Dickie paid for the second round of beer.

"Yes. On the first wave. The second wave began a little more than thirty minutes later and lasted until almost ten o'clock. That one was smaller, only about half the number of planes, and no dive or torpedo bombers. But they still did plenty of damage. When it was over, almost twenty-four hundred American military on the island had died and five of the eight battleships were sunk. Along with thirteen other ships and almost two hundred fighter planes, before the damned Japs headed back to their aircraft carriers."

"What kind of loss did they suffer?" Erwin asked.

"Practically none, by comparison. Fewer than sixty Japanese killed and only twenty-nine planes lost. And a couple of submarines."

We spent the entire evening talking with him, but we never saw Cecil again after that. He left to go home the following day.

Cecil's account of the attack on Pearl Harbor etched the horrors of battle into our brains, with only a few short weeks between us and our own fighting.

———

OUR BRIEFINGS AT OUR VARIOUS TRAINING CAMPS included significant events during the war, to give us context of how we fit in. Apparently, the higher-ups in Washington, specifically General Benjamin Lear, I was told, wanted to make certain we knew why the war was being fought. Personally, I thought that was a great idea. If we hadn't learned that Germany was intent on claiming world domination, we wouldn't have understood how crucial our participation was to the final outcome.

We already knew that President Roosevelt declared war on Japan the day after the Pearl Harbor attack, December 8, 1941. But most of us were unclear as to exactly when and why we went to war with Germany and Italy. To our surprise, we learned *they* both declared war on us. On December 11, 1941. And we reciprocated three hours later by declaring war on them.

With the advent of D-Day, the need for troops became both more massive and more urgent. Many soldiers, like Cecil, had already fought for five years and earned enough in the military point system to return home.

But for us, the need for men remained greater than ever before and the push to end the war became more pressing. Which is why we, as replacement soldiers, would face the field as green fighters and assume the positions of seasoned veterans who had either died or fought long enough to head back to the States. We were prime examples, along with the casualties of D-Day and the Pearl Harbor attack, of the expendability of soldiers to our government. In the big picture, we all understood that it's our government's job to supply an endless stream of fighters, and to have the most soldiers standing on the field at the end of the final battle. Mission over men, we were told. Our government couldn't afford to worry about the individual loss of life.

But dammit it all to hell, I could. And I did. Same as my fellow soldiers did.

I supported my government to do what it had to do to keep fighting. To win the war. But I also made a commitment to those around me to personally support them. To fight for them. I promised myself—made it a sacred vow—that none of the soldiers in my little band, not one, would die in battle because I had failed to fight hard enough to defend them.

I prayed that when our time in battle came, I could fulfill that promise.

CHAPTER
ELEVEN

SAM

A chill hung in the early winter air at Camp Shanks, the huge base that straddled the borders of New York and New Jersey, our last stop before shipping overseas. December in the north hosts lower temperatures, of course. But it was more than that.

The war was close. Awfully close. And heartbreakingly real after hearing Cecil's story.

We joined the forty thousand soldiers per month staged at Camp Shanks prior to heading overseas. Which earned it the nickname of "Last Stop U.S.A."

Our staging area was one of seven, which included an area for the Women's Army Corps and another for the Black Engineering Corps. There was even an area for prisoners of war. But with more than fifty thousand people in the camp, we mostly stuck to our own space and kept our heads down. Our status as members of the 89th Infantry Division told us the European Theater Operation—ETO in Army-speak—was our destination with Berlin, Germany, our final target.

We were headed for the heart of Hitler.

Regardless of which base we occupied, we regularly received news from the front. The Allies suffered defeats at the beginning of November, with the sinking of the American destroyer *Abner Read* in the Leyte Gulf by a Japanese kamikaze, followed by the British frigate *Whitaker*, off the coast of Ireland, and the American tanker, *Fort Lee*, in the Indian Ocean, both sunk by German submarines.

But a few days later, the Japanese cruiser *Nachi* was sunk in Manila

Bay by U.S. aircraft, and shortly after that, the United States bombarded Iwo Jima.

By the second week of December, Patton's Third Army, our destined division, captured the V-rocket factory at Wittring in eastern France.

"Man," Simon griped, "there won't be any fighting left by the time we get there."

We walked from the base theater after seeing the movie *Thirty Seconds Over Tokyo* starring Van Johnson and Robert Walker. The newsreel shown before it played fresh in our minds.

"Yeah," Eddie agreed. "What the hell else do we gotta learn about how to kill Krauts?"

Eddie and Simon crouched, assuming assault stance, and pretended to shoot at each other.

Dickie and I continued to walk and left Eddie's question hanging. Dickie lost a brother to D-Day, as I had, making the tragedies associated with war very personal to us. We were as ready to defend our country as Simon and Eddie, but we also wanted to soak up every bit of training that could give us an advantage over our enemy.

On our way from the theater, we passed the landmarks of the massive Quonset hut base—the ball field and bowling alley, a couple of USO clubs, the chapel, some stores, a bakery, and the hospital. The camp was a miniature city, erected in 1942. Our orientation had included a history lesson and we learned the camp's location was chosen due to its proximity to several rail lines and Piermont Pier, both of which allowed for easy access down the Hudson River to Manhattan and Hoboken harbors where large military ships could dock and then transport their cargo—us soldiers—to the front lines.

We ambled along in the direction of our favorite USO spot, the one closest to our barracks. Experience taught us that when Simon and Eddie got liquored up, we needed to get them to bed pronto to avoid trouble.

In our short stay there, we had seen entertainers Frank Sinatra and Jimmy Durante, and sports greats Joe DiMaggio and Joe Louis. The camp rubbed elbows with New York City, so it was an easy trip for celebrities to pop over and visit us. We really enjoyed their entertainment, but nothing could beat listening to our own USO girls singing "I'll be Seeing You," or dancing with them to Al Dexter's "Pistol Packin' Mama."

To our delight, the marquee in front of our club proclaimed "USO Show Girl Revue" and we knew we were in for a treat.

We squeezed into a packed house where stage lights focused on a dozen of our favorite USO ladies in a mock march, harmonizing to a medley of World War I songs. The last notes of "Pack Up Your Troubles in Your Old Kit-Bag" died out and we found a table in the back. Dickie cleaned up the remnants of the last occupants and Simon and I found two more chairs, so we could all sit. The music changed, and the girls went directly into "Oh How I Hate to Get Up in the Morning." It brought the men to their feet. The last line, "And then I'll get the dirty pup—the guy who wakes the bugler up—and spend the rest of my life in bed" elicited cheers and whistles that rang through the rafters. We all suffered from too little sleep, so that song was always popular with the troops.

The ladies picked up the tune of "Over There" and the men quieted slightly. Another forty thousand soldiers would ship out by the end of the week. The song was a somber reminder that, for us, the war closed in with frightening speed.

We sipped our beers and the girls marched off the stage to thunderous applause. Then the announcer came out. He was met with boos and jeers, probably because he didn't have a pretty face or shapely legs. But he quieted the men enough to introduce a new act—somebody we didn't recognize, named Elizabeth Booth Windsor. I didn't normally like new acts. That's why we chose that particular USO. We knew the girls and could count on their talent. New people didn't always deliver. I rose to go to the men's room.

And that's when it happened. Another one of those "moments in time." Like the one when I found out Walter had been killed. One of those rare times when I understood, as it happened, that my life would never be the same again.

She assumed her position at center stage and bent provocatively toward the audience. She was the most beautiful creature I had ever seen.

Spotlights reflected from the red sequins on her tight, knee-length dress and projected rosy sparkles to every corner of the room. The newsreel we had seen earlier that night detailed how women made sacrifices to raise their hems to the knee so there was more fabric for soldiers' uniforms. For the life of me, however, I couldn't remember seeing a uniform made with red sequins.

But it certainly worked for her. The shorter hemline revealed the most shapely legs I'd ever had the pleasure to ogle.

She hovered over an empty chair on the stage beside her, but I was so awestruck, I didn't hear what she said. Not a word. Regardless, I would have sworn she looked right at me and even raised her hand in my direction.

Suddenly there was commotion behind me and Simon and Eddie slapped me on the back and pushed me down the aisle toward her.

"What the hell?" I said.

"It's you, Old Man," Simon told me, guiding me to the front of the room. "She crooked her finger to you. She wants you on stage with her."

I looked up and her perfect smile almost blinded me. Her huge dark eyes looked black in the spotlight, and her short dark hair curled around her head like a halo. Hands all around me pushed me onto the stage and suddenly there I was, face-to-face with the woman of my dreams. The woman against whom all other women would be compared.

Until the end of time. Amen.

"Hiya, soldier," she said. "What's your name?"

My tongue refused to work so my buddies called it out and she smiled again.

"Sam?" she asked. "Is that it?" She was so tiny, she must have looked like an angelic elf beside me. And she smelled good. Fresh. Like my mother's flower garden in a spring breeze.

I nodded, and she reached up to my shoulders and gently pushed me onto the chair.

"So, Sam," she crooned, "may I sing you a song?"

My mouth went as dry as if cotton filled it. I couldn't swallow. But I nodded again. The music, which only vaguely registered in the background, strengthened and took on a definite beat. She moved around me, touching one shoulder and then the other.

Her lips whispered to her microphone and I'll never forget the throaty words. "I wanna be loved by you, just you, and nobody else but you."

Cheers erupted from the whole place and I'm sure I turned bright red. Probably matched her dress.

As she sang, she brought her sweet face inches from mine and looked deeply into my eyes. With the next line, "I wanna be kissed by you," I granted her wish and planted a huge one on her bright red lips. The soldiers went wild. They stood and cheered.

I was hooked. Hopelessly. Helplessly. In love with Elizabeth Booth Windsor.

My own little *Betty Boop*.

I decided then and there that she would be my wife. Before the song even finished, I devised a plan to take her home and meet my mother then marry her by the end of the year.

She gave me a quick hug and I snapped back to reality. Everyone in the place was still standing, cheering, stamping their feet.

She pulled me up from the chair and I leaned in and said, "I have to talk to you. Please find me when you finish on stage." She didn't answer but turned to the crowd.

"Come on, fellas," she said. "Let's hear it for Sam." And the cheering swelled again.

I managed to leave the stage without falling on my head and found my buddies, all of whom clapped me on the back and gave me some good-natured ribbing.

But I didn't care.

I was in love.

My future was clear.

CHAPTER
TWELVE

GERDA

Gerda visited the concentration camp at Buchenwald weekly, taking bread and fresh-baked confections to the commandant and his wife, along with his officers and the German personnel acting as administrators. The camp had expanded in the months Gerda visited and Aldrik gave her a tour of the new facilities. He showed her the indoor riding arena, a theater, a casino for the troops, dog kennels, and a zoo for the SS families, along with shooting ranges and at least one brothel. She knew other buildings existed, primarily for the torture of inmates, but Aldrik never mentioned those. So she didn't ask.

The last building he showed her was a mews, where a few carrier pigeons rested among the falcons. "The pigeons are sometimes used for communications," Aldrik said, "when we receive intelligence that our regular methods could be intercepted."

Gerda was delighted. "We used carrier pigeons on the farm when I was young," she told him. "My cousin, Ulrich, and I sent each other messages all the time."

While Gerda's rescue efforts during the previous two years had proven dramatically successful and saved more lives than she had dared hope, she hadn't been able to save everyone she would have liked. Both of Rebekah's parents had been sent to Buchenwald in late 1943. But, already weakened from too little food, Rebekah's father contracted typhus from the louse-infested barracks, despite being stripped and shaved of all hair as soon as he arrived. On the first day of December 1944, he and twenty-five others were forced from the barracks and shot. Rebekah's brother, Jakob, found out when he over-heard guards talking on his work detail in the quarry. When Gerda showed up the following week, he motioned her over to the fence and told her, then asked her to find a way to let his mother know.

Although she actively worked against the Nazi guards to save the lives of the children they planned to execute, Gerda enjoyed her time with Aldrik. He was so much kinder than the other officers she met. Gradually, their kisses had elevated their passions, but on that after-noon, when Aldrik discovered her talking to Jakob, he turned suspi-cious eyes toward her. Then he took her arm roughly and guided her to his small house.

They sat together on the sofa and he took her hands in his.

"Gerda," he said, after filling her face with kisses, "why were you talking to that boy?"

"Oh, Aldrik," she said. She reached up to twirl one of his curls around her fingers and then fixed him with a winning smile. She gave him a small kiss on his lips. "I saw him here the first time I came. He's Rebekah's brother—you remember her from the Jewish-only sector in Zwickau, right?" Gerda had visited Rebekah every day for months and Aldrik had assisted her. "He used to be my neighbor. He told me his father died. It was gossip. Nothing more."

"I hope so," he said, putting his hand on her knee. "Consorting with the prisoners without a guard around could get you into trouble, you know." His hands moved under her skirt and he continued to kiss her. "Serious trouble," he said, nuzzling her neck. Both hands found her underwear and gently tugged. "More trouble than even I could get you out of."

"Aldrik…"

She pushed at his hands, but they became insistent, rubbing her skin, his thumbs firm on her hips, pulling her toward him. His fingers explored every inch of her and she found she no longer wanted to resist. He took her hand and placed it between his legs and she moaned involuntarily. In one swift movement, he shed his trousers and entered her. She responded by shoving against him and welcomed his thrusts then relaxed into her emotions and shut out all other thoughts. She loved Aldrik and refused to examine her feelings about his part in keeping Jewish people captive. Or worse.

After several minutes, he leaned away from her and pulled her dress down over her knees, then rearranged his pants. "I love you," he said.

"I love you, too," she breathed into his ear, happy in the knowledge that he returned her feelings.

"And I don't want to lose you," he continued. "So please don't do anything to get yourself into trouble. I may not be able to save you."

"Yes...no...I won't," she added, her brain still clouded.

"We will get married," he said. "Soon. We will live here."

"Yes," she whispered, her lips kissing his ear.

She sat up straight. "Wait." She shook her head. "Yes," she repeated. "I agree. We'll be married. But I need to stay with my parents. They can't manage the bakery without me. I'll still come here once a week as I always do. And even spend the night sometimes," she added, resuming her soft kisses. "But I just can't leave them yet. Maybe when the war is over."

He didn't argue and she was relieved. She still had work to do, children to save. She believed she could compartmentalize her feelings and love the sweet young man with her while at the same time, continue her silent crusade against Nazi atrocities. She avoided linking the Nazi beliefs to Aldrik. She had to keep them separate.

They strolled through the courtyard. "Aldrik," she said, entwining her arm with his. "Before I go, will you find *Frau* Rosenbaum for me? Rebekah's mother?" He stopped and frowned at her. "She doesn't know her husband is dead. Her son asked me to tell her." She reached up and kissed him again. "Will you do it for me? You said it would be okay as long as a guard was present."

He shrugged. "Wait here," he told her and entered the prisoner compound.

He returned with Rebekah's mother and she looked at Gerda warily. Gerda faced her through the fence. "*Frau* Rosenbaum," she said kindly, "I saw Jakob today and he gave me some bad news." She didn't wait for Mrs. Rosenbaum to respond but rushed ahead. "I'm sorry to have to tell you this, but your husband died earlier this month. Again, I am sorry." She tried to ignore Mrs. Rosenbaum's sharp intake of breath and the tears that built in her eyes. Aldrik watched her, so she hid her feelings. The Rosenbaums had been her family's friends for decades and watching her friend suffer hurt her heart. But she didn't show it. She simply nodded, thanked Aldrik and walked away.

She made her deliveries quickly and drove the bakery truck back to Zwickau, then collapsed into her mother's arms and cried with her over the same sad news.

CHAPTER
THIRTEEN

GERDA

Gerda and Aldrik married less than a month later in a quiet ceremony with only her mother and father present. They exchanged matching gold wedding bands, set with a row of diamonds.

Within a week, her Resistance friends suggested she stop her activities on their behalf.

She fixed them with hard eyes. "On your behalf?" she asked. "Is that what you think? That I'm only doing this for you?" She stood firm, her hands on her hips. "I couldn't care less about your mission," she said, her voice rising. "I do what I do because I care about people. Because it's the right thing for one human being to do for another. Because our government is wrong."

"Then we agree, *Fräulein*," Michel Baudelaire, her main contact for more than two years, told her after a short silence. "Excuse me...*Frau* Ziegler," he amended. "We, too, believe the German government is wrong in its beliefs, its tactics. And we, too, care about each person being able to live a humane life, free from constant fear of execution." He studied her face. "I only thought it may be too hard on you to continue. That your loyalties may be torn." He turned away from her. "And that should you be caught, it might now be easier for you to give up names and locations for the Resistance movement that we would not wish to fall into German hands."

"I understand your concern," she said through clenched teeth. "Although, truthfully," she continued, her irritation building, "the fact that you put it into words angers me. That you could possibly think, after all we've been through together, after all the people we've saved together, that I would ever name names... Well, I can't believe that thought would even enter your head. So *nein*," she said. "I will not have a problem continuing to save as many people as I can." She crossed her arms over her chest, but moments later reached out to Michel. "I wish I could make you understand. I love my husband. But, as a person, not as part of the Nazi SS Guard. Besides, he's not like the others."

Gerda's cousin, Ulrich, and Michel exchanged a look. Michel heaved a long sigh. "If you say so, *Frau* Ziegler. I hope you are correct." He was silent for a moment, then sighed again. "Very well. We will continue."

And they did. Twice a week, Gerda got word to Jakob, who arranged with Antonin Kalina and Gustav Schiller, the elders of Block 66, to select three to four children and then make certain they were able to escape the barracks in the middle of the night. Through funds from the Resistance, bribes to the guard assigned to Block 66 had increased threefold so he would dispense with morning and evening *appells* altogether.

New children arrived almost weekly, from the sub-camp of Ohrdruf, an hour away, but not enough to make up for the number that had been rescued. If the guard at Block 66 had conducted daily roll call and noticed how drastically the number of children had dwindled, the whole operation might have unraveled and all those involved arrested. And probably executed.

The elders agreed to give the children French names, to teach them a few French words and to let them know what to expect during their journey, that they would have to walk for hours through dark forests and would probably not be able to rest or eat while maintaining complete silence. Until they were out of Germany and into Vichy, France. Or Luxembourg. The children needed to know the trip wouldn't be easy and that they risked capture and death with every step they took. Gerda impressed on the elders the need to choose carefully and to pair babies with children who were old enough to take care of them. If even one child were caught, the whole operation would be shut down. And they would all hang.

Everyone in the chain accepted the risk. The elders passed the children's Jewish names and their new French names to Gerda, who recorded them, along with the names of the families who received them. Mostly in free Europe, but occasionally outside the continent. She always returned her lists to the glass jars that had housed them for so many years and then buried them, waiting for the end of the war and a reunion of scattered children and the families that remained.

So far, Gerda acknowledged, the children chosen for the journey had proven worthy.

To date, she thought with satisfaction, almost one thousand children had been rescued and removed from Germany.

CHAPTER
FOURTEEN

SAM

For the two weeks after we met, the love of my life, whom I'd officially dubbed "Betty," and I spent every spare minute together. Imagine my surprise when I learned she returned my feelings and again, after only a week and a half, when she agreed to marry me.

I received an unexpected Christmas furlough and took Betty home to Prospect Park to meet my family. The farmhouse didn't have a telephone, so I couldn't let them know to expect us. Besides, I liked the idea of surprising them. Once we arrived at the bus station, we splurged on the only taxi in town, drove out to the farm, and traveled up the long lane. My heart raced at the thought of introducing Betty to my mother.

We rounded the last bend and the large white farmhouse filled my vision, warming my soul as I knew it would. Its wraparound porches beckoned, welcoming and inviting. Only minutes separated me from my mother's arms.

Walter's jalopy rested in its normal place by the side steps. But several other cars joined it and filled the small patch of browned grass in the front yard.

"Looks like you have company," Betty said. "Did they know you were coming?"

"No," I answered. My heart's excitement waned and apprehension flew in. "Something's wrong. I feel it." We jumped out of the taxi, gathered our few bags and paid the driver. Too much, probably, because I had trouble focusing by then.

Little Freddie hunched on the porch steps without a coat, and at seeing me, burst into tears. "Hey, little guy," I said, folding him in my arms. "What's the matter?"

He continued to cry. Deep, choking sobs. Fear stabbed my heart and left my breath shallow. I picked Freddie up. Mrs. Gibbons met us at the door.

"Oh Sam," she said. "You're here! We weren't expecting you. Come on in, honey."

She stood aside and Betty and I entered the warm kitchen, abuzz with my mother's church ladies. They all turned to look at us with cries of "Sam! It's Sam."

"Hi everybody," I said. "This is Betty." Then I turned to Mrs. Gibbons. "What's wrong?" I asked. "What's happened?"

"It's your mother, honey," she said, taking our coats. "Your sisters are with her."

"You go on, Sam," Betty said. "I'll get to know these ladies." I squeezed her hand and found my sisters in the parlor, clustered around my mother on the daybed.

"Sam!" Kathleen said. She rose to hug me and burst into tears. My other sisters crowded around, and more tears followed. "I was going to have Billy send you a telegram," Kathleen said, "but she got so much worse last night, I was afraid to leave her."

"What...?" Words failed me.

"She never recovered from the boys' funerals," Kathleen managed to choke out. "She'd improve for a day or two and then get sick again. Dr. Garrett told us yesterday it had gone into pneumonia, and it weakened her heart, her lungs. Well, everything. She died this morning." She stopped talking and hung her head. "I should have tried to let you know," she continued in a whisper. "So you could have seen her one last..." Her voice broke and her tears overflowed.

I couldn't believe how much my heart hurt. In fact, I was certain it was breaking. Losing my mother was devastating, of course, but I also grieved that the two most important women in my life would never have a chance to meet. I'd been so excited to introduce my wonderful mother to my darling Betty. And we'd missed it by only a few hours.

My sisters moved to make space for me and I knelt by my mother's side. I kissed her hand, cold to my touch, her skin translucent. The whiff of death floated over her like a cloud.

The girls had done a great job of decorating the house for Christmas, with the lighted tree set up in the room where my mother lay, directly in her line of sight. She loved Christmas, always had and it was obvious my sisters had been determined Mother would enjoy that one as well.

She almost did.

"Mr. Carruthers is here," Mrs. Gibbons said behind us.

The undertaker hovered at the door and my sisters left the room, allowing me a little while longer with Mother. I was vaguely aware of chatter from the kitchen and assumed my sisters met Betty. That was not the way I had hoped to introduce them, but I couldn't focus on that. I was still consumed with my heartache at having missed saying good-bye to my mother. My first thought was to curse the war that had kept me from her but I caught myself because that same war also brought me Betty.

Mrs. Gibbons found me in the parlor after a few minutes and put her hand on my shoulder. "Sam," she said, "I've made plates for you and Betty. Come into the kitchen and eat something. Mr. Carruthers will take care of your mother."

Mother's church friends busied themselves with making room at the table for us and Mrs. Wainwright gave me a hug. "Billy will be here to pick me up soon," she said. "He'll be so glad to see you." She smiled at Betty. "And to meet Betty."

One by one, my sisters joined us at the table. Despite their grief, I could tell they had warmed to her right away. But we were surprised when Freddie pushed himself between us and climbed onto Betty's lap. She hugged him to her and he settled into her curves.

"It's almost time for Santa, you know," she said in an obvious effort to take his mind off losing his mother.

He nodded.

"What do you want him to bring you?" she asked.

His shoulders lifted in a small shrug, but he remained silent.

Kathleen lowered her eyes and tears streaked her face. "We told Freddie Santa may not find us this year," she said, "what with Mother being sick and the war and all."

"Yeah," he agreed in a tiny voice, "the war and all..."

He put on such a brave front, I couldn't talk over the lump in my throat. Again, I wanted to curse the war that brought so much pain. The poor little guy had already suffered enough in his young life. It simply wasn't fair. I decided to talk to Kathleen later and figure out a way to get Freddie *something* for Christmas.

"Betty, from Elizabeth, right?" Mrs. Wainwright asked in the silence that followed. "In the Bible, that name translates to 'Oath of God.'"

"Pardon me?" Betty asked.

"Mrs. Wainwright," I told Betty, "knows the true meaning of names from their biblical origins."

"I love that," Betty said. "What does Sam's name mean?"

"'Name of God,'" Mrs. Wainwright replied. "You two are a great match."

"That's good to hear," I said. I took Betty's hand and turned to my sisters and my mother's friends, "because Betty has agreed to marry me."

Smiles lit their tear-stained faces and we shared hugs all around the kitchen.

Mr. Carruthers cleared his throat from the parlor doorway. "We're finished here," he said. "When can we get together to make the, uh, final arrangements?" His words unleashed new tears.

"I'll go," Kathleen said. "I'll follow you into town."

"I'll join you," I told her.

We headed out to Walter's jalopy. "You drive, Sam," Kathleen said and climbed into the back seat. Betty eased in beside me and rested her hand on my knee.

"Katie," I said, "I know it's hard to think about right now, but I'd like to get Freddie something for Christmas. What would he like?"

"Before Mother took a turn for the worse," Kathleen said, "all he could talk about was a Radio Flyer wagon. But Sam, the department store sells them for nine dollars. We couldn't spend that kind of money right now. Especially with having to pay for Mother's...well, you know."

"We'll get it for him," Betty said. "If that's okay with you," she added quickly.

Kathleen's silence worried me, so I turned to look at her. A smile curved her lips and lit her eyes. "That would be great," she said softly. "He would love that. We all would." She put her hand on Betty's shoulder. "Thank you. I would be incredibly grateful."

Kathleen and I went to meet Mr. Carruthers and Betty left us to go to Harrington's Department Store. We made the necessary decisions and settled on Sunday, Christmas Eve, for Mother's funeral. Reverend Purdue would handle the service as he had for my brothers.

We left the funeral home, bundled up against the cold, and walked toward the department store to find Betty. There hadn't been snow for a couple of weeks, Kathleen had told me, so despite the bitter temperatures, the sidewalks were clear of ice.

"So, when are you planning to hold the wedding?" Kathleen asked.

"Not sure," I answered. "We had hoped to get married here before I have to return to camp. Before I go overseas. But now..."

She stopped walking and took my arm. "Sam," she said, "that would be perfect."

"What?" I asked. "How do you figure that? It seems disrespectful."

"No," Kathleen said. "No, it isn't. Look, even if you had gotten here while Mother was still alive, she probably wouldn't have known it. In fact, I hadn't told you this, but at the end, during those last few days she was able to talk, she went on all the time about Walter and Richard coming to see her."

Shivers found my spine and I put my arms around her. She slumped into me and let her grief flow. I shared her pain. Even at my age, I felt like an orphan.

"Do you think they came to get her, Sam?" she whispered. "Do things like that really happen?"

"Yes, Katie," I said, rubbing her back. "I think they do."

Truth was, I didn't know if my brothers showed up to escort my mother to heaven or not, but I sure hoped so. What a wonderfully comforting thought.

Kathleen worked to control her tears. "We knew she wouldn't get any better. And honestly," she said with effort, "now that I think about it, I'm glad you didn't see how she was at the end. I would have hated it if you'd made a special effort to get here and then she hadn't recognized you."

We started walking again and she continued to talk. "So, I don't think having your wedding before you return would be disrespectful at all. In fact, what a great way to celebrate her life. With a new beginning." She wiped her eyes. "Think about it," she said, "the whole family will be here, the town will already be assembled, and Reverend Purdue will already be with us. It makes perfect sense. I mean since you were going to get married during this time, anyway."

"Let's see what Betty thinks," I said, draping an arm across her shoulder. We entered the department store and found Betty coming toward us, her arms full of packages.

The smile left her face when she saw us. "How did it go?" she asked. "I'm so sorry you're both having to go through this."

We filled her in on the arrangements and I suggested we sit at the lunch counter for a soft drink. I took her packages to the car and Betty and Kathleen found stools. Several people came over to shake my hand and to ask about our mother. They all promised to come to her funeral.

"Betty," Kathleen said, "Sam and I were talking on the way here." She took a deep breath. "We—I—think you two should go ahead and get married on Sunday. Right after Mother's funeral." She didn't wait for a reaction. "I told Sam, the whole town will already be together and Reverend Purdue will be on hand..." Her words tapered off and silence followed.

"Kathleen thought the celebration of our new beginning," I told Betty, "would be a fitting tribute to our mother. What do you think?"

Betty closed her eyes. "I don't believe it," she said with a small smile. "The exact same thought has been going through my head. Do you think anyone would mind?"

"Everyone would love it," Kathleen told her.

"Then I think it's a fine idea. But only under one condition." She took Kathleen's hands in hers. "I have no family left," she said. "Both my parents are dead, and I was an only child. So my condition is that you agree to be my Maid of Honor." They hugged and it was settled.

Mr. Harrington found us and told us how sorry he was about our mother. He also congratulated me on my engagement to Betty. Then he turned to her. "And I found that wheel we talked about, young lady," he told her.

"What?" I asked.

"The only Radio Flyer wagon Mr. Harrington had left in the store was missing a wheel," she said. "He told me if he could find it, we could have the wagon at a discount." She turned to him. "Thank you so much. I'm sure Sam can fix it."

We visited the jewelry department and purchased matching gold bands. Then we stopped by the courthouse for a marriage license. We returned to the house and found my sisters and my mother's friends in the kitchen, organizing the food brought by neighbors. Kathleen told them about our marriage plans and they gathered around us, all chattering at once. They put their heads together and in minutes, the plan was in place. My head spun at how fast it happened.

Later, I sat at the table with a cup of coffee. Mrs. Gibbons eased into the chair beside me.

"I don't mean to get into your business," she said, "but I wanted to make you aware of something."

"Go on."

"Kathleen has an opportunity for a position at the shirt factory. The one that's been vacant since your mother got sick. They held off filling it to see if your mother recovered, but now..."

"That she's gone," I finished. "I guess we need to get used to saying it."

"Yes," she said. "Well, with that, they told me they need to fill her position soon and want to offer the job to Kathleen. She would be great at it and it pays well."

"That's wonderful," I said. "What's the problem?"

"She doesn't think she can accept it because of Freddie. Someone needs to stay with him."

"Oh yeah," I said. "And the Army allotment Mother received from my service will start going to Betty."

"Right," she said. "I thought of that too."

I had learned about other families in the county that lost their sources of income, and in many cases, the younger children were sent to live with relatives or neighbors and the farms sold to help with their upkeep. I didn't want that to happen to my family.

"Betty still has her USO job," I said, "so I'm certain I can have the bulk of my allotment continue to come here, to Kathleen. At eighteen, she's legally old enough to receive it. That would help, right?" I frowned. "I hate for Kathleen to give up a job she wants that would also mean more money for the family. But, she's right. I don't know what we'd do about Freddie." I looked over at her. "Any ideas?" I asked.

"Yes," she said. "That's what I wanted to talk to you about. The factory is adding a second shift and they've asked me to be the supervisor."

"Congratulations," I said. "I hope you get a raise."

"I do. Which will come in handy. But my hours will change. I'll be working from three to ten instead of eight to three. So, I was thinking, if you agree, Sarah and Winnie could walk Freddie to my house on their way to school and pick him up on their way home. At fourteen, Sarah's old enough to care for him and to even start dinner before Kathleen gets home. And the arrangement would only be for five months, since Freddie starts school in the fall and the younger girls can care for him during the summer months. Right? What do you think?"

Tears filled my eyes and I covered her hand with mine. "We'll be happy to pay you," I said quietly. "I can't believe you would help us out like this."

"Honey," she said, "your mother was like a sister to me and she would have done the same thing if the situation had been reversed."

"Yes," I said. "I know she would have."

"In fact," Mrs. Gibbons continued, "she was always doing things for everybody. It didn't matter who the family was, if they had a life event happen—a death, a birth, or anything in between—there was Maudie, with a right hot pie."

I smiled at that. At the simple things that meant so much to the folks in these parts.

"And you won't have to pay me anything," she continued, "but have the girls send a snack with him so we know he always has his favorite treats." She pushed her chair back. "Let's talk to Kathleen about it," she said. "I wanted to clear it with you first."

———

I WOKE TO GRAY SKIES THE FOLLOWING MORNING. THE tantalizing smell of frying bacon—a treat left over from Winnie's "Pigmalion"—drew me to the kitchen where I was the last to arrive. My sisters busied themselves with breakfast and Betty sat at the table, holding Freddie on her lap. I kissed her forehead and tousled his hair. "Hey, Sport," I said to him. "Want to play catch later?"

"Too cold," he said and snuggled deeper into Betty's chest.

"Is it too cold for a walk?" Betty asked. She pulled him in closer. "After breakfast. I'd like to see the family cemetery and be introduced to your brothers. Could you take me there, Freddie?" He nodded and climbed down.

"And you'll come too, Sam?" he asked. His tiny hand slid into mine.

"I'd love to," I croaked, unshed tears interfering with my voice.

We took Betty to the family burial plot and visited with my brothers for a while but left as the funeral crew arrived to dig my mother's grave. Wind whipped at our coats and stung our faces on our walk back to the house and our little group was somber.

But we entered the warm kitchen and found it humming with activity and wonderful aromas. Kathleen simmered a stew for dinner, made with one of Winnie's chickens, and Mrs. Wainwright delivered our wedding cake, fresh from the oven. Mrs. Gibbons and her daughters had cut the last of Mother's white camellias and arranged them throughout the house to celebrate our wedding the following day. Mother would have basked in the love radiating from her domain.

———

CHRISTMAS EVE DAWNED BRIGHT AND CRISP, WITH A NEW layer of powdery snow that transformed our rutted yard into a fairyland. Little Freddie christened it with the first footprints.

We met in the kitchen and wolfed down a quick breakfast before piling into Billy's Packard and Walter's jalopy to attend Mother's funeral. After the service, we all shed tears at the family cemetery as she was lowered into the ground next to my brothers. I hated leaving her there and wished for the hundredth time I could have hugged her once more before she died. Kathleen's story about Mother believing Walter and Richard had come to see her filled my head, and again, I hoped it was true. I saluted them both before walking back to the house where everyone else had already reassembled.

Warmth and love created an inviting atmosphere when I walked into our big kitchen. My heart still missed my mother, but the festive joy surrounding my wedding was contagious. And welcome, after a third burial in six months.

Reverend Purdue took his place in front of the Christmas tree in the freshly cleaned parlor, the hovering scent of Pine-Sol dispelling the stench of death.

But I noticed something else. The calendar showed late December, but I swear, when I walked into that room, the fragrance of jasmine and roses was so strong, I looked around to see if someone else had brought flowers. Mrs. Wainwright put her hand on my shoulder.

"You smell it, don't you?" she asked.

"What?"

"Don't play with me, Sam. I see it on your face. You smell the jasmine and roses, right?"

"How did you—?"

"It's the angels," she answered. "They're here for your mother."

To my credit, I didn't roll my eyes. Mrs. Wainwright had always worn her spiritual beliefs on her sleeve and experienced more of the unseen than the rest of us. But, truth be told, I *did* smell roses and jasmine. In addition to the camellias. So if angels really did come to escort Mother, that struck me as totally appropriate.

Billy, my best man, and I took our places beside the reverend while Mrs. Wainwright played the wedding march on the upright piano in the corner. It needed tuning, but no one else seemed to notice. Or care. Then my siblings filed into the room. Sarah and Winnie sprinkled camellia petals as they walked slowly toward us with Freddie, who carried the rings, between them. Next came Kathleen, with my beautiful Betty behind her.

The ceremony was short and when the reverend pronounced us husband and wife, everyone applauded.

Happiness surrounded me. Except for the gaping hole the size of my mother. Still, Kathleen had been correct. Even with Mother gone, it was right to proceed with my marriage. She would have wanted it that way.

Our well-wishers filled themselves from the abundance of food, gifts from our caring neighbors, then departed, and the family sat in the kitchen. The girls drifted off to bed and took Freddie with them.

Betty and I placed the Christmas presents she bought under the tree, including Freddie's red wagon. With all four wheels intact. As an added bonus, Betty placed crayons, thick tablets of drawing paper, and coloring books inside it. I knew Freddie would love them.

I wouldn't have had a clue what to get the girls, but I believed Betty's choices were perfect. A bright colored scarf and matching hat and gloves for Kathleen; three Nancy Drew mysteries for Sarah, including the newest one, *The Secret in the Old Attic;* and for ten-year-old Winnie, a large, colorful box titled "Paper Doll Party," featuring six dolls, Betty said, and at least a dozen sheets of printed clothes.

When at last I was alone with the love of my life, our union was everything I had ever hoped for. We didn't sleep until almost dawn.

Freddie's shrieks jolted us awake.

We shrugged into our robes and flew down the stairs, fear plain on our faces.

But we found him, unharmed, sitting in his new red wagon with the biggest grin I'd ever seen on his tiny face. The girls waited until we joined them to open their presents and then planted countless hugs and kisses on us. They even had gifts for Betty and me—hand-knit hats and scarves for both of us.

Snow fell all morning and we spent a lazy day playing games and enjoying each other's company. I savored every minute, knowing that in a few short days, I'd be on my way to Europe.

My orders called for me to return to Camp Shanks on New Year's Eve for my final physical and equipment check prior to shipping out. I hugged my siblings tight before leaving them and all too soon, the reality of war smacked me in the face again.

Betty made the return trip with me and we spent our last night together in the Hotel Chelsea on Twenty-third Street in New York. The manager reduced the regular room charge from two dollars and a quarter to two dollars, because I was in uniform. Betty and I held each other and tried to cram the next few months' worth of love into a single night. Time was short when I caught the trolley and then the bus back to Camp Shanks.

I left my new wife standing at the door of our hotel room, waving and crying, with no idea how long it might be until I saw her again.

For the second time in less than a week, I was certain my heart was breaking.

CHAPTER
FIFTEEN

SAM

In the first week of 1945, we marched aboard our transport ferry on Piermont Pier and crammed the top deck. Our trip down the Hudson River took us under the George Washington Bridge and over the Lincoln Tunnel on our way to Hoboken Harbor where we would board the *Queen Mary* for our trip across the Atlantic.

My buddies and I stood together at the rail of the ferry, looking out over the water. Even with them surrounding me, the black shroud of grief that accompanied me on my initial trip to Fort Meade six months earlier found me again and hung heavy on my heart. I was thrilled to have married my darling Betty, but I missed her so much my whole body hurt.

Plus, I missed my mother and sisters and little Freddie. Before the war, I had taken for granted that they were always there, and that I would spend time with them again. Now, that was no longer possible. Mother was gone and I truly didn't know if I would get back home to the rest of them after I joined the battle in Europe. We had been trained that once we touched the soil of France and prepared to engage in our first battle, we needed to operate as if we were already dead. Without hope of returning.

"Come on, Old Man," Simon said with an arm around my shoulder. "You Old Married Man. Let's get off this tub and get on a real boat." We had all heard about the splendor aboard the luxurious *Queen Mary* and had seen the pictures of her in *Life* magazine, proudly sporting her bright red, black, and white coloring. I didn't much care about her interior, but Betty read the *Life* article to me and she was really impressed with the thick carpeting and chandeliers, "each one," she read, "with thousands of prisms that reflected light in millions of tiny rainbows." So we anticipated a comfortable voyage across the ocean.

Our last little bit of luxury before marching through mud to meet Hitler.

Moments later, we caught our first glimpse of the glorious ship and Simon laughed out loud. "Man," he said with a shake of his head. "I don't believe it. Go figure."

The massive ship, eighty-one thousand tons, I remember reading, with her sun deck an impressive seventy-five feet above the water line, looked like a poor caricature of her former self. Gone was the bright, distinctive coloring, replaced with a drab, cloudy-day gray. Even as close as we were, her outlines blurred into the cold waters of Hoboken Harbor.

"They call her the *Gray Ghost* now," Dickie said. "One of her crew members told me."

"That makes sense," I said. "But did they have to change her that drastically?"

"I guess so," Dickie answered. "Given Hitler's attitude."

"What's that damned Kraut gotta do with it?" Eddie asked.

"I talked to some sailors last night at the Enlisted Club," Dickie continued. "They said Hitler's furious that the *Mary* can deliver ten to fifteen thousand fresh soldiers to the war each time she crosses the Atlantic. So he's supposed to have offered a two-hundred-and-fifty-thousand-dollar reward to the Nazi submarine gunner who can sink her."

"Whew," Simon whistled, "for that kinda dough, I'd consider doing it myself."

"Except he wouldn't pay you to blow her up," Erwin Davis said with a laugh. "And, even if you did it anyway, he wouldn't rescue you when you landed in the water."

The Davis twins had rejoined our company at the completion of their training. "But with that kind of reward at stake," Erwin added, "I wonder how much longer her luck will hold out?"

"You're right about the rescue part," Dickie said. "If the Germans ever do get her, our chances of being rescued, even as prisoners of war, are nonexistent. We need to say our prayers, boys, that she keeps avoiding those U-boats. If that ship goes down," he pointed to the ocean liner waiting for us, "and ten thousand soldiers with her, that would be a crushing blow for the Allies and a decisive victory for Adolf Hitler."

A cloud of worry enveloped us as Dickie's words sank in and we shuffled toward the massive gray shape in silence.

We boarded her in full combat gear—cartridge belt, canteen, rifle— and carried our heavy duffle bags. On the ship, we each received a letter from President Roosevelt letting us know we were "soldiers in the United States Army, embarking for distant lands where the war is being fought." As if that were a surprise to us.

In keeping with the changes to her outward appearance, the spartan conditions onboard shocked us. Gone were the miles of carpeting we'd read about, the deck chairs, even the china and silver, we found out later. Instead, walls of sandbags greeted us. We stepped through rows of hinged metal doors and found our way to the bowels of the ship where we would spend our journey across the Atlantic. Our sleeping quarters consisted of bunks stacked six high with only eighteen inches between them. "Racks," seasoned soldiers called them.

Claustrophobic my whole life, I immediately chose a top bunk. Little space separated the bed from the ceiling, but it was more than the foot and a half in·the choices below.

"Good thinking," Eddie said when I scrambled up to test the mattress. "At least up there you won't have five other guys puking their guts out on top of you."

In truth, that hadn't occurred to me. I'd never before crossed an ocean, or been on a large boat, so I didn't even know if I suffered from seasickness. But what Eddie said made sense and I decided I'd rather be the one emptying my stomach from the top instead of the recipient of other stomachs emptied on me. I settled in and tried to find a comfortable position but gave it up after a few minutes. The tiny mattress was too thin and the stuffing painfully lacking. I'd had more comfortable sleeping arrangements in deer stands while waiting for a prize buck.

Regardless, we had orders to stay below until we heard the signal that we could move around on the upper decks. When the bell clanged, we climbed several flights of stairs to the sun deck, already crammed with soldiers. A thick cloud of cigarette smoke engulfed them and rendered them almost invisible. The smokers lit up nonstop in daylight since they couldn't smoke during nighttime blackouts.

Dickie and I inched close to the rail and watched the landscape slide by as the Queen Mary sailed down the final miles of the Hudson River to the Atlantic. Our last glimpse of American soil. For how long, we had no way of knowing.

We drifted past the Statue of Liberty, her torch dark since the beginning of the war, and without warning, hot tears slid down my cheeks. The crush of men went silent and I figured we all shared the same thought, wondering if we would ever see her again. Or return to our families.

Or live through the fighting.

I didn't allow myself to focus on the fear, although I certainly felt it. I figured when the time came, I would do what I'd been trained to do. I figured we all would. At least I hoped so. Our lives depended on it.

Our voyage lasted eight days and for every minute of every day, I gave thanks I had chosen a top bunk. I did, I found out, suffer from seasickness. In addition to claustrophobia. The regular pitch-and-roll of winter waves in the Atlantic was bad enough, but to keep from being discovered by searching German U-boats, the Queen Mary zigzagged across the waves and changed direction every eight minutes, which made for constant motion and no way to ever brace oneself against it. Countless times during the night, men rolled from their bunks with the sharp movement only to slide several feet after that on the vomit covering the floor. Large bruises popped up daily on all parts of the soldiers and broken arms became commonplace.

We cleaned the floor often, but the smell made it almost impossible to accomplish the task without adding to the problem. Many of the men in my area threw up so often they couldn't eat, so the mess area was seldom crowded. Only two meals a day were served and those consisted of greasy meat and crusty vegetables drowned in thick gravy. All of which needed salt. Many days I found my stomach fared better with crackers and toast. Not filling, but at least it stayed down.

The final straw was the fact that we weren't allowed to shower. Only officers had that privilege. And they usually skipped it. I tried to filter out the smell by sleeping with a damp washcloth over my nose and mouth but by morning, the stench saturated the flimsy material anyway and I woke up choking to breathe.

Simon and Eddie, regulars in the ongoing poker games, played daily to pass the time. They taught me to shoot craps and I played a little. Until the day the *Queen Mary* pitched to her side so violently, we thought we were finished. We genuinely believed she had capsized and that ten thousand soldiers would never make it to the front. Dice and cards and men slid across the floor, knocking into whatever was in their path—furniture, rails, stairs. But mostly each other. We all knotted together in one big heap until she righted herself again, as suddenly as she had pitched over. After that, there wasn't a clean spot on the floor large enough to throw the dice anyway.

With little to keep us busy on the ship, I thought about my family constantly. No letters came in while we were at sea but I wrote several in my spare moments. Mostly to Betty, but also to Kathleen. I even wrote a note to little Freddie. I thought he would get a kick out of having something delivered with his name on it.

We stood on the top deck the morning of our last day at sea and enjoyed the fresh air, relatively free from vomit and body odor, with the view of the Scottish countryside growing more distinct. We saw ships approaching and heard from one of the *Queen Mary's* crew that the fleet consisted of a British anti-aircraft cruiser and five destroyers, there to escort us into Port Glasgow.

Escort or not, they kept their distance.

"If they're supposed to escort us," I asked one of the British crew members close to me, "why are they staying so far away?"

"Oh," he quipped. "Because of what happened with the HMS *Curacoa* two years ago." At my blank look, he said, "You never heard about that? October 2, 1942, it were. What a terrible day. Terrible. Just terrible." His voice trailed off, apparently caught up in the memory.

"Well?" I asked. "What happened?"

"She were a British cruiser, the *Curacoa*, exactly like that one." He pointed to the largest of the ships sailing toward us. "And she joined us about five miles or so from port. I heard later her captain radioed that her top speed was only twenty-five knots, so she planned to try and get ahead and then stay alongside as best she could since she couldn't match our zigzag speed of twenty-six and a half knots." I nodded. "But that day," he continued, "we was going much faster than that." He shook his head again. "Protocol said we had to stay close to the *Curacoa* for her guns to be effective, but she was pretty old by then. Didn't maneuver real quick. And we was forbidden from slowing down, headed into the most dangerous part of our trip, as we was. Captain received intel that a nest of German U-boats hovered close."

He stopped talking to tend to his station and then continued. "It still makes my blood run cold. Many of us, and thousands of the soldiers traveling with us, watched from this very spot. The *Curacoa* drifted into our path. Both ship captains turned hard to avoid a collision, but it were too late." He stopped talking and wiped his brow. "The most horrible thing I ever seen, it were. The *Mary* plowed right into the *Curacoa* about a hunnert and fifty feet from her stern. Without slowing down. Without missing a beat. The *Curacoa's* armor were three inches thick. But it split apart like it were matchsticks, erupted into the air as if a bomb blasted it. We was all horrified. Hundreds of her crew was on her top deck and we seen the disbelief in their eyes as we pulled closer." He closed his own eyes and shivered. "And then we heard their screams as they tumbled into the ocean."

"And you couldn't go back and help them?" I asked.

"The soldiers with us that day asked the same thing. But we couldn't. We would have been sitting ducks for the Germans if we tried that. And we had eleven thousand men to protect and deliver to the front."

"How many did they have?"

"Their crew were four hundred and thirty-nine souls. And I know your next question," he added quietly. "Scarce a hunnert sailors was saved. We threw as many life jackets as we could, but when the *Curacoa's* steam pipes ruptured, oil spurted from her fuel tanks onto the water's surface. Covered everything. Men clinging to wreckage for their lives lost their grip and slipped into the ocean." He wiped his brow again before continuing. "Both pieces of the ship went down in minutes. We was all in shock. Many of us was sick. But, of course, them sailors on the *Curacoa* suffered the worst." He hung his head. "It were terrible," he repeated. "Just terrible."

I thought about the men aboard the *Mary* during that trip and imagined the anguish and horror the soldiers must have felt. I also thought of the sacrifice from the men on the *Curacoa*, who gave their lives so eleven thousand Allied soldiers could survive.

To fight on D-Day. Many of whom never made it back from Normandy's beaches.

Another grim reminder of the expendability of men during war.

The *Queen Mary* continued her zigzag pattern until she reached the River Clyde for her final leg to Glasgow Pier, where she slowed and then snugged in close. The engines died and silence filled the air, only to be replaced seconds later with cheers erupting from the ten thousand of us aboard. We rejoiced at the thought of stepping onto dry land. Stable, un-pitchy, dry land.

The *Queen Mary* had survived one more trip. And we survived with her.

We marched off the ship in full gear exactly as we had marched on. Except that eight days of grime and stench clung to us.

We boarded trains in Glasgow, then rumbled across the countryside to the port of Southampton on the English Channel. Fortunately, they were troop trains, which spared civilians from our smelly, disheveled lot. We were tired. We were cold. We were filthy. And our morale was low. I couldn't believe that only a week had passed since my mother died and I held my beautiful Betty in my arms.

Surely it had been a lifetime.

Barrage balloons, which, in my mind, resembled a tiny dirigible convoy, filled the sky around the station, their network of cables to deter German fighter planes barely visible in the waning light.

We left the train in Southampton and marched to the dock where vessels waited to take us across the English Channel. The thought of getting back on a boat—any kind of boat—made me nauseous. I hated our conditions and simply wanted to rest.

A cold, biting wind accompanied us as we stumbled down the dock in the black of night on January 22, 1945. Some of our company boarded Higgins Boats, similar to the ones that delivered men to the beaches during the D-Day landing. My buddies and I boarded the large Landing Craft Tanks, or LCT's, in Army-speak. We'd already learned that they carried tanks, vehicles, cargo, and troops directly onto shore without the need for docks or piers. They worked great for that but once we were on board, they offered no escape from the wind and cold. We huddled together in the bitter temperatures for almost eight hours and didn't see land again until dawn streaked gray in the Eastern sky.

We reached the French shore at Le Havre.

CHAPTER
SIXTEEN

SUZANNE
2015

We reached the French shore at Le Havre.

We'd taken the red-eye from Philadelphia and, after a quick stop in Ireland, landed in Southampton, England, before six o'clock on the morning of May 2, 2015. We had time before catching our ferry, so we opted for a traditional English breakfast. I'd never been to England and was shocked to see the bacon that accompanied my eggs. I had told the waiter I wanted it crispy. In fact, what I actually said was, "If you think you've burned it and you're about to throw it away, those are the pieces I want." In spite of my instructions, what they put in front of me was practically raw.

My fork hung in mid-air spiking my last bite of black pudding, a spicy English sausage, when my dear father took that opportunity to let me know how it was made. "It's primarily pork blood," he said. "Mixed with oatmeal and special herbs. But it's the blood that makes it look so black." I choked, and it was all I could do to keep it from coming back up. Fortunately, the coffee was good, despite the fact that the English were most famous for their tea.

We left the restaurant and Dad put on a baseball cap that identified him as a World War II veteran. Every soldier who signed up for the trip received one.

We boarded the train for Portsmouth and then our ferry across the English Channel. The spring breeze cut through my thin coat and I shivered.

"Ugh," I said. "I can't believe how chilly it is."

"You think this is bad?" Dad asked. "You should have felt the weather when we came across here in January of 'forty-five. I thought I'd never stop shaking."

I expected to get a lot of comments like that during this trip. "And did you have to walk five miles through the snow?" I kidded him. "Uphill? Both ways?"

He grinned his crooked little grin and said, "You think you're being funny, Suzie. But that wasn't far from the truth. You'll see when we go through France and Luxembourg on our way to Germany. Hundreds of miles. And yes, there was snow. Lots of it. And hills. Mountains, actually. On the east bank of the Rhine. I didn't think we'd ever get out of those damned mountains."

"Well, you're right. I will see. I'm looking forward to that part of your story. And," I covered his hand with mine, "thanks. I'm glad you're telling me about it, Dad. I had no idea your conditions were so bad."

"Wait till I tell you about the battles."

We searched for an interior compartment to escape the wind and spoke to several veterans along the way who wore caps identical to Dad's. He knew many of them, but even the ones he didn't know stopped to introduce themselves. They shared a common experience, a historic experience. Despite the fact that most of the former soldiers were in their nineties, they exuded high spirits and joyful camaraderie. I found myself caught up in their excitement.

We chose a compartment and settled in for the eight-hour crossing. Dad stood and looked out the window. I saw that his mind was far away. Perhaps decades away.

"What is it, Dad?" I asked. "What's on your mind?"

He answered without turning. "My last crossing. Seventy years ago. You have no idea how much I hated being on that big, open cattle car they called a boat. The thought of traveling in luxury like this wouldn't have entered my head."

"I would imagine lots of things are much better now. Like flying across the ocean in seven hours instead of eight days on a boat that zigzagged every eight minutes with you throwing up almost as often."

I rose and stood beside him at the window, then rested my head on his shoulder. "What you and your fellow soldiers did during World War II hasn't happened in any wars since. Your entire generation had a common purpose. Have you ever thought about that?"

He shrugged.

"Or taken the time to appreciate what a significant part you played in making the world free? In saving hundreds of thousands of lives? Especially Jewish ones?"

"Probably not." He was quiet.

"Well, I have," I told him. "Ever since Mom asked me to come with you, I've been researching World War II. You're a hero, Dad. You all are."

His snort came from deep in his chest.

"I'm serious. Did you know, for example, that the 89th Infantry Division was heralded as 'The Last Line of Defense'?"

"No," he answered. "I didn't."

"And that out of some thirty divisions set up to finish the war, the commanding generals considered the 89th Infantry the best of the best under their control?"

"Nope. Didn't know that, either."

"The thing I found so interesting, and you haven't really talked about this part, is that the history books call you 'citizen soldiers.' It took me a while to figure out what they meant, but I got it. That you fellas in the 89th Infantry, and especially you and your buddies, as replacements toward the end of the war, were ordinary men. Men plucked out of your everyday lives who *learned* how to be soldiers, with the knowledge that your final training would be 'on the job.' And yet, you came together well enough with the rest of the Allies to push the final defeat of Hitler's professional armies, who were better armed, better trained, and better dressed. What a monumental task. Seriously, Dad. That's huge."

"Yeah, I guess. We didn't think of ourselves as regular soldiers. And, you're right, as replacements, we weren't considered regular soldiers by the career Army guys. With so much of the war already over, our job was to wipe out the final German resistance—those

zealots who weren't ready to admit defeat. We called it 'mopping up.'"
He cut his eyes toward me and his lips curved in a tiny smile. "That's
a career soldier term, you know." He sighed and crossed his arms
before continuing. "But in our hearts, we simply thought of ourselves
as men forced to wear uniforms—filthy uniforms most of the time. We
were aware of what we had to do but we really only cared about
winning the war and going back home to those we loved. We would
have helped the same way even if we hadn't been soldiers."

"That's my point," I said. "That's why they called you 'citizen
soldiers.' You always kept your connection to home and family and
were only in uniform for the duration of the war and then you were
done. No more soldier."

"That's true. I think we all felt that way. Don't get me wrong,
Suzie, we were all patriotic. And we'd been hardened by the depres-
sion, but our thoughts were certainly more civilian than militaristic
and often led to conflict with career Army." He chuckled. "I remember
meeting some of those fellows. They weren't too pleased at having to
depend on us. Thought we were brash and undisciplined. And it got
worse after they found out our training had been reduced to thirty-five
weeks. My group actually had less than that."

"How long was theirs?"

"Oh, most of a year in 1940 and '41."

"So, did their attitudes ever change—the career Army guys?"

"Most times, after they fought in battles with us, they came
around. But you know what? We didn't much care how they felt about
us. We were there to do a job and we did it."

"And thank goodness you did. Have I told you about a television
show I've recently started watching? The one called *The Man in the High
Castle*?"

"I don't think so. What's it about?"

"The aftermath of World War II. Only in this scenario, the Allies
lost and Germany and Japan divided the United States into two zones,
each governed by their mother countries. Kind of like East and West
Germany. It portrays what might have happened if that had actually
been the outcome. And it's scary as hell, Dad. I'll get it set up so you

can watch it when we get home. It will make you really appreciate your role in freeing the world."

⋯⋯

WE PLANNED TO MEET DAD'S ARMY BUDDIES AT THE HOTEL for dinner, so after freshening up, I found Dad in the bar, nursing a vodka sour, the crook of his cane draped over his knee. I kissed the top of his head and sat down beside him.

"Hey, Old Man." The voice behind us, thick with a New York accent, belonged to a wiry man who leaned heavily on his own cane. "You made it."

A smile filled my father's face and he stood and hugged the slender man in front of him. The crown of thick, curly white hair rose no higher than my father's nose. And when Dad held him away to get a better look, I saw snow-colored eyebrows that all but met. Exactly as Dad described him.

"Simon," Dad said, "great to see you again."

"You too, Old Man." Still holding Dad's hand, he turned and stared at me. Leered actually. "Who's this young chickie?"

I threw back my head and laughed. "You're one of my new best friends," I told him, "especially given the fact that I turned seventy several months ago. I'm Sam's daughter, Suzanne. Great to meet you, Simon."

"And I'm Simon's son, Liam." The man behind him held out his hand and I shook it. Liam resembled his father, but taller with softer features. And a less pronounced Brooklyn accent.

"Haven't seen you since Dickie's ninetieth birthday party," Simon said. "You talked to him lately? He still planning to come?"

"Last week," Dad told him. "And yes, he said he'd be here by tonight or tomorrow."

"And how about Ervin's funeral? Did you make it?" Simon asked.

"Yeah, I did. A nice affair. Erwin spoke. Very moving. Ervin would have loved it. Have you seen Erwin yet?"

"No, he probably came over early. I talked to him last month, though. He said there'd be around fifty of us from the 353rd Regiment. But several hundred from the 89th Infantry Division. Not a bad number after seventy years, right?"

"Not a bad number at all. How many from K Company?"

"The four of us and Sarge." He referred to Sergeant Randolph Noonan, I found out later, who had been with them through most of the worst fighting. "Oh, and that guy Fred Fordham from the Midwest."

"I love it," I said, "that you're all still invested enough in your service years and each other to make such a big trip. All the way to Zwickau."

"Zwickau," my father said. He spoke so softly, I had to lean in to make certain I'd heard correctly. "Yes, I look forward to returning there."

⚬

MY DAD HAD A WONDERFUL TIME AT DINNER WITH SIMON. I loved watching them and hearing the bawdier stories that Dad hadn't, and probably wouldn't have, told me about their times together. And of course, Simon's New York accent added exactly the right spice.

I loved seeing Dad enjoying himself and I laughed until my jaws hurt. We stayed together way too long since our bus was scheduled to arrive early in the morning. Not quite "zero-dark-thirty," but earlier than I normally made myself presentable enough to meet the world. Or in this case, Erwin Davis and Dickie Dickinson.

The next morning, I joined Dad, Simon and his son in the lobby and we all went out to catch our charter. I couldn't believe how cold it was this time of year until I remembered Le Havre shared a latitude with Canada. But rather than express my discomfort and risk an onslaught about the frigid temperatures the soldiers encountered during the war, I pulled my coat tighter and tugged on my gloves.

My teeth chattered nonstop and my jaws ached from trying to hold them still.

CHAPTER
SEVENTEEN

SAM

1945

My teeth chattered nonstop and my jaws ached from trying to hold them still.

Bleary-eyed from lack of sleep, we boarded troop trucks almost as soon as we landed at Le Havre and crammed in tight...men, field packs, rifles, radio equipment, and anything else the Army thought we couldn't do without. The trucks opened to the sky with wood slats along the sides that were supposed to serve as seats. But they left a lot to be desired since their narrow width prevented us from leaning back with our field packs still strapped on our shoulders, a necessity since duffle bags filled the floor. We hunched forward and planted our feet in whatever tiny space we could find.

Our trucks rolled through Le Havre in the gray morning light. I had already learned that five thousand of its civilians had lost their lives and more than eighty-five thousand buildings suffered damage or destruction because of bombings from both sides of the war. But nothing could have prepared me for the devastation I witnessed. Empty shells of former homes bared their souls to us through the remaining one or two walls and exposed the remnants of lives cut short. Black filth covered everything except the trash, unearthed and blowing in the cold wet wind.

For hours, we traveled through sleet and snow, over ice-covered roads and through unoccupied villages, their mutilated remains a grim reminder of why we were there. When my heart couldn't take any more, I closed my eyes and caught an uneasy nap, jolting awake when we reached Camp Lucky Strike, near the village of St. Valery-en-Caux.

The large tent city looked like heaven to me and I jumped off the truck into ankle-deep mud, anxious to stow my gear and find a little warmth. A long line formed and I took my place with the other men who'd recently arrived. Wind whipped around us and produced tears, freezing our lashes and gluing our eyes shut. We bent away from its bite and huddled together.

We shuffled along. Minutes passed before we realized the line no longer moved. More minutes dragged on until we learned that several large tents had collapsed from the weight of a recent snowfall, so the camp organizers scrambled to find room for us. Hours passed before we found a place to stow our gear and grab some sleep.

We woke to find that in addition to a tent shortage, the camp also suffered a food shortage, so we scrounged for anything we could find. I was luckier than most. My mother had taught me to recognize edible greens, like watercress, and I pulled enough of it to make a scant salad. In the days that followed, the shortage continued, so I trapped a few rabbits—scrawny little things—and cooked them on my alcohol stove until our food supply caught up with us. My cooking abilities increased my popularity among the men and at the end of our famine period, I banked quite a stash of candy bars and cigarettes, traded to me for some of my rabbit stew.

Which, we discovered, wreaked havoc on our digestive systems. Doubly bad when we found our latrine consisted of an open trench at the end of our row of tents. Several times per day and into the night, one or the other of us took off running and barely made it in time to squat and do our business while the wind blasted icy gusts between our legs.

"Gives the term 'blue balls' a whole new meaning, don't it?" Eddie said.

We were accustomed to Eddie's crude humor by then and it struck us as funny that even amid the conditions we endured, Eddie could still make jokes. He was good for us, made us laugh. We needed that.

We settled into our new routine. As steamy heat and slippery mud had been a way of life during our training in the States, bitter cold and crunchy mud became the norm in France. We trained in ankle-deep mud daily, perfecting our maneuvers and then cleaning our equipment and keeping it well-oiled.

Mail caught up with us at the camp too, and I was one of the lucky ones with twenty-one letters in one twine-tied parcel thrown into my hands. I had a date for bubble dancing that afternoon, Army-speak for kitchen duty. Which worked out great because I left the kitchen area with a little extra food stuffed in my pockets for my buddies and me, but I couldn't read my letters until that evening. Then I devoured them.

The stack included eleven letters from my beautiful Betty, newsy little notes about her day and a description of the family during her one visit out to the farm. I read them so many times, they practically disintegrated in my hands.

Four of the letters were from Kathleen, detailing how much she loved her new job and how well Freddie was doing with Mrs. Gibbons, who had already taught him his letters and how to spell his colors and the names of our animals on the farm. There were even a few pages from Freddie himself, with large, wavy letters that sloped downhill, and several pictures, done in vivid colors, created with his Christmas crayons, I was certain. One showed him in his new wagon with Winnie pulling him. I figured that was his ride to get to Mrs. Gibbons each day. What a smart little girl Winnie was to think of that. Another one showed a person who must have been a soldier, dressed in brown and holding a long black stick that I assumed was a gun. Red dots dripped from its end. He obviously didn't know how guns worked. Thank goodness. The figure's black boots stood on the word "SAM."

My vision swam when I thought of that sweet little guy and I truly hoped his life was happier now than it had been his last few months after losing two of his brothers and his mother. The note from Mrs. Gibbons indicated that it was. The rest of the letters were from the other girls and Billy. There was even a prayer card from Reverend Purdue, which I tucked into my boot so it would always be handy. Just in case.

IN EARLY FEBRUARY WE LEARNED WE WOULD RECEIVE A visit from General George Patton himself. I had never seen an officer with a higher rank than captain, so I looked forward to a real-live major general.

Excitement raced through Camp Lucky Strike and we spent time cleaning up and getting ready. Our officers inspected our weapons and ordered us to clean and oil them again and again, until the sunlight glinted off every square inch, be it wood or metal. One of the tents was even refitted and equipped so we could clean our uniforms. We wanted to look our best for the general.

The Engineering Corps erected a temporary stage so he would be visible to each of the sixty thousand men in camp. Music blasted from the makeshift sound system and prior to Patton's arrival, we enjoyed a combination of both popular and military music.

The morning of February 20, 1945, the sun actually made an appearance and the lack of rain for the previous two days rendered our muddy roads less troublesome than normal. When lookouts alerted our officers at first sight of the general's jeep, the camp speakers switched to "There'll Be a Hot Time in the Town of Berlin (When the Yanks Go Marching In)," by Bing Crosby and the Andrews Sisters. We had heard the song before, but it took on a special meaning, since, we'd been told, it was the general's favorite.

He stepped out of the Jeep looking exactly the way we expected— brown riding pants with shiny brown knee-high boots, his crisp uniform coat decorated down one whole side of his chest with medals —fruit salad, the career guys told us—and his pearl-handled Colt .45 holstered at his side. I'd never seen such an impressive-looking man before and found myself grinning from ear-to-ear.

He marched to the platform and took the steps two at a time. Our parade of soldiers moved rhythmically around the camp, shouting our cadences for his benefit. K Company stood directly in front of his platform when he halted the marching and gave the "At ease" command.

He stepped up to the microphone and we turned toward him with rapt attention, standing silently.

"Men," the general began, "this stuff that some sources sling around about America wanting out of this war, not wanting to fight, is a crock of bullshit."

A ripple of laughter flowed through the ranks.

"Americans," he continued, "love to fight, traditionally. All real Americans love the sting and clash of battle. Americans love a winner. Americans will not tolerate a loser. Americans despise cowards. Americans play to win all the time. I wouldn't give a hoot in hell for a man who lost and laughed. That's why Americans have never lost nor will ever lose a war; for the very idea of losing is hateful to an American."

The general paused and looked over the crowd.

"You are not all going to die," he said slowly. "Only two percent of you right here today will die in a major battle. Death must not be feared. Death, in time, comes to all men. Yes, every man is scared in his first battle. If he says he's not, he's a liar. But a real man will never let his fear of death overpower his honor, his sense of duty to his country, and his innate manhood. Remember that the enemy is just as frightened as you are, and probably more so. They are not supermen."

His voice was strong and we hung on every word. He spoke to each one of us, individually. At least that's how he came across. And we ate it up, ready to march through the gates of hell if it would please the charismatic man in front of us.

"An Army is a team," he continued. "It lives, sleeps, eats, and fights as a team. This individual heroic stuff is pure horseshit. The bilious bastards who write that kind of stuff for the *Saturday Evening Post* don't know any more about real fighting under fire than they know about fornicating!"

That one really got to us. We howled. Although he didn't use the word "fornicating." He used the real word—the one that motivated my mother to wash Richard's mouth out with soap the one time he dared use it in front of her.

Yes, Patton's speech was everything we had anticipated.

He lost us for a minute with his next words, when he said we received the finest food, considering we had endured starvation conditions when we first arrived. But when he moved on to how he felt about the men we would fight against, we were back. In full force.

"Why, by God, I actually pity those poor sons of bitches we're going up against. By God, I do."

Again, we howled. He had us in the palm of his hand and his confidence in us was the most important thing in the world. The next few lines he spoke hit many of us where we lived, including me, touching on things we couldn't help thinking now that battle was only days away.

"Some of you men are wondering whether or not you'll chicken out under fire. Don't worry about it. I can assure you that you'll all do your duty. War is a bloody business, a killing business. The Nazis are the enemy. Wade into them, spill their blood or they will spill yours. Shoot them in the guts. Rip open their belly and rip out their living guts and use them to grease the treads of our tanks. When shells are hitting all around you and you wipe the dirt from your face and you realize that it's not dirt, but it's the blood and guts of what was once your best friend, you'll know what to do.

"Each man must not think only of himself, but also his buddy fighting beside him."

I had already made my own promise to my buddies. With General Patton's speech, I renewed my silent commitment to them. Not only the ones I was close friends with, but also the ones whose names I might not yet know.

"The quicker we clean up this mess," the general continued, "the quicker we can take a little jaunt against the purple-pissing Japs and clean out their nest too. Before the damned Marines get all the credit."

That line brought more cheers. The Army's reputation was less respected than that of the Marines and less exotic than that of the Navy. But we were the ones on the ground, fighting the battle for all Americans, and the general's deep sincerity in how he felt about his men conveyed real significance for us. He continued quietly.

"Sure, we want to go home. We want this war over with. The quickest way to get it over with is to go get the bastards who started it. The quicker they are whipped, the quicker we can go home. The shortest way home is through Berlin and Tokyo." He paused. "And when we get to Berlin," he yelled, "I am personally going to shoot that paper hanging son-of-a-bitch Hitler. Just like I'd shoot a snake!

"There is one great thing that you men will all be able to say after this war is over and you are home once again. You may be thankful that twenty years from now when you are sitting by the fireplace with your grandson on your knee and he asks you what you did in the great World War II, you WON'T have to cough, shift him to the other knee and say, 'Well, your Granddaddy shoveled shit in Louisiana.' No sir, you can look him straight in the eye and say, 'Son, your Granddaddy rode with the Great Third Army and a Son of a Bitch named Georgie Patton!'

"All right you sons of bitches. You know how I feel. I'll be proud to lead you wonderful guys in battle—anytime—anywhere. That's all."

The cheers must have roared on for a good five minutes while he stood there and welcomed them swirling around him. His words hit the exact right note with us. They were what we needed to hear to pull us out of the doldrums created by too much cold, too much mud, and too little praise coming from our own officers. We needed to know that someone believed in us, so we could do a better job of believing in ourselves.

And the timing of his magnificent motivation couldn't have been more perfect.

The next day we received orders to move across France.

To take our places on the front lines.

CHAPTER
EIGHTEEN

GERDA

"This is wonderful news," Aldrik said. He held Gerda's hands in his and then stroked her belly, finding the small bump which held his first child. "I thought I loved you with all my heart already," he added, his eyes tearing, "but I never realized how much that love would grow with the new life of my baby inside you."

She returned his excitement. "Oh Aldrik, you're right. This is so great for us. I can hardly wait until this war is over so we can live together in Zwickau. You and I can both work at the bakery and take care of our child in the bosom of family. Like my parents and grandparents did."

He frowned. "But Gerda, I plan to remain in the German military service after the war. I will be needed more than ever to maintain order in the new Reich."

That hadn't occurred to her and unfortunately, they hadn't discussed it before they married. She had assumed Aldrik would be finished with the military when the war ended just as she knew she would. The thought of remaining around the people among whom Aldrik lived and worked unsettled her, as did the thought of having to move to wherever the new job took them rather than putting down roots.

"And we don't have to wait until the war is over to live together," Aldrik continued, apparently oblivious to her hesitation. "You can move to Buchenwald at once and live here with me. Our child will be born here."

She forced a smile. She was very content with their current

arrangement and really wanted her mother with her when she gave birth. She couldn't imagine Karla putting up with the attitudes of the arrogant doctors at the camp.

"Plus," he continued, "with my promotion to the REIMAHG and my added responsibility, I'll be earning a lot more money." His eyes sought hers. "Please, Gerda, be reasonable. We can give the extra money to your parents so they can hire someone to take your place at the bakery. That will satisfy everyone."

Gerda let it drop. She was thrilled to be having a child with the man she loved, but they would have to have another conversation about what she wanted from their life together rather than have him blindly believe she would obediently follow him wherever he went.

But that would have to wait until the war was over.

———

FOR DAYS AFTER HER CONVERSATION WITH ALDRIK, GERDA worried. She was happy he was promoted, of course, but his news brought fear to her heart. The REIMAHG he spoke of, an airplane factory named *Flugzeugwerke Reichsmarschall Hermann Göring* in honor of the Nazi officer, was being constructed in a recently expanded mining tunnel via forced labor by the Buchenwald inmates.

Aldrik had given her details about the ongoing work, but it had been her Resistance contact, Michel, who told her when they met at her family's farm in Baden-Baden, why the work had begun.

"The Allies are winning," he said excitedly. "For months, we've made progress in the skies and German industrial centers are being wiped out in air strikes, almost daily." He stopped talking and began pacing. "That's the good news. The bad news is that because of the increased Allied activity, German manufacturing is being relocated underground. To build newer, more powerful fighter planes. *Messerschmitts*, they're calling them. *ME 262s* for short. But that means the workload will increase and the tunnels will be occupied around the clock. The same tunnels, unfortunately, we're using for the children."

He almost collided with Gerda, who paced in the opposite direction, a frown filling her face. "The Germans say the *MEs* are the first jet-powered fighters," he continued, "faster and more heavily armed than any of their enemy's planes. They've been working on this strategy for a while, but ran into problems with materials shortages and design issues that led to reliability—"

"Will you stop prattling?" Gerda turned on him abruptly, impatience filling her voice. "Don't you see? None of that matters, now." She resumed pacing, but Michel stood, following her with his eyes. "We have to find an alternate route. With inmates at the tunnels around the clock, there's no way we can get any of the children through. And Aldrik said that with Hitler's Army pushed back at every turn, the remaining prisoners at Buchenwald will be sent on forced marches to other camps and more and more of the barracks will be emptied." She stopped pacing again and faced him. "We can't slow our work, Michel. We must increase it. Get more children out as fast as..."

Words failed her and tears filled her eyes. The fate of children in the camps bothered her more than ever now that a child of her own was ready to enter the world. She couldn't stand the thought of children dying at all, but it was even worse for them to be cut down ruthlessly as if they were worthless blights on society.

She had to do more. They all had to do more. And they had to do it faster.

But they couldn't get caught.

"You're right, of course," Michel said. "But we will have to be incredibly careful. Highly creative. We really should explore alternate routes."

"Yes," Gerda agreed. "And I have an idea. But we have another couple of weeks before workers begin their round-the-clock shifts at REIMAHG." She faced Michel, urgency tensing her body. "Let's do one more run. Next week. With bigger numbers." Her frown found its way back to her face. "Do we have enough families ready to take as many as a dozen children? Jakob says he overheard the guard at Block 66 telling the elders he might have to reimplement *appells*."

"He's probably shaking them down for more money," Michel said.

"Maybe. But I'm not sure we can take that chance. If he discovers how many children are actually missing..."

"Right," Michel said. "We're all in trouble. Let me check. I agree, let's take the maximum number. But after that, we may need to move our operation to the camp at Ohrdruf."

"That's exactly what I thought," Gerda said. "There's activity going on there. I'll go see the camp's officer in a couple of days and see if I can begin making bread deliveries. Maybe we can set up something there too."

"You'll have to be really careful, Gerda," Michel told her. "Our intelligence tells us the tunnels at Ohrdruf are for an underground Nazi headquarters in case Hitler has to leave Berlin in a hurry. And we know the Russians are closing in."

"The *Führer*," Gerda said softly. "In our part of Germany." She eased into a nearby chair. "Good Lord. That would ruin everything."

⸻

AFTER THE COLDEST WINTER GERMANY HAD SEEN IN almost fifty years, the fresh scent of an early spring filled the air and fireflies returned to blink away the darkness.

But the war raged on. Tiny new green shoots disappeared daily, ground into the earth by muddy boots while flowering buds exploded into the sky as bullets severed them from branches.

Gerda's due date neared, but still she worked. She'd been able to stall Aldrik's plan for her move to Buchenwald by telling him her father was slowing down and her younger brother, Ernst, couldn't keep up with all the orders. Her family needed her more than ever, she told him, because there wasn't anyone available to hire with all the able-bodied men off fighting.

Plus, the local military commandeered the bulk of the bread produced by her family's bakery, which kept Ernst busy at the ovens rather than the front lines. She'd been successful at convincing the Ohrdruf kommandant to allow her to deliver her family's bread there and as a result, the orders had piled in. Not only for bread. Many of the officers' wives had a sweet tooth, so the demand for strudel and stollen, even *Lebkuchen,* had increased by more than a third. The bakery's ovens ran constantly.

The drive to Ohrdruf was more than two hours from Zwickau so she combined it with her deliveries at Buchenwald, a mere hour away. Some bombing had occurred, but the roads remained clear and she had no trouble navigating the ruts and mud. Her father became increasingly insistent that she refrain from putting herself in such danger, but her mother soothed him, understanding the importance of Gerda's work. Her *real* work in the war.

There had been another benefit to her time at the Ohrdruf camp. She hated the conditions there and what it represented, but on her first visit, Kommandant Hermann Ostermann gave her a cursory tour of the grounds. At the fence surrounding the courtyard where prisoners walked for fifteen minutes daily, a tall girl in filthy striped prison garb stood by the gate. Her head had been shaved and her body was nothing more than skin and bones with her right hand drawn up like a claw. But behind the tortured, vacant eyes, Gerda recognized the soul of her long-lost childhood neighbor and companion.

Rebekah. At Ohrdruf.

Gerda's heart soared even while it broke at the sight of her emaciated friend.

She would figure out a way, she decided, to save Rebekah along with the children.

CHAPTER
NINETEEN

GERDA

A massive escape, the last they thought feasible, was set for the Buchenwald camp with a dozen children chosen and coached. After that, the operation would shift to Ohrdruf. Michel and Gerda, along with her cousin, Ulrich, prepared every step and personally interviewed the children outside the gates of the camp during their practice breakout the night before. One of the children broke down and cried uncontrollably and Gerda made the painful decision to leave him behind. She had to. She couldn't risk that same behavior the following night.

The escape was strategically scheduled during the anniversary celebration for the kommandant and his wife at their sprawling house on the square, within sight of Aldrik's house. But as far away from Block 66 as was possible within the confines of the compound.

Gerda's cousin Ulrich sent her cases of the family's pear brandy and she convinced Aldrik to contribute that to the celebration. His status rose several notches with the kommandant.

During her months at the camp, Gerda had spent time with Elsa Krueger, the kommandant's wife. Despite her repeated attempts to ingratiate herself with *Frau* Krueger, Gerda sensed a reluctance on the *Frau's* part to fully accept her. So she showed up at the house early to help with the final party preparations. She opened the first bottle of brandy immediately and poured a generous glass for the kommandant's wife.

"*Danke, Liebe,*" *Frau* Krueger said. She drained the glass in one swallow and Gerda poured another. And another and another. After several glasses, the kommandant joined her, and Gerda continued to pour. Their guests arrived and Gerda, along with the *kapos*, the camp prisoners who acted as servants for the officers, made the rounds, keeping the glasses filled with the strong, clear liquid. With the fourth round, words slurred and laughter increased in volume.

"*Hier, Liebling.*" Aldrik's fingers closed around the glass she offered but he stumbled backward and brandy sloshed over the tumbler's side.

Gut, she thought. The guard staff was light, but she had bribed one of the junior officers to take brandy to those on duty as well. To cover all the bases.

MICHEL AND HIS TEAM HID AMONG THE TREES, THEIR faces blackened to avoid reflections from the moonlit sky. One by one, children appeared and his teammates whisked them away to the darkness of the forest, many of them hoisting the children to their backs for the arduous trip through the REIMAHG tunnels.

"*Dix*...ten," Michel said under his breath. One more to go. Thus far, the children had appeared at regular intervals, but a lull ensued after the tenth child. Michel risked a few steps outside the trees, straining in the darkness to find movement. He saw none.

"What do you want to do, Michel?" Ulrich whispered at his shoulder.

"I hate to leave one," Michel answered. "Let's give it another minute."

INSIDE BLOCK 66, ELDERS ANTONIN KALINA AND GUSTAV Schiller dealt with a meltdown. Erich, the child told he couldn't go with the others, begged to be taken. His tears escalated to the level of screams and he clung to Klaus, the eleventh child. Kalina tried reasoning with the sobbing boy while Schiller watched the door, hoping to intercept the guard if he showed up to see about the commotion.

"*Bitte*...please," Klaus said. "I'll keep him quiet. Please let us go." He turned to the smaller child and knelt, getting right in his face. "Erich, you must stop crying or neither of us will get to go." He shook the boy's shoulders. "Stop. You must stop now."

Erich's sobs waned to coughing hiccups, so the elder agreed.

"But hurry or they'll leave you," Kalina said.

———

THE TWO BOYS SLID INTO THE HOLE UNDER THE STOVE AND scrambled through the tunnel, coming up slightly short of the forest. Klaus' face had been blackened, but there hadn't been time to take care of Erich's face, so it and his blond hair shone bright in the moonlight. They ran for the cover of the trees, but Erich slipped and cried out. Klaus ran back to help him up, but Erich lay there, whimpering, broken bone visible through the gash in his shin.

Michel appeared at Klaus' side. "Run into the forest. Ulrich will take you to the tunnels," he whispered.

"I can't leave Erich," Klaus answered.

"I'll take care of him," Michel said. "Run."

Klaus took off and Michel bent to get Erich.

"Halt! Stop where you are!" A distant light shone on Michel's face. He hesitated for only a moment and then scooped the boy up and ran for the trees.

Shots rang out and the thud of bullets ripped into Michel's body, his right leg, and his left shoulder and arm. Still he ran. Blood dripped from his arm and fell to his ankles, coating his boots then trickling off them to the grass, making it slippery and impeding his footing. He ran on. Dogs barked behind him, but he continued forward, limping badly as the blood from his leg wound flowed freely. He stopped to tie his belt around it to lessen the trail for the dogs.

"You must be quiet, Erich," he said softly. "I have to put you down for a minute. Lie still and we'll be on our way again in no time."

He laid the boy gently on a patch of grass, quickly removed his belt and tied it as a tourniquet above the wound on his leg. The sound of barking dogs grew louder. He bent to retrieve the boy.

The moon shone briefly on Erich through a break in the trees and Michel gasped. The little boy's face was missing. Replaced by a gaping black cavity. He turned the boy over to reveal the bullet hole in the back of his skull and understanding flashed. Erich's blood was what dripped down his arm, then mixed with his own.

He had no choice. There was nothing he could do to help the boy anyway, so he left him in the grass and ran. The boy's body would slow the dogs, giving the others a better chance of getting away. His heart hurt at the thought of losing a child. But Gerda had been right to deny the dead youngster the final spot in their escape. He reacted exactly the way she had predicted he would. And it cost him his life. And possibly the lives of others if the dogs caught up with them.

Blood continued to ooze from Michel's wounds and his progress slowed. He only needed to make it to the mouth of the tunnels within the REIMAHG. Just a short distance.

A stick snapped and he tripped, sending a tree branch through the open wound in his leg. He gasped and cried out. And then lay there, unable to move, surrounded by growling dogs and shouting guards.

⊹

A COLUMN OF CHILDREN AND RESISTANCE VOLUNTEERS made their way steadily through the tunnels. Electric lights, low in the night, softly illuminated the darkness, casting eerie shadows which helped conceal the escapees' progress. Following the leader's hand movements, the column moved soundlessly past outer offices with glass walls into larger chambers.

They spent no time staring at the airplane parts scattered throughout the rooms but continued deeper into the complex until they reached the tunnel that led them outside to the Elster River and the route to their destination.

The volunteers and children faced a grueling four-day trip on foot through forests while avoiding roads and populated areas until they reached the borders of Vichy, France, still under German occupation but loosely governed by Marshall Pétain. Finding families to take the children had been easier with the German rule slightly less strict. Even there, however, if discovered, all parties contributing to the operation were certain to be executed.

MERRIMENT AT THE KOMMANDANT'S PARTY CEASED abruptly with pounding on the door. "*Herr* Krueger," the shouts sounded from outside. *Frau* Krueger answered the door, weaving from side to side as she did so with the kommandant only steps behind her.

"*Heil* Hitler," Gerda heard at the door. Her heart thudded in her chest.

"*Ja,*" the kommandant said, "*Was ist es*...what's going on?" His voice was sharp. He didn't like being interrupted.

"An escape, sir. We captured a Resistance fighter."

Gerda sat down hard, hearing words she had dreaded. Words from her worst nightmare. She wondered who had been captured.

The kommandant's wife, known for her sadistic streak, told the guard. "Bring the traitor here." Then, turning to her guests, she asked, "Shall we have some fun with him?" A cheer sounded among them.

Gerda thought she might throw up.

In the next instant, as Michel, wounded and savagely beaten, was pushed through the door, she did. All over *Frau* Krueger's expensive carpet. Her stomach heaved with a contraction and she screamed out in pain. All eyes turned to her, the prisoner momentarily forgotten, and Aldrik rushed to her side and helped her stand. Gerda made eye contact with Frieda, one of the prisoners who worked at the kommandant's house, and received an almost imperceptible nod in return.

Gerda continued to cry out and more and more of the guests clustered around her with offers of help. The bewildered guard stood alone with Michel, who struggled to remain upright. Frieda approached the guard with several glasses of brandy on a tray, along with some cookies. He readily accepted and when he drained one glass, she encouraged him to take another. She reached up and slapped Michel, drawing her hand across his mouth.

From her peripheral vision, Gerda saw his one good eye widen and his jaw tighten. The guard worked on his second glass of brandy and Michel slumped to the floor. Frieda screamed and most of the group left Gerda to crowd around Michel. The guard tried to stand him up, but he was too far gone so they all took turns kicking him.

Gerda's tears flowed freely.

Frau Krueger, her eyes narrowed, turned to look at her.

"Oh, my poor *Liebling,*" her husband crooned in her ear. "I'm sorry you're in so much pain. Let's get you to the house and then find the doctor." Aldrik paid no attention to the Resistance fighter at the door, beaten almost unrecognizable by then, but Gerda couldn't resist a quick glance from her husband's arms, her heart breaking at the loss of her friend.

CHAPTER
TWENTY

SAM

The day after Patton's speech, we could talk of nothing else, although we were supposed to keep it a secret. The major general told us the enemy was not supposed to know he had been with us. They thought he was in England and the higher-ups had chosen to let them believe that. So as much as we wanted to write home about his impressive speech, we knew that any attempt to do so would be cut by the censors.

I tried to outsmart them. I told Betty before I left that there would be times when our positions would be confidential and I couldn't let her know where I was. So we worked out a code to keep her from worrying. I decided to try the same pattern to tell her about Patton. In my letter to her that afternoon, I wrote the following:

Good afternoon, my darling Betty. Everything is fine here. Nothing new. Even the weather is better. Rain stopped. And not as cold. Looks like we could move out soon.

Probably in the next two weeks. And then further east. To Germany. Through the mountains. Or over the river. Near as I can figure. We're good here. All the men are in fine spirits. Saw some grim sights when we first arrived, though.

Hope you're doing well there. Every night I think about you before I go to sleep. Remembering our last night together. Everything about it. I know

*our reunion will be as good when we're together again. Nothing will
stand between us.*

*Can hardly wait to hold you again, my love. And to really start our lives
together. Might write again later. Pucker up, Sweetheart, because I'm
sending you a kiss.*

Of course, I couldn't tell her I used the code, I'd simply have to
trust that she figured it out. And that the Army censors didn't. If she
deciphered it correctly, she would record the first letter of the first
word of each sentence and understand that my secret message read:
GENERAL PATTON WAS HERE IN CAMP.

WHEN WE PULLED OUT, WE WEREN'T TOLD OUR
destination, only that we would travel across France. Part of our
preparation included standing in long lines so the quartermaster could
exchange whatever currency we carried for both French *francs* and
Luxembourgish *francs*. And a few German *marks* thrown in for good
measure. All of which gave us a good indication of our target location.
I took my place with the others to receive my currency, although I
didn't believe we'd have an opportunity to spend any of it.

A lot of chatter accompanied our preparation and morale remained
high from the stirring message we'd received earlier. We considered
ourselves lucky to have seen the commander of our Army and to know
he was right there with us. We packed our gear and stuffed it into the
jeeps and deuce and a halfs, Army-speak for the two and a half ton
trucks that waited for us.

I wasn't sure how the rest of my little band felt about fighting, but
for me, it would be a relief to put my training to work. I was ready and
I believed the men beside me were too.

We moved out at dawn on the morning of February 22, 1945, with
two C-rations and one K-ration per man and rumbled along on a six-
hour journey up Highway North Twenty-five, through Dieppe, to a

cluster of coastal villages in the Somme region around Le Tréport. Or what was left of it. We moved slowly over poor roads and through dense forests, past farmhouses and tiny villages reduced to rubble where we watched children and dogs root through garbage for food. Many of the children lacked boots or coats and we threw our candy bars to them and an occasional blanket. I imagined Freddie having to look for food in trash bins and struggled to keep my eyes dry. It struck me then that regardless of the tough life my little brother had suffered in his few short years, it couldn't compare to the horror the kids in front of me had faced. The sights we passed worked on me and made me more determined than ever to end this conflict here rather than let it travel to my home and my family.

For the couple of days after General Patton's speech, Simon and I joked constantly about the part Patton listed as "the best" of several things he considered Army perks. One of which was food. Maybe that was true for three-star generals, but for us, and especially someone like me who was raised on home-grown, farm-cooked hearty meals, the thought of one more can of C-Ration's cold, greasy spaghetti or corned beef hash turned my stomach. I knew I should have been grateful, given the fact that we had *no* food when we first arrived at Camp Lucky Strike, and that I had watched children search through garbage to find enough to eat. And I was. But, I'd been forced to leave my little alcohol stove behind so a cold meal had become my only option. And it made me cranky.

"Hey Sammy," Eddie said beside me when we stopped for a stretch break. "I got a idea."

"Yeah, little buddy? What?"

"You lookin' forward to eating cold spaghetti tonight?"

I whipped my head toward him. "How'd you know I was thinking about that?" He grinned. "But, no," I continued, "to answer your question, I'm not."

"Well, what if we could heat it up?"

I frowned. "Out here? How would we do that? We sure as hell won't be allowed to build a fire. Even if we could find enough dry wood."

His grin filled his face. "What if we tied our Cs together and then put 'em on the truck manifolds so they'd be nice and warm when we stop for our evening meal? You think that would work?"

I actually grabbed him with both hands and kissed his cheeks. "I sure as hell do, you crazy kid. In fact, I think that's brilliant. Let's tell the others."

Eddie's idea flew through the ranks and many of our friends, including the truck drivers, joined us in "Operation Hot Meal." Soldiers emptied their pockets and we pooled whatever we thought might work to tie cans together—twine, string, mesh sheets. The engineers contributed fuse wire and even stuck around to advise on the best way to link our meals so they'd ride without falling. When we stopped at dusk, we met at one of the trucks and feasted. I couldn't believe the difference in the aroma of that spaghetti, wafting from the can like it had come straight from Mama Rosa herself, rather than the odorless, tinny, greasy mess we normally ate. We might as well have dined at a five-star restaurant, we enjoyed it that much.

That one small thing, a hot entrée rather than cold, greasy food, worked wonders for us and morale soared.

———————

AS PART OF THE 3RD BATTALION, OUR COMPANY STOPPED IN Mers-les-Bains at the end of our road trip, where we billeted in abandoned bombed-out buildings.

We couldn't believe our good fortune. I thought by now we'd be squatting in foxholes and breathing mud, but our lieutenant, Boyd Cooper from Indiana, said we had to wait for the rest of the 89th Infantry to catch up with us. So once we reached Luxembourg we stayed in real buildings. Most of the windows were broken and inches of dust coated everything. Plus, the toilet didn't work and we were still stuck with C-Rations. But it was the closest thing we'd had to home for months. By the time we left, the house we occupied had been cleaned from top to bottom and the toilet repaired. We even set up a kitchen and managed to hook up a feeble line of electricity so we could enjoy another night of hot spaghetti or corned beef hash.

While we waited for the rest of our division, Simon and Eddie found their way, almost nightly, to a certain house in town where half the regiment joined them for the favors of local ladies. So, for one reason or another, we all found it hard to leave the area.

But our orders to move came on March 2. We packed up and were told to board the forty-and-eights. We stood around, frowns on our faces.

"Forty-and-eights?" I asked. "What the heck are those?"

A regular Army corporal happened to walk by and grinned at my question. He pointed to boxy train cars. "Those are forty-and-eights," he said. "The name originated in the eighteen hundreds. That's what they called the old French cargo wagons used to haul men and horses —either forty men or—"

"Eight horses," I finished. I picked up my gear and headed toward the train car.

"That's stupid," Simon said.

"Because...?" Erwin asked.

"Well, if that's what they meant, then they shoulda called 'em 'forty-or-eights.'"

We all agreed, but then none of us ever did fully grasp Army-speak.

We arrived at Mersch, Luxembourg, and were met by more deuce and a halfs and taken to Consdorf for billeting. I had no idea, when we arrived, where we were supposed to stay, but found out from Lieutenant Cooper that our regiment commander, Lieutenant Colonel Tyler, told the town's burgomaster that his citizens had an hour to pack their belongings and leave the buildings and, in a few cases, their homes so soldiers could occupy them. Normally, we filled municipal buildings since we were forbidden to occupy German residences except as a last resort. Apparently, Lieutenant Colonel Tyler figured it was a last resort.

I was horrified. All I could think about was someone driving up to my farmhouse in Pennsylvania and forcing Kathleen and the younger ones to leave our home and find another place to stay. To be thrown out in the cold so some strangers from across the ocean could sleep in our beds and eat our food.

Worse, our headquarters had issued a document, drummed into us at Camp Lucky Strike, with governing regulations for our encounters with Germans. It stated that all Germans, including civilians, were considered active enemies, that a strict curfew and blackout was enforced for civilians encountered in a town we occupied, that the Army could seize not only public buildings, but private ones as well. *Unless* those homes were occupied by German families. That was prohibited.

Lieutenant Cooper must have noticed the look on my face because he came up beside me and said, "Don't worry about it, Ryan. It's part of war. These people are German sympathizers, even though the German Army made them leave their homes too. They'll be able to come back when we move on."

The house we occupied was comfortable, although my guilt at how we got there kept me from relaxing. I was shocked when I ran into an elderly man in the hallway. He raised his arms and anxiety filled his eyes. "Coca-Cola," he said with a heavy German accent. "Mickey Mouse...Joe DiMaggio..."

Before I could say anything in return, the Lieutenant came up behind me. "We allowed him to stay. Come with me. I'll show you why." The Lieutenant beckoned to the old man and we returned to the kitchen where he moved the crude wooden table and lifted a section of the floor. Light from the kitchen spilled into the darkness, dispelling it like sun racing across a field on a cloudy day. Bright eyes, five sets of them, filled with fear, looked up at me and then retreated against the wall, regaining the shadows.

"This man," Lieutenant Cooper said, "has hidden boys and old men in this cellar for more than a year. To keep the Nazis from finding them."

"Why?" I asked. "Why would they have to hide from their own people?"

"The Nazis are a different breed," the lieutenant said. "They come through periodically and grab everyone strong enough to hold a rifle, whether they're sixteen or sixty, and then force them to be part of the fighting unit known as the *Volkssturm*. Around headquarters, it's known as the Nazi version of 'Custer's last stand.' The *Volkssturm* receives virtually no training and has the highest incidence of casualties of any of the German forces. This man saved these people from that fate, so we allowed him to stay."

The old man's name was Meinhard and I shook his hand. His eyes fixed on me, clear and kind, and he validated my belief that not all Germans were like Hitler. That they were, first and foremost, people trying to live their lives and take care of the people they loved. Just as I was.

My heart eased at having to take over his home and I joined the others in the kitchen, where we prepared a huge meal, laughing in easy camaraderie, and enjoying a night out of the mud. The larder was well stocked and our meal turned out even better than our C-rations heated on manifolds. I sat beside Eddie and again, marveled at his ability to shovel the food in. I didn't know where he put it. Until dark, that is, when I heard him running for the bathroom with what we called the "GIs" from that rich food rolling around in a stomach unused to it.

For the next few days we honed our preparations and, more importantly, bonded with our fellow soldiers and officers, a necessary element designed to serve us well in combat. But on March 9 we entered the ranks of "cornplaster commandos," the Army-speak name reserved for those of us who moved from location to location via leg muscles and boot leather. We set out around noon and marched thirty-one miles through fields of early crops. Mostly cabbages, which made me think of my sisters' Victory Garden back home.

Our progress constantly slowed, as every few miles, we discovered bridges destroyed by the Germans that forced us to find new routes over canyons, cut deep from ancient rivers. We crossed the German border, reaching Newel close to midnight, only six or eight miles from the Moselle River, our first strategic target.

The German Army had left the area so we only encountered stragglers who offered no threat. We took them prisoner.

But our officers took no chances. As green soldiers who had yet to see combat, we were not allowed to chamber any rounds that day for fear we would inadvertently shoot each other. It worked for me.

On March 10, we were officially committed to enemy action and the next day we replaced the 76th Infantry Division.

We had arrived.

In Germany.

On the front line.

We were, I heard whispered through the ranks, "locked and loaded" and ready for combat.

CHAPTER
TWENTY-ONE

GERDA

"**H**err Ziegler," *Frau* Krueger greeted Aldrik. "Please come in." He saluted her with the *Heil* Hitler motion and stood at attention. "I believe the kommandant wished to see me," he said.

"*Nein, Herr* Ziegler," she responded. "I sent for you." She led the way into the living room past the freshly cleaned section of carpet where Gerda had been sick. "Please," she said, indicating the couch. "Sit."

He perched on the edge of the cushions, uncomfortable alone in her presence.

"How is your wife?" she asked. "No baby yet?"

"*Nein, Frau.* The doctor said it was false labor. But thank you for asking." He twirled his hat in his hands, his fingers betraying the nervousness he felt.

"*Gut, gut,*" she said. "I'm glad our little...commotion...last night didn't harm her." She stopped talking and leaned back in her chair. "I know so little about her. About either of you. Where did you meet?"

"In Zwickau," he said. "At Flossenbürg, the Jewish-only sector."

"Oh?" She leaned forward and studied him intently. "What was she doing there?"

His heart sank. It had been a mistake to tell her that. "She had brought her bread cart there—to sell her family's bread to the Jews. Many of them still had money and she—"

"The Jews? The filthy Jews? And you let her talk to them?"

He shifted in his seat. He had made things worse, but he wasn't sure what to do about it. "Well…I…"

"Was she there to see any particular Jews? Did she know them?"

"Well…yes, I think…a family had recently arrived. They had been her neighbors."

"*Herr* Ziegler," the kommandant's wife said sharply, "I hope you know that is not acceptable behavior for an officer's wife."

"*Ja, Frau* Krueger. But we weren't married then. She hasn't—"

"Seen any Jews since then, *Herr* Ziegler? Is that what you were going to say?"

Aldrik hung his head.

"It is my understanding," *Frau* Krueger continued, "that she has spoken to Jewish inmates here at this camp, once without an officer present." She leaned closer, inches from his face. "And once," she continued, "with you standing beside her. Is that true?"

"*Ja*," he said, his voice barely audible.

"*Herr* Ziegler…" Her breath brushed his nostrils, her voice menacing, "I would hate for mistakes on your wife's part to halt your rising career. The kommandant thinks very highly of you. At least for now. I sincerely hope you will take immediate actions to keep your wife in line."

"*Frau* Krueger, this position is incredibly important to me. I will do whatever I can—"

"*Gut*," *Frau* Krueger interrupted. "Very good. I'm certain you will come up with something to convince us of your sincerity, *ja*?"

"*Jawohl!*" Aldrik answered and stood at attention again, clicking his heels together as he did. "*Danke, Frau* Krueger. I will take care of it right away."

"Fine," she said. "You may go."

He left the kommandant's house shaken. *Frau* Krueger exerted a great deal of influence over her husband and Aldrik considered himself lucky she had offered him a way to get back in their good graces. She could as easily have suggested he be shipped to the front lines.

Gerda's pregnancy had changed her, he realized. Had made her more belligerent, harder to deal with.

He had to show her who was in charge.

CHAPTER
TWENTY-TWO

GERDA

Gerda hadn't faked her labor. She really had doubled over with the pain of contractions, brought on, she believed, by the capture of her friend and fellow Resistance fighter, Michel Baudelaire. But her false labor provided Michel enough time to swallow a suicide pill which allowed him to die with slightly more dignity than he would have at the hands of the officers in charge of torture at Buchenwald.

Prior to the large-scale escape, Michel and Ulrich had agreed that if they were captured, they would ingest a potassium cyanide capsule. Gerda volunteered to take one too, but the men chastised her for even having such a thought.

"You're about to give birth," Ulrich said. "Taking your own life is one thing, but you can't take the life of your baby. Your child is Germany's future. I'll hear no more about it."

Gerda puffed herself up at his tone. She wasn't accustomed to being told what to do. Not even by Aldrik. But Michel put his hand on her arm and said, "Gerda, the movement needs you. It can continue without us, but you are the backbone of ensuring that children are saved from these atrocities. You can't join us in this."

"You're right, of course," she said. "I truly hope it doesn't come to that."

But unfortunately for Michel, it had.

They all carried the capsules with them, but they understood that if capture came suddenly, there might not be time to transfer the capsule to the mouth, so they also made plans to have them hidden in several places. Gerda had given three capsules to Frieda, the Krueger's maid, selected from among the camp's inmates. If the worst happened, she instructed Frieda, one of the capsules would go to the captured Resistance fighter, whoever that was, and one would be available for Frieda, herself, in case her involvement came to light. Without Ulrich's or Michel's knowledge, Gerda also told Frieda that one should be given to her if she were discovered as a Resistance member. She didn't believe she would be tortured as badly as the others since she was pregnant with a German officer's child, but she didn't want to take any chances.

Once Michel was dragged into the kommandant's house, Gerda caught the maid's eye. While her false labor created a distraction, Frieda approached Michel to slap him and used that movement to insert a capsule into his mouth, a thin-walled glass ampule filled with a concentrated solution of potassium cyanide. Gerda watched his face change when he felt the capsule. He bit down and the poison acted right away.

Ulrich had explained how it worked. "Once one bites the ampule and breaks the thin glass, the person quickly passes out, especially if they are already weak. Brain activity stops within minutes and the heart stops shortly after."

Gerda shuddered at the thought of her friend's death. But she genuinely believed he was better off than he would have been with the torture that awaited him. She hadn't been able to avoid seeing some of their methods during her time at the camp with Aldrik, and she was glad Michel had been saved from that.

Jurgen Reiner, the camp doctor, had insisted she rest and stay off her feet. For the day after Michel's death she lay in bed, fretting that she hadn't been able to contact anyone to see if the children made it out safely. A growing fear began in her stomach that something bad, in addition to Michel's capture, had happened and she couldn't do anything about it. The memory of *Frau* Krueger's eyes on her the previous night haunted her and a feeling of helplessness overtook her and squeezed her heart.

From her bed, her window offered a direct view into the open space near the gatehouse where a portable gallows had been set up. To her horror, five of the camp's inmates hung from it. But only two of them hung by the neck. By piano wire, Aldrik had told her, rather than rope.

The other three hung there in one of the Nazi's favorite torture positions, with their wrists tied at their backs and then their arms roped up at a grotesque angle behind them, leaving their feet dangling about a foot from the gallows platform. Even with her windows closed, their screams, as their arms stretched beyond reason and then dislocated, penetrated her walls.

Enough, she thought. She had to do something.

She flung the covers off and swung her feet to the floor. Married or not, she didn't want her baby born under the conditions that surrounded her.

"*Liebling.*" Aldrik entered the room and looked at her, his eyes full of questions. "What are you doing? You should be resting."

"I'm going home," she told him. "I will not have our child born here where I can hear the screams of the inmates from my bed." She opened drawers and threw clothes into a bag.

Aldrik covered the distance between them in an instant, his hand firm on her arm, stopping its motion. "I can't let you do that," he said. His voice was quiet but laced with steel.

"You can't...what...?" She couldn't believe what she had heard. Her head jerked up to search his eyes. A hard glitter replaced the warmth that normally greeted her. "What do you mean you can't 'let me' do that? The last I heard, I was still a free citizen of this state." She jerked her arm from his grasp and backed away. He advanced, menacingly.

"I'm asking you to be reasonable, Gerda," he said. "You can no longer leave here. You're too ingrained in this camp now."

"Aldrik, have you gone mad? This is me. Us. You've never spoken to me like this before. What's gotten into you?"

"*Frau* Krueger is suspicious of you, that you had friends who were dirty Jews. She warned me to watch you, to keep you hidden until the baby is born. To keep you under control."

"Under...? I'm a person, Aldrik. Not your property. You can't—"

His face hovered inches from hers, his voice like ice. "I can. And I will." He grabbed her arm and forced her to the window. "I want you to look at the yard by the gatehouse."

She hung her head. "I've already seen it," she said. "I don't need to see any more."

"Oh, but you do," he told her. He jerked her head up roughly. "Look at the faces of the ones hanging by their necks. Really look."

"I don't want to." She clamped her eyes shut.

He grabbed her hair and forced her head up, then thrust field glasses in front of her eyes. "Look," he commanded again. "Do as I tell you. This is important."

Gerda opened her eyes and couldn't help but see the faces of the five inmates on the gallows. The faces of those hanging with their arms behind their backs twisted in pain, their mouths open wide with their screams. But she caught her breath at the faces of the two who hung by their necks. She was shocked. And devastated. They were her friends, Jakob and Ruth Rosenbaum. Rebekah's mother and brother.

And she knew, from Aldrik's words, they were there because of her.

"No...no," she cried. "Why? How could you? I don't understand..." She flung the field glasses away from her and stood there, sobbing. Aldrik released her and she crumpled to the floor.

Calmly, he turned his back to her and removed the clothes she had already packed, replacing them in her dresser drawers. Without turning, he said, "I've arranged for the delivery van to be returned to your parents' bakery, along with a note from me informing them that Dr. Reiner has placed you on mandatory bed rest." He faced her again and crossed his arms. "You will stay here," he continued. "Our baby will be born here. There will be no discussion."

She no longer recognized him, the soldier in him overriding the loving husband he had always been. "And you will do as I say," he added, his voice harsh. "Without question."

The trickle of fear she had experienced earlier exploded and her body shook uncontrollably. Aldrik strode from the room without a backward glance and the door locked behind him. From the outside.

She was trapped. A prisoner in what had been her home. Cut off from communications with the outside world. She sank onto the bed and her sobs flowed.

CHAPTER
TWENTY-THREE

SAM

Early on March 12, we moved forward toward the Moselle River with the goal of securing the high ground on the river's west bank. Once we were across, our lieutenant told us, the Ruhr industrial region, critical to Hitler, would lay open to the Allies and hasten the war's end.

General Patton had described himself as "relentless in pursuit of a wounded enemy," and it must have been true. Our reconnaissance group reported that the regular German Army had retreated, but pockets of German zealots, not ready to give up, fought with a fury to provide time for their retreating Armies to get out of our way and regroup.

We weren't surprised when Evans, one of our forward scouts, reported machine gun nests, roadblocks, and minefields along the road banks and hillsides. We moved out carefully, rifles ready, rounds chambered. Nerves gurgled my stomach and a rotten odor reached my nose. With two more steps, my boot barely missed the stomach of a dead German soldier, shot in the head, his still-open eyes crusted with dried blood. Someone had already gone through his pockets but the faces of a young woman and two small children smiled up from a picture beside him. That got me in the gut. The poor woman probably had no idea her husband lay dead and abandoned beside a road in the middle of Germany. I wondered if she'd even get his body back.

I hoped my sweet Betty never had to experience such a fate.

I forced myself to return my focus to the road ahead. At its first turn, we left it and headed straight into dense woods. Under other circumstances, I would have relished a walk through the woods, enjoying the leafy-musk scent and a glimpse of early spring buds, but on that day, my head swiveled from side-to-side, alert for shadows or motion since the likelihood of hearing our enemy's movement was nonexistent. The sound of our forward progress resembled a herd of cattle thrashing through thick brush and the thought struck me, too late, that our training didn't include nearly enough stealth tactics. The lieutenant held up his hand and we halted, the swish of soft wind humming in our ears. After a moment, we continued to scurry along, bent low on our haunches.

I told myself I was alert, but the sudden machine gun fire startled me. Ahead and to my left, small branches flew from trees and a flock of birds swooped up, darkening what little sky we could see. I fell to my stomach and bellied my way to the cover of a sturdy pine. Bullets struck dirt on both sides of me and I eased my rifle into position. Anguished groans reached me and shouts of "Medic!" sounded throughout the company.

I remained motionless until the next spate of bullets, then searched for their origin. I followed the sound and hit pattern to a small berm, part of a network of piled earth that broke for a footpath, then picked up again on my right only a few feet away. I trained my scope on the bullets' origin and found the top of a German helmet. It bobbed to the surface then disappeared. The process repeated three times. The same helmet in the same spot. Each time it became visible, the machine gun fire stopped, leading me to believe we only faced one gunner. Two at the most.

I eased my field pack from my shoulders and retrieved more ammunition. The second the helmet popped up again, I rolled to the berm beside me and scrambled over it, then crawled toward the shooter. At the break, where the path intersected, I risked a look and saw the left half of a German uniform. The helmet lifted once more, and I plowed half my ammunition into it. The soldier rose, showing me his stunned face and I finished him off.

He fell and I reloaded.

Within seconds, his body changed positions. Pushed away, obviously, and confirming my suspicion of a second shooter. Then of all fool things, a head popped out and looked in my direction. His eyes held the same mixture of shock and disbelief as my only twelve-point buck, whose head hangs over the fireplace in the family farmhouse. I shot the German in the same spot that had downed the deer. Right in the middle of those emotions.

The sound from my rifle deafened me and time slowed to a halt. I heard nothing. No shots, no bird calls, no wind, no shouts. Only roaring in my ears heightened by the sound of my heart slamming against my rib cage. A sharp odor reached me and turned my stomach. Cordite, my training taught me. Sickly sweet, not dry and smoky like the smell of gunpowder that reached my nose and mouth when I found Richard. The smell of cordite irritated my nose and caught in my throat, which was bone dry. As were my lips. I reached up to touch them and my hands shook.

After what may have only been seconds, my ears eased back to normal and the sounds of soft whimpering and rapid panting reached me. My vision cleared and I saw Simon climbing the berm toward me. Other soldiers marched a few Germans toward the back of the line while still others bent over the ones who'd been wounded.

"Hey, Old Man, you okay?" Simon pressed his nose close, almost touching mine and then looked anxiously into my eyes. "You did great. Once you took out those dudes, the rest of them Krauts just walked out with their hands up." He patted my shoulder and helped me stand. "I sure am glad you're on my side."

My focus on that machine gun and its shooters had been so intense, I'd missed the rest of the battle around me. Several of our guys were hit, Simon said. Dickie had a surface wound on his left arm and one guy lost an ear. Our losses weren't too bad, except for one.

Lieutenant Cooper didn't make it.

"When you took out the first machine gunner...ow..." Dickie said, wincing as the medic applied antiseptic and bandaged his arm, "...the lieutenant stood to rally the rest of us forward. A lone sniper fired a round and got him in the back of the head."

"And then, Sergeant Hanley took the sniper out," Eddie said, "and had us keep the rest of them Krauts busy whilst you finished off the other gunner. Great job, man." He patted my back.

I was sorry to hear about Lieutenant Cooper. He was a good man and we worked well as a unit. Who knew how well someone else would fit in with our squad?

But something else occupied my mind.

Something big.

I recognized that I had—that we all had—experienced something profound.

Our "baptism by fire."

Our first experience of actual combat in a war.

My first experience of killing another human being.

General Patton had been right. When the moment came there was no time to be afraid. Training kicked in and I did what I was supposed to. Without thinking about it.

Until it was all over.

After that, I struggled to keep from throwing up. I couldn't dwell on the fact that I had taken someone's life. Someone who would never return to his mother or his wife, who would never see his children again. I had to put it out of my mind. I *had* to.

I focused on what I had been trained to do and knew I had done the right thing.

I also knew I could do it again.

———

BY MARCH 14, WE HAD CROSSED FIFTY MILES OF ROUGH terrain in three days, keeping mostly to forests and only double-timing on real roads for scant miles before returning to the cover of the trees. We encountered little pockets of Germans, but they didn't put up much of a fight and, for the most part, gladly surrendered. I didn't speak German, but from their body language, they looked like they were bone-tired and ready for it to be over.

We also cleared several towns along the way, among them Wispelt and Krinkhof, which required house-to-house searches where we isolated and evacuated civilians who may have harbored German resistance. Our lieutenant hadn't been replaced, so our captain spent more time with us.

Captain Powell. A true professional. He carried out his orders according to protocol, giving the evacuation notice to the correct officials in the towns we cleared and then giving the residents the proper amount of time to vacate. So my pangs of remorse when we had to commandeer homes lessened.

The next night, however, we camped beside the town of Aldegund, north of the Moselle River. It flowed slowly at our crossing site, but spanned two hundred yards, then wound through a deep gorge, its banks terraced with vineyards that rose steeply to three hundred feet on each side and ended in thick woods. The perfect hiding place for snipers. Our capture target, the town of Alf, sat on the river at the point where it abruptly turned southeast for a few miles and then doubled back, almost meeting itself again and forming what the Army termed "the teardrop." Finally, Army-speak I understood. A teardrop is exactly what it looked like on the map.

In the pre-dawn hours of March 16, we joined three other battalions. The captain told us we faced one of the most difficult of combat operations, that of launching an assault by crossing a hostile river line. The boats to ferry us across could only take a few soldiers at a time and exposed us to possible German fire. But worse, the first soldiers to arrive on the opposite shore suffered the risk of being driven back into the river by the enemy.

With that knowledge, we launched under the cover of darkness and stayed quiet at the edge of the water until three boatloads made it across. Regardless of our stealth, we encountered small arms fire during our crossing but no one sustained serious injury.

We regrouped on the eastern shore and as we began our punch inland, we encountered a wounded German soldier. The Davis twins were the first to reach him.

"Please," he said in perfect English, "don't kill me." Eddie held his gun steady on the soldier's head as the German unbuttoned the top of his uniform and removed a picture. He held it up so we could see a smiling woman with three small children surrounding her. "Please take me prisoner," he begged. "I want to return to my wife and children when the war is over."

And there it was. An enemy soldier actually voicing the words I had always believed. He didn't want to fight us any more than we wanted to fight him. I couldn't help but remember the dead German I had encountered earlier who also had a picture of his family. My heart went out to the one in front of us.

Eddie cocked his weapon but Erwin called for a medic and Ervin put his hand on Eddie's arm. "We don't need to kill this one," he said. "But we will keep him from killing any more of us." Eddie lowered his gun and Ervin helped load the wounded man onto the stretcher to be patched up and then imprisoned.

We regrouped and charged the teardrop with Captain Powell leading the way. Our target was the remnants of the 14th *Nebelwerfer* Regiment, holed up in both the *Marienburg* and the *Prinzenkopf* Towers, located less than a mile northwest of our position, but higher on the same ridge. We climbed toward them for three miles up steep terrain.

The Germans had the advantage of a higher elevation, with a panoramic view, so they saw every move in our rank and file. And exacted a heavy price for each yard we gained. They hit us not only with rifle fire but also with machine guns and grenades. For two days, we'd advance three feet and be driven back two. We hadn't expected them to have so much fight left in them.

On the morning of March 18, the first rays of the sun shone on a few white flags, flying from windows on several levels of the *Marienburg* Tower.

"Cease fire!" Captain Powell stood and, with Sergeant Hanley and a dozen other troops, moved toward the tower to receive the surrendered soldiers. But after three steps, the Germans mowed them down like dominoes.

We couldn't believe it.

That went against everything we had been taught about the rules of engagement. And our sense of fair play.

They fought dirty.

That wounded German soldier we encountered earlier, I thought, was certainly lucky we hadn't seen this treachery first. We might never have let him live.

Determined to do something to avenge our slain brothers, Dickie and Simon and I skirted the mountain, hiding under grape vines and creeping ever higher. Eddie, Ervin and Erwin, along with their superior firepower, crept up the ridge about two hundred yards to our left.

Two more times while we inched up the side of the mountain, German soldiers waved their white flags.

To our horror, two more times our guys came out of hiding only to be shot down.

We got mad. And vowed to get even. They couldn't treat General Patton's Third Army that way.

The six of us made a final push and our bazooka brothers gained ground high enough to see into the German machine gunner nest. They loaded and shot. The shell landed perfectly, taking out the gunners. We covered them with rifle fire from our position and Dickie and I took out several snipers ready to shoot. Simon threw grenades and we all unloaded on them with our small supply of TNT. The tower crumbled and we watched the few remaining soldiers scramble down the slopes on the other side of the hill.

The Moselle crossing was successful and the road to the Rhine, the last stronghold between the Allied Army and Berlin, lay open.

We had passed another test, one of nerves and endurance.

Even more important, the 89th Infantry opened a vital supply route across the Moselle, cleared more than one hundred towns and villages, along with several hundred square miles of territory, and captured more than five thousand Germans.

The next big hurdle we faced was the Rhine River crossing.

And then on to Hitler.

CHAPTER
TWENTY-FOUR

SAM

Ⓦe marched nonstop for the next two days with practically no rest.

Our unit surged from the Moselle Gorge into Enkirch and Briedel, through forests and patches of pine during nights so dark, since we marched under blackout conditions, you literally couldn't see your hand in front of your face. I know that's true because I held mine up to look.

We'd been instructed to put our hand on the shoulder of the man in front of us to keep from wandering off the path in the pitch black. We couldn't see, so our other senses sharpened. The silence was deafening. Sure, an occasional grunt from a soldier whose foot caught on a vine and the slight squeak of backpack straps being rearranged. But we heard no bird calls, no insect chirps, no distant animal movement. The lack of sound unnerved us.

Eddie marched at my front with Simon at my back. I wasn't sure where Dickie and the twins were in the line-up but I didn't have time to think about them. Fortunately, we marched in what my mother would have called a "dark moon," so no light reflected off our guns or bayonets.

We must have moved for three quarters of an hour and I remember wondering how the person at the front of the line could see to lead us. Or how he even knew where we were headed. While I certainly didn't understand the inner workings of the Army, I also remembered marveling at how anything got done with so many of us in the dark—

literally, at that point—about the strategy. I moved steadily along, one foot in front of the other, my hand never leaving Eddie's shoulder.

Until he disappeared.

He was there one second and gone the next. With no explanation and no sound. I couldn't see where I was headed.

I took one step forward and tumbled down a steep embankment, end over end, and landed on Eddie's pack as he attempted to pull it up, which took my legs out from under me. Before I could rise, Simon landed on my head.

We all scrambled to our feet and felt our way, like blind men, until Eddie found his soldier again, then regrouped as before, hand to shoulder. I wished I could have seen what we looked like, because the picture I had in my head was of the chain formed by the elephants in the circus, the one time I had seen them. Trunk to tail. I was certain we looked funny but I didn't dare laugh.

We marched through the rest of the night and at dawn reached the small town of Walhausen, where we cleaned out the enemy and captured more than one hundred prisoners. We took a quick break to have our C-rations, at which time I vowed that once the war was over, I would never again eat cold spaghetti or corned beef hash, and then moved ahead that afternoon to take Loffelscheid and Schwarzen.

MANY OF THE VILLAGES AND HAMLETS WE ENCOUNTERED already reeled from bombs dropped by the American P-47 Thunderbolts that wiped out the enemy convoys assigned to protect them and unfortunately, parts of the towns as well. The villages were so small, I figured it must be impossible to make certain that civilians were out of the way when pilots dropped bombs from thousands of feet up. I tried to steel my heart against it, but again, it hit me in the gut when I saw small children without shoes searching through garbage for food. Funny thing about that. Every time I shared my cold spaghetti with them, *they* seemed to love it. I gave away more than I ate.

Occasionally, we heard some of the fighter planes overhead, returning to their base. That afternoon, during a quick break, a P-47 flew low over us and its engine struggled, sputtered, and then stopped altogether. Within seconds, the tops of trees to our left sheared off and we heard a crash.

"Sam," Dickie said, "let's go find the pilot." We took off at a trot through the field and crept into the tree cover.

We found the downed plane after only a few steps and the pilot after that. One hand moved his flying goggles to the top of his leather helmet and the other hand reached for the sky. Three German Lugers zeroed in on his chest.

I motioned to Dickie that I would take the one on the right. Soundlessly, we stood and caught the pilot's eye. In a single motion, we broke through the trees and seconds later, our guns rested squarely in the backs of two of the Germans. The pilot whipped out his pistol and trained it on the third.

"Drop your weapons," I said. Slowly, they raised their arms, their guns falling to the ground. Dickie scooped them up and stuck them in his knapsack. "Remove your belts," he told them. We belted their hands behind their backs as Eddie burst through the trees. After making certain we were all okay, he marched the German soldiers back to our unit, where they were added to the cage.

"I sure am glad to see you guys," the pilot said. "I've been told Germans shoot fighter pilots."

"Yeah," Dickie grinned. "We heard that too. I'm Dickinson, by the way." He jerked his thumb toward me. "This is Ryan. We're part of the 89th Infantry Division. You okay?"

The pilot, about my height at six-foot-two, removed his helmet and goggles in one swipe and his brown hair lay plastered to his forehead in damp clumps. He produced a handkerchief and wiped his wet face with a hand that shook slightly. Then he moved his arms as if to hug himself and stretched sideways, first to his right and then to his left. "Yeah," he said finally. "But now that it's all over, I realize it rattled me a little more than I had imagined it would." He reached out his hand. "I'm Spencer. Mike Spencer. 405th Army Air Corps. And yeah," he repeated. "I'm okay. But my crew chief will be mad as hell when he sees the condition of his plane."

The fuselage sported holes everywhere. Same with the wings.

"What happened?" I asked him. "It's not normal for you guys to get shot up like this."

"No," he said. "It isn't. We were strafing a freight train outside of Seiburg. Trains are our favorite targets," he said absently, rubbing his hands over the fuselage. "When we cripple one," he continued, "that keeps supplies from getting to the German troops. But we don't usually see them in the daylight. Normally, they only come out in the dark."

He shook his head at the number of pock-marks in the aluminum. "Our G-2 told us to be on the lookout and sure enough, there it was, coming out of the tunnel. We circled around it and then banked in for a fast dive from around fifteen thousand feet and leveled off at five hundred. We hit it hard with our fifty-caliber guns." He patted one of the eight massive machine guns mounted under his wing. "I sent bullets all the way down the length of it and pulled up to make another pass. But then the sides of several boxcars dropped open and showed me row after row of twenty-millimeter flak guns. I screamed a warning to the others in my radio, increased my prop pitch and pulled back hard on the stick to get the heck out of there. But," he said, surveying the damage again, "not fast enough."

"What about the others?" Dickie asked. "Did they get hit?"

He shook his head. "I was the lead, so I got it the worst. Normally, something in the emergency procedures works to get the engine back on track. I got it running again on my third attempt to start the fuel transfer pump. But the tanks had been hit and what fuel there was leaked out. Not enough to get back to Metz. You guys have a radio in your unit?"

"Yeah," I said. "Come on. Through the trees."

On our way back through the sparse forest, Spencer told us about being chased by a new German fighter. "A *Messerschmitt—ME-262*. He chased me for a while, but I had gotten rid of my payload, so I was able to stay far enough away from him. We've been told those guys will fly faster and be more heavily armed than anything the Allies have in the sky yet. I sure hope this war is finished before they have those babies ready."

We never saw Spencer again, but always imagined he looked out for us from above.

———

WE BIVOUACKED AT A SMALL FARM OUTSIDE SCHWARZEN and I remember being impressed with how neat the farmer kept the place, even in the middle of a war. I marveled that the barn was an extension of the house, not a separate building behind the house like the one at our farm.

We slept in the hayloft with cows, pigs, and chickens below us. It made me homesick for my sisters, Sarah and Winnie, and their animals.

At the edge of dusk, the farmer's two little girls crept into the barn to take care of the livestock. We weren't supposed to talk to the German people, but Dickie and I pooled our candy bars and offered them to the girls to wash our clothes for us. They agreed, with so much chocolate as a reward.

Which amazed me. Honestly, it was the worst tasting chocolate I'd ever had. At a briefing, one of the officers told us the Army made a deal with the Hershey Company to use less sugar than normal so the soldiers would eat them slowly, for sustained energy, as opposed to scarfing them down the way we used to do on the rare occasions Mother could afford them. The idea, we learned, was to make them taste only slightly better than a boiled potato. I can't imagine who came up with that plan, but it worked. They were not good. But for those little German girls, I suppose even bad tasting chocolate was better than none.

We stayed at the farm until the edge of dark the next evening which gave our mail a chance to catch up with us. My packet contained seven letters. One from each of my sisters—with pictures from Freddie—and four from my darling Betty. I loved the letters from the girls and replaced the last picture from Freddie I had tucked in my boots with one of the new ones, six baby ducks marching behind their mother. I arranged the letters from Betty in date order and read them slowly.

Her tidbits from the USO Club and visits to the farm brought a smile to my face, but I let out a whoop at the news in her final letter.

Erwin, sleeping in the hay, raised his head and looked at me through bleary eyes.

"What is it, Sam? Are you all right? Did you get news from home?"

I couldn't stop smiling. "I sure did," I said. "I'm going to be a father."

They all crowded around me, slapping me on the back and giving me hugs.

"Okay," Eddie said. "This calls for a toast." We scrambled to get our canteens, then each poured a small amount of water into the attached cups.

"Here's to the Old Man and his offspring," Simon said.

"And," Eddie added, "to keeping him alive so he gets to meet his little one."

We clicked our cups the best we could and then drank. I was thrilled.

And worried. I hated the thought of Betty having to go through childbirth with me stuck in Europe. I knew I'd never make it home in time. Of course, Betty had a plan. She would work at the USO as long as she could, then go to the farm to live with the girls and Freddie. She had already spoken with Mrs. Gibbons and Mrs. Wainwright and they had promised to be there to help her. She would be fine. Still, I wished I could have been with her.

My smile stayed with me until I met our new commanding officer, Lieutenant Jerome Scott. He was career military, unlike Lieutenant Cooper, who had come up through the ranks.

I couldn't believe the difference in their personalities. And in their treatment of us. Lieutenant Scott gave us the impression that we were dirt under his feet and it was all he could do to even tolerate the sight of us. We had formed a tight band by the time he arrived and I worried that his "by-the-book" attitude wouldn't work well with our group.

CHAPTER
TWENTY-FIVE

SAM

For the hundredth time or so, I was thankful for our training at Fort Butner where we practiced river crossings. Two days after meeting our new lieutenant, we faced yet another river —the Nahe—and still had the Rhine in front of us. One of our sister regiments, the 355th, had already made it across and wiped out the bulk of machine gun nests, so by the time we got there, we forded easily with only moderate opposition.

Almost immediately, we learned that another small river, the Glan, stood between us and the Rhine. But to get to it, we had a day or so of moving through sparse thickets and over large tracts of exposed ground. With plenty of hiding places for German snipers.

We reached Limbacher Höhe. Lieutenant Scott referred to it as elevated ground. But to me, it looked like mountains. More mountains.

"Move out, men," Lieutenant Scott shouted at us. Which was weird. We'd gotten hand signals from Lieutenant Cooper to keep from exposing our position.

But Lieutenant Scott was in charge. So we did as we were told.

My little band fell in at the head of the pack. We crept through the scant tree cover, bent over and scurrying from one trunk to the next. I started up a steep rise, my rifle ready, but a small snap sounded to my right, as if a squirrel moved from branch to branch. I raised my eyes and found a pair of German boots right in front of them, hanging out of a tree. I fell to the ground, discharging my weapon on my way down and then lay still. Within seconds, a crash assured me my bullets had found their mark.

I lay still until Dickie crawled up behind me. "Great shooting, Sam," he whispered. "That sniper was reloading. If you hadn't gotten him, he'd have gotten you. And probably the rest of us as well."

Taking the life of another human still unsettled me, even though I knew he would have shot me if he hadn't run out of ammunition. Regardless, my stomach turned over a few times and it took me a minute before I could continue. Soldiers on either side of me advanced.

Dickie stayed beside me and we moved forward in parallel. All too soon, we ran out of cover and into direct fire. This time we both fell to the earth and I grabbed my little shovel from my pack. I dug into the soft earth at my side and piled it in front of me. To my right, Dickie did the same. Bullets whizzed over us and I thought of Hanson, who took one to the head during our barbed-wire, belly-crawl training. I damned sure wasn't going to let that happen to me. I rested the side of my face directly on the ground and continued to dig. Before long, Dickie and I had a deep hole and we both rolled into it.

Despite the gravity of the situation, I couldn't resist flashing Dickie a grin. The look he returned told me he thought I had lost my mind. "The day I met you," I whispered, "my first thought was that if I had to share a foxhole with somebody, you would be the one." I grinned again. "And here we are." He grinned back.

We lay there amid the firestorm until word came from the foxholes around us to move. We scampered forward toward a rock outcropping a hundred yards up the mountain.

Always up. Annoyingly up.

Soldiers ran toward the rocks and I put my head down and ran along with them. The Germans fired from above, so we made good targets. Our training taught us the art of zigzagging, so I scurried to my left in a kind of crab scuttle and then turned to my right again. Bullets pelted the ground around us and it came alive with their impact.

The rocks beckoned and I made my final push to reach them as a machine gunner opened up from above. There's something about that sound that makes your blood run cold. And your teeth clench. It's so different from the sound of a regular rifle. And so much more deadly.

I turned on the speed with only fifteen or so yards to go when I saw Eddie get hit. To me, it looked like the Germans turned the gun full on him. The staccato sound of bullets raced through the air and cut his legs right out from under him. As I watched he spiraled up, the stumps of his knees turning over and over as if he were doing cartwheels. But his helmet was gone, along with a large chunk of his face. Before he could land, more shots tore into his chest and severed an arm.

I must have hesitated. Or maybe I stopped running entirely. I'm not sure, because time stood still. I'd been lucky. Except for my brothers, I'd never had anyone close to me get shot. But even then, I didn't watch them die. I couldn't have imagined how much worse it was to witness the devastation of bullets tearing through a body. From the first time I met Eddie, I thought he was too young, too small to have to fight in a war. Seeing him killed was almost more than I could stand.

I'm lucky the bullets didn't hit me too. And, honestly, I'm not sure how I escaped it. But as I was ready to go gather up what was left of Eddie, Dickie came up beside me and physically forced me to keep moving, the way we'd been instructed, instead of stopping to help Eddie the way I wanted. He pushed me ahead of him, all the while telling me there was nothing we could do for our little buddy. And that if we tried, it could mean the end of us as well.

He was right. I knew he was. And yet, I wanted to punch him in the face for making me leave one of our brothers behind.

Who knows? Maybe some part of me thought I should have been the one to go. A stupid thought, of course, because in a perfect world, none of us should have died. But that wasn't an option in March of 1945. In Germany. During a global conflict.

Dickie and I reached the outcropping of rock and then slipped around the side and crawled up the hill until we were below the German machine gunner. We both hurled grenades until he stopped shooting. Ironic how much I'd been bothered earlier by taking a life. After wiping out that gunner's nest I felt immense satisfaction.

The battled raged on the rest of the day until the remnants of that unit waved white flags and marched out with their hands up. Given the ambush our company encountered in earlier surrender trickery, I hollered at those around me to stay put rather than get suckered in again. So we didn't leave our positions until we confirmed they were unarmed and serious about surrendering.

Lieutenant Scott marched up to the highest ranking German and hit him in the head with the butt of his rifle. He fell to the ground, a great gash dripping blood all over him. And then the lieutenant kicked him.

"Okay, you sons of bitches," he said to the Germans who had surrendered. "Who's next? Who still feels like fighting? Come on. Come at me." He was screaming by then. "All I want is for one of you assholes to give me an excuse to blow a hole in you. Who will it be? Who?"

Not one German moved. The lieutenant even pushed a couple, apparently trying to get a reaction to justify beating the hell out of them. But they stayed put. With their eyes straight ahead.

We all felt like beating the hell out of them. But it didn't seem right when they had surrendered. We chalked up the lieutenant's reaction to being new to command. And to the heat of the battle. And to his anger at losing so many men.

THAT NIGHT, WE HAD K-RATIONS INSTEAD OF THE GREASY C-rations. I'm not sure why, but they were so much better. Even cold, they tasted like a treat. Or would have if I could have swallowed. I sat on my pack in the field with the remaining four soldiers in my personal little band of brothers and mourned my little buddy. I would miss his quick grin and crude humor.

Erwin and Ervin were especially quiet and from time to time Erwin touched his twin's shoulder and then gave him a quick hug. He left our circle for a few minutes to relieve himself and Ervin told us what had happened.

"When we all dug foxholes in that open field, I was scared to death. So I didn't move. Not a muscle. I was so still, in fact, Erwin thought I had been hit. Killed."

"True," Erwin said, coming up behind him. He touched his brother's shoulder again and his voice shook. "We made a deal before we ever left the States that if either of us didn't make it, the other would remove the high school ring from his finger and take it home to our mother. I was so afraid I was going to have to do that." His voice broke. "I didn't know how I would make it without him."

Dickie stood and patted his arm. "I'm glad you didn't have to, Erwin. But you'd have done it," he said. "You'd have made it without Ervin the same way we will make it without Eddie."

Tears filled my eyes. I had made a vow to myself that no one in our group would suffer because of something I had failed to do. My mind couldn't let go of that, wondering what I could have done differently, what I could have done to save him.

Everyone else left to catch some sleep, but I sat. And Dickie sat with me.

"The answer is 'nothing,' Sam," he said quietly.

"Huh?" I said. "What are you talking about?"

"I know you," Dickie said. "You're sitting there wondering what you could have done differently to save your little buddy."

My head whipped toward him. "Dammit all to hell, Dickie. You don't understand," I said, my voice near breaking. "I made myself a promise that—"

"Sam." He cut me off and laid his huge hand on my arm. "You did all you could. We all did. There was no way we could have taken that machine gunner's nest out before we did. Eddie's death was the rotten luck of the draw. It was just his time. And he'd be really pissed to know you're sitting here beating yourself up over something that wasn't your fault. You've got to find a way to let it go, Sam. Or it could get you killed too."

He stood and patted me on the head. Not condescendingly. Brotherly.

While I didn't let it go completely, his words were enough to get me back on track. One more time, Eugene "Dickie" Dickinson brought me back from deep inside myself and pointed me in the right direction.

I still had a job to do. And I needed to have my head on straight to do it.

CHAPTER
TWENTY-SIX

GERDA

"*T*ante Karla," Ulrich said into the phone, "have you spoken with Gerda lately?"

"*Nein*," Gerda's mother answered. "But Aldrik sent the van back, along with a note that said she went into false labor and her doctor placed her on mandatory bed rest. Why do you ask?"

"We had some trouble a few days ago. And my contacts at Buchenwald tell me she hasn't left the camp since. Hasn't left her room, actually."

"Well," Karla said, "it's probably as Aldrik's note stated, that she's on bed rest."

Silence greeted her on the other end of the line. "What is it, Ulrich?" Karla asked.

"I'm worried about her," Ulrich said. "That maybe she is being held against her will."

Karla gasped. "*Ach du großer Gott!*" she said. "Why do you think that?"

Ulrich hesitated. "*Tut mir leid*...sorry, *Tante*. I didn't mean to upset you. But we have some insiders there and even they are worried about her. I can't get in to see her. But I think someone should." More hesitation. "Would you be willing to drive out there? To make certain she's okay? I can't imagine that even Aldrik would turn away her own mother."

"*Ja*," Karla said softly. "I will go tomorrow."

"*Gut*," he said. "That will be good."

"HALT," THE GUARD ORDERED KARLA. "*WAS GEHT SIE HIER AN?* State your business."

"Well, I would think that would be obvious," Karla said, indicating the lettering on the bakery van. "I'm here to make deliveries. Your kommandant has approved our company to deliver our baked goods here."

"*Warten,*" the guard said. "I will check."

Within minutes, Aldrik came to the checkpoint to greet Karla. "*Frau* Berghmann," he said. "Welcome." He nodded to the guard and the gate opened. "Please come in. I'm sure the kommandant will be pleased to have fresh bread."

"I'd like to see my daughter as well," she said.

"Of course," he answered. "Go ahead and make your delivery to the kommandant's house and then I will meet you at Gerda's and my home."

She would have preferred to accompany him then and there but did as she was told. After dropping off her goods with the kommandant's maid, she moved her van to the nearby house her daughter shared with Aldrik.

GERDA HEARD THE KEY IN THE LOCK AND SAT UP IN BED. Since it wasn't time for a meal, an unexpected visit might mean trouble. In the days of her involuntary confinement, her mind raced constantly, going through every minute of her time with the kommandant's wife and with Aldrik to figure out where their suspicions had originated. She didn't believe the elders in Block 66 had been discovered, so the doubts must have come from her conversations with the Rosenbaums.

Almost a week had passed since Aldrik locked her in their room, during which time he refrained from sharing it with her.

Which suited her fine. She didn't understand his new harshness, but she didn't like it.

"Gerda," Aldrik said from the door. "Get up and put on your robe. Your mother is coming to see you."

"Oh," she said. A smile found her face and her heart soared. She threw the covers off and planted her feet on the floor. "I'll get dr—"

"No." Aldrik's voice was firm. "She knows you've been assigned to bed rest. That's what I told her. So she will expect you to be in your bedclothes."

Gerda's anger rose. "But that's not true," she said. "I am perfectly fine and you know it. You're just—"

He closed the distance between them in one step and grabbed her arm. She tried to pull away. "Aldrik, you're hurting me. Why are you acting—?"

He jerked her arm cruelly and she cried out in pain.

"I'm getting a lot of pressure from my superiors, Gerda. You will not do anything to harm my position with the kommandant. Now put on your robe."

A knock sounded on the outer door. Again, Gerda tried to pull away but he held her tight. Then Aldrik leaned in, his mouth inches from her ear. "You will tell your mother that you have been ordered to stay in bed until our child is born. And you will tell her that everything is fine and that you feel privileged to have the great care you are receiving here. That she needn't worry."

"And if I don't?"

He released her arm. "Then I can't be held responsible for what could happen to her."

She gasped, unable to reconcile the man in front of her with the Aldrik she had loved.

A second knock. Louder, more insistent.

"Put on your robe," he said again and left her. She shrugged into her robe, ran her fingers through her hair and went into the living room. She did her best to arrange her face in a pleasant expression and moved toward her mother.

"*Mutti*," Gerda said taking her hands. "I'm so happy to see you."

"*Ja,*" Aldrik agreed. "This is certainly a nice surprise, *Frau* Berghmann."

"So, why have you come, *Mutti?*"

"Aldrik told me you'd been ordered to bed rest, and I thought the kommandant and his wife must be missing the fresh bread and treats from our bakery. So I brought some with me. I didn't get to meet them, but I'm sure they will be pleased. Don't you think so, Aldrik?"

"*Ja,*" he said. "They are really fond of your family's baked goods."

"That reminds me," Gerda's mother said. She reached into her large fabric bag and pulled out a tin of *Lebkuchen.* "I thought you two might enjoy this."

"*Danke, Mutti,*" Gerda said, accepting the box of treats.

"Well," Karla said. "Aren't you going to open it? I've never known my Gerda to turn down the taste of *Lebkuchen.* I also brought some of our *Birnen-Brand,* our pear brandy."

Aldrik reached for the brandy, tore away the paper seal and eased the stopper out, then held the bottle up to the light. "I always wondered how you get that big pear in the bottom of the bottle through such a small neck."

"It's a trade secret, Aldrik," Karla said, "but since you're family, we can tell you. Gerda, why don't you explain it to him?"

"Explain how the pear becomes imprisoned?" she asked. Her lips smiled at her mother, but her eyes remained serious. "You've never told me how that happens, *Mutti,*" Gerda said. "So I guess you'd better tell him."

"Of course," Karla said.

"Before you do that, *Mutti,*" Gerda said turning to face her husband, "will you get the good glasses, Aldrik? They're in the cupboard over the stove."

"Sure," he answered, "but don't you girls talk about anything while I'm gone. I don't want to miss the family news." He strode to the kitchen.

As soon as he was out of sight, Karla mouthed "What's going on?" Gerda sent a distressed look toward the door. She pointed to the kitchen, then herself, and jerked her head toward the bedroom door, pantomiming the motion of turning a key in a lock. Her mother's eyes widened.

Aldrik returned with the glasses and poured generous servings of brandy into each. "Okay, Karla, you were going to tell me about getting the pear into the bottle?"

"Right," she said. "In the early spring, when the fruit begins to bud, Gerda's cousins take the bottles to the orchard and select one bud from the cluster of fruit and then pinch off everything else so they only have one tiny pear at the end of a branch. Then they thread that into the bottle and wire it to a higher branch so the large end of the bottle points upward."

"Why?" Aldrik asked. "Why above?"

"Because if rainwater got into the bottle the pear could swell and split. A lot of precautions are taken to keep the pear healthy," she added. "Once the bottle is secured, for example, a little fabric is attached over the end of it so the sun doesn't scald the young fruit. And then at harvest time, the bottle is unwired from the tree, the pear's stem is cut and a full-grown pear rests in the bottom of the bottle. After that, our double-distilled and aged brandy is poured on top of it and we're ready to sell it." She turned her hands, palms up at her sides. "And that's how it's done."

Aldrik finished his brandy and Gerda poured him more. A very generous pour. He downed that as well.

Karla stayed a little longer, then stood and told the young people she needed to leave so she could get back to the bakery before dark. Gerda and her mother hugged in a long embrace.

"Help me," Gerda whispered to her mother.

Karla pulled away and took Gerda's chin in her hand, then looked into her eyes. "Take care of yourself, *mein Liebchen*. You will be fine. I promise it."

GERDA WAS BEING HELD AGAINST HER WILL. WHEN SHE feigned ignorance of the pear brandy process—which she had known since she was a small child—and used the word "imprisoned," Karla suspected something was wrong. But Gerda's pantomime with the key when Aldrik was in the kitchen clinched it. Karla cleared the gate before she allowed her tears to flow.

She called Ulrich the minute she got home. "You were right," she said. "Something's going on with Gerda and Aldrik. I don't know what yet, except that apparently he's locking her in her room. We need a plan."

"I agree," Ulrich said. "Let me speak with my contacts and I'll get back to you." He heaved a sigh. "Don't worry, *Tante*. I am certain they won't hurt her while she's still pregnant."

"I think you're right," Karla said. "But she only has a couple of weeks to go. We need to move quickly."

CHAPTER
TWENTY-SEVEN

SAM

We had covered a large distance since Eddie's death and I was able, for the most part, to focus on my job without my gut going completely nuts with grief for that sweet little guy.

Only hours separated us from the Rhine River, the last big hurdle that, once conquered, opened the road straight to Berlin. After Germany's access to the Ruhr Valley was severed, their primary manufacturing center would be lost to them and their ability to ship war materials crippled.

At our briefing the previous night, our commanding officer told us that General Patton wanted river crossings made via what he called "on the jump," that is, to accomplish them so quickly the Germans couldn't respond with a prepared counterattack. He followed that up by telling us that two days earlier, on March 24, General Patton reached the Rhine and took that opportunity to urinate in it. We all cheered. It sounded like something the NOT-by-the-book general would do. And when he completed his crossing, he reached down, picked up a handful of dirt and shook it in the air. When I heard that, I thought of Scarlett O'Hara during her "As God is my witness" speech in *Gone with the Wind*. Mother had won tickets to it because her camellias placed first in the 1939 county fair and she took the four oldest of us with her. But thank goodness I kept that thought to myself because right after that, our CO told us the general did that to emulate his favorite historical figure, William the Conqueror. Had nothing to do with Scarlett O'Hara. I felt foolish at how little I knew about classic warfare.

Our regiment crossed the river by units. The First Battalion led the way with a surprise attack and made it across with light casualties. The Second Battalion crossed, scaled the cliffs on the eastern side of the river, and then worked its way toward Bornich.

My battalion, the Third, waited at the edge of the river at three o'clock in the morning, under strict light and sound discipline, for the boats that would ferry us across. On the other side, we would turn south and make our way into Kaub. The first boat loaded and started the trip while the rest of us hunkered down to scramble onto the second boat as soon as it got close enough.

Without warning, machine gun fire ripped into the small craft bobbing along the swift current of the Rhine. It sank, along with several of our fellow soldiers, churning the small white caps red, their screams adding to the din of constant gunfire. We watched helplessly as the men without wounds helped the others float down to a safer spot where they emerged on the enemy-side of the river.

"Engineers!" The command came from Sergeant Gordon, who had replaced Sergeant Hanley after the Battle of the Teardrop. "We need smoke screens over here."

We had met several of the guys who launched the smoke bombs, a great group from the Black Engineering Corps who'd been with us since we crossed the Moselle. But after several minutes, nothing happened. No one appeared. The rat-tat-tat of German machine guns continued to spray the water right where our boat was supposed to cross.

"Sarge." The corporal's voice was low. "There's an issue with the smoke bombs."

"What the hell?" The sergeant addressed Lieutenant Scott's special aide. "I don't want excuses. Bring them here and get them deployed. What's the holdup?"

"We don't have the bombs anymore," the corporal said.

Even in the semi-darkness, I saw the sergeant puff himself up, ready to tear that poor corporal a new ass, but the corporal continued talking.

"Lieutenant Scott had me take them out of his vehicle. We left them at the last camp."

"Now why in holy hell would he have you do that?"

The corporal appeared to squirm. "He found some champagne at the last town we passed through, so he had me take out the smoke bombs and fill their space with the wine. He said he planned to share it with everyone as soon as we got across the river."

I've heard of people being "hopping mad." I even saw my father illustrate it once. But nobody could hold a candle to the fit Sergeant Gordon threw that morning. If the sergeant had spoken to the lieutenant that way, he would have been court-martialed for certain.

We couldn't believe it, either. None of my little group had warmed to the new lieutenant anyway, and the news delivered by that corporal made any warm-up more unlikely. It might have been nice to have champagne after a successful battle, but to sabotage the tools that would have made that battle a success was unforgiveable.

Without a smoke cover, my whole battalion would have to cross against the rough current while German machine gunners pelted us. With the sun an hour or so from rising, and only one boat left to take us across, we would be mercilessly exposed, the perfect targets for shooters with unlimited ammunition.

"Sergeant," Erwin Davis said with his twin at his shoulder. "My brother and I will distract them with our bazooka fire. Maybe the rest of the company could move a little farther south and make it across."

"Good God, man," Sergeant Gordon said. "You'll never be able to hit any of them from this distance."

"We know that," Ervin chimed in. "But all we have to do is to make them think we can hit them. At least the shooting won't be so one-sided then. And if we can distract them long enough, some of us can get across."

"Plus," I added, "that first boat has floated back up. It's too full of holes to support anyone, but I think I can hold onto it and swim it across for cover. Once I'm on the other side, I'll work on that machine gun nest."

"And I'll go with him," Dickie said, one of his big hands solid on my shoulder.

"Me too," Simon chimed in.

The sergeant looked at us like we'd sprouted another nose but agreed to the plan. I don't think he had much choice, given the fact that our lieutenant had totally screwed up the original plan. Interesting, I thought, that I hadn't even seen the lieutenant yet that day.

The Davis brothers waited for the three of us to wade into the river behind the disabled boat and then set up their bazooka on the shore. Too much in the open, I thought, but they were the experts and I needed to focus on my part. Ice cold water filled my boots and when it reached my chest, my breath left me.

The gray streaks of dawn shone on us by then, but heavy cloud cover blotted the brightest rays of the sun. I took the lead position beside the bullet-riddled boat with Dickie in the middle and Simon at the back. We didn't have boats on the farm, so I wasn't sure which was bow and which was stern, but we had both parts covered.

Our rifles rested as high on our shoulders as possible to keep them dry enough to fire when we needed them. We followed the shoreline south for several yards and then pointed our little craft toward the middle of the river. Several feet into the water the first bazooka blast sounded and almost right away, the machine gun fire slowed. Before we had time to get cocky, however, the Rhine's current kicked in, so our paddling intensified. Several times I had to nose us back toward the opposite bank rather than let us drift farther south down the middle of the river.

The Germans spotted us and pointed their guns in our direction. The impact of the bullets startled me and the boat's hull smacked into my head full force. I was dazed but kept moving.

"The side of your head is bleeding," Dickie said. "Did you take a bullet?"

"No," I answered, "the boat hit me. Hurt like hell."

My boots and field pack weighed me down and my legs worked

harder to keep my torso afloat. I assumed the others experienced the same issue but we made steady progress and kept the boat between us and the eastern shore. Bullets lodged harmlessly into the hull, although I occasionally felt water swish extra fast around my legs when a stray shot entered the river. The Davis brothers blasted another bazooka rocket and once it was clear the Germans had spotted us, the brothers discharged their rockets steadily.

I lifted my head slightly during a lull in the firing and saw our objective, closer than I expected. A movement on the opposite shore caught my eye and I lifted my head several more times to figure out what it was. On the third time a loud pop reached my ears, along with a sharp pinging sound. My head flew back and I went under. The water in front of my face clouded with red and the boat's forward motion stopped.

I waited for the pain from the bullet.

Or the oblivion of death.

Neither of which happened.

Dickie's free hand hooked one of my arms and yanked, pulling my head out of the water.

"Sam," he said. "Talk to me, man. Where were you hit?"

"My head," I answered.

I wiped water from my eyes, but they refilled immediately with blood.

"Simon," Dickie said, "keep paddling. I'm going to see how bad Sam's wound is."

"Right," he answered with a grunt.

I unlatched my chin strap and Dickie lifted my helmet. "Thank God," he said and smiled.

"What?" I asked.

"Well, you have a new part in your hair above your ear. But it looks like the bullet only grazed your scalp."

"Good to know. But dammit all to hell, it stings."

"Thank goodness you can feel it sting," he said. "An inch to the left and you wouldn't have felt anything. Why'd you hold your head up, anyhow?"

"Movement," I said. "On the far shore. Couldn't quite see what it was."

"Oh yeah," he said. "I see it. Some of our guys from this boat's first trip. Waving us a little farther south. That's good. We can all attack that machine gunner's nest together."

Another bazooka blast reached us, followed by more machine gun fire. I put my helmet back on and we hauled ass to get the hell out of that water.

Two men from our company helped us get ashore and the five of us headed north in search of machine gunners. The Davis brothers continued to blast away on the other bank.

We crept through tree cover and up the side of the steep hill, using the sound from the German machine guns in the orchard above us, as our guide. We angled upward and must have climbed at least a thousand feet, which worked to our benefit because the soldiers below us couldn't adjust their shots quickly enough to keep up with us. We reached a position above the machine gunners and I took aim at the one with his finger on the firing button. Dickie zeroed in on the other —the one who feeds the bullets through and our shots found their targets at the same instant. The other three unloaded grenades on the soldiers around the machine gunners.

One by one, we picked off the Germans who remained in the orchard and even took out two twenty millimeter anti-aircraft guns. Every few minutes, I had to wipe blood clouding my vision before I could continue. But we cleared enough Germans that our sergeant, recognizing the slowdown, sent another load across on our only boat. He'd attached a series of ropes so he could pull it back for the next load. After three more loads, my whole battalion was across.

The rest of the Germans ran to the hills outside Kaub.

We chased them.

Almost immediately, we ran into a Russian prisoner of war who offered to lead us to a pocket of Germans. The two men who helped us get ashore agreed to follow him, but the other three of us circled away from the path the POW took and again, angled up the hill. Within minutes, we heard voices and looked down to see more than a dozen

Germans, flat on the ground with their rifles pointed toward the path the POW had taken. With hand signals, we each chose a target and shot at the same time. The remaining Germans rose from their positions and whipped their heads around, trying to find us. But we all shot again. And again.

After several rounds of firing, the soldiers who could stand did so, threw down their guns and held their hands high just as the POW and the other two men from our company rounded the corner. Our guys saw they'd been led into an ambush and before we could stop them, shot the POW in the head.

The Germans held on stubbornly. We met up with the rest of our unit, including by now Lieutenant Scott, and fought off flak gunners, prison guards, and large groups of *Volkssturm*—the units run by the SS troops comprised of Hitler Youth and old men the SS forced into service. They fought hard but couldn't match our grit and we overpowered them easily. We rounded up the remainder of the Germans and marched them into Kaub.

From there, we seized Auf der Hohe, then broke off and headed for the higher ground of Wolfsheck and Lorchausen, where we routed all the Nazi sympathizers and took a few more prisoners.

Town after town in the German countryside fell to one of our infantry divisions, then my battalion crossed the Ernst and Wisper Rivers, a skip across a puddle compared to our battle crossing the Rhine. We beat our way through heavily forested Ranseler Wald and in quick succession, captured all the towns in our path for the Allies.

More and more cities in the German countryside fell—many of them without a shot—and by March 30, four days after we crossed the Rhine, the hamlets, villages, and towns in our path were free of German soldiers and Nazi sympathizers. In another three days, after driving across the province of Thuringia, the 89th Infantry became the easternmost Division in Germany. And the one closest to the Russian Army that steadily closed in on Berlin from the north.

Chapter Twenty-Eight

GERDA

"*Gut gemacht, Herr* Ziegler," Frau Krueger told Aldrik. "Well done. We can't have your wife telling tales about our work here. You did well to take care of her like that."

"*Danke, Frau* Krueger," Aldrik said. "I guarantee you, she will not be a problem."

"The kommandant has big plans for you," *Frau* Krueger said. "In fact, he's waiting for you in his office now."

Aldrik clicked his heels together, said, "*Heil* Hitler," and left.

He knocked on the kommandant's office door.

"*Eintreten,*" the kommandant said. "Enter."

"*Heil* Hitler," Aldrik said, his hand high. He wasn't happy about treating Gerda the way he had, but he wanted to advance within the Nazi party for their future and *Frau* Krueger had given him his opportunity. He would figure out the rest once the baby was born. He and Gerda would be fine when the war ended, when she'd be ready to listen to reason. He was certain of it.

"*Herr* Ziegler," the kommandant said, "*Kommen sie.* My wife tells me you have handled a situation that concerned us. Well done." He indicated a chair and Aldrik sat down, his hands in his lap. One-on-one time with the kommandant was new for him and he tried to hide his nervousness.

"*Danke,* Kommandant Krueger," Aldrik answered. "I will do anything to help the party and the war effort."

"*Gut, gut.* I'm happy to hear that. In fact, that's what I wanted to talk to you about."

Aldrik's stomach tightened, but his face remained expressionless.

"There is a meeting near Eisenach, a couple hours' drive from here. I'd like you to accompany me and several of the other officers from the camp. We will be meeting with *Herr* Himmler about how to speed up our 'Final Solution' for the Jewish pestilence that pervades our realm. I'd like for Himmler and the others to know how you dealt with your, er, personal problem with Jews."

Aldrik recognized the importance of the meeting. He would meet the *Führer's* second-in-command. What a great stepping-stone for him.

"*Danke*, Kommandant," Aldrik said. "It would be my pleasure."

That night and the next, Aldrik returned to his small house. But he kept Gerda locked in their bedroom. He had arranged for Dr. Reiner, the camp doctor, to visit her every other day, but always unlocked the door prior to the doctor's arrival and never left her side during the examination. In the presence of others, he acted as if he and his wife were a happy couple expecting their first child. And if anyone ever questioned his wife's attitude, he chalked it up to hormones and dismissed it.

Alone with his wife, Aldrik steeled himself to ignore her tears and her pleas to return to Zwickau and her parents. Their situation was temporary, he told himself, but necessary to accomplish his goals. Surely she would understand once this was behind them.

⸻

ON THE DAY OF HIS TRIP, ALDRIK SLIPPED INTO THE bedroom to pack. Gerda faced the wall away from the window and didn't lift her head when he entered.

"I want you to know, *Liebling*," he said, "I will be away for a day or two." He couldn't keep the excitement from his voice. "The kommandant has invited me to a meeting with *Herr* Himmler himself. Quite an honor for me." He stopped packing and turned to her. "And good for us, Gerda. For our future. For our baby's future. I really hope you will try to understand."

Gerda didn't turn toward him. "The only thing I understand,

Aldrik, is that you are keeping me prisoner." Her voice held no spark of life.

He wished she shared his excitement at his opportunity, but he didn't try to convince her. He finished packing and turned to leave. "Dr. Reiner will continue to look in on you," he said.

Gerda turned and heaved herself upright, more and more difficult with her increased bulk. "Aldrik," she said in a quiet voice. "If you're leaving the camp, won't you please let me visit my parents? It's Easter and we have a family tradition of going to the farm in Baden-Baden and seeing all the relatives. I won't say anything you don't want me to, Aldrik. I promise. Won't you please let me go?"

His heart went out to her and he almost believed her. But he couldn't take that chance. Especially since he would be with the kommandant.

He walked over to the bed and sat down beside her. "My darling Gerda," he said stroking her belly. "I wish I could. But I can't."

She started to turn toward the wall again, but he stopped her. "Gerda, the main reason is that it's not safe. The Allied Armies have taken over that area and anyone who travels those roads risks capture."

"Do you really think anyone would capture a pregnant woman eight and a half months along? Please, Aldrik. They would know I'm no threat to them."

"The answer is 'no,' Gerda. I can't allow it."

He watched her eyes narrow. She took a deep breath, then let it go and turned from him.

"You will be fine, Gerda," he said. He rubbed her arm, but she pulled away. "And," he continued, standing, "*Frau* Krueger has been kind enough to allow Frieda to see to your needs while I am gone. I'll be back the day after tomorrow. We'll have dinner together. A belated Easter celebration, if you wish, and I'll give you all the news from the meeting."

She said nothing, her face turned to the wall. He hesitated in the doorway, hoping for some response, but at her continued silence, he shrugged his shoulders and left, locking the door behind him.

Minutes later, he stowed his bag in the kommandant's car and climbed into the back seat with his superior officer. The kommandant gave the signal to his driver and they rolled out through the gate. Several bottles of the pear brandy from Gerda's family rested on the floor. The kommandant poured from an open bottle and handed a glass to Aldrik, then toasted with his own.

As always happened, the strong liquid burned Aldrik's throat and calmed his nerves.

For more than two hours the beautiful German landscape passed by their windows and the kommandant regaled Aldrik with stories of the early days of the Reich, with how he met his wife and how fortunate he was to have her by his side. About how lucky he was she shared his ideas of the purity of the Aryan race and the steps needed to protect it. He didn't come right out and say so, but Aldrik believed the kommandant jabbed at him because his own wife had been friends with Jews. Since Aldrik couldn't refute it, he tried to change the subject.

"What is our final destination?" he asked the kommandant. "For today's meeting, I mean," he added. "Not for Germany," he said with a smile. "I believe I am aware of that."

The kommandant smiled back and poured more brandy for the two of them. "We're headed to Wartburg Castle, overlooking Eisenach in Thuringia." The kommandant took a long drink, almost draining his glass. "Do you know anything about it?"

"A little," Aldrik answered. "We had to study it in school. I remember it was founded by Duke Ludwig of Thuringia. I don't remember the year..."

"One thousand sixty-seven," the kommandant said. "History of the area is one of my passions. Do you know what it's famous for?"

"Not really," Aldrik said, taking his own drink.

"It's where Martin Luther translated the Bible," the kommandant said. "And later Goethe expanded on it."

"Oh," Aldrik said. "Right." He knew nothing about the Bible other than stories he had learned as a child, so he studied the landscape. They reached the small town of Eisenach and began their climb to the castle through the Thuringian Forest. At a bend in the road, the main part of the structure materialized before them, its five-story tower dominating the edifice.

"Well, look at that," the kommandant said with a smile.

A large swastika blew in the breeze above the tower, replacing a cross that had stood there for centuries. "The *Führer* has been working on that with the local townspeople," he said, his smile widening, "but I wasn't aware he'd accomplished it."

They continued along the drive and approached the large arched entrance to the castle's courtyard. A swastika hung there as well. Several men stood below it, hands on hips.

"Stop the car," the kommandant told his driver. "*Herr* Ziegler," he said. "Come."

They scrambled out of the car and the kommandant clicked his heels and raised his right arm. "*Heil* Hitler," he said. Then he bowed. "*Mein Führer*," he added.

Aldrik couldn't believe his good fortune. Not only was he about to meet the *Reichsführer*, Heinrich Himmler, but there stood the *Führer* himself, Adolf Hitler.

Aldrik's nervousness overtook him. He too clicked his heels and raised his right hand. His throat was dry, but he managed to voice "*Heil* Hitler," and received a curt nod in return. The kommandant appeared to be familiar with the country's leaders, so he chatted with them while Aldrik, still tense, followed meekly behind them.

During that afternoon, the camp's kommandant reported on activities at Buchenwald. The *Führer* had come to the meeting, Aldrik learned, since he was in the area to inspect the progress on the tunnels near Ohrdruf, the site of his Western Headquarters if he were forced to flee Berlin.

Aldrik wished his parents could have seen him in such grand company. Especially when the kommandant asked him to say a few words about his part in the camp's activities and his personal elimination of Jews. His presentation brought a slight smile, the first from the *Führer*, along with a second nod. He wished Gerda could see him too, and more important, be proud of him for his success. He pushed that from his mind to focus on the plans being outlined for Germany to win the war.

At the conclusion of the meetings, a sumptuous dinner was served, along with strong spirits and endless wine. Every time Aldrik's glass emptied, it was immediately filled. But the most surprising thing to him was that a number of beautiful women joined them. Women Aldrik could talk to. Women who didn't argue with him and cause him worry about who their friends were. Women who shared his views of his job and what it meant to be German.

He drank and danced well into the evening and then watched as the other officers climbed the stairs with one of the beauties on each arm. After several more drinks, Aldrik did the same.

The following morning he woke alone in his bed. His head throbbed as if a thousand boots marched through it. He shaved, dressed, and made his way downstairs to the dining room, where a huge breakfast waited. Several officers greeted him and he helped himself to coffee. A waiter found him and handed him a note.

Herr Ziegler, I have had to return to the camp early, but have arranged a ride for you with another group of officers. Enjoy your breakfast. I will see you when you return.

Relief flooded him. He seldom drank to the extent he had the night before and was so sick, he was glad he didn't have to keep up a conversation with his superior officer.

Two hours later, he boarded one of three open air touring cars with other junior officers and pulled his hat down low over his face. His head fell to his chest and within minutes, he slept.

CHAPTER
TWENTY-NINE

SAM

O n Easter Sunday we attended a memorial service to honor our fallen friends. I said a prayer for my little buddy, Eddie, Lieutenant Cooper, Captain Powell, Sergeant Hanley, and all the others I had met and fought beside who were no longer with us. The chaplain cited statistics about how many soldiers had been lost so far in the fighting. There were more American casualties, he said, in the Battle of the Bulge, than during D-Day, which surprised me because that loss was huge. It didn't happen often, but that day, I struggled to remember why we were there.

It would make more sense, it occurred to me, if those who called the shots—Roosevelt, Churchill and Stalin—met somewhere and duked it out with Hitler, Hirohito, and Mussolini.

I almost laughed at the thought. Roosevelt would have to fight from his wheelchair and Churchill was grossly out of shape. So until I had a better idea, I decided I'd put one foot in front of the other and try to keep my nose clean.

We received mail after the memorial service and I found a quiet spot where I could enjoy Betty's letters alone. She wrote her last one from the farm and told me about the family's plans for Easter and how excited Freddie was for the Easter Bunny to visit. She included a picture he'd drawn of a bunny carrying a basket of brightly colored eggs. I had to smile.

"Good news?" Dickie said. He sat down beside me, several letters in his hands.

"Yeah," I answered. "Anytime I get a letter from Betty, it's good news. And she sent me this picture." I held up Freddie's drawing and he smiled too. "How about your news?" I asked. "Everything okay with your family?"

"Mom has a cold. New York had a late frost." He shrugged. "Other than that, everything's fine. Which is great." He grinned at me. "Wouldn't it be awful if our families had to go through the same kinds of things we're going through?" he asked. "And then tell us about it in letters?" He shook his head. "How much do you tell your family about all this?" he asked.

"Practically nothing," I answered. "Don't want to worry them. They have enough stuff to think about right now."

"Yeah, same here."

The late morning peace was suddenly shattered by Lieutenant Scott's voice.

"All right, you lazy maggots," he shouted. "Get the hell up and let's move out."

A collective groan rippled through the ranks.

"What?" the lieutenant said. "Do I hear complaining? Would you prefer to march in double-time?"

No one responded, but several of us exchanged looks. I still hadn't forgotten about the men who died because he replaced the smoke bombs in his jeep with champagne. None of which he had yet shared with us.

We got to our feet and shouldered our packs. The spring day was gorgeous, high up in the Thuringian Forest. Beauty surrounded us, complete with a castle in the distance that could have come straight out of a fairy tale. But we didn't have time to appreciate such sights, given the reason we were there. Rather than enjoying the countryside, we had to be vigilant, always on the lookout for the enemy. They could pounce on us at any second.

The relative quiet of the forest slipped away behind us and we reached an opening before the trees picked up again a couple of hundred yards in front of us. We scattered from the road we'd been following, but studied the landscape around us, keeping a sharp lookout for Germans.

The first shots rang out and we dove for the ground, hiding behind what little scrub bushes we could find. We fought our way across the open stretch, lobbing grenades when we could get close enough, hunkering down when we couldn't. We made it to the next stretch of woods and took up defensive positions. Foot by foot, we crept forward through the trees, gaining several yards and then retreating for a few feet. Forward and back. Forward and back. Always watching for where the bullets originated and then aiming in that direction.

We edged farther up the side of the mountain, sticking to the trees, hiding in little ravines when possible. At a lull in the shooting, I heard motors and stopped to listen, then made my way over to Lieutenant Scott and pointed to the east. Gunfire erupted behind us and a big German touring car full of officers became visible on the road we had recently left. I lowered my head to duck bullets and when I looked again, the car was empty.

"Ryan," the lieutenant said at my elbow. "Take three guys and go see where those Krauts went." I motioned to the men closest to me and we crab-crawled across the forest floor, until we got close to the road. A bullet rang out behind me and Earl Jones, a young fellow from Kentucky, fell. The rest of us regrouped and changed our focus to our rear when a shot sounded in front of us. I risked a quick look and saw a second and third touring car, also empty. Which meant we had even more Germans surrounding us and trying to take us out.

I worked my way back to the lieutenant and reported the additional soldiers. He gave orders to keep firing. The Davis brothers fired a bazooka shell and landed a direct hit on the lead car, blowing it all to smithereens. My group maintained our position to the lieutenant's left, while another group crept to his right. With a second bazooka missile, another car disintegrated.

Machine gun fire sounded, followed by screams, making it impossible to tell which side had been hit. Our machine gunners were taken out in our last battle and hadn't been replaced, so I feared the worst. We had burp guns. The sound a burp gun made was distinctive. And terrifying. But that wasn't what I'd heard.

We continued to trade fire for the next hour, with neither side making progress.

Gradually, I became aware of additional Allied soldiers surrounding us and recognized some of the men in B and C Companies from a different regiment. They filled in our ranks and together, we pushed toward the Germans. In less than half an hour, they stopped returning fire and minutes after that we heard shouting.

"Halt! Stop firing. We surrender."

Lieutenant Scott issued the "Cease fire" order and shouted, "Throw down your weapons and come out with your hands up."

Bushes swayed and then parted and a dozen or so young German men, many of them unshaven, all of them in officer's uniforms, stumbled out into the open, their arms high, their hands empty. Behind them several women in fancy clothes and heavy makeup stepped out with their arms raised as well.

Lieutenant Scott strutted up to the first officers out of the trees.

"Who's in charge here?" he demanded.

A German stepped forward. "*Hauptmann* Auerbach," he said. And then he snapped to attention, clicked his heels, raised his right arm and said, "*Heil* Hitler."

"Oh no. You didn't just do that," the lieutenant said. "You damned stupid Kraut."

The lieutenant raised his arm and I saw his Colt revolver, pointed like an extension of his hand. He squeezed the trigger and a hole appeared between the German's eyes.

My breath caught in my throat and I started forward, but Dickie put his arm across my chest. I jerked my head around sharply but he mouthed the words, "He'll shoot you too."

I swallowed hard but didn't move.

"The rest of you," Lieutenant Scott screamed at them. "Over here."

He chose four of them and lined them up facing the edge of a small ravine we had used for cover. "Taylor, McIntyre," he called. "Front and center."

The men appeared beside him, each equipped with a burp gun. "Take care of this scum," he ordered. McIntyre's eyes widened, but he

THE ROAD REMEMBERED | 179

raised his gun and stood there. To his right, Taylor shot two of the officers, but McIntyre lowered his gun and turned back toward Lieutenant Scott.

"Lieutenant," he said. "I can't do it. I just can't."

The lieutenant strode over to him, twisted the gun from his hands and knocked McIntyre to his knees. "Well, goddam it, I don't have any trouble doing it." He shot the other two Germans in the back and swiveled around to the remaining officers who stood frozen at the edge of the forest, their hands raised, their eyes filled with horror.

Before they had time to act, the lieutenant's finger pressed the burp gun's trigger and held it down, spraying its devastation from one side of the group to the other. As if engaged in a macabre dance, the soldiers' bodies jerked from the impact of the bullets tearing into them. Then they crashed to the ground in a bloody heap, several of them continuing to twitch. One of the women lay dead among them.

I was sickened at the spectacle.

The lieutenant turned to us. "I'm sure you all saw what I saw," he screamed. "Those damned Krauts tried to escape." He fixed us with a hard look and focused on each one of us up and down the line, the burp gun ready in his arms. "Anybody see anything different?" He continued to stare at us. "Well?" he screamed again. "Anybody?"

We were silent.

The rest of the women whimpered and he whipped around, his gun aimed at them. "You whores have anything to say?" He looked at each of them as he had done with us and then moved closer, touching the barrel of the gun to their stomachs, one by one. "Well? Do you?"

They shook their heads vehemently, tears streaming, but didn't say a word.

He handed the burp gun back to McIntyre and jerked his head toward the dead soldiers. "Anybody who wants German souvenirs, now's your chance." He strode away without a backward glance.

Some of the Americans, Simon among them, scrambled to take knives, insignia, Lugers—anything that appealed to them—from the bodies of the dead soldiers.

I bent over and threw up.

Dickie did the same.

I was numb. I thought the lieutenant was by-the-book when we first met him, but I couldn't have been more wrong. There was no book in the history of war that condoned such behavior.

My whole being rebelled at having to follow a man who took the war into his own hands like that. Who shot people down where they stood simply because he thought he could.

It was still Easter Sunday. I began the day by mourning my fallen friends.

I ended the day by mourning my fallen enemies.

Then I prayed hard for the twisted soul of Lieutenant Scott. I asked God to touch his heart and change his ways, so he wouldn't commit such atrocities again. And that we wouldn't have to be a part of them.

He gave the order to move out and we did. The German women who had accompanied the dead officers, stumbled along in their high heels, openly weeping.

Which was exactly what I wanted to do.

CHAPTER THIRTY

GERDA

"**F**rieda," Gerda said, her voice low. "Will you help me?"

The woman lowered her head and avoided Gerda's eyes. She placed the breakfast tray on the small table in the corner.

"Frieda, please. Bring me the transmitter so I can get a code to—"

"Gerda. *Frau* Ziegler," Frieda whispered. "You know I cannot. *Frau* Krueger has me watched. She has us both watched. Since the night Michel died. She wouldn't hurt you, but she would have me executed."

"She might not hurt me, but she has convinced my husband to keep me prisoner." Gerda stopped talking while Frieda laid out the meal. Then she tried again. "Frieda, I have to get word to my *mutti*. My baby can't be born here. Not with all the horrible things that have happened. *Bitte*, Frieda. Please."

Frieda hesitated. Then she squared her shoulders. "*Nein, Frau* Ziegler. Please do not ask me again." She stood still, her back to Gerda. "Dr. Reiner will be here soon. *Frau* Krueger wanted me to make certain you had eaten first. So please..." Frieda turned back toward Gerda. "She will find a way to blame me, *Frau* Ziegler, if you don't eat. Please, have your breakfast. Please." She hurried through the door.

The lock clicked.

Gerda pushed her bulk from the bed and lumbered over to the table. She glanced out the window on her way past and saw the kommandant enter his house.

They're back. Aldrik will be here soon. Maybe he'll be in a good mood from his meeting and I can convince him to let me go home.

Her stomach rolled, but she sat at the table where her breakfast was laid out and attempted a few bites of the toast and a forkful or two of the scrambled eggs. She was lucky to have such good food and she didn't want Frieda to get in trouble. During most of the children's escapes, Frieda had been a great ally and a tremendous help in passing information back and forth from Block 66. But Gerda also knew Freida was right. Everything changed the night Michel died. Both women squirmed under constant surveillance since then.

In addition, Gerda didn't want to waste the food on the tray. Frieda was a wonderful cook and the Krueger's pantry was well stocked. All the officers of the camp, in fact, could get whatever food they wanted with no threat of rationing like Gerda's parents experienced in Zwickau. But with almost ten thousand underfed prisoners on the camp's premises, any food not eaten by the privileged few was fed to the animals. None of the inmates, including Frieda, were allowed to have the kind of fare on Gerda's tray. Frieda had told her, in one of the rare moments they could talk without fear, that meals for the prisoners consisted of a tiny slice of sawdust-laced bread and a lukewarm cup of liquid that served as coffee or tea. Lunch consisted of the same and usually included a thin soup made from grass and turnips that did more to produce stomach distress than to ease the prisoners' hunger. On rare occasions, the inmates might get a small piece of sausage. But even that, Frieda said, tasted rotten, as if it had been made from condemned meat.

Gerda forced the fork to her mouth again and again. Frieda aside, she also believed it was her duty to eat, to nourish her baby. She drained her glass of milk and shoved herself back from the tray.

A small knock sounded, the lock clicked and her door opened. Gerda expected to see Aldrik, so her eyes widened when *Frau* Krueger entered.

"*Frau* Ziegler, how nice to see you up. Did you enjoy your breakfast?" *Frau* Krueger bustled into the room with Frieda trailing behind her, head down, eyes averted. *Frau* Krueger inspected Gerda's plate, then nodded to Frieda, who picked up the tray and left.

"Since *Herr* Ziegler is away," *Frau* Krueger said, "I thought I would accompany the doctor on his visit. It wouldn't do for him to examine you without either your husband or a trusted female friend with you, right?" She smiled sweetly. Gerda's stomach rolled again. But she forced her voice to be pleasant.

"How nice to see you, *Frau* Krueger," Gerda said. "Thank you for coming. Especially since your husband just got home." *Frau* Krueger whipped around, surprise showing on her face. "I saw him through the window," Gerda explained, "when he entered your house. I thought Aldrik went with him."

"You are quite right, of course," *Frau* Krueger said, "but my husband asked Aldrik to stay for another meeting. He should be home sometime today or tonight. I am happy to stand in for him with Dr. Reiner."

Frieda showed the doctor into the room.

"Will you lie down, *Frau* Ziegler?" Dr. Reiner asked, after a few stilted pleasantries. "I don't want to keep you any longer than necessary."

"So, Dr. Reiner," *Frau* Krueger said, "how much longer before our girl here will go into labor?"

"Hard to tell," he said. "First babies are always tricky. And usually late."

"Oh," *Frau* Krueger said. "We're all so anxious."

At Gerda's surprised look, *Frau* Krueger added, "I've never had any children of my own, so I'm looking forward to having a baby here with us. You will share, won't you, *Freundin*? And I know you'll want to show the child to your family. When can the baby travel, doctor?"

"Oh, four to six weeks, I would think" he answered.

Gerda frowned, but kept quiet. She had never known *Frau* Krueger to talk so much.

"And if the child doesn't nurse? I've heard that some children can't or won't, Gerda," she said and turned back to the doctor. "What happens then? How should it be fed?"

The doctor gave her a quizzical look, but said, "I don't think that will be a problem, *Frau* Krueger, but we can address that if necessary. There are formulas and baby bottles the *Frau* could use if such a thing should happen. Everything looks good for now so I don't see a need to worry." He patted Gerda's knee and helped her sit up. "If you ladies will excuse me, I will show myself out."

He left and *Frau* Krueger turned to Gerda, her face wiped clean of her former friendly expression. "Continue to take care of your baby," she said. "For your husband's sake. It will all be over soon."

She left without another word and locked the door behind her.

Her frustration mounting, Gerda lay still on the bed and fitful sleep overtook her. When she woke, the bedside clock showed two hours had passed.

With effort, Gerda rose and went to the window again. The main square, the *Appellplatz*, where roll call took place twice daily, was empty, with only a few *kapos* calling out to each other. An official-looking car stopped in front of the kommandant's house and an officer got out and opened the back door. Gerda was shocked to see a woman in fancy clothes emerge from the back seat. Even from a distance, Gerda saw that the woman's clothes hung in disarray and her hair was disheveled, her makeup in need of repair. She stood with the officer on the kommandant's steps, then they both disappeared inside.

Gerda paced the room, racking her brain to come up with an escape plan. She'd been the master of formulating intricate arrangements. But with her advanced pregnancy, no communications at her disposal and no allies to count on, nothing that had worked for the countless others she had helped would work for her. She couldn't think of a way to get a message to her usual sources.

When her pacing brought her back to the bed, she heaved a deep sigh and lay down again. Her body felt heavy, drained and sleep returned within minutes.

"*JA*," *FRAU* KRUEGER SAID TO THE OFFICER AT THE DOOR. "*Was ist es*? What is it?"

The officer clicked his heels and his right hand flew to the air, his left firmly clutching the woman with him. She hung her head and tears spilled down her cheeks. *"Heil Hitler, Frau* Krueger. I need to see the kommandant. Right away. It's urgent."

"Hold on. I'll get him."

"Frau, if we could see him in private..."

"He has no secrets from me," she huffed. "Wait here."

The two of them returned to the front hallway moments later. The kommandant glared at the officer. *"Ja?"* he said. "Why do you bother me when I am at home with my wife?"

"Herr Kommandant," the officer said. "As I told *Frau* Krueger, this is urgent." He took out a handkerchief and wiped his brow. "We found this woman on the road through the Thuringian Forest. She was, she said..." The officer took a deep breath. "Tell him," he commanded.

The kommandant fixed her with a stern scowl. "Well?" he said. "What is it, woman? I'm a busy man."

The woman's face crumbled and she dropped her head to her hands, ragged sobs tearing from her. The officer beside her shifted from foot to foot, then handed her his already damp handkerchief. She accepted it and blew her nose, a large lipstick stain prominent when she returned it.

Gradually, her crying lessened, and she spoke. "The Americans," she said. "We saw them on our way from Wartburg Castle. Someone from the first car fired on them, and they, they..." Tears resumed control of her voice.

"Tell me," the kommandant said. "Those were my men, my officers. What happened?"

"The Americans fired back. So the officers left the cars and took us with them. They positioned themselves behind trees and fired again. One of the cars had a machine gun. But the rest only used handguns. They fired as long as they could..."

"Good God, woman." The kommandant lost patience.

"When your officers ran out of ammunition, sir," the officer present said, "this woman said they surrendered. All of them. And the women with them. Except for this one."

"Why were these women—?"

"Not now, Elsa," the kommandant addressed his wife harshly. "Then what happened?" he asked, turning back to the woman at the door.

"They surrendered," the woman said in a small voice. "Walked right out. But I had to pee, couldn't hold it. So I squatted where I was. Then I heard the American ask who was in charge and when I peeped over the bushes, I saw your officer step forward. With no warning, the American raised his gun and shot him. Then the American called two men with big guns and gave the order to shoot. But one stood there, so the American grabbed his gun and shot your men. All of them. And Thrude with them." The kommandant drew in his breath. "Those guns sounded like nothing I ever heard before. Like a long belch." The woman attempted to demonstrate the sound until the soldier with her shook her arm.

"And then the American officer screamed at his own men," the woman continued. "I know a few English words, and I heard 'escape.' But that wasn't true. They didn't try to escape. The American just shot them where they stood. Then he rounded up the rest of the girls and moved out. Looked like they headed in this direction."

"*Mein Gott,*" *Frau* Krueger said in a whisper.

"Headed here?" the kommandant said.

"*Ja,*" the officer at the door said. "They're on foot with rugged terrain in front of them, accompanied by women in high heels. So they're probably a day or day and a half away."

"*Danke,*" the kommandant said. "With so many of my men gone," he added, "I need your help. Truck in everyone you can find. We have a lot of work to do before the Americans arrive."

"*Heil* Hitler," the officer said and left.

"What about me?" the woman whined.

"Get out," *Frau* Krueger spat at her. "Get out or we'll shoot you too."

"Sound the sirens," the kommandant said into his phone. "Immediately."

"Hush, baby," Gerda crooned. "Please stop screaming."

She rocked the infant, but the screaming continued. Constant. Loud. Annoying. The baby pushed into her shoulder, soft at first and then harder. It shook her. The sound continued. She couldn't think. "Gerda," the baby said. "Gerda, wake up!"

SHE JOLTED AWAKE. BUT THE CRYING BABY CONTINUED TO wail.

"What...?" Frieda's eyes hovered above her in the semi-darkness of dusk. Gradually, Gerda recognized the sound of the camp's sirens.

"Gerda." Freida's voice conveyed urgency. "The Americans are coming. The kommandant is marching the prisoners to another camp. I may have to leave soon."

Gerda sat up. "I need to get word to my family. Can you get to a telephone?"

"*Nein*," Frieda said. She set a picnic basket on the bed. "But I brought this."

At the sight of the basket, Gerda realized she hadn't had lunch and her stomach growled. Frieda unpacked cold chicken and boiled pota-toes, then gently reached into the basket once more and brought out a pigeon. "This is the one Ulrich sent months ago. It's been hidden in the mews with the falcons," Frieda said. "It's all we can do for now. But we must hurry."

Frieda handed a small piece of paper to Gerda, along with a pencil.

Americans are coming, she wrote. *Camp being cleared. Have Mutti come get me.*

Frieda took the paper, rolled it up tight and attached it to the pigeon's leg. She went to the upstairs window facing away from the kommandant's house and released it into the darkening sky, then watched as it winged its way southwest to the Black Forest.

THE SIRENS STOPPED SCREECHING AND GERDA WATCHED the scene in the *Appellplatz*, frenzied activity filling every corner. Guards berated prisoners as they scurried into lines, then bullied them to tighten their formation. As soon as one large group assembled, the prisoners double-timed out of the gate, and another group filled the space in the square. Those who fell or lagged were shoved to the side by the empty gallows. After three groups trotted out through the gate, other guards marched the forty or so remaining prisoners in the *platz* out of Gerda's sight. Within minutes the rapid fire of machine guns reached her ears and the guards returned alone.

Bile filled her throat at the picture her head painted of what must have happened.

Frieda rejoined her and stood at the window beside her. She pointed toward the east and Gerda saw the orange glow in the sky at the edge of the surrounding forest.

"They reopened the graves," Frieda said. "I heard the kommandant demand it. They're burning the bodies—decomposed or not. He told *Frau* Krueger they had to hide the evidence of the killings as much as possible. I believe they will leave the camp shortly. Certainly before the Americans arrive. That's how I was able to come here. They are focused on saving themselves."

"Frieda," Gerda said, "I can't believe I was so stupid. I should have implored Ulrich to get the rest of the children out. The guards just marched prisoners to one of the back sheds. And then I heard gunfire. I think they will kill all those they can't get out in time. We have to save the children."

Gerda left the window and headed for the door, but Frieda stopped her. "I will do it, *Frau* Ziegler. You cannot go. You are too large. You would slow their progress. I will work with the elders in Block 66 and we will get as many children out as possible."

Gerda squeezed Frieda's hand and then hugged her. "Thank you," she said. "Get me as many names as you can. If the war is almost over, we will need a way to reunite these children with their families. And be careful. You can no longer take them through the Reimahg tunnels unless they too have been abandoned."

"I'll find out," Frieda said. She stared intently at Gerda. "This is probably good-bye, *Frau* Ziegler," she said. "Please eat the food I brought you and then rest. I'm sure tomorrow will be a very hectic day. A crazy day. You need to take care of your baby." The two women hugged again and Frieda was gone.

Gerda reached under the bed and hauled out a suitcase, then opened drawers and threw items into it. She wasn't sure where she would go, but she had to take advantage of her unlocked door and the confusion within the camp. The last thing she saw out her window was another group of prisoners being herded into the square.

She had almost finished her packing when an acrid odor reached her nose and settled in her lungs. *The smell of burning bodies.* She ran to the basin on her washstand and threw up. Wave after wave of nausea assaulted her and she emptied her stomach and then dry-heaved.

She struggled to remain standing and moved slowly toward her bed. The outside door opened again. "Frieda," she called weakly. "Did you forget something?"

"It isn't Frieda," Gerda heard, and looked up to see *Frau* Krueger standing in the doorway. "But I see she was derelict in her duty to lock your door. Are you ill?"

Gerda nodded and eased herself down to the mattress. She closed her eyes.

"We've received some bad news," *Frau* Krueger told her. "The Americans are headed this way." *Frau* Krueger looked pointedly at Gerda's hastily packed suitcase. "Oh," she said. "I see you already knew that." Gerda nodded again and Frau Krueger continued, "We will leave the compound at first light. You will accompany us."

"Thank you, but no." Gerda kept her eyes closed.

"That choice is not yours to make, *Frau* Ziegler. You will do as we say. We will make you comfortable and we will care for your baby once it is born."

Sudden insight clicked in her head and Gerda understood why *Frau* Krueger had asked the doctor so many questions about the baby's ability to travel and what it could eat if it didn't nurse. The woman never mentioned caring for Gerda. Only her baby.

Frau Krueger left the room and locked the door behind her. Taking Gerda's opportunity for escape with her.

CHAPTER
THIRTY-ONE

GERDA

Rosy streaks of early dawn painted the sky as the Berghmann van motored toward Buchenwald with Gerda's mother, Karla, at the wheel. Many miles lay between her and the camp, but she met hundreds of prisoners in their tattered striped uniforms marching in formation to the shouts of guards who struck them with cattle prods and whips. She drove slowly past them.

"*Tante* Karla," Ulrich had said in his pre-dawn phone call, "something has happened at Buchenwald. I received a message via pigeon that said the Americans are headed their way. Gerda asked me to have you go get her."

"Really?" Karla asked. "Why couldn't she have called me herself?"

"I don't know. I don't know why she didn't call me either. But it's been too long since I've heard from her or spoken with her."

"Same for me," Karla said. "Since I went to see her last."

"I believe the situation is urgent," Ulrich said. "I doubt the camp kommandant will want the Americans to see how they treated their prisoners, so who knows what they might be doing?"

"I will go right away," Karla said. "Thank you, dear boy, for calling me."

"I have friends headed there now," Ulrich said. "To see if we can help those who are left. But I doubt they will arrive before you do."

Karla readied herself and left within the hour, driving as fast as she dared, given the age of the van and the need to avoid being stopped.

Before she reached the compound, black smoke billowed, thick and high, to her right and a rancid odor found her nose even with her windows closed. She had carefully rehearsed her story to get past the guards but she needn't have bothered. The gates hung open and the guards' only objective appeared to be herding out a wave of prisoners in their tattered garb past her. No one paid her any attention so she drove straight to the house where her daughter lived.

The door to Gerda's bedroom was closed. She hesitated, then knocked lightly. No sound greeted her from the other side. She knocked again and called softly, "Gerda, are you in there?" She tried the knob, but it was locked. She rattled it. "Gerda," she called louder. "Are you there? Is Aldrik with you? Why is your door locked?"

"*Mutti.*" The sound was soft. "*Mutti,* are you really here?" Louder. Muffled sounds of movement floated through the door, followed by a sound like something falling against it.

"Gerda," Karla shouted. "Open the door. Please let me in."

"Lock...on your side." The voice was faint.

Sudden understanding flashed and Karla saw Gerda was right. She turned the bolt and gently pushed the door. It didn't move. "Gerda, you're blocking the door," she said. "Can you move to the side? Maybe try rolling. I don't want to hurt you." Shuffling sounds reached Karla, along with soft groans. She pushed again, gently, and the door opened to reveal her daughter's legs on the floor. In one motion, she cleared the door and knelt beside Gerda, who lay slumped against the wall, her hair stringy and her clothes soiled. Droplets of sweat coated Gerda's forehead and she smelled of vomit. "Oh, my goodness," Karla said, "let's open a window."

"No," Gerda said. "Can't. Nailed shut. From outside. And they're burning the bodies. Smell made me sick."

"Oh, that's what the smoke was," Karla said. The same choking odor she had noticed on her drive permeated the air in the closed bedroom. Helping Gerda stand, she continued, "Come on. We're going home. I can't believe you've been kept a prisoner in your own house."

"Nonsense," a voice behind them said.

Karla whipped toward the door. *Frau* Krueger stood there, her arms folded. "*Frau* Berghmann, I presume," she said. "How nice to meet you." Her stony face belied her pleasant words. "We didn't expect you. And I can't imagine why you thought your daughter was a prisoner."

"I'll tell you why," Karla said. "Because I had to unlock the door myself to get to her. And look at her. She's a mess. She's been sick." She put her arm protectively around Gerda's shoulder. "I will thank you to kindly get out of my way so I can take my daughter to the van. Where is her husband, anyway? Why isn't he here?"

"Oh," *Frau* Krueger said. She tapped her lip with her finger. "Yes, that's right. You don't know."

Gerda and her mother both looked at the woman in the doorway, their expressions wary.

"Know what?" Gerda asked.

"About your husband. Aldrik is dead. Killed by Americans."

Gerda drew in her breath and tears filled her eyes.

Her stomach spasmed and she bent double with her scream.

"Good Lord, woman," Karla said. "You could have found a kinder way to tell her. Stand aside. I'm taking her home."

She hugged Gerda under her shoulders to help her stand, but before her daughter made it all the way to her feet, her stomach spasmed again and her water broke. Liquid whooshed down Gerda's legs and drenched her bare feet and Karla's shoes. A contraction took hold seconds later, bending Gerda double again.

"Honey," Karla said. "First babies usually take a long time. Let's try to get you home."

But another contraction seized Gerda and she sank to her knees. Blood seeped onto the carpet and grew larger with every second.

"Get the doctor," Karla told *Frau* Krueger.

"No," *Frau* Krueger said. "Even if I wanted to, he's already gone. Left early this morning with his patients."

"Well, will you at least help me get her on the bed?"

Gerda moaned and then screamed as another contraction spasmed her stomach.

Frau Krueger grabbed the other woman's arm and held her in place. "No, *Frau* Berghmann," the kommandant's wife said. "She is having the child of a German officer. She will stay with us until the baby is born. Then she can do as she likes. But we will raise the baby as a pure Aryan."

"Like hell you will." With her free arm, Gerda's mother pulled back to slap the kommandant's wife, but *Frau* Krueger was faster and landed a solid punch in *Frau* Berghmann's stomach.

Karla sagged and Gerda screamed again.

"See here," said a voice from the door. "What the hell is going on?"

"Kommandant," Gerda's mother gasped, "your wife thinks she can keep my grandchild. I will not have it."

The kommandant looked from one woman to the other and then to Gerda, balled up in pain on the floor.

"Elsa," he said quietly. "We don't have time for this. We must leave now. Come."

He turned toward the door.

"But, Karl," *Frau* Krueger whined. "You promised. The baby."

"It is too late," he answered without turning. "We have to go. *Now.*"

Frau Krueger fixed Gerda and her mother with a final hate-filled stare and kicked Gerda in her back where she lay. Gerda screamed in agony and Karla rushed the kommandant's wife. But she was too slow. *Frau* Krueger turned abruptly and left the room. Without another word.

The lock clicked behind her.

Karla rushed to the door. "Come back," she screamed. Her fists battered the wood. "You can't leave us like this. My daughter is in labor."

Karla pounded the door, then ran to the window when a motor roared to life. Minutes later, after the kommandant and his wife entered his car with several suitcases and a large picnic basket, the car rolled down the lane and through the gate.

Frantically, Karla searched for a way out.

She inspected the bottom windows first. As Gerda had said, they were nailed shut, but even worse, heavy metal screens in a small diamond pattern covered them from the outside, so breaking the glass would be no help. Then she removed items from the washstand and dragged it to over to inspect the top windows, which she could see didn't have the screens. She climbed on the small table, but even standing on her tip-toes, she couldn't reach the window latch. Gerda's next scream grabbed her attention and forced her to give up her search.

Karla climbed down, then helped Gerda up and bodily moved her to the bed. She pushed her daughter down and swiveled her legs so she lay fully on the mattress then raised Gerda's nightgown and removed her underwear to check the baby's progress. Blood oozed onto the coverlet. She wanted to get her daughter home, to take care of her there, but she had to work within the reality of their situation.

"Okay, *Liebling*," Karla said in as calm a voice as she could manage. "It's all right. You'll be fine, but the baby is coming so we'll deliver it ourselves. Babies are tough little creatures," she added. "It will be okay."

Karla checked the pitcher she had moved from the washstand and found it had a little water left in it. She moved the vomit-filled basin as far away from them as the room allowed and then removed a pillowcase to use as a washcloth. She stuffed the naked pillow under Gerda's knees then found a spare blanket in the chest at the end of the bed for the baby. The top drawer of Gerda's bureau revealed her sewing kit, so Karla removed the scissors and a spool of strong thread and laid them out with the blanket.

Under normal circumstances, delivering babies was not hard, but Karla worried about the constant flow of blood. She swabbed Gerda's face with the drenched pillowcase.

"Do you have any clothes for the baby?" Karla asked.

Gerda shook her head. "We were supposed to gather some things when Aldrik returned." Tears eased from the corners of her eyes and fell into her ears. "They wouldn't let me go anywhere while he was gone. And even he kept me locked in here for days."

"Okay," Karla said. "It's not a problem. We'll be fine."

Karla rummaged through the chest where she had found the blanket, moving items aside to look under them. She found a shawl and decided to use it for a diaper, but more important, she found a bottle of Berghmann *Birnen-Brand*. Using the glass from Gerda's lunch tray, Karla popped the seal, then filled the glass to the rim and tipped it to Gerda's lips. Over and over. She didn't want Gerda drunk, but she hoped the brandy would ease the pain somewhat.

Gerda screamed again then stopped, as if she tried to hold back.

"Honey," Karla told her. "Go on and scream. There's practically no one here now. And certainly no one who will care. They all have their own problems with the Americans coming."

"Will the Americans kill us, too, *Mutti*?" Gerda whispered. "Like they killed Aldrik?"

"No, my child," Karla answered. "They will know we are not a threat to them. Let's concentrate on bringing my grandchild into the world." She smiled at Gerda. "We can figure out the rest later."

Gerda screamed again.

And again. And again.

The blood slowed and Karla continued to drizzle pear brandy down her daughter's throat until Gerda fell into a twilight-type slumber between contractions.

Karla used that time to return to the window, to search for someone who could unlock the door. Prisoners continued to fill the square and then jog out through the gate. But the only people who could help, Karla saw, already had their hands full and didn't hear her shouts the few times she tried to get their attention.

Between Gerda's contractions, Karla also poked and prodded into every corner of the room to find a key or something to unlock the door from their side. She found and tried bobby pins, but they bent and broke before turning any of the tumblers. And the knife from Gerda's lunch was too wide. She even tried using the blade as a screwdriver on the door hinges and when that didn't work, tried inserting it between the door jamb and the lock, but that failed as well.

She reconciled her day, and possibly her night, to swabbing Gerda's brow and delivering the baby with the items at her disposal. She couldn't count on anything beyond that.

During one of Gerda's brief naps, Karla watched as prisoners lined up in the square. Many of them hobbled into place, filthy and emaciated. She couldn't hear what was said, but she saw them bow their heads. After a second command they turned around.

Shots rang out and the first line of prisoners fell. Then the second. And the third. All the way to the back line. Karla jerked involuntarily as each row hit the dirt. She used the last ounce of her willpower to keep from being sick.

What had happened to the world? To her beautiful Germany?

She turned back to her daughter, who moaned again, and her eyes filled with tears. A new life, a product of love, was about to burst forth within the walls that surrounded her. But seconds earlier she had watched countless other lives, victims of hate and prejudice, unceremoniously executed on the other side of them.

CHAPTER
THIRTY-TWO

SAM

Normally, I had no idea of our destination as we marched, but during one of our breaks, I relieved myself behind a tree and overheard the lieutenant talking with our scouts. They squatted, studying a map and discussing various routes.

"There's something large over here," the scout named Perry said. "Lots of buildings, fences. Looked like a prisoner of war camp to me."

"How far?" the lieutenant asked. "And is it still on the route to Gotha? I'm not sure how much longer I can stand having these damned women with us. We can drop them off there."

"Another half to three-quarters of a day's march," Evans, the second scout answered. "Near the town of Ohrdruf. And directly on the path to Gotha. Probably not much more than half an hour from it."

"Okay," the lieutenant said. "I want you to go back there, take a couple of squads from K Company. Find out how many Germans remain." He sat back on his heels for a moment. "In fact, you guys double-time it, get there as quick as you can. I'll take B Company on to Gotha with the whores and then we'll join you in Ohrdruf. Get what you need and move out."

We assembled to follow the scouts. Germans had surrendered in record numbers, but I worried about storming a camp with watch towers, machine guns, and lookouts.

I'd never seen a prisoner of war camp before and had no idea what the inmates might look like. Or how well they were guarded. Regardless, the scouts gathered up our squad and two others from K

Company, with Sergeant Gordon acting as our commanding officer. Frankly, I liked that plan and was glad to be away from the lieutenant for a while. We moved out, through the remainder of the Thuringian Forest, at as fast a pace as the rugged terrain allowed.

Little daylight reached us through the trees, and by dusk, we had cleared the forest and reached the road. The scouts took us northwest and we kept our eyes sharp, ever on the lookout for small groups of Germans. Most of the regular soldiers we'd seen marched out with their hands up, but we wanted to avoid the zealots who fought to the last breath.

We moved along the road for an hour or two, diving into steep ditches paralleling it whenever cars passed. We only saw three of them, a German officer's car piled high with luggage, along with escorts, front and back. Soldiers armed with machine guns hung outside the cars and kept watch as vigilantly as we did. The Davis twins moved up to Sergeant Gordon and asked about taking a shot, but he decided to let the German group go since our band was small and had no capacity to take prisoners.

Personally, I figured he wanted to stay on the good side of Lieutenant Scott and carry out our mission to the letter, rather than get sidetracked. After the display we had all witnessed that afternoon, we honestly believed he could as easily—and would, without qualms—shoot any of us. The sergeant did report the German officer's position to the lieutenant, however.

Around midnight, the moon, only a day or two past full and waning gibbous, spilled such bright light on the road, we crept back to the cover of the trees. We hugged the edge of the forest, always heading north and west. A couple hours later, Sergeant Gordon called a break and the guys who smoked lit up, using their helmets to hide the cigarette's glow. Lieutenant Scott would never have allowed that, but since Sergeant Gordon smoked, he gave the okay. He huddled with the rest of the smokers and the scouts squatted beside him.

"We have another two and a half to three hours," Perry said. He unfolded a small map and used the glow of the sergeant's cigarette to indicate our route with his finger. We all provided cover with our helmets.

"Okay," the sergeant said. "Listen up. We'll take an hour to rest and then move out. That will put us there slightly before dawn. We'll get a good picture of how many soldiers remain when they begin their morning routines. Levy, Carlson, Myers—take the first watch. After thirty minutes, Hummel, Thomas, Anderson, you relieve them. Fall out."

Dickie and I leaned back against nearby trees and made ourselves as comfortable as possible. Funny thing about sleep when you hardly got any. You learned how to pick it up under almost any conditions. I settled in and drifted off immediately only to jerk myself awake again.

"Dammit all to hell." I thought I whispered it, but Dickie roused.

"What?"

"Sorry. I have to go to the bathroom again." I pulled myself up and searched for a tree that didn't have a soldier leaning against the other side of it. My stream hitting the dead leaves on the forest floor sounded especially loud in the stillness of the night.

My senses shot to red alert.

The air was too quiet. No trilling of insects. No chirping of night birds. Not even the stealthy sound of small nocturnal hunters. There was a reason those sounds had gone still and I didn't think it was because of us.

I finished my business, zipped up, and eased my rifle from my shoulder. My ears strained to pick up something that didn't belong. I remembered one of my early campouts with Walter and Richard in the Appalachian foothills behind our house in Pennsylvania. That night presented the same kind of eerie quiet. Nothing moved. Or called. Or scurried. Silence blanketed the night as if all the woodland creatures held their collective breaths and didn't dare stir until they found out what spooked them. In seconds, a big black bear roared out from behind a boulder and then crashed through the brush toward us. Walter got him in the shoulder with our dad's shotgun. It didn't kill him, but it did send him packing in another direction and gave us time to escape.

The lack of sound in the German forest mimicked that night exactly, although I didn't expect to see a bear.

Little patches of moonlight found their way to the forest floor and my eyes, accustomed to the dark, raked through them. No movement. I stood a moment longer and almost decided I was imagining things when I heard a shuffle. Very faint.

Quietly, I moved through the trees to the path we had taken from the road and found the position I sought, a break in the trees that allowed for a clear view of the moonlit night with bare sky behind it. With my rifle at the ready, I stood perfectly still and watched. Nothing moved, but the shuffle continued. Slightly louder.

My back stiffened at a presence behind me.

"It's Dickie," he whispered. "When you didn't come back, I thought I should look for you. What's up?"

"Listen," I said. "Can you hear it?"

We stood still, every sense at attention.

"Sounds like footsteps shuffling along," he said after a minute. "A lot of them."

"Right. Watch the moonlight through those trees."

"What's going on?" The Davis twins crept up behind us.

"Look," I whispered, pointing to the bare moonlight. We watched and a dark figure shadowed into it, slowly, stealthily. It crept to the other side and before it disappeared into the trees, raised its arm as if it beckoned someone to follow. Rifles readied behind me.

We maintained our position and in a few more seconds, another figure moved into the moonlight. And then another. And another. One by one and then two by two.

But curiously, those figures were small. They scampered through the moonlit sky.

I lowered my gun and felt Dickie's movement beside me as he did the same. I started forward, creeping along and making certain to keep the trees behind me so I wasn't as visible to them as they were to me. We made practically no sound, but I could tell Dickie and the Davises kept up with me.

The closer we got to them, the more we heard. Some of them

whispered, but mostly we heard sounds of shushing. More and more of them scurried across the path to disappear in the trees on the other side. A larger figure broke the moonlight again and I called out.

"Halt. Who goes there?"

We heard a loud gasp. As if they all sucked in their breaths at once. The larger figure shoved smaller figures behind it.

"Stop," I said.

The larger figure stepped forward. I trained my rifle in the middle of it.

"Who are you and where are you headed?" I demanded. The others had moved beside me and had their rifles trained on the dark figures as well.

"*Bitte*," the large figure said, its voice small. "Please," it added in English. "We escaping children from labor camp. To save from shoot." The voice was feminine and the English heavily accented and broken.

But her meaning came through loud and clear.

My blood ran cold.

"Who's in charge?" Dickie asked beside me.

"I. Frieda."

"Who else is with you?" Erwin asked.

"Elders, Antonin Kalina *und* Gustav Schiller. Block 66. Buchenwald."

Two additional tall figures materialized beside her. The small figures huddled behind them. We lowered our rifles.

"How many of you are there?" I asked her. I started digging in my backpack for chocolate. I knew they should have real food first, but I had more chocolate than rations.

"Thirty. Was all we could get before guards ..." She stopped talking and her voice broke.

"I'll get the sergeant," Ervin said and took off at a trot.

The three of us handed out chocolate. We had enough among us so each child got half a bar. The almost full moon brought their little faces into focus and the sight of them broke my heart. They resembled tiny skeletons dressed for Halloween in oversized, filthy clothing which reeked of urine and body odor. Some of them reached bony arms out for their share and tattooed numbers became visible in the pale night. I imagined my little Freddie being marched through the forest at night, hungry and dirty. I wanted to cry.

"Why were these little guys locked up? What did they do wrong?" I asked.

"Born as Jews," Frieda answered with a shrug.

"What?" I asked. "I don't under—"

"What's going on here?" Sergeant Gordon asked. "Who are you people? And why do you have all these children out in a forest in the middle of the night? Good God, woman, what were you thinking?"

Perry, one of the scouts, joined us. "Are you from Ohrdruf?" he asked Frieda.

"*Nein,*" she answered. "Buchenwald. Maybe three hour walk from Ohrdruf. That one—" she hesitated, then finished in German. "*Klein lager.*"

"Small camp?" he asked her. "So Ohrdruf is a prisoner of war camp, right? *Der Kriegsgefangener...da?*"

"*Nein,*" she answered. "*Konzentrationslager.*"

Perry shrugged, then turned to us. "That's a term I haven't heard. I guess we'll find out what it means when we get there. But I didn't realize they kept children in POW camps."

"What's your story?" the sergeant asked Frieda. "Who are you?"

"Born in Poland," she said. "Arrested and sent to Auschwitz, transferred to Buchenwald."

"Why?" the sergeant asked. "What did you do?"

"Worked with Resistance effort against Germans."

"Why are all these children with you?"

"She rescued them," Dickie said quietly. "Kept them from getting shot."

"They know you're coming," Frieda said. "Cleared out camp. Kill anybody no leave."

By this time, most of the K Company squads had gathered behind us. The camp cook whispered something to the sergeant, and he grinned. "Yeah," he said. "Good idea." He turned back to Frieda. "Some of the boys have donated their C-rations," he said. "It's not great, but probably better food than these children have had in a while. Follow him and he'll dish it up. You can stay with us until we head out and then we'll arrange an escort for you. Where you headed, anyhow?"

"Away," she said.

CHAPTER
THIRTY-THREE

SAM

Frieda and the two men, both of whom carried babies in backpack harnesses, herded their charges into the middle of our camp. The sergeant doubled the lookout. We all understood how traumatic it would be for the children to have escaped the terrible abuse they had endured only to be caught and taken back. With the added sound of thirty-three extra people, we didn't want to give the Germans an advantage to sneak up on us.

Although, I was amazed at how quiet the children were. I figured it hadn't hit them yet they'd been freed. Just as well. It helped us get a few more minutes' sleep with them scattered among us, cuddled in. I held one of the babies for a while. A little girl. Her tiny eyes searched mine and after several seconds her lips lifted in a slow smile. Her grip on my fingers tightened and my heart melted. I hoped my child would be a girl. In fact, if we hadn't been in the middle of a war, I would have taken the one in my arms home with me.

I handed the baby back to the elder and several of us continued to talk with Frieda as she related the conditions of the camp she had recently escaped. She told us the camp commander and his wife had left hours earlier and that most of their officers had been killed by Americans in the Thuringian Forest.

Killed by Americans? The thought hit me between the eyes. *By us.*

By Lieutenant Scott, actually.

But we kept that fact to ourselves.

Frieda also talked a little about Ohrdruf, a satellite camp of the larger one at Buchenwald from which she had escaped. Series of tunnels by each camp provided a shortcut, she said, and would save us time getting there, in addition to concealing our approach. They had traveled both sets of tunnels and confirmed that soldiers no longer guarded them. She gave the scouts specific directions through each set of twisted passageways.

"What were they for?" I asked.

She shrugged. "Resistance says tunnels by Ohrdruf for Hitler. If he escape Berlin."

"There are also theories," our scout, Perry, added, "that they were bomb testing sites. But the tunnels near Buchenwald were designed to build jet-powered planes. We know that for certain from reconnaissance photos."

The sergeant radioed the lieutenant for a small party to meet Frieda and the children and take them to safety, then designated four soldiers to travel with them until they met the escort. With only a couple of hours until dawn, the rest of us packed our gear and prepared to move out.

Frieda's hand found my arm. Her sleeve shifted and a tattooed number became visible. Like the one on some of the children. I had no idea what it meant but determined to find out when I could.

"*Bitte*," she said. Her eyes pleaded with me. "After you leave Ohrdruf, you must go to Buchenwald. When you get there, find Gerda. *Frau* Ziegler. She is..." The woman hesitated as if searching for a word. "*Schwanger*...I think you say...pregnant. In small house by parade grounds. Locked in room. No food. Find her. Please."

"Why?" I asked. "Who is she?"

"Wife of killed officer."

"I'm not sure I can help her," I said. "That makes her one of the enemy."

"*Nein*," she answered. "No enemy. She save Jewish children." I saw her struggle before she said, "*Zwölfhundert*."

"I don't understand," I said. "Is that a number?"

"It is," Perry said as he passed. "Sorry, but I couldn't help overhearing. She told you that the woman she wants you to help has saved twelve hundred Jewish children."

OUR K COMPANY SQUADS FOLLOWED THE ROUTE FRIEDA described and after a couple of hours, entered the tunnels at Jonastal, along the road between Krawinkel and Arnstadt, southeast of the city of Gotha. We found the entrance, hidden with dense brush as she said we would, in the forest beside railroad tracks. We followed our scouts deeper and deeper into the ground and gradually the walls transformed from rough-hewn rock to smooth stone and then tiles, like those I had seen in pictures of a subway.

The tiled part of the tunnel also sported lights, which burned brightly and raised the hair on the back of my neck. We had trusted Frieda without question, and I hoped we hadn't been set up. She seemed so sincere.

I took a deep breath and forced my nerves to calm. There was no way she worked for the enemy. Not when she traveled with those starving children. And wanted me to help her pregnant friend.

Evans led the way from the map he drew under Frieda's guidance. We turned right and entered a larger corridor with rooms leading off. Dozens of doors and windows lined the hallway and appeared to be offices. One of them seemed especially large with a gold plate on its door. The plate was blank, but I couldn't help but wonder if that had been the one designated for Hitler.

We kept walking and after another couple of turns entered a cavernous chamber. Tables, spread with blueprints, occupied the room's center and a large pile of gears and cylinders rested on the floor beside them. I didn't know anything about reading blueprints, but Erwin studied them and let out a low whistle.

"I can't be certain," he said, "but I believe these plans are what they told us about in bazooka school. The Germans were testing various rockets and bombs." He turned the page and studied it. "Even atomic bombs," he said. "I think that's what this plan is for."

We crowded around, but it made no sense to me.

After a few minutes, we continued through the tunnel and at an intersection, turned left. We entered several other chambers set up as factories like the one where I had worked, only these appeared to be set up for something I had never seen before. Small, two-wheeled platforms leaned against the wall with a hollow tube protruding from the middle of them. This time, it was Ervin who enlightened us. He pointed to a word at the top of one of the diagrams that littered the table, along with countless gun parts. "Look at this," he said. "*Raketenwerfer 43*, a reusable anti-tank rocket launcher. For the infantry, we were told. To enhance their ability to fend off tank warfare. The grenades those guns fired," he said, pointing to the hollow tubes protruding from the wheeled platform, "were stabilized with little fins and produced less kickback."

"Come on, fellas," Sergeant Gordon said. "Let's move. We'll send some guys back here once we've completed our objective. For now, leave everything as is."

In the next chamber, we saw the parts that appeared to be for aerial cameras—at least according to the drawings on the walls. And the chamber after that revealed sophisticated ammunition—we didn't even have the kinds of weapons that would fire such stuff. There were also stacks of other equipment—bazooka parts, grenades—which Sergeant Gordon did let us take—and mortar stands. It all sat there. So close to being useful, but most of it useless in its current state. I couldn't help but wonder why these items hadn't been finished and sent out to the field. I was glad, of course. But puzzled.

The scouts led us through that room and back into a short tunnel that ended abruptly. Perry opened the door to find the outside.

We flattened ourselves against the wall in the early dawn, then crouched and scurried along on our haunches. When we exited the tunnel, Sergeant Gordon gave the all-clear and we stood and continued toward our destination. According to Frieda's directions, once out of the tunnels, we were less than a mile from the first camp, Ohrdruf, the satellite camp of Buchenwald. I had no idea what to expect when we got there, but I kept my rifle ready.

I was glad to be outside in the early dawn after the confines of the tunnels.

It was April. The fourth, I think. A day when spring breezes should have brought forth the fresh scent of new beginnings. Fresh flowers in my mother's gardens in Pennsylvania. New growth everywhere.

Instead, the breeze blew a rotten stench our way. Something burned.

"Bodies," Simon said. "One of my buddies died in a burning car. Smelled the same."

Every step closer to Ohrdruf magnified the odor of death which filled our nostrils, leaving no room for fresh air. We couldn't breathe. We scrambled to cover our mouths and noses so we could keep going. Within half a mile, we saw the smoke and in two more turns down the road, the gates came into view. The watch towers stood empty and no one moved in the large facility.

Miles of chain-link fence topped with thick, rolled barbed wire enclosed the camp, but did nothing to obstruct our view through it. The large, open area on the inside greeted us with unbelievable horror.

Dead bodies, some piled three and four deep, littered the entire space in what looked like a square. A gallows rested at one side, but its five nooses hung empty. Everyone on the ground appeared to have been shot.

"Davis," the sergeant hollered when we reached the gates, "bazooka. Front and center."

Ervin planted a perfect shot in the middle of the metal structure, but it held firm.

A second shot yielded no better results, so we worked together and forced the gates open.

I had seen shocking sights during the war, but nothing that even came close to the magnitude of the carnage surrounding me. So much death.

None of us spoke. Words couldn't adequately describe the revulsion we felt.

There appeared to be no guards at all, but some of the bodies lay in pools of blood that hadn't yet congealed. I had visions of guards in the middle of a crowd, shooting everyone around them and then running to cars and hightailing it away from their slaughter. There couldn't have been much time between their wreaking this devastation and our opening the gates. Sergeant Gordon radioed the lieutenant to tell him what we had found, and the lieutenant said he would pass it up the chain. We couldn't make any decisions as to what to do with the bodies, so we simply stood. Gaping. Immobile. Horrified.

The scene was mind numbing. Unthinkable.

I ran out of words.

So I threw up. Along with most of my fellow soldiers. I was glad the Germans were gone because we would have made perfect targets for them, bent to the ground and emptying our insides all the way to our toes.

When nothing else came out, I straightened and leaned against the chain-link fence.

But movement caught my eye. From one of the buildings to my right, a face appeared. I pulled my rifle from my shoulder and aimed. So did others. But while we stood there, a sound reached us. A cheer. Low at first, building to a crescendo. People appeared from around the square. Scrawny, bony people in filthy, tattered striped uniforms. Some wore caps, most had no shoes. But they moved toward us, their arms held high, their hollow faces wreathed in smiles. Mouths opened in huge grins to reveal rotten teeth. Or no teeth at all. A few of them limped. Many of them fell to the ground and wept. Most of them tried to touch us. To shake our hands. To offer thanks.

I looked around our ranks. To a man, tears streaked our cheeks. We reached into our packs and shared whatever food we had left with the grizzled men and the few women. We cautioned them to eat slowly. To no avail. Many of the prisoners gulped down all the food they were given and immediately it came back up.

Sergeant Gordon dispatched us in small groups to search the rest of the camp and see what else we could find. Simon and Erwin and I headed left with one of the freed prisoners, a woman. Which surprised me. Her head had obviously been shaved at some point because her hair growth was no more than muddy stubble. Her right arm was drawn up, her hand like a claw. She wore a dirty striped uniform that resembled pajamas and her face was skeletal, with tortured, vacant eyes. But her English was excellent.

We forced the door of a small shed open and were confronted with forty naked bodies sprinkled liberally with lime. We backed out and the prisoner told us it was a holding facility. "German guards piled dead prisoners here until shed is full—two hundred corpses," she told us. "Then bodies removed and buried in pit about a mile from camp." More than three thousand inmates had suffered this fate, she said, since January of that year.

We continued our search and the smell of burning bodies strengthened. The prisoner explained that some of the burial pits had been opened and bodies exhumed so they could be burned. In hopes they wouldn't be found, she thought, although no one had told her that. We turned a corner and found a large, still-smoking pit ringed with empty five-gallon drums, their labels indicating they had contained pitch. Bones and partial bodies piled high across railroad ties laid on brick foundations showed evidence of having been drenched with it. So they would burn faster, I guessed. That's probably also why they started the fire from pinewood and coal. For a quick burn. Piles of both fuels rested near the still smoldering embers beneath the bodies. But apparently they ran out of time and the place cleared before the evidence of their deeds had been destroyed.

I was shocked at how immune I had become to the sight of such atrocities in only the short time since my arrival. The scene around me was surreal and after the initial shock that greeted me at the gate, I wandered through the rest of the camp in a sort of self-induced numbness to keep from dwelling on the devastating scenes I witnessed. I could tell from their body language that my buddies reacted the same way. Even street-hardened Simon.

We searched several more areas and poked our heads into a building with a large concrete pool and the strong smell of creosote.

"What was this for?" Erwin asked our guide.

"Cleansing. Delousing." She turned her head.

"For everyone?" I asked.

"Ja. We were shaved when we first got here." She reached up and demonstrated the strokes the barber used. "He put shaver here," she touched her forehead, "and made quick stroke all the way to here." Her hand reached the back of her neck. "Five strokes. No more hair. Next part was worse." She hesitated and we waited for her to continue. "They shaved arms, legs, underarms. Even genital and anal areas. After that, we were forced to get in pool filled with creosote. Our bodies throbbed with pain from the nicks and cuts left by razor. But anyone who screamed or cried was beaten, naked, in front of everyone."

My heart went out to her. I couldn't resist touching her arm to give her reassurance. She shrank away, fearfully, and covered her head with her hands. The striped sleeve of her shirt pulled up to reveal a line of tattooed numbers on her left arm.

"I'm sorry," I said, my throat tight. "I wasn't trying to hurt you."

She lowered her arms and appeared to be embarrassed. We resumed our search, heading in the direction of the main area, when a scuffle broke out behind me. Several prisoners held another one down while still others beat him with rocks. I recognized the prisoner under attack. He had hung around the gate as we entered and chatted up several of the soldiers. I remember noticing that he appeared to be better fed and better dressed than the others. His pants sported no holes and his jacket and scarf were relatively clean. I started toward him to help, but the prisoner who had joined us laid her hand on my arm.

"Would be best if you did not interfere," she said. "That man was *kapo*, one of privileged prisoners who carried out German's orders. He beat other prisoners and took their food for himself. He even took jewels they smuggled in. Prisoners beating him now suffered at his hands." Her face hardened as she watched. "Let justice play out."

I would never even have imagined a scene like this before stepping through the gates of the Ohrdruf hellhole hours earlier.

When the beaten man could no longer stand, the prisoners holding him let him fall to the ground where an emaciated man finished him off with a tire iron. The last I saw, the head of the beaten man looked like a squashed melon, the features of his face unrecognizable as pulpy mush.

I steeled myself to keep walking and made it back to the main square.

"What kinds of activities took place here?" I asked.

"*Appells*," she said. "You would say 'roll call.' Two times per day, morning and evening. Made us leave barracks and run through tunnel of guards and *kapos* who hit us with rubber hoses. The scum you saw beaten to death," she said fixing her eyes on mine, "was one of the worst. If prisoners fell while running through, he and guards set upon them and gave them real beating. Even sick inmates had to appear for roll call and were beaten because they couldn't stand at attention. We had to look straight ahead, thumbs lined up with seams of trousers. Anyone who moved, even coughed or sneezed, was beaten savagely."

"Even you?" I asked. I couldn't keep the shock from my voice.

"*Ja*. There were few women here and they were lighter on me with beatings. But they made up for it with...by..."

She stopped talking and hung her head. Shame overtook her whole being. I touched her arm again. Lightly. This time she didn't flinch.

"And not only me," she continued. "Some of women submitted willingly for special privileges. Until they got pregnant. Then babies sent to other camp and women forced into hard labor. I was lucky. No babies."

"Whatever happened to you," I said, "wasn't your fault. You'll be safe now."

She recounted the rest of the roll call routine, ridiculously precise actions expected of civilians who were too weak and sick to even stand, much less remember military-type movements. The exercise sometimes took hours, she said, especially since the guards had to add the numbers of prisoners in each row and then collect them to get the total in the camp. They were almost never right the first time, so the whole process would be repeated. Then the prisoners had to go to work. With practically no food. They worked all day, only to repeat the roll call fiasco again in the evening.

I remembered the woman, Frieda, and the children in the woods from the night before. Some of them had the same kinds of numbers as our guide. I pointed to her left arm. "Did they do this to you here?"

"*Nein*," she said. "At Auschwitz. Sent me there first, then here."

"We saw someone else with numbers like that," Erwin said. "What was her name, Sam?"

"Frieda," I said.

Our guide drew her breath in. "You saw Frieda? Alive?"

"Yes," I told her. "She was with children from the camp at Buchenwald. You know her?"

She nodded. "We were at Auschwitz together. Then they sent her to Buchenwald and sent me here. I thought she was dead. My brother and parents were sent to Buchenwald too."

"Do you think they're still there?"

"I don't know. I hope so."

"What's your name?" I asked, ashamed I hadn't thought of asking that earlier.

"Rebekah," she said. "Rebekah Rosenbaum."

CHAPTER
THIRTY-FOUR

SAM

A ctivity at the main gate caught our attention. We joined other soldiers there, including Lieutenant Scott and the rest of our unit, minus the German women. Soldiers moved to form columns and allowed jeeps with stars on their little flags to pass.

I couldn't believe it. The Supreme Allied Commander, General Dwight D. Eisenhower, hopped out of the first jeep and none other than General George Patton strode from the second. The whole place snapped to attention. At least the Americans did. The prisoners didn't have a clue who they were, so they milled around as they had been.

Photographers traveled in the generals' entourage and after the same kind of initial reaction we all had, they began snapping pictures. General Patton left the area and Simon told me later he saw the general throwing up behind the shed with the naked bodies strewn with lime.

I understood. Most of us had thrown up as well when we first entered the gate.

The generals toured the camp while we waited for orders and after an hour or so, General Eisenhower climbed on his jeep. His aide blew a whistle to alert us that the general was about to speak. We assembled to attention in front of him until he gave us the order to stand "At ease."

"Men," he said, "I'm sure we all share revulsion at what we are witnessing here today. Prior to coming here, I had seen written reports of atrocities, but I assure you, after touring this area, I can state unequivocally that those reports did not paint a picture of the full horrors. As you have seen for yourselves. I want you to know that I am ordering every unit nearby that is not on the front lines to tour this camp, as you have done today. I have been told that the American soldier does not know what he is fighting for. Now, at least, you will all know what you are fighting against."

He saluted and we saluted back. Then he was driven out. We heard sometime later that he carried through with his order and the camp was toured time and again by every unit in the area. He worried, we were told, that at some point in the future, propaganda might be created to say that the mass executions enacted by the Germans were fake, a big lie to make the German people look bad to the rest of the world. He wanted to ensure that never happened.

We were all witnesses to the truth of the horror.

CHAPTER
THIRTY-FIVE

SAM

"Sergeant Gordon," I said, "have you spoken with the lieutenant about us going to the other camp we were told about? The one at Buchenwald?"

"Yeah," he answered. "General Patton heard about it too and wants to inspect it like he did this one. The lieutenant's sending a platoon to join the 6th Armored Division. They're headed to a town about two miles northwest of where we believe the other camp to be. A place called Hottelstedt. You looking to volunteer?"

"Yes sir."

Which surprised me. I mostly tried to keep my head down and get through the day. But the woman Frieda told me about, someone named Gerda, wouldn't leave my head. She had somehow managed to save twelve hundred Jewish children, and now she was pregnant and locked in her room. I knew Betty was being well cared for at the farm with my sisters, but I hoped someone would have come to her aid if she'd been in the same situation as this Gerda person.

"You got it," he said. "Find three or four people to go with you. And we'll need to find a guide. Someone who speaks German."

Something brushed up against my elbow. "I will be guide," Rebekah said beside me. She looked at the sergeant and added. "My family was sent there two years ago. I hope to find them."

He looked her over and made up his mind. "Fine," he said. "Can you get hold of some regular clothes?"

She nodded and said to me. "I will return in fifteen minutes."

"We'll move out in twenty," the sergeant said.

I asked my band of buddies to accompany me and they all agreed. As an added precaution, I approached Sergeant Randolph Noonan, one of our company medics, to join us. "Sarge, there's a pregnant woman there who's been locked in her room. She might need help."

"I don't have a lot of experience delivering babies," he said with a smile. "But I volunteered with our ambulance crew at home and did it once. Well, I helped, anyway."

About twenty of us waited by the gate for a ride with the armored crew when the inmate, Rebekah, joined us. Her transformation was astounding. She had washed and dressed in dark clothes with a black beret to hide her stubble. Her face was still hollow, but otherwise, she looked surprisingly good for the abuse she'd endured.

We climbed aboard the trucks that accompanied the tanks and the sergeant instructed them to drop us off before we reached Hottelstedt. We intended to follow the tunnels Frieda told us about to conceal ourselves from the enemy for as long as possible. Like the tunnels outside Ohrdruf, Frieda had said, the ones close to Buchenwald were no longer occupied.

At the base of Etterberg hill, we hopped off our transport and headed up, searching for the entrance to the tunnels. Rebekah kept up, surprising us all.

Sergeant Gordon located the entrance and we entered, encountering much of the same terrain as in the other tunnel. Rough-hewn walls gave way to smooth tiled corridors with lights no longer lit. But this time, the trail led up rather than deep into the ground.

We didn't find office complexes as we had with the first set of tunnels, but there were additional manufacturing rooms, which we hurried through. For the most part, nothing surprised us during our journey.

Until we reached the last chamber, a huge room with a high ceiling. The walls boasted pictures of modern airplanes, labeled "*Messerschmitt Me* 262." Something about that rang a bell. Dickie's voice came from behind me, "These are the planes that pilot told us about. What was his name?"

"Spencer," I said.

"Right. He said these planes were faster and more heavily armed than any of the Allied fighter planes."

We walked around the room, amazed at its efficiency. Several fuselages for the new planes were strategically placed at angles. To me, they looked complete except for their wings, which rested in another part of the huge chamber on wheeled dollies. Display panels were arranged in precision on tables to our right, with everything numbered that, at a quick glance, appeared to be specifically designated for a fuselage bearing the same number.

"They told us about this in bazooka school too," Ervin said softly. "These could have been devastating on our air corps if the Germans hadn't suffered from strategic materials and fuel shortages. A lot of which stemmed from Allied bombing. And apparently, from what we learned, the Germans couldn't agree on the final design of the turbojet engines, so the ones produced suffered from reliability problems. Thank goodness."

I agreed. If the Germans had been a little farther along with this work, we might have been the ones surrendering to them at this point instead of the other way around. The thought made me shudder.

We moved through the room to the outer tunnel door. Positioned above it was a huge banner that read *"Flugzeugwerke Reichsmarschall Hermann Göring"* and under that was the single word, "REIMAHG."

Ervin pointed to it and said, "It's a subsidiary company of the Nazi industrial complex under the leadership and direction of Hermann Göring, Hitler's *Reichsmarschall.*"

"This way, men," Sergeant Gordon called.

We followed him and found ourselves back in a short tunnel of rough-hewn stone that opened to the outside. Once out of the tunnel, we were amazed to see many other buildings in the industrial complex, with bridges, office buildings, airplane hangars, and even a short runway.

Near the top of the hill, we struggled through a thick stand of beech trees, the literal translation of buchenwald, Rebekah whispered to me. We cleared it and Rebekah used her good arm to point out the Bismarck Tower to the south, along with the beautiful palace of Anna Amelia to the north. It struck me as a great spot for a picnic.

Shouts reached us as we cleared the last clump of beeches and the concentration camp complex lay in front of us, a massive system of long, low buildings with houses clustered around a main square, like the one at Ohrdruf. But much larger. We moved closer and the sound of machine gun fire reached us, along with distant mortar fire and more shouting.

We shouldered our weapons and continued toward the gates of Buchenwald, reaching them at the same time as an M-8 armored car with a captain and three other officers. Men in striped prison garb hung off the sides of the car and cheered while waving their weapons in the air. Behind it was a German officer's car like the one we'd encountered on the road to Ohrdruf. Men in striped uniforms hung off that car too, and I saw two people slumped in its back seat.

Both vehicles were greeted by thousands of similarly dressed inmates within the complex, who also waved their weapons and cheered.

"What the hell?" Simon said. "Where did those guys get guns?"

The sergeant quickly told the group our mission and we all entered the complex together. The prisoners picked up the leader of the other group, Captain Frederic Keffer, and threw him in the air, then caught him and threw him again. I never heard such cheering.

Rebekah found a prisoner nearby and learned what had happened.

"When they heard the sounds of fighting nearby," she said, "a secret resistance group inside the camp revolted against the guards. They plotted for months, he told me, stashing stolen weapons and making plans for each fighter when time came. This morning, they broke into the guards' armory and stole rifles, machine guns, even anti-tank weapons, and took over the camp. They have the guards under lock and key in one of barracks."

"Did they tell you anything about this German officer's car?" I asked.

"Ja. The kommandant of the camp. And his wife. Trying to escape but captured by Americans. When the prisoners saw them, they hauled them out of car and beat them. They would have killed them, he said, but Americans made them stop."

Soldiers removed the German officer and his wife from the back of their car and tied them to the nearby gallows posts. Their faces bloodied, the man stared straight ahead, but the woman struggled against her restraints and screamed at everyone who passed. The soldier assigned to guard them turned his back to them.

The captain met with the prison resistance leaders and promised to radio ahead for food and medical help. His soldiers unloaded all the food they had. We did the same.

We wandered around the large complex, amazed at what the prisoners had accomplished. Especially in their weakened condition. The captain and his men left to get help and Sergeant Noonan tended to some of the weakest inmates.

Rebekah appeared at my side. "I'd like to look for my family," she said. "But let's find your pregnant woman first and then I'll go."

"Right," I said. I motioned to my small group and headed for the houses that faced the square, as Frieda described. I approached the first house and found the door unlocked, so I entered and searched every room shouting *"Fräulein."*

In the first three houses, no one shouted back.

Before I reached the fourth house, a scream greeted me, along with another voice. Quieter, calmer. I opened the door and shouted again. *"Fräulein."* The sound stopped. "Americans," I added. "Frieda sent me."

"Hier!" Pounding accompanied the voice.

I followed the sound to a closed door and turned the knob. Locked.

"Will you let me in? Unlock the door."

"Nein. Locked on your side."

That puzzled me, but she was right. The bolt on the door was in the locked position. I turned it and opened the door then stepped into the room just in time to catch a woman who collapsed in my arms. "Oh, thank *Gott!* Help us."

I heard Rebekah's gasp behind me and in seconds, she engulfed the woman in a huge hug.

"*Frau* Berghmann," she said. Tears streamed down her face.

Another woman writhed on the bed, her belly huge. A large pool of blood stained the coverlet under her and sweat coated her face and drenched her hair. She screamed again.

Rebekah rushed over to her. "Gerda," she cried. "The Americans are here. To help."

I sent up a silent prayer of gratitude that Sergeant Noonan had accompanied us. "Hang on," I said. "I'll be right back."

I raced out and found him, still ministering to those around him. "It's what I was afraid of, Sarge. I need your help. The woman's in labor and she's struggling. You need to deliver the baby."

His eyes bulged. "I know I said I did it before, but..."

"But nothing," I said. "You have to do this. Come on." I pulled him into the house with the screaming woman. Dickie, Simon and the Davis twins followed us.

The older woman, who had spoken to me first, met us at the door, a full pitcher of water in her hands. "*Kommen Sie*," she said and led us back into the bedroom. "I'll do my best," the sergeant said, "but I'll need help. Ryan, are you up for it?"

"Sure," I said. I had delivered piglets and calves on the farm. How much different could it be?

"What's her name?" Sarge asked the older woman.

"Gerda," the woman answered. "She's my daughter. Please help her."

Rebekah sat beside the pregnant woman and held her hand. "She's my best friend. For my whole life. You must help."

"Okay, Gerda," Sarge said, all calm efficiency. "Let's birth this baby. What do you say?"

But another contraction overtook her and the woman's only response was a scream.

CHAPTER
THIRTY-SIX

GERDA

"Breathe, *Liebling,*" Karla told her daughter. "These nice men will help us."

She continued to bathe Gerda's face with cool water while the soldier the others referred to as "Sarge" checked her daughter's progress.

"I think I found the problem," Sarge said. "The baby's crooked. Not breach, but not properly lined up in the birth canal, either." He looked up at Karla. "I have to turn the baby a little. But it's going to hurt like he—a lot. Be prepared. She's going to scream again."

"She's screaming all night," Karla said. "I don't know how she has voice left. Shall I give her more brandy?"

"Good idea," he answered. "I would give her something for the pain, but I'm afraid it might harm the baby. Okay, here we go."

"Squeeze my hand, Gerda," Rebekah said, offering her good one to her friend. "Don't worry. You can't hurt me."

The soldier called Sarge began by pushing on Gerda's stomach to try and shove the baby into the proper position. As he expected, Gerda's screams intensified and she pulled her legs up and tried to roll over. Karla said soothing words in her ear and trickled more brandy through Gerda's lips. It dribbled down her chin onto the front of her nightgown.

"Ryan," Sarge said. "Hold her legs. We have to get this baby out of her."

The other soldier sat beside Gerda on the bed with his back to her face and held her thighs still with both hands.

"That's good. *Fräulein*," Sarge added. "Can you push? I need to see what else I have to move."

"*Drücken*," Gerda's mother told her. "Push." She wiped her daughter's brow again and Rebekah whispered soothing words to her friend.

Gerda pushed, screaming as she did, her face screwed into a mask of misery.

"I see it," Sarge said. "One of the shoulders is caught." He reached his fingers gently into the birth canal and pushed the tiny shoulder closer to the middle. As he expected, Gerda let out another scream. But the following contraction moved the baby along and the head popped out.

"Great," Sarge told her. "You're doing great. We have a head." He looked at Gerda's mother. "Will you have her push again? We're really close."

"*Drücken*," Karla said again. She held her daughter's other hand. Gerda gave another push and the baby's shoulders joined the head.

"Okay," Sarge said. "It's going great. We're almost finished. Once again." He glanced at Karla. "What was the word you used? *Drücken?*"

"*Ja*," Karla answered. The two of them and Rebekah said the word together and Gerda strained to push out the life from inside her.

"Wonderful," Sarge said. "We have half a baby. Another couple of times should do it."

By this time, other soldiers filled the doorway. When Sarge gave the "push" command, they all said "*drücken*" right along with him. Even the big soldier who held Gerda's legs. The one Sarge called "Ryan."

Gerda screwed up her face with her effort and the rest of the baby popped into Sarge's waiting hands.

"It's a girl! Congratulations."

"*Das Mädchen*," Karla told her daughter. "Your *tochter*."

Rebekah leaned in and kissed her friend on the forehead. Tears streamed from the faces of all the women and the soldiers in the doorway cheered. Sarge asked Karla to cut the cord and he tied the end still attached to the baby's navel.

"Sarge," the one called Ryan said. "The baby hasn't cried. She hasn't made a sound yet. Is that okay?"

The tension in his voice filled the room.

Sarge turned the baby over and gently tapped her back, then her tiny buttocks.

Nothing happened.

He turned the baby back over and looked at her face. Her eyes were closed and no sign of movement sprung from her chest. Gently, he massaged the area above her heart and her color improved slightly, but still no chest movement. He pushed. Nothing.

"Sarge!" Ryan said quietly. "Do something!"

The men from the doorway watched and Karla's face paled. Rebekah squeezed Gerda's hand.

"*Was ist falsch?*" Gerda asked. "What's wrong?"

Sarge wiped out the baby's nose the best he could, then covered her nose and mouth with his and gently blew. Nothing. He rhythmically compressed her chest to a count of thirty, then blew into her nose and mouth again. Still nothing.

No one moved. Or said a word. But heads bowed. And tears flowed. Not only from the bed, but also from those filling the doorway.

Once more, Sarge gently compressed the baby's chest and blew.

Then he did it again.

"Sarge," someone said from the door. "Maybe you should let her go. You've done all you can."

Karla drew in her breath.

"No," Sarge said. "She's going to live. She *needs* to live. For all of us."

He went through his routine.

Again.

And again.

The eighth time he blew into the baby's nose and mouth, her eyes flew open. And as soon as his mouth left hers, she gave out a howl. Long and loud.

The men in the doorway slapped each other on the back and the man called Ryan grabbed Gerda's hand and kissed it, tears streaming down his face to match hers.

Sarge used the cloth and water Karla had brought and cleaned up the rest of the baby. He wrapped her in the shawl laid out for her and held her up for Gerda to see, then turned her toward the door. The men cheered again.

Several of the men ventured in and slapped Sarge on the back. Then Karla moved around to him and hugged him as if she'd never let him go.

"*Danke*," Karla said. "I can't thank you enough. I couldn't have saved the baby the way you did." Tears overtook her and she couldn't say more.

"What's her name?" the man they called Ryan asked Gerda.

"Etta," Gerda said. "Etta 'Sarge' Ziegler."

AFTER THE BIRTH OF HER GRANDDAUGHTER, KARLA retrieved bottles of pear brandy from her van and handed one to Sergeant Noonan with thanks for delivering the baby and for keeping her daughter and granddaughter alive. She also gave a bottle to the man called Ryan and several bottles to Sergeant Gordon to distribute among his men, many of whom offered her and Gerda small trinkets from their field packs—chewing gum, chocolate bars, cigarettes— whatever they thought might be welcomed.

Karla busied herself, packing Gerda's things for the trip home, while her daughter nursed baby Etta. Rebekah stayed with Gerda, rubbing her arm, then patting the baby's back.

"I'm so glad to see you, Bekah," Gerda said. "But you're very thin. Have you had any food?"

"Yes," Rebekah said. "The Americans have been wonderful. The ones here found me at Ohrdruf. When they said they were going to Buchenwald and needed an interpreter, I volunteered. Did you know that the prisoners staged a revolt and took over the camp outside? They have the guards locked up and the Americans have called for food and medical help." She squeezed Gerda's arm. "It's almost over," she added. "We can go home soon."

Gerda smiled at her.

"I heard you got married," Rebekah said. At Gerda's surprised expression, she added, "The prisoner's grapevine is alive and well. You'd be amazed at the things we heard behind our bars." She let out a long sigh. "I'll bet it was that young soldier, wasn't it? The one who helped us the very first day in Zwickau. Where is he?" She looked around and then gasped. "Oh no," she said. "Is he one of the ones locked up by the prisoners?"

"No," Gerda said, her voice sounding strangled. "He was killed. A couple of days ago. By the Americans."

"I'm so sorry," Rebekah said.

"He had changed," Gerda told her. "His ambitions got the best of him and he bought in to the party line. He kept me locked here in this room. Even after he was killed, the kommandant's wife, a horrible woman, locked me in as well." Gerda kissed the top of her baby's head. "I'm sorry Etta won't ever know her father, but she will have a more loving life with my family than she would have as a Nazi."

"That's one of the reasons I volunteered to come here," Rebekah said. "I didn't know you were the one we were trying to find but I was hoping to get word of *my* family. Do you know if they're still here?"

Rebekah looked at Gerda's face, but Gerda dropped her eyes. "You *do* know," Rebekah said. "You must tell me, Gerda. You must."

"Your father," Gerda said haltingly, "contracted typhoid fever almost right away, as soon as he got here, and died quickly."

A small sob left Rebekah's throat. "And my mother? Jakob?"

New tears eased down Gerda's cheeks. "Jakob was here. He was wonderful. He worked with us to identify the children we saved. And then your mother was sent here. But…"

"Gerda…"

"Jakob and your mother were killed," Gerda choked out. "And it was my fault." Gerda's grief spilled over and she sobbed into the soft down of her baby's head.

Rebekah bowed her head and joined her friend in grief. "I'm sure you didn't have anything to do with their deaths, Gerda. The Nazis..."

"But I did," Gerda said. "You need to know about it. And, Bekah, if you no longer want to be friends, I will understand."

"What happened?"

"Aldrik saw me talking to Jakob a couple of times. And your mother once. He even found her for me so I could tell her about your father."

Gerda stopped talking and new tears soaked her face, already wet from her ordeal. Haltingly, she related the details that led to the deaths of Rebekah's family and her own incarceration.

"When Aldrik made me look out the window at the gallows..." Gerda said at the end of her story, "it was...I saw..."

"Jakob and my mother there," Rebekah finished.

Gerda nodded, unable to speak.

The two women sat in silence and then Rebekah reached out and took Gerda's hand. "Don't worry, my friend. I know it wasn't your fault. You did what you had to do to save the children. If my family hadn't been killed then, they could as easily have died on any of the days since. I'm sure the guards here were as bad as ours. They didn't need a reason to kill people. They could do whatever brutal thing they wanted whenever they wanted to. With no consequences. Especially to Jews. They all hated us. I never understood why. But the why no longer matters. They just did."

Gerda raised her reddened eyes. "Can we still be friends?" she said in a small voice.

Rebekah reached over and kissed her on the cheek. "I think we have to be friends. You're all I have left." She managed a small smile and Gerda smiled back.

Gerda's mother bustled into the room, followed by one of the soldiers who had helped deliver the baby. Karla lifted Gerda's suitcase and put it into his hands.

"I really appreciate your help," Karla said. "Ryan, isn't it? I heard Sarge call you that."

"Yes, ma'am," he answered. "That's my last name. My first name is

Sam." He had trouble tearing his eyes away from Gerda and the baby. "My wife is pregnant," he added. "I'm hoping we have a daughter too."

Karla reached up and hugged him, then she pulled back and studied his face. "Sam," she said. "When you first came to the door, you said someone sent you. Who was it again?"

"Frieda."

Gerda gasped. "You found Frieda? Where was she?"

"We saw her in the forest south of Ohrdruf. She was with two men and a bunch of children, including a couple of babies. Thirty altogether, I think she said."

"Oh, thank *Gott*," Gerda answered. "Thirty? I would have hoped for more, but still *gut*. Please," she added. "You must check Block 66 to see if there are any children left. Maybe the guards didn't kill them all before the takeover."

"They shot children?" Sam asked. His voice was no more than a whisper.

"They shot everybody they could," Karla said. "Whenever they wanted. Then most of them left, the cowards, so they wouldn't be discovered when your Army arrived. There must have only been a skeleton staff when the resistance prisoners overthrew them."

"Yeah," he said, "we saw a lot of that at Ohrdruf. The guards there took off too."

"*Bitte*," Gerda said again. "Please go. Block 66 is at the back of the camp, near the woods. Whoever is still there will need help."

Sam placed the last few items in Karla's van and left in search of the building Gerda told him about.

"Rebekah," Karla said, "Gerda told me about your family. I am so sorry. You will come home with us."

"Oh, I couldn't," she said. "It could be so bad for you to have a Jew in your home."

"I know the war isn't totally over yet," Karla said, "but I think it's close enough and I understand the Americans are headed for Zwickau. Please. Let us be your family now."

"Please, Bekah," Gerda added, reaching for her friend's hand.

"Do you really think it will be okay?"

"Yes," the other two women said in unison.

"Then, yes. Yes! I would love to. Thank you." New tears streaked her face.

Sergeant Noonan stuck his head in the door. "Everything going okay here?" he asked.

"*Ja,*" Gerda said with a smile. "Very okay." Little Etta continued to nurse, her tiny fingers wrapped around one of her mother's.

"Sarge," Karla said. "I'm going to take my daughter and grand-daughter home now. Will you carry them to the van for me?"

Karla took a blanket to the back seat of the van and Sergeant Noonan placed Gerda, still holding Etta, gently on it. He straightened up and Karla hugged him again. "Thank you, Sarge. I will never forget you."

He left and something caught Karla's attention at the edge of the square. Two people, filthy and bloodied, slumped against the gallows posts.

The kommandant and his wife.

Karla walked over and put her face close to that of the woman who no longer screamed.

"How does it feel, *Frau* Krueger? To be a prisoner in your own space? Not fun, is it?" The other woman kept her head down. "Well, despite your best efforts, my granddaughter was born and will be going home with me now." Karla narrowed her eyes. "I sincerely hope you get everything you deserve. I will make certain the Americans know that Gerda and I will gladly testify at your trial."

She headed back toward the van but stopped and returned. She stared at the kommandant's wife until the bound woman raised her head. Karla drew back and struck the woman's face with every ounce of strength she possessed. A bright red mark, immediately visible, brought her immense satisfaction.

CHAPTER
THIRTY-SEVEN

SAM

My buddies and I left Gerda and searched for the area she called Block 66. We asked one of the nearby prisoners to take us there and on the way, he introduced himself as Rudy—Jewish and a former newspaperman. Like most of the other inmates we encountered, his filthy striped uniform bore tatters along the edges of his shirt and pants and his body bent from the waist. He twisted his head up to look at us when he talked and the smile he flashed revealed rotten teeth along with a number of empty spaces where teeth should have been. We slowed our pace to allow for his pronounced limp, which didn't seem to dampen his spirits at all. I was amazed he could be so upbeat, considering what he had experienced.

"Block 66 is way at the back of the camp," Rudy said. "The Resistance leaders decided to leave the children locked in so they couldn't get caught in the cross fire when we revolted against the guards. The little guys should be safe."

We passed signs of carnage even worse than those from Ohrdruf. Stacks of corpses lay scattered throughout the complex, some of which had been sprinkled with lime. But most hadn't. As much as I thought the sights from Ohrdruf had numbed me from being moved by further atrocities, I couldn't have been more wrong. Passing by so much death triggered constant gagging and overwhelming sadness at the faces of the corpses with their vacant eyes staring up at me. The thought never left me that if we had only arrived sooner, some of them might still be alive.

We also passed the crematorium, a facility missing from the other camp, with the charred skeletons of its latest victims still visible. Our guide showed us the gallows and the whipping bench and then convinced us to stick our heads into the pathology lab.

At first, I thought it couldn't get worse than the jars filled with human organs and shrunken heads. Until I saw the room that housed the tattooed skin, some stretched on metal frames and hanging like shirts in a closet. Other skins formed lampshades or were encased in glass ashtrays scattered around the room.

"They looked for vivid colors," Rudy said. "The kommandant's wife was especially fierce about wanting trinkets in her home made from the tattooed skin of prisoners here. Some inmates were killed for that reason alone, that they had colorful skin."

That did it for me. I shot past the others to reach the outside. And threw up until my throat was raw. Before discovering these atrocities, I hadn't considered myself a weak person, but I leaned against the building when I could stand again and cried. Deep, racking sobs. After several minutes, some of the soldiers in our group joined me at the wall and either retched or cried along with me. Sometimes both.

I was totally spent. The past two days had been an emotional upheaval with the death and devastation we saw in the concentration camps and the near-death of the German woman's baby.

Then the anger set in, first at Rudy, who brought us to view these appalling areas. But my anger transformed very quickly into under- standing that he wanted witnesses to the brutalities he had lived with for years. That I didn't want to see it, or even acknowledge it, didn't change the fact that it had happened. Showing us these horrible things was his way of ensuring the world found out about it and never forgot. Much like Eisenhower's press corps taking pictures for posterity.

So my anger switched to where it belonged, to the sick Nazi minds that could somehow justify behavior like this in the modern world. To the camp commander and his wife, still tied to the gallows by the gate. If I hadn't seen these outrageous murders with my own eyes, I would never have been able to wrap my head around the fact that one human being could so coldly and callously treat another human being in such a heinous manner. Where I came from, I had never even seen an animal treated so horribly.

Those of us leaning against the wall didn't speak. But the body language of the other soldiers convinced me they struggled with the same feelings I had.

"Do you still want to see the children?" Rudy asked quietly.

"Yes," I said, speaking for the group.

He led us deeper into the recesses of the massive complex to Block 66. The door remained locked, so we broke it down and discovered dozens of children crammed into the room, cowering against the walls. They were all male, but of various ages and in different stages of starvation. Seeing those skeletal little tykes still alive after the sights we'd witnessed on our way there, filled me with joy and I reached down and hugged some of them. I couldn't help it.

"Don't be afraid, little guys," Rudy told them. "These are American soldiers and they've come to set us free." Those who were strong enough cheered and the others smiled. My heart went out to them, the poor little things.

I couldn't help but wonder, however, what freedom would actually mean for them. I had no idea where they would go. Most of their parents, Rudy said, were dead and their houses confiscated for the state, so I couldn't imagine what would happen to those little souls once they left that horrible place.

I watched them file out of the barracks and again, Freddie leaped into my head. I couldn't stomach the thought of his having to go through what these small children had endured for most of their lives.

But seeing them was especially hard on Simon. As an American soldier, he wasn't treated any differently from the rest of us because he was Jewish. But the deeper we got into Germany, the number of atrocities we saw inflicted on Jewish people multiplied.

They were his heritage's people. His religion's people. His people. And it ate at him.

He leaned against the wall as the children cleared the door, his face pale.

"You okay?" I asked him.

"No," he said. "I'm not. Why do you think this happened, Sam? I mean, it's all horrible. But with adults, you can almost convince yourself that they at least had the ability to irritate the damned Krauts. What did these little guys do that made them end up here? How could they have bothered anybody?"

"I don't know, Simon."

"I mean, think about it. An accident of birth is all that separated me from those walking skeletons or the piles of dead bodies out there. And if I'd been born into this, I would have fought back, so I'm sure I would have been one of the first ones to go."

"Maybe," I said, "but you would sure as hell have taken a lot of Germans out with you."

"What we saw makes me want to take a bunch of them out right now. I can't understand..."

"Me neither."

We accompanied Rudy and the boys from Block 66 to the front of the camp and as we got close, the German bakery van pulled out through the gates. Gerda raised her head and her smile told me she had seen us.

Cooking aromas reached us from the square and the children ran toward the steaming pots where soldiers dished stew into cups, bowls, or whatever vessel appeared in front of them.

Sergeant Noonan approached us. "The German woman told us the camp commander's pantry was well stocked, so some of the guys raided it."

I enjoyed the pleasure on the children's faces and sent up a silent thanks that Gerda had sent us to find them. The fact that she had already saved twelve hundred children did a lot to renew my faith in the German people. They didn't all, thank God, share the same view of humanity as their wretched *Führer*. My mother would have been appalled, but I prayed to God that the soul of the horrible man responsible for the atrocities we'd uncovered would rot in hell.

CHAPTER
THIRTY-EIGHT

GERDA

Karla settled behind the wheel and Rebekah climbed into the front seat beside her. They moved, unimpeded, toward the gate and Karla recognized some of the soldiers who motioned her through. She got one last look at the soldier named Sam Ryan, who herded a group of children toward the square. In the mirror, she noticed Gerda rise up and then settle back down with a satisfied smile.

"Gerda," Karla said, "I'm sorry Etta will never see her father. I know you loved him."

"*Ja, Mutti,*" Gerda answered, "I did. At first, anyway. But at the end, our philosophies differed so widely, I'm not sure how happy our future would have been anyway."

"Right," Rebekah offered, "with you trying to save the world and him set on killing it."

Gerda smiled at Rebekah's snort. "That's a funny way to put it, Bekah. But what it comes down to is that Aldrik got caught up in the warped frenzy of hate and prejudice Hitler spread."

Karla drove away from the camp and every mile that separated her from its horror lightened her heart. She had called her husband to tell him about their ordeal and let him know they were on their way home. With his granddaughter and Rebekah.

"*Mutti,*" Gerda said softly from the backseat. "Thank you for coming to get me. I would have died there by myself. And so would Etta."

"*Frau* Krueger made it sound like she wanted to take you with them," Karla said. "She would have had a doctor handy to deliver your baby."

"Maybe," Gerda said, "but you heard her. She only wanted the baby. They would probably have killed me after she was born. And I can't imagine the life my little girl would have had living with them. They were horrible people. Someday I'll tell you about them. But not today."

Karla maneuvered the van over the rough roads to avoid as many bumps as possible. With Rebekah smiling beside her, she smiled, too, at the sound of Gerda's even breathing and Etta's soft little wheezes.

Her mind told her the worst was over.

If only she could make her heart believe it.

CHAPTER
THIRTY-NINE

SAM

"Listen up," Sergeant Gordon told us. "We have a new assignment. A temporary one. General Patton plans to tour this camp like he did Ohrdruf. But he has instructed us to accompany the 6th Armored Division down the hill to the town of Weimar in the morning. To bring the citizens here and, in his words, 'rub their noses' in the rotting flesh and scenes of horror, to see the death and mutilation firsthand." He stopped talking, put his hands on his hips and stared at us, one by one. "I don't know about you guys," he continued, "but from what I've seen here, I think that's a damned fine idea."

We cheered.

We made ourselves useful, helping to feed prisoners, making certain everyone could come and go freely from their barracks, and taking turns with the prison resistance group to keep the German guards locked up.

In addition, we eagerly anticipated our task of rounding up Weimar's citizens and marching them up Etterberg Hill to tour Buchenwald. The previous afternoon, I caught a glimpse of General Patton as he strode around the camp with his entourage, his face like a thundercloud. Seeing him like that validated all the emotions I felt when I viewed the savagery that had taken place there.

While Karla and her daughter were not like the ones who ran this camp, it occurred to me that a lot of others must have been or they would have tried to change what was going on. Like Frieda did by helping the Resistance fighters. Or like Gerda did by saving Jewish children.

The following morning, we assembled at the gate and Sergeant Gordon told us that General Patton had motored into Weimar the previous afternoon and insisted the mayor convene a town meeting where Patton, himself, addressed the residents. He told them a little about what had happened at the top of the hill adjacent to their town and reported that many of the residents' faces registered shock as he talked about it. Regardless, he also insisted they make the climb, accompanied by his soldiers and tour the camp for themselves. In addition, he said, work details would be set up for the townspeople to come back to the camp and properly bury the massacred inmates. In individual graves. After having seen the remnants of some of the bodies, I thought that was a pretty tall order. But it wasn't up to me. And I loved the fact that he wanted the people of Germany to see what they had let happen to their country, what they had let their country's leaders get away with.

I walked the first group, led by Sergeant Gordon and accompanied by a dozen other soldiers, up the hill. They were all men, and older men at that, since their younger counterparts had been out fighting. Their silence surprised me and once we got into the camp, they filed through expressionless, their bodies rigid, their eyes straight forward. Halfway through the tour, Sergeant Gordon stopped them and asked them point-blank how many had been aware of the torture and abuse taking place virtually under their noses. Naturally, no one admitted knowing about it. In fact, one man said, "*Herr* Himmler outlawed beatings three years ago."

I thought the sergeant would burst a blood vessel. He grabbed that man by the arm and dragged him to the whipping block, a waist-high square table, the top of which was covered with inch-wide slats that curved downward in the middle. The sergeant bent the man over it until his nose almost touched the dark stains. "Then what do you make of this?" the sergeant asked. "The man whose blood spilled on this torture device is lying face-down right outside this door. Dead.

The slashes still in his back where the whip cut him." He jerked the man up and threw him roughly back into the group. "There may have been a statement issued on paper," he screamed in the elderly man's face, "but it didn't translate to reality. So I don't give a damn what Himmler, or even Hitler himself, *wanted* you to believe. I'm showing you what actually happened."

He turned away from the group in disgust.

The next stop was the morgue, where one whole wall was lined with sharp hooks positioned at the junction of the wall and ceiling. One of the resistance prisoners explained to the townspeople that guards hung inmates from the hooks with piano wire around their necks until they died. "And this," he said, pointing to the heavy club hanging from one of the hooks, "was what the guards used to finish the job if the prisoner didn't die fast enough to suit them."

I forced myself not to look away. I studied the faces of the residents to gauge their reactions and saw grim masks. Some of *them* even looked away.

I was livid. I don't normally have a violent bone in my body, but at that moment, facing the indifference in front of me amid such torture, I wanted to grab that club and wield it myself. To let them experience the horror felt by the people who had died there.

I was thankful Simon wasn't one of the soldiers accompanying this apathetic group. I don't think the sergeant and I, together, could have stopped him if he decided to take out his Jewish-justified anger on the townspeople. I prayed fervently that the group he escorted included women who would have the good sense to cry. Or throw up. Or both.

We finished the tour and the men in our group continued their emotionless shuffle.

Sergeant Gordon headed back to the gate and the rest of us herded our charges behind him. We had cleared the gates, but we weren't even out of sight of the gallows, for God's sake, when one of the men in the middle of the group made a comment in German and several of those around him laughed. As one, the soldiers in my unit turned our rifles on them. The sergeant exploded.

"Fine," he screamed. "We obviously didn't do our jobs to give you a thorough enough tour. So we'll do it again. Turn around. And this time," he said marching up and down the rows of them, "we'll take it nice and slow. We'll give you plenty of time to see everything. To smell the corpses up close. To feel the wire in the morgue. To hold the club and imagine how it would have felt slamming into your head."

I shared Sergeant Gordon's anger. I wanted to scream at the Germans myself and beat them to the ground.

Which scared me. Could I have carried out the same kind of vigilante justice on these Germans that my lieutenant served on the officers in the Thuringian Forest?

But I knew the answer. I *wanted* to hurt them. I was angry enough to hurt them. But I *didn't* hurt them.

We turned the group around and re-entered the camp to spend double the time at each station. Sergeant Gordon did a spectacular job of getting their attention the second time through.

In the pathology lab, for example, he dragged a man with tattoos out of the group and forced him to touch the skins hanging there. He described his version of how he believed the skins got there. In meticulous detail. None of us soldiers had any idea of the process to skin a human. Didn't even want to think about it. Regardless, the sergeant held everyone's attention with his descriptions. He made it sound like skinning a deer. But a whole lot creepier. When he finished, he shoved the old man back into the ranks and smiled in satisfaction as the man threw up all over the shoes of those closest to him.

I accompanied several other groups that day and was satisfied they were properly sickened, even though they continued to maintain their ignorance of the torture being carried out within walking distance of their homes.

When all the groups had come through and gone back home, Sergeant Gordon told several of us that General Patton ordered the same kinds of tours for the people of Ohrdruf. The burgomaster of that town, Albert Schneider, who had steadfastly denied knowledge of the atrocities, failed to show up for the tour. General Patton sent a detail to get him.

The detail returned and reported to the general that they found the mayor and his wife in their living room.

Where they had hanged themselves.

CHAPTER
FORTY

GERDA

After returning to her home, Gerda threw herself into bakery chores. Bread had become the main product produced and the German military procured great quantities of it, sometimes demanding it for free, but most times paying enough to cover expenses. Gerda had seen first-hand, however, that the Germans no longer controlled the war's outcome so the days of the German military as their main buyer were numbered. The Allied armies moved closer to Zwickau every day and rumors ran rampant that the Russians closed in on Berlin.

With Gerda's absence, Ernst had taken over the deliveries, so Gerda used her extra time to strategize with her father. "Papa," she said to him one evening when the ovens had cooled, "we need to plan for the future. I don't believe Germany will win the war." He patted her hand in a dismissive gesture. "This is important, Papa. When Germany loses, our main buyer will be eliminated. We have to figure out what products the new world order will want."

"Now how do you propose we do that?" he asked her.

"By finding out what the Allied nations will buy," she said. "I've already thought about this." She leaned back in her chair. "As soon as the war is over, I am going to order newspapers from England, France and Russia. Maybe even America. Once we see what is advertised there, we can produce similar things here. And we should make more *Lebkuchen*. Now. Before the American Army arrives. I met some of those soldiers, Papa, and I believe they will buy it. But we'll need the decorative tins so they can take the treats home to their wives and girlfriends. We'll make signs. And put them in the windows." Her eyes danced.

"Gerda, my love," her father said. "Where did you get these big ideas? We're a small *bäckerei.*"

"It's time we grew, Papa. I have my daughter to think about now. And Ernst will get married one day and have children and the business must be large enough to support all of us."

Karla came into the room, carrying Etta. "Look who was awake," she said.

Otto reached for his granddaughter. "Come and see Papa," he said. The infant settled into his arms and he studied her face, his own face glowing. "Gerda, she is so beautiful," he said in a hushed voice. "She looks exactly like you did when you were born."

Gerda rose and stood behind her father. "You can get lost in that little face, can't you?" she asked. Her father nodded. "When you look at her," Gerda added, "it's hard to believe that only a few kilometers away, men are still killing each other."

"You must have seen a lot of that where you were," he said quietly.

Neither Karla nor Gerda had shared the full story of her life with Aldrik, and her imprisonment at the end. The German military presence in Zwickau was still too strong and Gerda didn't want her father or brother to do something stupid that might lead to their arrest. Already, the family broke the law by having Rebekah with them and although she remained hidden as much as possible, there was always a chance something could slip and they would be found out. Regardless of how weak the German Army had become, the Nazis were still in charge and the penalty for harboring a Jewish person was still harsh— imprisonment and, in some cases, execution.

Air raid sirens presented the greatest danger when everyone scrambled to one of the cellars. The *bäckerei* had its own cellar, but it was also the designated area for most of their neighbors, which included the Kaisers, the military family that had taken over Rebekah's house when her family was forced to evacuate. The Berghmanns worked it out that Rebekah would either go to the cellar early to hide, and risk being seen, or remain upstairs and risk being bombed. Neither alternative was a good one, but fortunately, most sirens ended as false alarms when Allied fighter planes passed the city on their way to other targets.

"Yes," she answered his question about the horrors she had witnessed. "And I've even seen it here, on the outskirts of town."

He frowned at her.

"Oh," Gerda said. "I guess you haven't seen the results of the bombing from the middle of March. The nineteenth, *Mutti* said."

He waved his hand in the air. "Right, right," he said. "So many air raid sirens. I lose track of when bombs actually fall. There were bombs last year, I remember. September, I think. Didn't do much damage to the city. None to us. But you're right, more bombs fell a couple of weeks ago. We didn't let Ernst make deliveries that day."

"From what I saw, the bombs fell in the suburbs, mostly that village of single-family homes at the edge of town. Many of those pretty little houses are nothing more than shells now. We even saw smoke still rising from some of them." She sighed. "I only hope the war ends before the Allies drop any more bombs on us."

As if on cue, air raid sirens wailed up and down the street. Etta's little eyes popped open and she added to the din. Gerda's father cuddled her to his chest and rocked her.

Rebekah appeared in the doorway, her eyes large, her face pale. Her left hand supported her drawn up right arm.

"Gerda," Karla said, "you go down with Rebekah and get her hidden. We'll bring Etta."

The young women dashed for the stairs and Gerda positioned her friend in a corner, covered her with a black drape, and then leaned the box that had held the new counter unit against the wall to conceal her. It fit perfectly. Gerda pushed a stack of boxes in front of one side of the carton and stationed an old coat rack, complete with coats, on the other.

"Are you okay?" Gerda whispered. "Can you breathe?"

"*Ja*," Rebekah whispered back.

Gerda moved chairs in place for her parents and went back upstairs to get supplies for Etta in case they had to stay longer than normal. She met Ernst on his way down.

"I didn't get to fix all of the blackout curtains," she said. "Will you take care of them?"

"Sure," he said. "But hurry back. I saw the Ungers and the Kaisers in the backyard," he said in a low voice. "They'll be here any minute. Everything okay here?"

"*Ja*," she answered. "Thanks."

Otto and Karla moved down the basement stairs, holding Etta, who continued to howl. "I'll be right down, *Mutti*," Gerda said. "I'm going to get a few things for her. And I'll feed her when I get back."

She gathered her things for the baby and opened the door for the families designated to join them. They all filed in, along with their children. Gerda was dismayed to see a puppy with one of the Unger children since it introduced a new element that hadn't been tested with Rebekah's hiding places.

"*Frau* Unger, *Frau* Kaiser," she said with a little curtsy. "How nice to see you again. My parents are already downstairs. Please join them. Pepin," she added, "new puppy?" He nodded, his face happy.

"Why Gerda," *Frau* Unger said to her, "*Frau* Kaiser told me you had come home."

Frau Kaiser patted Gerda's stomach. "And look at you," she said, "all thin again. Where is the baby? And that handsome husband of yours?"

"My daughter is with *Mutti*—downstairs. I need to feed her. And Pepin, please keep your puppy in your lap. Etta is a tiny baby and we don't want to spread germs to her."

The families, their children, and the new puppy followed Gerda to the basement where Ernst had fixed the curtains and set up the rest of the chairs. An old mattress hugged one of the walls, far away from Rebekah, and the children, including Pepin and his puppy, bounced onto it. Gerda caught Ernst's eye and gave a quick nod toward the small dog. It wouldn't do for the animal to roam the basement and tug on the carton that hid her friend.

She moved her chair in front of the carton where Rebekah stood, invisible to the rest of the group. Then she covered her shoulder with a light blanket and let her daughter nurse, keeping a sharp eye on the puppy the whole time.

"So," *Frau* Unger said to Gerda while she searched the basement. "I didn't hear your answer before. Is your husband with you?"

A small silence filled the room and Karla studied her shoes. Otto cleared his throat. "What?" *Frau* Unger said. "What did I say?"

"My husband was killed," Gerda told her neighbor. "Last week. In a battle in the Thuringian Forest."

Frau Unger uttered a choking sound. "Oh no. I am so sorry. Is there a service scheduled?"

Gerda shook her head. "I'm not even certain his body was recovered," she said. Her voice broke. "I'm sorry," she added. "I'm still having trouble talking about it."

"Oh, you poor thing," *Frau* Kaiser said. "He seemed like such a nice boy too. This terrible war," she added. "Will it never end?"

"I hear the Americans are really close," *Herr* Kaiser said. "One of the clerks who worked at Ohrdruf said that pompous ass, Patton, ordered everybody in town to visit some prisoner of war complex close by. But the mayor showed him who was boss. He refused to go. Who does that Patton think he is, anyway?"

"Gerda has a lot of big ideas about how we can expand the *bäckerei*," Otto said to the group. "She thinks the war will be over soon."

"Maybe," *Herr* Kaiser said. "But I don't think the *Führer* will give up that quickly. Not as long as we still have the problem with the dirty Jews."

"The problem with—?" Gerda began.

"Gerda," Karla interrupted her. "Does Etta need to burp? Has she finished eating?"

Gerda moved the baby to her shoulder and patted Etta's back.

"Pepin," Ernst said, "where did you get your puppy? He sure is a cute little thing."

The others picked up previous conversations and filled the room with chatter. The subject of Jews didn't come up again, but internally,

Gerda seethed. The ignorance and blind obedience of her neighbors to the party line struck her as almost criminal and she would have liked nothing better than to tell how Rebekah and Frieda had aided in freeing so many children from almost certain death. But that would have meant incriminating herself, as well. Her mother had been right to change the subject.

She continued to pat her baby's back, no longer even attempting to take part in the ongoing conversation. Without warning, the "all clear" sounded, loud and jarring, and everyone jumped. The puppy yelped and shot out of Pepin's arms, making a beeline for Gerda's chair.

"Pepin! Your puppy," she said urgently. "Ernst," she added, turning to her brother, "will you get the dog away from here?"

Gerda shot out of her chair in an effort to keep Rebekah from being discovered and the blanket fell from her shoulder, leaving her breast exposed. The children stared and Ernst almost knocked into her on his way to retrieve the puppy. But the dog had already reached the corner where Rebekah hid and tugged on one of the coats. The rack and the rest of the coats toppled to the floor with a crash and the puppy dug in his heels and barked at it. All of which scared Etta, her wails adding to the din and echoing in every corner of the basement. Pepin came running and he and Ernst bumped heads as they both tried to reach the small dog. The carton hiding Rebekah skewed away from the wall.

"Why don't we all go up for pastries?" Gerda's mother said and physically ushered the families back up the stairs to the *bäckerei*. "Pepin and Ernst can join us when they get the dog under control." They filed up the stairs.

"Here you go, Pepin," Ernst said. He held the squirming puppy out to the boy. "You should probably take him outside to go to the bathroom after all the excitement he's had."

But Pepin stared at the corner and Gerda did the same, her heart in her throat. To her horror, Rebekah's shoes stuck out from beneath the black drape.

"Who's that?" Pepin asked.

Ernst shoved the carton back so it snugged up to the wall again and said. "Oh, it's only an extra pair of Gerda's shoes that she doesn't wear anymore. Her feet got too big when she was pregnant." He turned toward her and grinned.

"Oh, go on with you," she said, forcing a smile. "My feet are getting back to normal and I'll wear those shoes again any day now."

"Do you want me to take them upstairs for you?" Pepin asked.

"*Nein*," Gerda said quickly. "I'll get them later. You'd better hurry," she added. "You're going to miss the pastry."

Pepin shrugged, took the wriggling puppy from Ernst and bounded up the stairs.

"Whew," Ernst said. "That was close." He tapped on the carton. "You okay in there?"

"*Ja*," Rebekah said in a small voice. "But I think I'll stay in the attic next time. Bombs or not."

"I'll let you know when they're gone," Gerda said to the carton. "Oh, *Gott*," she added, "this war can't end soon enough to suit me. I wish the Americans would hurry up and get here so we can surrender. Having them here can't be any worse than this."

In only a few short days, those words would come back to haunt her.

CHAPTER
FORTY-ONE

SAM

Regardless of our sickening encounters from the previous few days, taking orders from Sergeant Gordon instead of Lieutenant Scott had been a welcome change. Once the lieutenant's group joined us at Buchenwald, however, our unit once again fell victim to the constant tension his style of bullying created. I was glad he hadn't been present for the birth of the German woman's baby. Or the townspeople's tours of the camp from nearby Weimar. Heaven knows what he might have done in those situations. But it wouldn't have been good, I was certain of that.

On April 14, he called us together and told us we had orders to move out, toward the Zwick-Mulde River. From finding the concentration camps abandoned, many of us had lulled ourselves into believing the German Army was ready to surrender everywhere. But the fighting during the next couple of days proved otherwise.

We left Buchenwald and the town of Weimar and moved at a rapid pace toward a bridgehead across our target river. More than twenty small towns separated us from our objective and we cleared each of them of enemy forces as we advanced. The closer we got to the river, the stiffer the fighting became and we faced our strongest resistance at the heights overlooking the small town of Greiz. There, we were met by hundreds of German troops—a combination, we found out later, of the final remnants of the German fighting force, including their national Army, the *Volkssturm*, and *Wehrmacht*, with soldiers from all branches of German military. Stirred up by the SS to make a valiant last stand, the rag-tag group met us with panzer and machine gun fire from a network of trenches. They fought with everything they had. But so did we. For twenty-four hours, we fought grimly to take out the eighty-eight millimeter artillery guns that kept us from reaching our goal. We dug in and inched our way forward, closing in on the outskirts of Reichenbach, weakened by air bombardment.

"We got these damned Germans now," Lieutenant Scott sneered during a break in the shooting. "Sergeant Noonan, grab a platoon and station your men behind these buildings," he said, pointing to the ones behind the main square. "Sergeant Gordon, you take a platoon and march right into the main street. Once you get there, those yellow-bellies will scramble out the back door and we'll be there to shoot them where they stand. It's time to show these Krauts who's in charge."

Dickie and I exchanged a long look. Sergeant Gordon's middle-of-town mission looked like a suicide march to us.

"Lieutenant," the scout Perry said, "our intelligence says there are still a number of units entrenched in this town. They'll have the advantage if we enter via the main street. It might be better if each platoon attacked from the rear and met in the middle."

I thought the lieutenant was going to strike him. He pulled himself up and I swear, I could almost see smoke coming from his ears.

"Are you questioning my orders?" he screamed in the man's face. "I think that makes you a coward. How dare you talk to me like that in front of my men? Well guess what, mister? You'll be leading the group down the main street."

Perry opened his mouth to say more and then closed it again. Right in front of my eyes, his face turned ashen. As if he were already dead. He turned on his heel and fell in with Sergeant Gordon's group.

Sergeant Noonan picked my team to go with him and while I was relieved, I felt a lot of guilt. I honestly believed the lieutenant had sent those men to pointless deaths. The German forces were weakened, so if we'd taken them by stealth, we could have suffered very few casualties. But flaunting ourselves in their faces begged for trouble.

My squad and I followed Sergeant Noonan through a little park with plenty of tree cover and secured positions behind the main street's buildings. Sergeant Gordon, with Perry beside him, marched into town.

We couldn't see the battle from our positions, but we heard the burp guns fire almost immediately and this time, we knew those guns weren't ours. Dickie and I crept closer and moved around the building on the end closest to our former position. He pointed up to the gun's barrel, visible from a fourth-floor window. I caught Sergeant Noonan's eye and indicated that we planned to go in and take the shooter out. When he nodded, Dickie and I belly crawled to the back door and covered each other through the first three floors.

A guard was posted at the bottom of the stairs leading to the fourth floor. I couldn't believe how young he was and figured he must be part of the Hitler Youth we had heard so much about. The poor little guy was ill-equipped and his face contorted with fear. Dickie dug in his knapsack and pulled out a little tin of potted meat, then skittered it across the floor to a spot away from us. The boy whirled toward the sound and I came up behind him, my rifle square in his back.

"Lower your weapon, son," I said quietly. When he did, Dickie grabbed it from him. I took his sidearm and tucked it into my waist. Dickie bound his hands behind him with a piece of twine he found in his pack and I removed the slender youth's belt and secured him to the banister with it. We used his own kerchief as a gag.

"You watch him," I said. "I'll go."

He nodded and I crept up the stairs, hoping to avoid any creaking boards. But shots erupted from the burp gun nonstop, so there was little chance for the shooter to hear me. I flattened myself outside the door but had a good view of the room's interior and was dismayed to see there were actually two shooters. One of the men pulled his weapon back and I saw he needed to reload. I shot and he fell. The other shooter whirled toward me and I ducked behind the door. I stuck my gun out, aimed where I had last seen him and pulled the trigger.

Nothing happened.

My gun jammed.

That had never happened before and I couldn't believe it. My gun stopped working. Right when I needed it most.

Another pull of the trigger yielded the same result. But by then, the shooter was on the move. His reflection in the window moved toward me, then hesitated on the other side of the door.

In less time than it took to take a breath, he threw himself into the hallway, his gun pointed at my chest.

Time slowed and every detail stood out, exaggerated, as if in a dream. Light brown stubble covered his cheeks and the space above his lips. Which greeted me in a snarl. Drops of sweat beaded on his forehead before trickling past his thick brows on their way to his eyes.

His finger closed on the trigger and I knew I was going to die.

With a last ditch "What the hell do I have to lose?" thought, I whipped the German youth's handgun from my waist, pointed and pulled the trigger.

The blast deafened me and blood splattered from the German's neck to cover my arm with poker-hot pain. Before he fell, I watched his sneer transform to shock and he stumbled backward and crashed to the floor. For a moment, quiet surrounded me.

Then footsteps pounded the stairs behind me. Ignoring them, I ran to the window to check on Sergeant Gordon's group. Shots continued to ring out and some of our soldiers crouched behind benches and trees. But at least a dozen of them lay in the street, face down. Sergeant Gordon was one of them. Perry was another.

Dammit all to hell.

"My God," Dickie said at my shoulder. "I knew that would happen."

"So did they."

"Sam, you're bleeding."

"What?" I checked my arm. It hadn't been the German's blood that hit me, but my own trickling down my arm. The German must have pulled the trigger as he fell back. "It's nothing," I said. "We need to help those guys."

"Right," Dickie said. "Look, let's go back to Sergeant Noonan, let him bandage you up and tell him what's happened. I'll see if a couple of the other fellas can come with me to move to the next building."

We descended to the third floor and found the boy we had bound in tears. I couldn't help but feel sorry for him. When he was recruited to be part of Hitler's glory, I'm sure no one ever explained the ugliness of battle to him. He wasn't much older than my sister, Sarah, and I couldn't imagine her in a situation like this. We made certain he was still secure and left the building to join the rest of the platoon. Sergeant Noonan sent Simon and one other fellow, Taylor, with Dickie and then took a look at my arm. "You're lucky," he said, "the bullet cut through your flesh but kept on going, nothing we have to dig out. It's gonna hurt like hell for a while, though." He patched me up with sulfa and a bandage. While he worked, I told him about Sergeant Gordon and Perry. He shook his head.

"They didn't have to die," he said. "I can't believe the lieutenant let his ego put his men in danger like that." He stopped talking and looked me in the eye. "We never had this conversation, Ryan," he added. "I really don't want to face court-martial this close to the end of the war."

"Sure, Sarge," I said. "I understand." I hesitated, then made up my mind. "But since we're not having this conversation anyway," I continued, "isn't there someone we can talk to about this? Someone in authority who could keep him from doing this same kind of thing in the future?"

"Who would that be, Ryan? Would you go to General Patton? Who got into trouble, himself, for hitting a soldier and calling him a coward? Or maybe you'd rather talk to General Eisenhower, who sent thousands of soldiers to their deaths on the beaches of Normandy. Of course, you could always go to President Roosevelt himself, who pulled the 'imminent attack alert' from the Pearl Harbor Base, resulting in the deaths of thousands of sailors when the Japanese dropped their bombs. It's the way of war. Mission before men. And enlisted men are expendable. It's unfortunate, but that's the way it is." He finished bandaging my arm and then looked me in the eyes again. "Look, I don't agree with his methods, either. But we have no way of knowing whether he has information we don't know about that influences his decisions. And the bottom line is, he's in charge. He gives the orders. And we have to follow. Or get court-martialed. And that's not something I want to volunteer for. How about you?"

"No sir," I answered. I appreciated his words. I'd always known we were considered expendable when it came to war. I guess people with all that responsibility had to look at it like that. To weigh the cost against the benefit. But from where I sat, I still considered my life, and the lives of those around me, important. And not expendable.

But I didn't get to decide.

I pushed my negative thoughts away and joined my group to scatter through the buildings facing the main street. In short order, we routed the rest of the Germans. They were mostly boys, anyway, like the one Dickie and I found. They had plenty of passion, but little of the wisdom of war, so they exposed themselves too easily and gave up without much of a fight.

Which suited us fine. We were certainly tired of fighting and hated the thought of killing boys. We marched them out into the street and swelled the number of prisoners we had taken by another four hundred. Then we helped gather up our dead from the street and met Lieutenant Scott on his way into town. I was so angry, I didn't dare look at him for fear my face would give my thoughts away. If he'd been a mind reader, he'd have shot me on the spot for what I was thinking.

By dusk, the town of Reichenbach, the last holdout between us and Zwickau, was ours.

We spread our sleeping bags in the cleared-out buildings to grab a few hours' sleep before starting our push toward what we hoped would be our last engagement in the European Theater Operation.

CHAPTER
FORTY-TWO

GERDA

Gerda nursed Etta while she sat with Rebekah in companionable silence at the kitchen table. Since returning to her old neighborhood, Rebekah spent a little time in the Berghmann family living quarters above the bakery, but most of her time in one of the bedrooms on an upper floor.

She rose and retrieved the coffee pot with her good arm, then divided the last of its contents into the two cups in front of her.

"Thanks," Gerda said. "But you don't have to wait on me, you know."

Rebekah smiled at her. "It's the least I can do while you're nursing Etta."

Gerda sipped her coffee and made a face. "Ugh," she said. "That's probably the one thing I miss about Buchenwald, the robust coffee. Mutti told me the supply was gone when she presented her ration card earlier. I can't believe how weak this is."

Rebekah threw back her head and laughed until tears streamed from her eyes.

"What?" Gerda asked. "What did I say?"

"That you thought the coffee was weak. It shows you the difference in our perspectives. I had just finished thinking how good it was, compared to what I was used to at Ohrdruf."

"Oh, Bekah," Gerda said, covering her friend's good hand with her own, "I'm sorry. That was so insensitive of me."

"It's not a problem," Rebekah said. She wiped her eyes and smiled at her friend. "I'm simply happy to be away from there. And grateful to be with you again. In fact," she added, "I'm going to see if I can help out with the ovens today. I don't think you should be standing that long yet."

Otto and Karla had been busy with the ovens for the past two hours. Their workload had increased, not only from the supply demanded by the military, but also from the fact that most people still had ration tickets for bread. The whole family worked to fulfill the extra orders.

A rumble sounded in the distance.

"Did you hear that?" Gerda asked.

"I heard it all night," Rebekah said. "Sounds like constant thunder rumbling."

"*Herr* Kaiser told *Mutti* earlier this morning that the Americans are awfully close. Reichenbach, he said." She sighed. "I know we're not supposed to hope our country loses the war, and I wouldn't even tell my parents this, but honestly, I only want it to end. Maybe then we can get on with our lives."

"Maybe," Rebekah said. "The Americans don't seem to have a problem with Jews. Of course if another country gets control of Zwickau, well, it's anybody's guess." She put her cup in the sink then returned to her chair. She rested her chin on her fist. "You know what, Gerda? Once the war is over, I might leave Germany. Go to America. Start over. There's nothing left for me here."

"Except me," Gerda said. "And my family." She placed her hand over that of her friend. "Let's see how things go before you make any decisions. The war still has to end first."

The bell from the bakery's front door tinkled the first few notes of *Edelweiss* and Rebekah ran for the stairs and her hiding space in the attic. Gerda added her cup to the sink and listened to see if one of her parents went to the bakery counter. But within seconds, the door to the upstairs living quarters opened and Ernst breezed in.

"Oh," Gerda said, "it's you. Finished with your deliveries so early?"

Ernst didn't answer and Gerda turned to look at him. He was distracted and paced the kitchen, picking things up and putting them down again.

"What's going on?" she asked.

"Hm? Oh, nothing."

"Yeah, right," she said. "I've known you all your life and I can tell, you've been up to something. What is it? Oh my goodness, please tell me you haven't done anything that will bring the Gestapo here."

"I hope not," he said.

"What? Ernst, *mein Gott*, tell me. Please."

"You can't tell *Mutti* and Papa." He put his hand on her arm, his eyes intense.

"Oh dear. What?"

"The Americans are close," he said.

"*Ja.* What about it?"

"With all the bombing going on and the airplanes flying right over us, and the American Army so close, we thought..."

"What? And who's 'we'?"

"That doesn't matter," he grinned. "I don't want you to have to testify about anybody but me if we get caught."

Gerda sat down hard, Etta at her shoulder. Alarm filled her face.

"Several of us climbed the tower of the *Marienkirche* and hung a white flag from the highest part of it. We hoped the planes would see it as they flew past and that it would be the first thing the Americans see when they get here."

"*Mein Gott*," Gerda said again, her eyes wide. "Ernst! What were you thinking? That's treason. An executable crime. Are you sure no one saw you?"

"As sure as I can be," he answered. "The interior is closed today, so we went in through the basement. That entrance is hidden. And we—"

Air raid sirens drowned out his next words and the two of them scrambled. Ernst went to find his parents and get the basement ready and Gerda climbed the stairs to the attic.

"Rebekah," she whispered. "Will you stay here or come down to the basement?"

"I'll stay," she said. "I'll get under my mattress. Don't worry. I'll be fine."

Gerda gathered a few things for Etta, but before she made it down to the basement, the drone of planes flying low overhead reached her ears. She hoped Ernst was right and that the pilots would see the white flag flying from the thousand-year-old cathedral's Gothic tower, but she also hoped no one in the neighborhood found out who put it there.

CHAPTER
FORTY-THREE

SAM

The date was April 17. I remember that clearly because it would have been my mother's birthday. Her fortieth. She had loved celebrating her birthday because we always made a big deal of it. Kathleen would arrange to have a beautiful cake from Mrs. Wainwright and the rest of us would work together to prepare a special dinner for her. Mother always did that for us too. Although four of us had birthdays close together—Richard and Kathleen first and then Freddie and me two days later. So she would often do a large, combined birthday dinner and invite all our friends.

I loved the memories of those gatherings.

That day, however, there was no time to dwell on them as we prepared for our march into Zwickau, some three or so hours east. I had done my best to avoid being around Lieutenant Scott after his ridiculous orders in Reichenbach that cost so many lives, but I couldn't escape the early muster where we received our final orders before starting our journey. A couple of the recon units, along with artillery, had already double-timed into the heart of Zwickau to seize the bridges over the Zwick-Mulde River, led by two British paratroopers who knew the bridges had been mined for demolition. Their goal was to disarm the mines so we could come behind and clear the town of enemy troops.

The lieutenant was quiet that morning, but I feared it was only temporary.

By the time we reached the city, we marched straight through to the riverbanks and routed the enemy out of their hiding places along the way. We captured more than seventeen hundred German troops and freed close to five thousand Allied prisoners in temporary prison camps close to the city, five hundred of whom were Americans.

I was surprised at the reaction of the German civilians as we marched into town. For one thing, white flags flew throughout the main street in Zwickau, including from the top of the highest church steeple. Other flags flew from second and third-story windows, with children sitting beside or under them, smiling and waving. I don't know who started it, but we waved back, then threw candy bars to them.

By then, dusk had settled and a small unit of us conducted the last few house-to-house searches on one of the side streets off the main square. We had worked our way through several houses when Lieutenant Scott caught up with us.

"We need to secure our billet for the night," he said. Simply hearing his pompous, cocky voice confirmed I'd been right to stay away from him.

"We thought we would finish with these house checks first, Lieutenant," Sergeant Noonan said, "and then go to one of the buildings in the square. Or to a church."

The lieutenant fixed him with a venomous stare and jutted his nose to within centimeters of the sergeant's.

"We will do it now and we will do it here." He left no room for argument.

He shoved past our group and entered the building in front of us. A little bell attached to the door played the first few notes of a German melody I'd heard before but couldn't quite place. He marched up to the elderly gentleman standing behind the counter and said *"Achtung!* Attention! American soldiers will quarter here tonight and for the duration of the time we stay in Zwickau. Move out immediately! *Raus Mit!* Out! Out! Out!"

We had been briefed on the rules of engagement and protocol dictated that the commanding officer, in our case, the lieutenant, would meet with the mayor, or burgomaster, and give him thirty to sixty minutes to clear everyone out of commercial buildings where we would bunk. That's what our first lieutenant had done.

The eyes of the man behind the counter grew large. "Sir," he said in perfect English, "this building is not only my business, but also my home. I don't believe we are to be forced to leave when there are other buildings available for your use."

He was right. The rules of the Geneva Convention stated we were never to throw German citizens out of their own homes. Unless there was no alternative. Unfortunately, it happened a lot.

By this time, the lieutenant had sauntered over to the shelf that housed bottle after bottle of brandy, complete with a pear in the bottom of it. He picked up a bottle, and with his field knife, popped the wax closing from around it, then took a swallow. He stood for a long time with his back to the owner and silence filled the room. After a minute, he whirled around, his arm at shoulder height, his pistol pointed at the man's head.

"Are you really going to argue with me?" the lieutenant asked.

Those of us with him took a step back.

Slowly, the man raised his arms and a woman joined him from one of the back rooms. "Otto, what is—?" She stopped talking and uttered a sharp gasp.

He said something to her in German and the lieutenant took two menacing steps toward them. "When you speak in our presence, you will speak English!"

The man behind the counter closed his eyes, swallowed hard and said, "These soldiers want to stay in our home for a while."

The woman hadn't moved, but I was certain she recognized us as we did her. I caught her eye and gave her a slight shake of my head. There was no way to tell what the lieutenant's reaction might be if he knew we had helped deliver her grandchild.

"Of course," she said smoothly. "The rest of the family is upstairs. I'll get them."

"No," the lieutenant said, holding his gun steady. He took another long swallow, his eyes never leaving them. "You will leave. *We* will tell the rest of the people here to follow you."

"Our ovens are still on," the man said. "If we don't turn them off, the bread will burn and a fire could start."

"Fine," the lieutenant said. "Ryan, go with him to make certain he doesn't come back with a weapon."

My feet dragged as if weighted with concrete. I couldn't fathom what the lieutenant was thinking. That kind of behavior was not only wrong, it was also unnecessary. There were plenty of other places for us to stay. I followed the man through the room behind the counter and on to a smaller room that was hot as hell but smelled like heaven. The man turned dials on the huge ovens and then turned back to me. He shook his head and his face held a look of disgust. I couldn't argue with him. I felt the same way.

My mother always taught me never to hate anyone. But I hated Lieutenant Scott.

The man with me went back into the shop part of the bakery and the lieutenant told him again to leave. We were ordered upstairs to remove the rest of the family.

I reached the top of the stairs first, and as I expected, the woman whose baby we had helped deliver stood there, the baby against her chest, her eyes wide. A pot of something that smelled like stew bubbled on the stove behind her.

I mouthed the words "I'm sorry," but almost immediately, the lieutenant brushed past me. "*Raus mit!* We're taking over your house for our quarters. You must leave immediately."

She nodded and turned to one of the back rooms.

"Halt," the lieutenant shouted. "I said 'out.' Where do you think you're going?"

"To get a blanket and diapers for my baby," she answered.

"Oh hell no," he said. "I could kill that little son-of-a-bitch with my bare hands. And I will if you don't leave immediately. Now. Go!"

Gerda drew in her breath sharply and I saw Sergeant Noonan's eyes bulge. All I could think about was how hard he had worked to keep that baby alive. And our lieutenant was talking about killing it.

I'd never personally known anyone other than Lieutenant Scott who went to military officer's school, but I would have bet my life on the fact that the way he acted around the enemy was not the way he'd been taught there.

A teenager came into the room from another part of the house and his eyes widened when he saw us.

"You," the lieutenant told him, waving the pistol at him, "leave the premises. Immediately. You really don't want to make me mad right now."

The woman and boy headed to the same stairs we had used to enter the family quarters.

"Is anybody else here?" the lieutenant asked.

"*Nein,*" Gerda said, shaking her head.

"In English, you swine bitch," the lieutenant screamed.

I could actually imagine my fingers closing around his throat and shutting his damned mouth forever. But I knew better. Yes, it was bad for the Germans to be thrown out of their home without being allowed to take anything with them. But I honestly believed that if one of us tried to interfere, he would as soon have shot us as look at us. And then figured out a way to blame it on the Germans.

"No," she said without looking at him, "no one else is here." She brushed past me and I could tell the baby needed a change of diapers, although she hadn't been allowed to get one. The teenager followed her. Neither spoke another word.

"Ryan, Levy, you two search the upstairs," the lieutenant barked. He took another big drink from the brandy bottle. "The rest of us will search every room on this floor."

Simon and I climbed the stairs and looked in every bedroom there, in wardrobes, under beds, and behind drapes. But didn't find anyone else. I was really glad. I was afraid it would have gone badly for Gerda and her family if she'd been lying.

"What about this?" Simon asked, pointing to a small door. He opened it to reveal another set of stairs. We assumed they led to an attic.

"I guess we'd better look," I said. "It would go badly for us if a

German soldier was hiding up there and snuck down in the middle of the night and killed us."

"Unless we could convince him to only take out the lieutenant," he whispered. I stifled a laugh.

We crept up the attic stairs and let our eyes adjust to the dark. We poked around behind a few things and Simon put a foot on an old mattress to look behind a cupboard beside it. A grunt sounded from under the mattress. I drew my weapon and held it steady while Simon slowly pulled the mattress up. Something moved under it and he reached down and hauled a woman up by her arm. We both recognized her. Rebekah. Our guide from Ohrdruf to Buchenwald.

I put my finger to my lips. We had heard it was a criminal offense for German families to harbor Jewish people. If we made her leave, not only would that be bad for her, since she had nowhere to go, but the family she was with would also be arrested.

I made a motion to Simon to let her stay and he agreed. We would simply say we hadn't found anyone. We did ask her if anyone else was there, although it didn't make sense that she would be a party to hiding a German soldier since she had spent years trying to escape them. We whispered to her to make no noise and left her there.

A small thing, I remember thinking, one little kindness for another human being. But the fact that we had defied the lieutenant's ridiculous orders made me feel slightly better.

OUR STAY IN THE BAKERY STRETCHED INTO ALMOST A week. We left the house for daily details and occasionally ran into one of the Berghmanns. But we always let them know with a gesture or two that it was unsafe for them to come back home.

Our lieutenant had gone through several bottles of the pear brandy and after several days, some of our company joined him. We had enough food, with what the family already had stored and the bread from the ovens, which was slightly undercooked, but better than anything we had eaten in a long, long time.

Simon and I didn't tell another soul about Rebekah in the attic. Not even Dickie. We didn't want to take any chances. We chose the bedrooms closest to the attic door, so every night after the lieutenant drank himself to sleep, we snuck food up to her and emptied her chamber pot.

The second night we were there, we found diapers and when the lieutenant went out for an officers' meeting, we took them, along with blankets and baby clothes to the house we had seen the mother return to.

"Ma'am," I said to Karla as I handed her the baby's things. "I'm really sorry about your house. But we've been with this lieutenant for quite a while now and we know him. He wouldn't have any qualms about shooting us if we got in his way. I hope you understand that we're not all like him."

"*Ja*," she said. "I do. And we're not all like *Herr* Hitler."

Because so many of us had been involved in the delivery of Karla's grandchild, we kept the rest of the soldiers from breaking stuff or messing up the house as much as some of the ones I had seen in the vicinity.

At the end of that week, Lieutenant Scott's superior came to Zwickau and ordered the troops to leave the town and bivouac at a camp on the outskirts of the city. Lieutenant Scott was nowhere to be found. The Berghmann family returned home, but before we left the bakery, I found Karla standing in the shop with her hands on her hips. She pointed to a wall of empty shelves and then shook her head in disgust. Brandy had filled more than half of them when we arrived. Apparently Lieutenant Scott had carted off all the remaining bottles. I couldn't imagine where he would even store them.

"*Arschloch*," she said in a quiet voice.

"What does that mean?" I asked.

"I believe you Americans say 'asshole.'"

Dickie and Simon came up behind me and heard our exchange. We all looked at each other and burst out laughing. That description fit him perfectly.

THE END OF APRIL BROUGHT US NEWSPAPERS THAT HADN'T found us in the thick of the fighting. What we saw in them shocked us.

For one thing, Franklin Roosevelt had died in office and his vice-president, Harry Truman, replaced him. I wasn't sure what it would mean to the end of the war, but I hoped a change in leadership might speed it up.

Then the real shocker reached us. On April 28, Benito Mussolini, former dictator of Italy and part of the Axis powers, was shot while trying to escape to Switzerland with his mistress.

Four days later, Sergeant Noonan came rushing into camp carrying an issue of our military newspaper, *Stars and Stripes*, that had been printed on a confiscated Zwickau press. The headlines covered half the front page and read "Hitler Dead." We all stood there and cheered. The article said Hitler and several of his highest officers, along with their wives and families, had committed suicide on April 30 in the Berlin bunker where he'd been living for weeks.

With two of the three Axis leaders gone, we believed it would be a matter of weeks until the whole thing was finished and we could go home.

Only five days after we received the news about Hitler, however, Germany signed an unconditional surrender at the Allied Headquarters in Reims, France. The news spread through the ranks like a hurricane. The cease-fire was called on May 7, 1945, at 2:41 PM German time with the Germans surrendering to Russia the following day. We rejoiced when we heard that official peacetime in Europe was set to begin at one minute after midnight on the morning of May 9, 1945.

In the early evening of May 8, 1945, we made our way into town and found the square filled with people.

Several of us found the Berghmann family in the square and apologized one more time for our lieutenant's behavior. Then we thanked them again for the use of their home.

Our company camped in town overnight and we celebrated into the early hours.

May 9 dawned bright and beautiful and we filled the large square in Zwickau—Americans and Germans alike—as jubilant friends.

CHAPTER
FORTY-FOUR

SUZANNE
2015

May 9 dawned bright and beautiful and we filled the large square in Zwickau—Americans and Germans alike—as jubilant friends.

A street bazaar greeted us, displaying wares from the shops that lined the perimeter of the marketplace and some of those from the side streets as well. Bright-colored umbrellas bloomed over each vendor's cart and I was reminded of the flower bulbs Dad and I had planted in the fall as our tribute to Mother. It included all her favorite spring flowers, yellow daffodils, red tulips, purple crocus, and pink hyacinths. They blossomed in a profusion of colors, like those umbrellas in the Zwickau square.

I found Dad, already seated at one of the long tables set up for the celebration that filled the center of the square. The tables, covered in bright fabric, reflected every color of the rainbow, similar to the umbrellas. I don't believe he planned it, but the blue of Dad's shirt perfectly complemented the tablecloth in front of him and the shine of sun smiling on his crisp white hair completed the scene perfectly. I fished out my phone, balanced the coffee tray I carried in one hand, and snapped a picture.

Simon Levy filled the chair beside him and Erwin Davis sat across from them. I set my tray down at the vacant chair next to Erwin and couldn't keep my feet from moving to the sound of the traditional German folk music.

Another man joined our table. "Sarge," the former soldiers said in unison.

He took the chair next to mine and I learned that his name was Randolph Noonan. He was alone but told us his wife would join him that afternoon for the evening presentation.

"You're right, Old Man," Simon said to my dad, continuing an earlier conversation. "I remember how I felt when we reached the edge of town with all those white flags flying. Especially after the battle a few miles east of here where the Germans threw everything they had at us."

"I'll never forget that either," Erwin said. "My brother fired several bazooka shots during that battle. Landed perfectly in the middle of the soldiers holed up on the other side of that house where the sniper was. He always said it was his most perfect shot of the war."

Dickie Dickinson, accompanied by his grandson, Adam, limped up next to the chair beside Dad and leaned heavily on his cane. "What I remember most vividly," Dickie said, jumping right into the conversation, "was subduing that boy at the bottom of the stairs in the house with the sniper. Remember, Sam? That poor child was scared to death. And rightfully so. I'm sure he'd been taught that dying for your country was a valiant and noble thing to do." He took a quick sip of the coffee I set in front of him and added, "I hope he made it through the rest of the war okay."

"Have you ever noticed," Dad said, "that no matter who you ask, any soldier who fought in the European Theater could tell you his exact location and what he was doing the very minute he received the news that the war in Europe had ended?"

"Yes, I have noticed that," Dickie answered. "As a matter of fact, we were sitting in the camp mess tent when a sergeant from one of the airborne divisions came to tell us. Remember?"

"Yeah," Erwin said. "What a great day that was."

"By the way, Sam," Dickie said, "guess who I ran into?"

Dad looked up at him expectantly.

"That fighter plane pilot we rescued from the Germans. Mike

Spencer. Remember him? I told him where our table was. He'll probably come by."

"Oh yeah," Dad said. "His plane was shot all to hell. Bullet holes everywhere."

"What I remember," Erwin said with a wicked smile, "was the way Simon and Eddie never had any trouble finding women who wanted company." They all laughed.

It had been like that the entire week. Soulful remembrances when we reached the field where their young friend, Eddie, was killed and good-natured ribbing everywhere else.

"Hey," Simon said. "Don't say things like that around my son. He thinks I'm perfect."

As if on cue, Simon's son, Liam, arrived with a variety of pastries. Dad's head shot up.

"Where did those come from?" he asked with a sharpness to his tone I didn't often hear.

"Over there," Liam pointed vaguely. "From some bakery cart."

My father's physical self remained at the table with us, occupying the seat across from me, but his eyes glazed and his mind left us.

"What, Dad? What is it?"

"I wonder if..." He closed the top on the pastry box and said, "I thought so. It had to be. Berghmann's. That's the only place on earth where you can find that combination of exotic smells." He stopped sniffing and looked around the table. "Anybody ever hear what happened to him?"

"You mean Lieutenant *Arschloch*?" Simon asked.

"I had to stick around after you guys left," Sergeant Noonan said. "I can't believe I never told you. You knew he was sent to the Pacific, right?" At the nods, he continued. "Well, he was captured by the Japanese almost right away. And shot on the spot."

"Serves him right," Simon said. "What goes around, comes around."

"So God does serve justice," Dad said. "He was one of the worst excuses for a human being I've ever had the misfortune to meet." They all agreed. "But I have thought, over the years, about what

General Patton said to the people in the towns near the concentration camps—that they must surely have known what was going on but didn't do anything to stop it. I feel like we were as guilty when it came to Lieutenant Asshole. We knew he didn't follow the rules of war and yet we didn't stop him."

"He would have shot us, too," Dickie said quietly. "Or court-martialed us at the very least."

"Yeah," Simon added. "And the same thing would have happened to anyone in the towns close to one of the camps. The SS would have snapped them up in nothing flat and thrown them in prison for disagreeing. I guess Patton didn't understand that."

"We all did what we had to do at the time to survive," Sarge said. "Right or wrong. I think that's what the people in towns close to the camps did as well. Things are different during war. Especially when one person has the power of life and death over others."

"Hey," Erwin said. "We're here for a celebration. Let's let Lieutenant *Arschloch* rest in peace—or purgatory, wherever he ended up—and celebrate what we came here to celebrate."

"Right," Dad said. "So, Berghmann's is still in business. We have to go see them."

"I hadn't put it together before," I said. "Isn't that the name on Mom's memory tin?"

"That's right, Suzie," Dad said. "I gave her that tin filled with cookies from Berghmann's when I returned from the war. Where was their cart, Liam?"

He pointed and we all turned.

"Recognize anybody?" Simon asked.

"Not there," Dad said, "but they're probably third or fourth generation." He stood, leaning on his cane until he found solid footing, then started walking, tapping his cane on the brick surface of the marketplace with each step. "I'm going to find the shop. Who wants to come?"

Sarge and I followed him across the square. He stopped a time or two to get his bearings and then headed for a side street off one of the corners. A bright-colored awning, along with matching umbrellas over outside tables welcomed us and I was enchanted. I could easily see why Dad wanted to return. He pushed the door open and we heard the first few notes of the song *Edelweiss*. I recognized it from the movie *The Sound of Music*.

Dad stood in the door with his eyes closed. "It's exactly the way I remembered," he said. "Get ready for a treat, my little Suzie. There's no place else on earth where this wonderful mixture of aromas reaches you the minute you open the door. Believe me, I've searched— been to many German bakeries all over the world. This is the only one."

I'd had no idea Dad searched for German bakeries. One more thing I learned about him.

The shop was abuzz with customers so while Dad waited his turn to speak with the person behind the counter, I wandered to the wall filled with pictures, complete with captions. The pictures appeared to be arranged in chronological order, beginning with a street cart and umbrella, like the one currently in the square, but an older version. Additional people filled the frames as the years rolled on and I was shocked to come to a group of pictures that included soldiers holding bottles high, as if they toasted something. The caption read, "The end of the war, May 9, 1945."

"Dad," I said. "You have to see this."

He left his spot and saw the picture I pointed to. Sarge stood beside us.

"Look," Dad said. "Us with Gerda and her baby. What was the little girl's name?"

"Etta," Sarge answered. "Etta Sarge Ziegler. You think she's still here?"

"Let's find out." They went back to the counter and spoke with the young woman there.

"We met some of the owners during the war," my dad said. "In fact, our picture's on the wall over there. We were wondering if any of the people we met are still here. Gerda or Ernst?"

"Or Etta?" Sarge added.

"Why yes," the woman said. "I'm Etta's daughter. She and Ernst are in the back. Wait here." She disappeared behind the curtain that separated the back from the front of the shop and returned a moment later with a woman about my age.

"Yes?" the woman said. "How can I help you?"

The sergeant stared at her. "Are you Etta?" he asked. When she nodded, I was shocked to see his eyes fill with tears.

Dad cleared his throat a couple of times before he could speak. "Etta, I'm Sam Ryan," he began, "and this is Sergeant Noonan. From the war. We were with your mother when you were born. In fact, Sergeant Noonan here is the one who delivered you and brought you back to life when you weren't breathing." My eyes filled with tears too.

Etta's eyes widened. "Yes," she whispered. "My mother told me about you. In fact," she said, turning her attention to Sarge, "I'm named for you." Tears threatened her as well.

"You did a lot for us that day," Dad told her. "We found your mother locked in her house at the Buchenwald prison camp. Your grandmother was with her. Karla, right?" Etta nodded. "When we found your mother, she was having a really hard time."

"You were stuck," Sarge said. "And I had to turn you before you popped out into my arms. We were all afraid you were going to die," he added.

"But we watched Sarge save you," Erwin said from behind us. We hadn't even realized they had followed us, but the whole group stood there, the former soldiers all sporting big grins. "We really needed to see new life that day after all the death we found there."

Etta came from around the counter and hugged each of them, lingering with Sarge. I snapped a picture. A man emerged from the curtain and Dad said, "Ernst, how great to see you again." They embraced and the seventy years that separated them from their last meeting disappeared. The whole group pointed out additional pictures and talked like old friends. They moved to a table and had been there for several minutes before my father asked, "So Gerda? How is she? Is she still...?"

"Yes," Ernst said. "Still alive and going strong."

"She's not here right now," Etta said. "She and my son went to the farm to pick up her cousin Ulrich and his wife, Rebekah, for tonight's presentation."

"Rebekah," Dad said, "the same one who was in Ohrdruf?"

"Yes," Etta answered with a smile. "I forgot you were the ones who rescued her. *Mutti* arranged for her to stay at the farm after the Russians took over East Germany and within a year, she and Ulrich were married. But they'll both be there tonight. Along with *Mutti*."

Dad and his buddies told Etta about their lieutenant throwing the family out of the house seventy years earlier and how they had worked behind the lieutenant's back to sneak diapers and other clothes to the family in their temporary quarters. Ernst added the part of the story from the family's perspective and talked about how his mother, Karla, wouldn't let anyone say anything bad about the Americans because of their help in delivering Etta. They all laughed when Simon told the story of Etta's grandmother calling their lieutenant an *"Arschloch."*

"You mentioned that word earlier," Liam said. "What does it mean?"

"Asshole," they answered in unison. Everyone laughed.

We spent a wonderful forty-five minutes with the bakery owners and then said our good-byes. Everyone else left to return to the square, but Dad stayed with me while I bought several tins of the famous *Lebkuchen* and a couple of bottles of the *Birnen-Brand*, pear brandy, both signature products of Berghmann's for more than one hundred years.

I opened the door to leave and the soft tinkling notes of the German song floated all around me. I took a step through it, but Dad stood there. A glazed, distant look filled his eyes before he spoke.

"I returned to the bakery about a month after the war was over."

CHAPTER
FORTY-FIVE

SAM
1945

I returned to the bakery about a month after the war was over.
I needed to see how Gerda and her family were doing after
what we—and Hitler's Nazis—had put them through.

My unit had bivouacked at the edge of town since before the cease-fire. Part of the armistice called for the division of the country into East Germany and West Germany with Zwickau falling into the eastern zone to be occupied by the Soviet Army. I wasn't sure, based on the few Russian soldiers I had met, that would be significantly better for the German people who lived there.

Regardless, a couple of weeks remained before the Americans totally pulled out of Zwickau on July 1. My group wondered if the Pacific front was in our future since the war still raged there. But our new orders called for us to first oversee the release of the prisoners in the Ohrdruf concentration camp and then return to the "cigarette camps" in France to operate a debarkation zone for soldiers with enough points to return home. Since none of us could leave that early, going back to France after a few more weeks in Germany, instead of being sent to Guam or the Philippines, or even Japan, sounded like a surprisingly good deal to us.

The 89th Infantry Division had been transferred to the 8th Infantry Division. We hated to see the end of the old "Rolling W," but the great thing about that was the loss of Lieutenant Scott, who was sent to the Pacific front. Without us. We didn't know why, but we didn't care. We simply rejoiced to be rid of him.

Leaves became easy to get, so I picked up a four-day pass. I sold all the rest of my cigarettes and chocolate and found a farmer an hour or so outside of Zwickau where I used the money to buy fresh milk, eggs, and vegetables. He even had some summer fruit for sale, so I bought that too. Best of all, he gave me a ride back to Zwickau and I took him with me to Berghmann's, where I bought some strudel and a tin of their famous *Lebkuchen* for his family.

The ornately decorated door opened to greet me with the same beautiful bell-like melody I remembered from earlier and as always, the spicy aromas welcomed me and delighted my nose.

"You come back," Gerda's father said. "Why?" I moved forward to shake his hand and he didn't refuse. His hand and the sleeve of his baker's coat wafted the robust scents out to meet me.

"Otto," Gerda's mother, Karla, said, "be nice. This young man helped deliver your granddaughter." She moved in for a quick hug and the heavenly bouquets floated from her hair.

"I hated the way your family was thrown out when we were here before," I told them. "That wasn't the correct procedure, but our lieutenant would as easily have turned on us if we had tried to stop him. I saw him do way worse things. I came to apologize again. And to bring fresh milk and eggs and vegetables for you. I have sisters and a brother at a small farm in Pennsylvania. In the States. I kept thinking how awful it would have been if something similar had happened to them. And my wife is pregnant, so seeing you put out in the street, especially with the baby so young, broke my heart. I'm sorry you had to go through that. And I hated being a part of it."

Gerda came into the room and put her hand on my arm. "My friend, Bekah, told me how nice you were to her. How you kept her presence secret from your lieutenant. And from the German soldiers as well. Thank you for that." Her blouse, her apron—even her smile fanned the aromatic fragrances in my direction.

I nodded. "Is she still here?" I asked.

"No," Gerda said. "She's at the family farm in Baden-Baden. She'll stay there for a while. At least until we find out how the Russians feel about Jews."

"And I want to thank you," Karla added, "for bringing diapers and clothes for the baby. For the things you brought to all of us while we were...away. You were all truly kind. At least you soldiers were. Your lieutenant, I didn't like."

I laughed. "Neither did we. He's been transferred to the Pacific, where the fighting is still going on. We're glad to be rid of him. He doesn't paint a good picture of Americans."

"Will you have dinner with us, son?" Karla asked. "I'll put some of these vegetables on to cook."

"I'd be honored," I said.

"Where are you staying?" Gerda's father asked, warming up slightly at hearing the good things the women said about my friends and me.

"I don't know yet," I said. "Maybe you can recommend a place for me? I have a four-day pass."

"You will stay with us," Gerda said. I saw her father's eyes widen. Gerda saw it too. "Papa, I would have died if it hadn't been for Sam. And so would Etta. He's the one who brought Sergeant Noonan to us and Sarge saved both of us." Her father nodded.

"Right," Karla agreed. "Then it's settled."

I graciously accepted their hospitality and Gerda showed me to a room on the third floor. I smiled at her. "This is the room I had before," I said. "My friend, Simon, and I stayed up here so we could look out for your friend, Rebekah. And to keep our lieutenant from poking around." I put my duffel bag at the foot of the bed. "Is it okay if I wash up?"

"Of course," she said. "You remember where, right?" she added with a smile.

I got myself cleaned up and joined the family at their dining room table in the apartment over the shop where I had my first taste of the German foods I would come to love for the rest of my life. Schnitzel, bratwurst, sauerkraut, and of course the red cabbage I brought, fragrant and tender.

"Try the spaetzle," Karla said. "I haven't been able to make it for a while because we needed our eggs for the bread. This is quite a treat for us."

The food was different from what I would have eaten on the farm, but I loved it. And requested the recipes to take home to Betty. They asked me a lot of questions about my life in the States and I told them about Mrs. Wainwright's award-winning cakes, my friend, Billy, and then described my sisters and little Freddie. Once I started talking, I found I needed to talk more—about my brothers' deaths, and my mother's. Then I told them about my darling Betty and they loved the story of how we met.

"The one thing I regret more than anything," I added, "is that I won't be there when my baby is born."

"She will be fine, Sam," Karla said, putting her hand over mine. "She will have lots of people to help her. And, as I told Gerda before Etta was born, babies are tough little creatures. They have a way of hanging in there."

I watched Gerda with Etta. She cradled the baby and whispered soothing words to her as she held a bottle to her tiny lips.

"We're really thankful for the things you brought," Gerda said. "I had to stop nursing because I couldn't produce enough milk and the poor little thing was starving. Look how much she's enjoying this."

The little girl was beautiful and I cringed at the thought of how close she had come to dying. Gerda caught me staring.

"Would you like to hold her?" she asked. "You can even give her the rest of this bottle. It might be good practice for you."

"I don't know if I—"

"You'll be fine," she said.

I was amazed at how much Etta's little legs had filled out in the two short months she had been alive. Gerda brought her to me and showed me how to support her head. I stared into her tiny blue eyes and it hit me again what a wonder that new life was amid all the death I had witnessed during the fighting. Her miniature fingers wrapped around mine and held on tight. My heart soared at the thought of holding my own baby.

"I think I told you," I said to Gerda, "that I hope my child is a girl.

And I hope she looks exactly like her mother." I stared into the baby's eyes and added, "Yes I do. I really do." In baby-talk. I'd never uttered any words in baby talk before. In my life. Freddie was the last baby I'd even seen and at fifteen, the age I was when he was born, I was too embarrassed to resort to such things.

Gerda laughed. "See," she said. "I told you it would be good practice for you."

We left the table while Gerda and her mother cleared it and I followed Mr. Berghmann and Ernst into the sitting room. I told them about hunting in the woods behind our house and how venison was a staple in our household. Neither of them had ever been hunting, they said, although they told me small deer roamed the family farm where the pear brandy was made. After making a pig of myself from the tray of pastries Gerda's mother brought us, I went upstairs to bed.

The following day, Gerda's father showed me around the ovens and the leavening room where yeast and baking powder were added to the dough to make it rise. My mother only made white bread, so I was surprised at how many different kinds there were, and Otto let me try all of them. I also saw how they made their famous *Lebkuchen*, but I was most intrigued with the tins that held it. Embossed with intricate flowers and vines, I knew immediately that Betty would love the romanticism of it, so I bought one to take home to her.

On my last night there, everyone except Gerda left to attend church services. I offered to stay with Etta so she could go, but she said Etta had been feverish that day and she didn't want to leave her. I went to my room to pack my things. I'd had a great visit with the family but needed to leave the next morning to find a ride back to camp. One by one, I rolled my clothes and stuffed them into my duffel. The last piece was my lightweight field jacket. We'd had a chilly spell, with temperatures in the low fifties each night, so I was happy to have had it with me. I folded the sleeves in to start my roll, but the bundle of letters I'd received before I left camp popped out from its front pocket. I opened them again, savoring the words on each page. Letters from Kathleen and Sarah, and a hastily scrawled note from Winnie all tucked into the same envelope along with another picture from Freddie of a black cat that appeared to be sitting on the front porch steps. Since we still had months until Halloween, I figured it was a new addition to the family. There was a quick note from Billy, telling me that a few of the guys we went to school with were killed in the last push before V-E Day. Two of them died only hours before the European cease-fire and two others died on the Pacific front. I sent up a silent prayer for their souls and added gratitude that I'd been so lucky during battles.

I picked up Betty's letters in the thin red-and-blue bordered envelopes and shuffled through them, remembering the contents of each. She kept a letter going to me every day and added to it as she could. At the farm full time, she painted great pictures of their lives there and I could hardly wait to get back to them. She also gave me regular progress reports about our baby, how big it was, when she had to get into larger maternity clothes, and other such things that always filled me with excitement and made me smile.

I had flipped through her letters when I noticed that one of them was thicker than the others. I had read them in a hurry because of my return to Zwickau, but I took the thicker envelope closer to the light and removed the letter again, only two pages of thin paper. But the envelope still felt thick. I turned it over and over and ran my finger along the red-and-blue edge, different from the others. Most of the envelopes were stamped with the red-and-blue border, but on this one, tape in the same two-colored stripe was attached all the way around. I had seen that tape from time to time, wrapped around several letters to keep them in a bundle, but never around all the edges of an envelope before. For some reason, two of Betty's letters were attached and then put into the bundle with the others. I worked a corner of the two-toned tape loose and an extra edge appeared. I couldn't believe my good fortune. Another letter to read. My heart soared again.

After a light tap on the door Gerda stuck her head in. "I finally got her to sleep," she said. "And I made a fresh pot of coffee. Would you like to join me for a cup and some strudel?" She hesitated and then added, "I'm feeling a little down tonight and could use the company. I know it sounds strange, considering how he treated me at the end, but I miss Etta's father."

"Not strange at all," I said. "And I would love to keep you company." I held up Betty's letter. "But I just found a letter from my wife that was stuck to another one. I'll read it quickly and join you right after."

"Okay." She closed the door quietly and I heard her footsteps on the stairs.

I tore the envelope open and felt a pang of guilt. Not only for my happiness with another letter from Betty, but also for being there when Gerda's husband was killed. Murdered, actually, by Lieutenant Scott. I still felt bad about it. Karla told me Gerda's time with her husband had mostly been good and with the cease-fire, they might have picked up the pieces and resumed a happy life.

I took the thin sheets out of the envelope and stopped thinking about Gerda and her husband. All I could think about was my darling Betty. I settled back against the headboard and opened the pages to read.

My darling Sam,
This is the hardest letter I have ever had to write.

Those words stoked fear in my chest and my hand shook so hard, the pages fluttered out of them. My first thought was that she had decided she couldn't stay with me for some reason. Or that something had happened to one of the girls. Or Freddie. Or Billy. I picked the pages back up and forced myself to read the rest.

Last week, I left the bedroom on my way to breakfast and slipped on a corner of the stair runner that had come loose. I noticed it earlier but hadn't taken the time to fix it. I will never forgive myself. I fell down the whole flight of stairs and bumped hard at the bottom. The girls came running, but I stayed down to test all my limbs and make sure nothing was broken. My extremities were fine, but before I got up, pain shot through my stomach.

I have to simply say it, Sam. I had a miscarriage. I lost our baby. It happened all at once, with practically no warning. That one pain and it came out. Our baby was a girl, Sam, just like you said you wanted. I still can't believe it.

The girls got Mrs. Wainwright and she called Dr. Garrett. He took care of me and I've been in bed ever since, except for the brief time of our baby's funeral. We buried her beside your mother, Sam. And I named her "Maud," in your mother's honor. The girls liked it. I hope you do as well.

The doctor told me over and over it was an accident and that I shouldn't blame myself. He said we can have other babies. But I can't stop crying. And I can't imagine how reading this is for you, there by yourself and us without a telephone.

I know you can't come home yet, but I really need to feel your arms around me. I am so, so sorry I let you down. Please forgive me, Sam, and know how much I love you. May God keep you safe to return to me.

Your loving wife, Betty

I read the letter again. And then again. I looked at the date of the postmark and found it had been mailed almost three weeks earlier and Betty said the accident happened a week before that. For the past month, my baby had been gone and I'd had no idea.

My heart hurt the same as if a giant hand had wrapped around it and squeezed. I really thought I might be having a heart attack. I couldn't breathe. And then the restriction around my heart eased and the pain flooded out and filled my whole body. The worst pain I've ever experienced. Sobs overtook me. Deep, racking sobs that boiled up from the bottom of my stomach and tore out of my throat in ragged, primitive sounds. I tried to keep them quiet but the strength of my grief was too great. I rolled myself into a ball and buried my face in the bedclothes while wave after wave of the sounds filled the room. My daughter was gone and my wife had to go through the ordeal without me. It wasn't fair. It just wasn't.

At some point, a hand patted my shoulder, then picked up the pages I had flung to the bed. I heard a sharp gasp and Gerda sat beside me. Her arms wound around me and she rocked me back and forth.

"She's right, Sam," Gerda said. "The two of you can certainly have more babies. It will all be okay."

Within seconds, I heard her sobs join mine and it wasn't until then I remembered that she was already upset about the death of her husband. Seeing my news must have triggered a similar response for her loss. I raised myself slightly and my arms circled her as well. Then we clung to each other, like two lost souls, unable to control our emotions and seeking comfort in the other.

I felt her tears fall on my neck and trickle into my shirt until my collar was soaked. I was certain my tears did the same to her. At some point soft little kisses rubbed new tears from my neck and our embrace tightened. She pushed into me and gradually, the kisses reached my lips. I'm embarrassed to say I responded.

At first.

But the thought of my wonderful Betty and the misery she had endured without me washed over me like a huge wave. It shocked me enough to make me realize what I was doing. I gently pushed Gerda's shoulders away.

"Gerda," I said. "This is wrong. And won't make anything better. I would simply be trading grief for guilt. And then I would feel both."

"Of course," she said. "You're right, Sam. I'm sorry."

"And so am I. I know you need comfort, without your husband, but I can't give it to you. Not like this, anyway. I'm sorry too."

She stood, straightened her skirt, and nodded at me. "I'm so sorry for your loss, Sam," she said and headed for the door.

I cried myself to sleep.

THE FOLLOWING MORNING, I FOUND KARLA IN THE DINING room. Before my duffel even left my hand, Karla was beside me, hugging me as if she'd never let me go.

"Oh, my goodness, Sam," she said. "Gerda told me about your baby. I can't tell you how sorry I am."

The pain was still fresh and I teared up. I couldn't talk, so I hugged her back. As always, wonderful aromas surrounded me, but I couldn't focus. Concern filled Karla's face and she touched mine with both of her hands. The spicy fragrances that clung to them reached my nose.

"I had a miscarriage once, Sam. Your Betty will be able to have other babies. And she will be healed by the time you get home to her. The hurt will get better for you, too, in time."

I nodded and she turned and handed me a fresh cup of coffee. I forced some of it down and tried to swallow. The liquid sat there, refusing to move past the lump in my throat. I waited, silent, and eventually it trickled down. I didn't try it again.

"Ernst has to make deliveries out your way," Karla said. "He'll give you a lift to camp."

"Thank you." The words sounded choked and I wondered how I would manage when I got back to my buddies. They'd know right away something had happened. "I'd like to tell Gerda good-bye. Is she here?"

"She took the baby for an early walk," Karla said. "She should be back any minute."

I hugged her again, stuck my head in to where Otto fed loaves into the ovens to tell him good-bye, and went outside. Ernst waited beside the bakery van, so I threw my duffel onto the floor in front.

"Sam," Gerda stood by the door with little Etta in the stroller. I went over to them.

"I apologize again for not spending time with you last night," I said. "I couldn't think…"

"No apologies necessary," she said. "Especially after all you did for me and my family. And I wanted to apologize for throwing myself at you," she added, her voice low. "I certainly hadn't intended for anything like that to happen. Mostly, I needed a hug." She dropped her head and I strained to catch her words. "But I let it get out of hand."

Lightly, I touched her shoulder and she looked up. "You're a good man, Sam Ryan," she said, "and you've become a friend I never expected to find in an American soldier. Thank you for that. For everything."

"You did a lot for me too, Gerda. You renewed my faith in humanity, for one thing, when you saved those children. You're quite a remarkable person."

She took my hands in hers. "Please travel safely on your return home," she said, "and have a wonderful life on your farm with Betty. I know you love her very much."

"That I do." I leaned down and kissed her on both cheeks, then touched little Etta's face and climbed into the van. Ernst put it in gear and we were gone. I never saw her again.

After a few moments, Ernst shot me a sideways glance and said, "Did Gerda ever tell you that I was the one who hung the white flag from the church steeple? We wanted to make certain you Americans would see it right away when you marched into town. And we hoped the planes would see it and spare us from their bombs."

I threw back my head and laughed. I couldn't help it.

"That could have gotten you killed if anyone had seen you, you know," I told him.

"Yeah, that's what Gerda said too. We haven't even told my parents."

We sat there in companionable silence for the rest of the trip. He was so young, I'm not sure he knew how to comfort a man who had recently lost a baby, so mostly he kept quiet.

I turned my attention back to the road and saw scores of people walking toward us. Filthy, emaciated people with tattered clothes and no shoes. My heart went out to those poor souls. They appeared to be beaten down, heads hanging, eyes vacant in the few faces I could see.

And then it hit me. They were prisoners from the concentration camps, probably from Buchenwald since we hadn't emptied Ohrdruf at that point. I figured they were trying to return home. To some semblance of their former lives.

While that didn't totally ease my pain, it did give me some perspective. The life I had waiting for me back in Prospect Park would be a whole lot easier to return to than the lives waiting for those pitiful people, many of whose homes were gone and their family members wiped out. I had known it for years, but it struck me again that war really was hell.

I sent up a silent prayer that the people I watched trying to return to an uncertain future would find peace and happiness wherever their journeys ended.

—⁘—

I WROTE LETTERS TO BETTY EVERY DAY TO TELL HER HOW devastated I was about the baby but that I knew it wasn't her fault and all I cared about was for her to get well and strong. And I assured her the doctor had been right and we would be able to have plenty more babies. I gave her all the news we had and after a month, told her what we'd been hoping for the whole time I was away. I had a ride on one of the ships returning soldiers to the States.

On August 20, I left Camp Twenty Grand and boarded the Liberty Ship *General Brooke*. The trip back across the ocean found the soldiers much happier than our trip in the other direction and as we sailed back up the Hudson River, night had fallen on the American shore. My heart leaped to see automobile lights on the turnpike and then soared when the lit torch of the Statue of Liberty came into view. I remembered wondering when I left the States if I would ever see her again. But there she was. All lit up.

The darkness of war had ended.

At least for me.

CHAPTER
FORTY-SIX

SAM

On the first day of September 1945, a little more than a year from when I left home for Fort Meade, I stepped off the bus in the center of my hometown.

Prospect Park had not changed at all in the time I'd been gone. Thank goodness. Not a single bombed-out building lined the street and the children I saw appeared to be well-fed and happy. Their laughter delighted my ears as they chased each other from tree to tree, and I sent up a grateful prayer that they were fully clothed and had shoes on. Except the ones who dashed in and out of the stream gushing from the hydrant in front of the park where the firemen had turned it on for them in the balmy Indian Summer afternoon. The whole scene painted a picture of small town life. Of peace. Hard won on Europe's soil.

"Sam! Is that really you?" Billy ran from the Selective Service Office and enveloped me in a big bear hug. I held tight to him too. Before long, I was surrounded by people. Mr. Harrington from the department store, Mr. Carruthers from the funeral home, and even Dr. Garrett, who must have been between patients. They all slapped me on the back and welcomed me home. Billy offered me a ride out to the house, so I hopped into his Packard.

"Sam..." He hesitated. "I'm really sorry about..." He seemed so genuinely uncomfortable with the topic, I felt bad for him. I put my hand on his shoulder.

"Thanks, Billy. I won't lie, it was quite a shock. But the thing I feel worst about is that I wasn't here to help her. I hate that she had to go through it alone."

"Trust me, she wasn't alone. She had your sisters. And most of the women in town, including my mother, took food out to the house and even volunteered to stay with her so Kathleen could go back to work. Dr. Garrett said she recovered beautifully. And that she was strong. He said future babies won't be any problem."

"Yeah, I've heard that too."

Billy turned into our long lane and my stomach did somersaults. Anticipation filled my chest and zapped tingles all the way to the ends of my fingers, rendering every square inch of me prickly with nerves. Tears formed in the corners of my eyes and I knew that in seconds I would have my darling Betty in my arms again. The thought made me so happy my whole body shook.

"Stop here," I told Billy. We hadn't quite cleared the woods that bordered the lawn. "I think I'll walk the rest of the way."

"I understand," he said. "It's really great to have you back, Sam."

I retrieved my duffle from his back seat and waved to him. He backed down our long drive while I stood there, staring at the house. I was more excited than I ever remembered in my life, so I didn't want to rush it. I wanted to soak up the pleasure of standing in front of my own home again, ready to receive my family into my arms.

I took the first tentative step. Then another and another. I cleared the trees to my right and I saw her. She stood at the clothesline, hanging sheets. Sunlight played in her hair, styled a little longer than I remembered, and tricked me into seeing blue highlights among the black curls. A simple housedress hung from her delicate shoulders and my mother's rubber garden shoes swallowed her tiny feet. That clinched it in my mind. My darling Betty was the most beautiful creature ever born. I was certain of it.

The screen door slammed and reluctantly, my gaze traveled to the porch.

"Sam! Sam! It's Sam—he's home! Come quick!"

Freddie flew down the steps without touching the last one and launched himself into my arms before Betty had fully turned from the clothesline. But I saw her hand fly to her mouth and heard a stifled scream before I fell to the ground with Freddie on top of me. He had grown and seemed to be all arms and legs, wiry and strong. His little mouth was ringed in chocolate that smudged my cheeks as he peppered my face with kisses. His tears mingled with mine. I squeezed his bony body and was acutely aware, once again, of how thankful I was that the ravages of war happened across the ocean rather than here in the heart of my family.

Seconds later, Betty was on her knees beside us, her arms hugging both of us, her tears hot on my chocolate-lined cheeks. I pulled her close and told her a thousand times how much I loved her, how happy I was to hold her again. We both cried harder.

"Oh Sam," she said. "I'm so sorry about the baby. Can you ever forgive me?"

"My darling," I whispered in her ear, "I'm so happy you're all right. I know it was an accident. If anyone should ask for forgiveness, it's me, for not being here when you needed me."

"You're here now," she said. "That's all that matters. You're here. You came back to me. Alive." Her hands never left me. Touching my face, my shoulders, then slipping around my waist.

"And once I've served my last few months here in the States," I said, "I don't plan to leave you ever again." My lips found her hair, her eyes, her lips.

By then, Sarah and Winnie had joined us and I was reminded of the last time we had all knelt in the grass. The day we found out Walter had been killed. But Mother and Richard had still been with us then. And that day had been sad. Incredibly sad. The day I got home from the war was happy. Maybe the happiest of my life. And I wished I had more arms so I could have hugged everyone at once.

"Betty found sugar when she went to the store," Freddie said excitedly. "We made cupcakes."

"And I'll bet you put chocolate icing on them," I answered, wiping some from my cheek.

"I made vegetable soup," Winnie said. "My first time. With fresh vegetables from our garden."

"And Betty's going to teach me how to roast a chicken," Sarah added.

"Well, it's a good thing I came home hungry, then, isn't it?" I said. We all struggled to our feet, gathered up my things and walked into the house, with Freddie riding on my back and Betty clinging to my side. I couldn't imagine that anyone had ever had a happier home-coming than this.

I spent the afternoon in the bosom of my family and when Kathleen arrived home from work that evening, we had a marvelous celebration dinner. I had brought little trinkets for each of them and handed them out while we still sat at the table. I put the ornate box of *Lebkuchen* in Betty's lap and, as I expected, she cried out with joy. With her first bite, she loved the earthy flavor of the spicy cookies. But also as I expected, the rectangular box that held them fascinated her and she ran her fingers over every surface of the tooled tin.

Many of our friends dropped in later that evening to shake my hand and ask about my war stories. I didn't tell them the worst of it, of course. There was no point in relaying the horrible scenes I had witnessed. They only needed to know that it was over in Europe and the Allies were victorious.

After dinner, Betty and I walked down to the small family cemetery, larger by four graves than it had been a little more than a year earlier with my two brothers in July and Mother in December. Then Betty buried our daughter there in May, four months before my return. We stood with our arms locked in front of the tiny grave.

"Maud Elizabeth Ryan," I read aloud. "What a beautiful name." I hugged Betty to me and we both shed tears for our poor little daughter who never experienced life or her parents' incredible love for her. There didn't seem to be anything else to say. So we both bowed our heads and said silent prayers for the souls resting there and then slowly went back to the house.

In our bedroom, I couldn't believe how nervous I was. I looked deeply into her eyes and pulled her down to sit beside me on the bed.

"My darling," I said to her, "how are you, really? Are you healed? Do you feel okay?"

A frisky smile played around her lips. In answer to my questions, she picked up my hands and slowly, deliberately, placed them on her breasts. From that simple act, desire flashed through me like a cyclone and as I watched, the look in her eyes transformed from playful to passionate. I'm sure my eyes must have held the same smoldering gaze. I covered her lips with mine and in no time at all, we lost ourselves to the urgency of our union.

The next few days passed by in a blur of bliss. I spent every waking moment soaking up family time, trying to stockpile it against the future. My obligation to Uncle Sam extended for another three and a half months, all of which would be served stateside. I'd be home by Christmas. After that, I determined it would take an act of Congress to get me to stay away from my beautiful Betty ever again, for even one more night.

CHAPTER
FORTY-SEVEN

SAM

2015

The reception prior to the formal celebration in Zwickau was in full swing when Suzanne and I finished our quick stroll through the sculpture garden and entered the *Concert and Ballhaus Neue Welt*. Built in 1903, according to the brochure we received ahead of time, the *Ballhaus* sported glittering chandeliers and elegant old world charm. Suzanne and I agreed it was the perfect venue for the occasion. We found Simon and Liam, who stood with Erwin, Sergeant Noonan and his wife, Madge. Before long, we saw Dickie and his grandson walking toward us with two new people.

"Remember this guy?" Dickie said to me.

The man offered his hand and I shook it.

"Mike Spencer," he said. "You took care of a couple of Germans who had me in their sights when I landed my plane in a hurry."

"I remember," I said. "You might have been in for a long haul in a POW camp if we hadn't come along."

"I also want you to meet Gloria Porter. Wait a minute, Gloria Porter Bowie," he said smiling at her. "This little lady is the magician who patched my plane up so I could fly it again."

"Nice to meet you," I said. "We didn't get to work with good-looking women when I was here. And you fixed airplanes too, huh?"

She laughed. "Yes. I was in the fifth class of WAVES once the Navy allowed women to join the service. They sent me from Hawaii to the front once these boys began bombing and occasionally getting their planes shot up. Quite an experience, I'll tell you. They kept us pretty busy."

The loudspeaker crackled to life and interrupted our conversation. "Ladies and gentlemen, please make your way to the auditorium. The program will begin in ten minutes." The message was repeated in several different languages.

We crowded into the beautiful two-level auditorium aglow with softly lit hanging lights and even grander chandeliers. Marble stairs dotted all sides of the room and led to statue-rich balconies overlooking the main floor. Ernst had told us that afternoon that the expected crowd for the *Ballhaus* was larger than they normally hosted, so the upstairs balcony was set theater style rather than the dinner style normally used there. Suzanne scooted up one set of stairs and when she came back down, told me chairs filled the area all the way to the back wall and in front of the windows.

Our level on the main floor held rows of red velvet chairs also set in theater style that faced the stage, which was draped with matching red velvet curtains. We found the seats designated for American soldiers and their companions. Some of the men wore their uniforms, but I hadn't even tried to fit into mine. My body didn't weigh a lot more than it had seventy years earlier, but the weight was distributed very differently. As it was with some of the men who did squeeze into their uniforms, most of which no longer buttoned or strained at the seams. Still, we were all happy to be there.

The mayor of Zwickau and other German officials welcomed us and it struck me again as odd that German people would honor us. It became easier to understand, however, after one elderly priest spoke of the country's feelings about Hitler and the Third Reich.

"When Adolf Hitler first spoke to us," the priest's voice boomed over the sound system, "he was exactly what we needed—a unifying voice for a people ravaged by the First World War. We needed to believe in ourselves again, with a reason to feel proud of who we were. He even brought us the swastika, an ancient symbol of good luck.

"But as the years progressed and his laws became more and more ridiculous, we knew we had supported the wrong person. Like the black hooked symbol in the center of the German flag, Hitler became a powerful spider who built a beautiful web and ensnared us all. And then after his own officers made an unsuccessful attempt on his life, he became even more powerful and turned on us. He began devouring us as a female spider devours its young. We didn't dare voice dissension even in our own homes behind closed doors for fear of retribution.

"So when you soldiers came over, you freed not only the prisoners who lived in horrible conditions within work and concentration camps, but you also freed the German people. To live without fear again. To be able to think for ourselves again. And for that, we thank you."

I'd never heard it put that way before but it made sense to me. It didn't justify the horrible things Hitler got away with, but it helped me understand *how* he got away with his atrocities.

A French officer took the stage next and awarded the French "Legion of Honor" to all the soldiers involved in liberating them from German occupation during World War II. That medal, he told us, the highest honor the French government gave out, had been awarded to many other people from all walks of life throughout the world since its inception in the eighteen hundreds. We walked across the stage to shake hands and receive the customary embrace and air kiss on each cheek. Even after all those years, that kind of grateful recognition brought tears to my eyes. And to Suzanne's, I found, when I returned to my seat.

Several other presentations were made and we reached the part of the program where civilians were recognized. I was shocked to see Rebekah, the woman we had rescued from Ohrdruf, take the stage. Older, of course, but totally recognizable.

Except that she had hair, lots of white hair, braided and piled on her head like a crown. She was a vision of grace, tall and slender, and the dress she wore flowed from her waist when she walked across the stage and gave the impression she floated.

"My name is Rebekah Rosenbaum Meier and I am here," she said, "to honor a German woman who did more for the Jewish people, my people, than anyone else I know. A woman who was not Jewish, but who has been my friend my whole life, regardless, and who helped me and my family when we were forcibly removed from our home in 1941. Her first rescue took place the very next day at the Flossenbürg sub-camp located in the Jewish-only sector right here in this city. I convinced her to rescue a baby in danger of being killed. She hid him in her bread wagon and spirited him away to her family's farm. That baby, now grown, is with us tonight. Please welcome Kurtiss Liebermann."

A tall, lean man about Suzanne's age went to the microphone. When the spotlight hit him, I saw that one whole side of his face was shaded by a dark birthmark.

"As *Frau* Meier told you, my name is Kurtiss Liebermann and, until tonight, I had never even met the woman who saved me, but I have been grateful to her my whole life. When the war was over, I learned the other members of my family, my parents and three sisters, were killed in concentration camps. I, alone, was left to not only carry on my family name, but to also tell my story so we never forget. I was supposed to be killed because of the birthmark that covers my face. Even so simple a thing was considered a flaw worthy of death by the Nazi belief in perfection. And I was Jewish. Two strikes. But Rebekah convinced her friend to remove me from the camp and I became the first of more than twelve hundred children to be saved by this remarkable woman."

They spoke about Gerda, of course. I knew from the first time I met her that she had facilitated the removal of Jewish children from the concentration camps, but it still amazed me there had been so many.

Others spoke about Gerda's accomplishments. Gerda's cousin Ulrich, who also happened to be Rebekah's husband, and the woman, Frieda, whom Dickie and I met in the forest not far from Ohrdruf when she herded the last thirty children who escaped from Buchenwald.

"Our friend, Michel," Ulrich Meier said, "who was captured and killed at Buchenwald, tried to talk this brave soul into discontinuing her effort, but she would have none of it. Even her pregnancy didn't stop her from saving the last two hundred children. At great peril to herself, I might add."

"I can testify to her peril," Frieda said when it was her turn to speak. "Her husband became suspicious of her and locked her in her room when she was eight and a half months pregnant. He was killed before he could return to her. If American soldiers hadn't come to her rescue, she and her baby would have died."

Rebekah came back to the microphone. "Before we bring this extraordinary woman to the stage, I would like for the children she saved to stand." Hundreds of people got to their feet and the crowd cheered.

Rebekah continued, "I would now like to introduce my lifelong friend, Gerda Berghmann Ziegler."

Five thousand people rose to their feet and cheered wildly as Gerda walked across the stage. Her hair was white and cut shorter around her face than I remembered, but she still radiated beauty and elegance. Tears trickled down my own cheeks and pride filled my heart. I couldn't have been happier that someone so deserving was receiving the recognition she earned. When she reached the microphone, the Chairman of *Yad Vashem's* Council from Israel's Holocaust Memorial Organization presented Gerda with its highest honor, its "Righteous Among the Nations" award and placed the medal around her neck. Then Gerda stepped up to the microphone.

"I'm not accustomed to giving speeches," she said, "and certainly don't feel like I did anything special. I did what I did—with a lot of help, I might add—because it was the right thing to do. Yes, I was a German who fit the Nazi's description of a pure Aryan. But the fact that my heritage fit their profile was the end of any similarities I shared with them. My mind screamed against their theories, against their inhuman beliefs. And most of all against their practices. Somebody had to do something. And I know I wasn't the only one. I simply happened to have access to both the children and places for them to go. None of it would have worked without the other people you've heard from tonight. And my parents, who disapproved of my actions for a long time, but who helped me, regardless. Earlier, you saw some of the children stand to be recognized. I would like for them to stand again, but this time with their families—their husbands, wives, children and grandchildren."

Two to three times as many people stood—almost half the audience. Again, the crowd cheered wildly.

"What you see here is the important part," Gerda continued, giving the signal for the crowd to take their seats again. "We all know that close to six million Jewish people lost their lives during the war and the holocaust within it. But fortunately, these folks, who were saved as children, are the backbone of the new Jewish population. From them and those who couldn't join us tonight, have come new generations, people who have contributed to the world in countless wonderful ways—as doctors, engineers, artists, entertainers, and everyday citizens, all of whom make the world a better place. So I thank you for your honors, but I would like to offer my applause for the soldiers here who helped end our horrible conflict all those years ago and for the concentration camp survivors—including the now-grown children and their families—who have gone on to rebuild their lives and a better Germany."

Again, the entire audience rose to its feet. Gerda remained in the spotlight, bowed, and blew kisses with both hands. Then Rebekah and Ulrich escorted her from the stage.

A few more items remained on the agenda, but within fifteen minutes, we retreated to the large lobby, where *hors d'oeuvres* and a bar had been set up. A small band played in the corner. My regular buddies surrounded me, and I remember thinking how great it was to be with them again after all those years. And how much I wished my little buddy, Eddie, had survived to join us.

I had come to remember myself as a young man and being with the ones who were young with me had worked like a tonic on me. We clinked glasses in toast after toast. I looked around at our group, seeing all the white hair, the canes some of us leaned on, and the wisdom that lined our faces and I couldn't help but wonder how many times we might all be together again. If ever. I drained my glass and felt a hand on my shoulder.

"Hello, soldier," I heard. "Buy a lady a drink?"

I turned and Gerda smiled up at me. She still smelled like rich spices and I bent and embraced her in a warm hug. Then I held her away. "Congratulations," I said to her. "I knew you were amazing, but I'm not sure I appreciated to what extent. Thank you for saving all those children."

She brushed my praise aside and said, "So, I understand you saw Etta and Ernst earlier? I'm so sorry I missed you. Is Betty here with you? I really want to meet her."

"No," I said. "I lost her last year. But my daughter is with me. Come and meet her."

I found Suzanne and introduced them. "Suzanne, this is my friend, Gerda. Etta's mother."

"Oh," Suzanne said. "I am so happy to meet you. And so impressed. It couldn't have been easy, doing what you did. So few people stood up to the Nazis, I understand. Congratulations on getting the recognition you deserve."

"I'm happy to meet you, too," Gerda said. "And I would like to invite you—all of you," she added, turning to include the rest of my soldier buddies, "to the house for a nightcap when this party ends. Will you come?"

"We'd love to," Suzanne said before the rest of us had a chance to reply.

Someone nudged my shoulder and then stood beside me.

"Gerda, may I have a minute?" Simon's voice was quiet and his expression serious.

"Of course," Gerda said. "It's Simon, right? I remember you."

He took one of her hands. "I am very embarrassed," he said, "that it's taken me so many years to get around to this, but I have something for you." He closed his eyes and took a deep breath before continuing. "I don't know if anyone ever told you, but it was our lieutenant, Lieutenant Scott—the one your mother referred to as the *arschloch*—who killed your husband."

Her eyes widened and she drew in her breath. "No," she said. "No one ever did. Not that it would have mattered, I suppose, to know who actually pulled the trigger."

"He killed all the officers from Buchenwald that day and then encouraged us to get souvenirs from them. As I said, I'm embarrassed to tell you I was one of the soldiers who took a few things. At the time, it seemed like an opportunity to get mementos I could pass on to my children. Then, when we toured the concentration camps and witnessed the horrible things those officers did to Jewish people, I became enraged. Later, when we were with you at the birth of your daughter, I knew your husband had been a German officer and I noticed you wore a ring that matched this one." He reached in his pocket and held out a gold band with a row of diamonds centered in it. It lay in his palm. "But I was still angry at the time and I associated you with the people who had committed those atrocities." He closed his eyes again and when he opened them, tears hovered around the edges. "But coming back here, I have learned two things." He cleared his throat. "First, I have learned I need to forgive the German people for the horrible things that happened so long ago, and second, I learned tonight, although I think I already knew, that you were nothing like those others. That you saved a generation from them. A generation that has produced other generations. Jewish people, like me, to carry on our heritage." He placed the ring in the palm of the hand he still held and closed her fingers around it. Then he put his other hand on top of the one that held hers and squeezed gently. "I understand it's probably too little, too late, but I pray you will accept this ring back, along with my most sincere apologies for ever having been so wrong about you. I hope you can forgive the Americans because you lost your husband. And I hope you can forgive me for taking so long to make this right."

I'd never heard Simon make such a long speech before. And I had no idea that all these years, he'd had the ring that belonged to Gerda's husband.

Her eyes shone too. She took the ring and then hugged Simon to her. "Thank you," she said. "I will pass this on to my daughter and grandchildren. And of course I forgive you, although there is no need. It was war, Simon. Things happened. But thank you. I will cherish this memory for the rest of my days." She hugged him again.

———

A LITTLE OVER AN HOUR LATER, SUZANNE AND I CLIMBED out of the taxi that took us to Berghmann's *Bäckerei* and joined the rest of my Army buddies there. I figured they also felt honored to be invited to this more intimate celebration for the special woman we had met seventy years earlier.

The familiar tune greeted us as we opened the door and within seconds, the heavenly aromas enveloped us. I was absolutely convinced that the fragrance surrounding me was the same one I would find in heaven.

The retail shop was filled with people. We accepted glasses of pear brandy and Suzanne coughed and wheezed when she downed hers.

"Oh," she said when she could talk again. "I hadn't expected it to burn so much. Whew."

"That means you need to drink another," Ernst said and handed her a second glass. She took it but didn't raise it to her lips right away. I introduced Suzanne to Freida, then Rebekah, who introduced us to her husband, Ulrich.

Most of the happy attendees belonged to Gerda's family, I found out, and worked on production of the pear brandy at the Black Forest farm or at the bakery in one capacity or another. Ernst told us his wife died before they had children, so when he passed, no one would actually possess the Berghmann name. But the business, he said, would continue as Berghmann's. Forever.

———

WE LEFT ZWICKAU THE FOLLOWING DAY AND SETTLED INTO the long flight home. The trip had been fantastic. I passed the test I set for myself...to travel the ground I trod as a young man and to reunite with people, both American and German, important to me seventy years earlier.

A chaotic chapter of life attained closure.

CHAPTER
FORTY-EIGHT

SUZANNE

A chaotic chapter of life attained closure. And it had been such a pleasure to watch it happen for Dad. The trip had been good for him and I had the distinct impression that it ticked off an important item on his bucket list.

The trip was also incredible for me. My head still spun from all the things I had learned and my eyes were opened to a part of my father I had never known before—a side of him I had never met, stemming from the experiences of the soldier that carved the character of the man. It made me think. I don't remember exactly when I had my first epiphany about Dad—the one every child experiences during a lifetime when the realization strikes that parents are not only the icons we place on pedestals to be feared or revered, but are also, first and foremost, people. People who do the best they can with what they're given. People whose lives consist of many different facets in addition to the one labeled "parents." I was extremely fortunate to have witnessed, first-hand, several of those different facets during our trip.

We arranged to have lunch together the Saturday after our return, May 16, 2015. My son, Steve, and my grandson, Sammy, went to the restaurant to get us a table and I went to get Dad. His side door was still locked, but I used my key and called out to him when I entered.

He didn't answer, so I figured he might still be in the bathroom and I crept down the hall to knock on the door. But it was open. And dark, although I could tell the shower had been used recently.

I called him again and found him in his favorite chair in the den.

His "Zen Zone," I called it. He lay back, fully dressed all the way down to his good shoes.

A sunbeam lit the smile on his face and as I walked farther into the room, I was greeted with the beautiful perfume of roses mixed with jasmine. Since I'm the one who buys his air freshener—apples and cinnamon—I knew the aroma that greeted me wasn't that. I looked around for fresh flowers but came up empty. Still, the fragrance persisted.

"Dad." I shook him slightly. "It's time to go."

He didn't move.

Mom's memory tin, Betty's Beautiful Box, lay open on his lap with a Kodachrome picture of Mom on top. She wore a red sequined dress and had short, dark hair that curled around her cheeks. I had seen that picture, taken on the day they met, hundreds of times and knew their love story by heart.

Beside that picture was the one of my grandmother, Maud, with Dad and all his siblings standing beside her in birth order. The smiles on their faces radiated from the faded photograph.

I leaned down to kiss Dad's forehead and found it cold under my lips.

Fear filled my heart and my sense of alarm spiked to high.

I felt his wrist for a pulse and when I didn't find one, tried his neck. Still nothing.

A small sob escaped me and I fell to my knees. I refused to believe he was gone.

He was too tough. Too vibrant. Too strong.

A memory from close to sixty-five years earlier seized me and I clearly saw him making the scrolled wrought iron posts that still supported the porch roof of this house. He made them within weeks of moving us here from the family farm in Prospect Park right after he finished his engineering degree. Each piece of the intricate design had been crafted earlier and I fit them together so he could weld them in place. He turned on his torch but plopped his oversized welding helmet on me, so heavy on my tiny neck, I tottered like a bobble-head. Mother snapped a picture and they laughed about it for years. He welded and then installed the columns. One at each corner of the porch.

"I don't know, Dad," my little girl-self told him. "Do you really think they're strong enough?"

He smiled his crooked little smile and grabbed the column's open scrollwork with his massive hands. To my amazement, he hoisted his legs up, using only his arm muscles, until his body paralleled the porch floor. Mother snapped a picture of that too.

So yes, he'd always been a strong man. The strongest man I'd ever seen, ever known.

And despite his age, I never imagined the world without him.

But the facts were clear.

My insides hollowed and tears streaked my face. I knew I should make phone calls, should try to resuscitate him, so he could stay with us a little longer. After all, we had a ninetieth birthday party planned for July.

I picked up his hand and a small slip of paper fluttered out of it. I picked it up from the floor and recognized it right away. Two words were printed on the tiny note. A name.

Our last night in Germany, as we celebrated with the Berghmann family in the bakery, Etta came and found us. The memory filled me.

"Oh good, I'm glad you're all still here," Etta said. "Mutti is hoping you'll come upstairs and join us in a little quieter setting."

"Oh," I said and looked around at the former soldiers with me. Dad and his friends, Simon and Dickie leaned heavily on canes. "Are you fellows okay with climbing a set of stairs?"

Before they could answer, Etta added, "How silly of me. I should have told you. We'll take the elevator, of course. We installed it a couple of years ago after Uncle Ernst bruised his hip and struggled to navigate the narrow steps."

We followed Etta to the elevator. "You guys go ahead," Dad said when he saw the size of the enclosed space. "That's a little too small for all of us at once." Dickie, Simon, Erwin, and Etta were the first to enter. "We'll send it back down for you," Etta said.

"Still claustrophobic, huh?" Sarge asked, directing his question to Dad.

"Guess I always will be," he answered.

The elevator car returned and Sergeant Noonan and his wife joined Dad and me for the short trip to the next floor. Etta waited for us when the doors opened and we followed her to the family quarters.

"Thank you for coming," Gerda said and passed among us with more brandy.

"It's nice to be back," Dad told her.

I joined Etta at the picture wall. "We kept these pictures here because they're more private family portraits. These are my grandparents, Karla and Otto," she said. She pointed to first one picture, then another. "This is a picture of my great-grandparents, Georg and Lise Berghmann. The ones who began the bakery. And these," Etta said, pointing to dozens of glass jars in a large old-fashioned china cabinet beside the photos, "contained the names of the children my mother saved." Her pride filled her voice and radiated throughout the room.

"Some of these jars only have one slip of paper," I said to her. "What happened to the rest?"

"When the war was over," Gerda told me, "we searched for the families of children taken to new homes." She heaved a sigh. "We worked hard to get children back together with any living relatives and to try and reunite siblings. Unfortunately, more times than not, their families had all been killed, so they stayed with their adoptive parents. Once their future was

certain, we removed the children's names from the jars and presented them to the families who'd taken them in as a concrete memento of the children's origins and what they had endured."

Gerda opened the china cabinet and removed one of the jars. "This one was for the final children rescued." She turned to Dad. "I'm sure you remember, Sam. You saw them in the Thuringian Forest with Frieda, the thirty children she spirited out of Buchenwald right before Etta was born."

My dad nodded. "I even held one of the babies," he told her. "A beautiful little girl."

"Both of those babies and three other children, all of whom were in their teens and related," Gerda said, "went to the United States with an American officer a month after the babies were rescued. His tour of duty was over and his wife had agreed to a ready-made family. When we searched for them, we found the tragic news that he and the three teens were killed in an automobile accident. They had just landed in America and caught a taxi at the dock. But the accident happened right outside the ship's terminal before he even made it home to see his wife. She was so devastated, she had a nervous breakdown. And the two babies were sent to a Catholic orphanage."

"That is so sad," I said.

"Unfortunately, it gets worse," Gerda told me. "Because these children were among the last to be rescued, almost two years had passed before we could research them. Their mothers, we found, had been imprisoned at Ohrdruf, and became pregnant when Nazi soldiers raped them. The babies were taken to Buchenwald when they were four months old, but both of the mothers died the day the Americans showed up. So we never learned anything about their families."

"What a horribly sad story," I said. "What happened to the babies once

they got to the orphanage? Were you able to find out?"

"Not really," she said. "One of the babies, the girl, was adopted, we learned, but before we could find out about her new parents, the orphanage burned and the fire destroyed all their records. Only a month or two after her adoption. Many of the nuns, and most of the children, including the baby boy who had escaped Buchenwald with her, perished in the flames."

"Where was the orphanage?" my dad asked, his voice only a whisper. "What city?" His face was white and he looked like he was choking.

"Philadelphia," Gerda answered. "We probably could have made a presentation of this one, for the little girl, if the records hadn't burned. She was close to a year and a half old when she was adopted and named—"

"Suzanne," Dad finished. His voice cracked and he sat down hard.

I whirled toward him. "What? How did you…"

"Your mother had a miscarriage while I was over here. I know we told you that, Suzie," he said to me. "We believed she could have more children." He took a sip of brandy. "But when nothing happened after another year, we decided to adopt. Our doctor put us in touch with the orphanage in Philadelphia. Saint Katherine's."

"Yes," Gerda said softly. "That's the one."

My eyes filled with tears as the truth hit me. I fell to my knees and took Dad's hands.

"They never told us where you came from," he said to me. "Only that your parents were dead. We didn't feel we needed to know more about you because we fell in love with you immediately." His voice cracked

again and he squeezed my hand. "You had a headful of little curls, not quite as dark as your mother's, but just as soft." His head snapped up and he looked at Gerda. "But wait a minute. If she came from a German concentration camp, why didn't she have a tattooed number?"

"Auschwitz was the only camp that did tattoos."

I let out a soft breath. "I can't believe…" I whispered.

"It has to be," Gerda said. "The orphanage didn't normally take children as young as the two babies. But because of the circumstances, they made an exception." She looked down at the paper she still held. "The mother named her baby Suzanne before the guards took her away. And her last name was—"

"Ryan," Dad interrupted. He stood and took the paper from Gerda's hand, then enclosed both of us in a hug. "And her mother's name was Betty," he added, kissing me on my temple. "We both loved her to distraction every second of her life." He pulled away and looked into Gerda's eyes. "A life, it turns out, for which we, along with twelve hundred others, have you to thank."

MY DAD HAD RETURNED TO GERMANY TO REVISIT HIS PAST, an important road that led him to the man he became. Before that moment, it never would have occurred to either of us that the road he revisited would also lead to finding my roots and the path that led me to him.

Dad and I talked most of the night and he told me how his heart reacted to me on the night of my escape and that he would have taken me home on the spot if he could have. We were both awestruck and so very thankful that one little German woman defied the Nazi government in a way that so profoundly affected our lives in America.

We hadn't shared the information with anyone else at that point. I was certain I would eventually tell my children and grandchildren, but for right then, it only belonged to Dad and me.

"And now...only to me," I whispered.

I fished my cell phone out of my pocket. But before I punched any numbers, I looked again at the smile on his face and remembered the story he had told me about smelling roses and jasmine at his mother's funeral.

"It's the angels," Mrs. Wainwright had said to him. "They're here for your mother." She'd almost made him believe, he told me, that his brothers had come to accompany his mother to heaven.

I understood. The angels had now come for Dad.

He'd done what he set out to do. He'd closed the circle on his earlier life by going back to Europe, visiting the places he'd gone as a young man and seeing Gerda again. He'd made peace with everything that happened during the war and received the added bonus of finding out where I came from and that Gerda is the one who gave me to him. He was finished.

And Mom needed him. I figured his own mother and brothers did too. Along with his first daughter, my lost sister, Maud.

I smiled through my tears at the thought of Mom showing up in her red sequined dress beside his mother in her housedress, both beaming as they came to get him. I would have given anything to find a tiny red sequin or a clump of farm grass on Dad's carpet.

I sat there with him a while longer and memories of our final trip together flooded in. I had learned so much about him. About us. And about the German woman who became our life connection. I had come to know the man as a soldier, certainly, but mostly, I had come to know the man as a man. A strong man. A good man. A man I liked and respected.

My father's name was Sam Ryan and I had adored him my whole life. But I learned much more about Sam, the man, on our final trip together than I had learned about Sam, my father, during my entire lifetime.

And, for that, I would be eternally grateful.

ACKNOWLEDGEMENTS

Many people helped me in the process of writing this book and I am grateful to them all.

Huge and special thanks to all the veterans who allowed me to interview them, all of whom also granted me permission to use their names and stories as some of my characters and plot points. They include Erwin Davis from Austin, TX. I found Mr. Davis via the Internet (please see Letter to my Readers) and he allowed me to use him and his late twin brother, Ervin, as characters. Mr. Davis and his daughter, RuthAnn Koepcke, have both read the manuscript and offered wonderful editing (in RuthAnn's case) and valuable insights (in Mr. Erwin's case).

Another veteran was Gloria Porter Bowie, who was living in a veteran's assisted living facility near me. I met with Mrs. Bowie and her daughter, Kim Veitch, and they spent valuable time with me, sharing countless pictures and regaling me with stories of Mrs. Bowie's time as a member of the fifth class of WAVES in Hawaii, where she repaired airplanes.

Thanks also to the other veterans I interviewed, along with the people who helped me find them: my mother-in-law, Penny Zaphel, and her friend, John Shepherd, who put me in touch with the late Cecil Reese, who was present at the battle of Pearl Harbor. Penny also introduced me to Mabel Toth, who traveled to Canada to join the service because she was too young to join in the United States. Danielle Johnson, Senior Center Programs Coordinator for the Council on Aging in St. Johns County, FL, arranged for me to interview Joe D'Aloia, who fought in the Pacific, and the late Mike Spencer, a fighter pilot who supported Patton's Third Army from the air over

Europe. In addition, thanks to Penny Davis for sending me the written history from her father, Victor Barber, who was also a pilot.

Thanks to my cousin, Ann Bloom, who interviewed my father, Herman Dykes, for an oral history class she took in college. Ann's transcribed account of Dad's time during World War II gave me first-hand insight into his thoughts and feelings about the war. Ann also read the completed novel and offered additional input.

Huge thanks go to my siblings, Noel Dykes, from Seaford, DE; Dr. Patricia Walker, from Richmond, VA; and Alan Dykes, from Arkansas City, KS, all of whom read this novel and offered feedback to make it better. My younger brother Alan, for example, who is a firearms expert and Hunter Safety Instructor, told me about the sounds bullets make from different firearms when they whiz overhead and my older brother, Noel, a lifelong hunter, taught me about deer stands and prize bucks. My sister, Pat, a former magazine editor, did my final proof-reading and offered nuts-and-bolts feedback. It was especially mean-ingful to me, as I believe it was to them, to share our thoughts about Dad's war stories, some of which we'd heard all our lives.

Heartfelt thanks to my friend, Scott Sylvester, a veteran, pilot, and World War II buff, who lent me stacks of books and movies, maps and pamphlets from his extensive collection. He was also one of my first readers and was invaluable in making certain I had my facts straight. He taught me, for example, that the firing of guns at a soldier's funeral is *not* considered a twenty-one gun salute, since that is reserved for presidents and officers, but is a holdover of a much older tradition. Scott also taught me about the difference between bombers and fighter planes, among many other such facts to make my story more believable.

Much appreciation to Corinne Hoisington, Professor at Central Virginia Community College, Lynchburg, VA, who introduced me to the book *The Bedford Boys*, from which came some of my descriptions—notably crossing the Atlantic on the *Queen Mary* and the carnage on the beaches of Normandy.

Thank you to David Lane from Kingsport, TN, the Facebook Administrator of the 353rd Infantry Regiment Facebook Page, who actually called me to help with some details and confirm such items as the name of the Burgomaster (mayor) of Ohrdruf, Albert Schneider, who hung himself, rather than be forced to witness the atrocities evident in the Ohrdruf camp. David's father served in the 353rd Regiment of the 89th Infantry Division, as did my father.

Thanks to both The National Archives and Records Administration, Cartographic Branch, College Park, MD, for the use of the 89th Infantry Division map and to CMG Worldwide for permission to use parts of General George Patton's and General Dwight Eisenhower's speeches.

As always, sincere thanks to my agent, Julie Gwinn of the Seymour Literary Agency, who helped me with internal structure and who gave me the idea of Suzanne's origin in Germany. I really loved that idea.

Thanks to my father-in-law, Ron Zaphel, who gave me the idea, based on stories from his late mother-in-law, for Gerda to work at a bakery; I expanded that idea for her to use her delivery wagon to save the children.

Thanks to Glenda Blake for helping me figure out the proper term for African Americans in 1945.

Thanks to my early readers: Larry McDorman, one of my best friends since first grade, and his wife, Vivian, who got me straightened out on what constitutes a Jewish name and the difference in one that is purely German. Thanks to members of my Street Team, Kathy Granieri, Susan Foster, Lorna Jones, and Candi Lennox, and to my children, Tracy Lewis and Rusty Bozman, all of whom were supportive and provided feedback to improve the story.

A heartfelt thank you to my mother's cousin, Pearl Layton, who told me about the code she and her husband, Jimmy, used to communicate when his location was supposed to be secret.

A big shout out to Eddie Jones, with whom I have worked on marketing strategy and who introduced me to both Ann Tatlock, my wonderful editor for this novel, who made it so much better than it was, and to Hannah Linder, my cover designer. Endless thanks go to both of those remarkable, talented women.

And, of course, my undying gratitude to my darling husband,

Michael, who reads every word I write and gives me honest feedback —especially when he doesn't like the direction I've taken with a character. He will sit me down and present his case about why I should change something. So far, he's been right every time. Michael is also a huge factor in my social media and in helping me to navigate the publishing world. Even after all of our years together, my Mikey is still my most ardent fan, my loudest cheerleader, and always, always, my best friend.

Veterans Interviewed

Private First Class Herman N. Dykes; U.S. Army; 89th Infantry Division, 353rd Regiment, K Company; part of General Patton's Third Army operating in the European Theater. The late Herman Dykes was my father and the inspiration for Sam Ryan.

Additional pictures of Dad with his Army buddies at Fort Meade. My Dad is the soldier to the far right in both pictures. These pictures served as inspiration for the soldier camaraderie described within my story. I never learned the names of the other soldiers.

Left: *Pfc. Erwin Davis;* Middle: *Erwin on left and twin Ervin on right;* Right: *Erwin and me The Davis twins served in the U. S. Army; 89th Infantry Division, 354th Regiment, B Company; part of General Patton's Third Army, serving as bazooka gunners. Erwin Davis became acting Sergeant Major before his discharge.*

Gunner Sergeant, Cecil Reese, U.S. Army; 9th Infantry Division, Battery H, 64th CA. Mr. Reese's first battle was the attack on Pearl Harbor and it so devastated him, he never had the desire to return to Hawaii. He was 99 when I interviewed him and he lived to be 100 but passed away in September 2020.

Major Howard "Mike" Spencer enlisted in the Army Air Corps and supported Patton's Third Army from a P-47 Thunderbolt. He allowed me to alter his story. The day he was hit by German flak guns, he didn't crash, but got his engine restarted and made it back to base. His book, One Man's Journey, *is an account of his life and service. Mr. Spencer passed away in November 2020 at the age of 99.*

Gloria Porter Bowie joined the fifth class of WAVES once the Navy allowed women in. After training, she was sent to Hawaii where she repaired gull wings on Corsair airplanes. She allowed me to take liberties with her story so she could meet my main characters.

Joe D'Aloia served in the 3rd Division of the Marines and spent his entire military career in the Pacific Front. He advanced to Sergeant when he was sent to Samoa. His other bases included Guadalcanal and the island of Bougainville. He is now 99.

Mabel Toth was only 18 when war broke out with Germany so she traveled from her home in Detroit, Michigan, to join the Canadian Women's Army Corps. She served her entire time in Ottawa, with the Adjutant General's office.

AUTHOR'S NOTE

This book is based on true events, and many of the characters are real people. In the list below, I indicate where some literary license has been taken and some events changed or condensed for the sake of story. Battles described are actual battles, unless indicated otherwise, but they were not all fought by the 353rd Regiment of the 89th Infantry Division. They may have been fought by the 354th or 355th Regiments. For literary purposes, I attributed all the battles to the soldiers I wrote about.

If explanation for a chapter has been skipped, that simply means there was nothing that needed to be explained or verified.

CHAPTER ONE:

- K Company was part of the 353rd Regiment in the 89th Infantry Division.
- 2005 was the last year the Buick Park Avenue was manufactured in the United States.
- On a cross-country trip we took together in 1998, my father actually told me that the Appalachian foothills in Pennsylvania looked like the ranges he crossed in Germany.

CHAPTER THREE:

- After D-Day, it took up to a month for folks in small towns to find out about their loved ones.

- Welders, including my father, had military deferments to make parts for Liberty Ships.
- Women sweetened cakes with Karo syrup when sugar became scarce.
- The animal's names in this chapter, Inky, the black sheep, and the cows, Bonnie and Belle, were real and belonged to my older brother, Noel Dykes, when he was a boy.
- Some men, especially in small towns, chose to commit suicide when their draft status was 4-F; soldiers who did go to war felt sorry for the ones who couldn't/didn't (source is Erwin Davis).
- Events on the beaches of Normandy are taken from actual accounts, especially in the book *The Bedford Boys*, written by Alex Kershaw.
- The description of *The Atlantic Wall*, ordered by Rommel, of the German Army, is accurate.
- Description of Walter's "jalopy" came from the description of a "car" my father described that he and his brothers made from scavenged parts, including the fact that there were no floor boards.

CHAPTER FOUR:

- A national boycott of Jewish businesses was declared in Germany on April 1, 1933.
- The 1935 Nuremburg Laws declared the Jewish people "enemies of the state."
- The doors of Jewish residents and businesses were painted with the word *Jude* and people were forced to leave their homes and relocate in Jewish-only city sectors; Flossenbürg was the sub-camp in Zwickau for its Jewish people.
- Jewish people were forced to wear gold stars, outlined in black, with the word *Jude* printed on them.

- The description of the treatment the Jewish people received at the hands of German soldiers is, unfortunately, accurate.

CHAPTER FIVE:

- Large birthmarks were considered imperfections by the Nazis and were considered reasons to murder people, especially Jewish people.

CHAPTER SIX:

- The Western Maryland Railway existed as described.
- The description of Army regulations, such as boots being handed out too large, is taken from firsthand accounts.
- The description of Fort Meade is accurate.
- The description of the Davis twins, along with their hometown, is accurate.

CHAPTER SEVEN:

- The 89th Infantry Division was known as the "Rolling W" and was part of General George Patton's Third Army.
- Descriptions of the M-1 Garand rifles at Fort McClellan as well as that of the World War I Enfield rifle, including the sickly sweet smell of cordite being emitted rather than gunpowder, are all accurate.
- The description of the exercise under barbed wire, with empty rounds being fired prior to live ammunition, is accurate.

CHAPTER EIGHT:

- The Wannsee Conference in 1942 introduced the "Final Solution to the Jewish Question."
- Block 66, where Jewish children were protected at Buchenwald concentration camp, was real; in fact, the real names for the elders in that block during the timeframe written about, Antonin Kalina and Gustav Schiller, were used.
- Real-life Irena Sendler, on whom the character of Gerda Ziegler is based, recorded all the names of the children she rescued, along with the families who received them, and put them in glass jars, which she buried behind her house; she also insisted that when the war was over, the children would be returned to whatever family members they had left.
- The commandant's wife at Buchenwald (real name not used in my story) had lamp shades and other trinkets made from colorful tattooed human skin.
- The description of the tunnels near Walpersberg and their relation to Buchenwald concentration camp are accurate.

CHAPTER NINE:

- The Davis twins received bazooka training and spent their time in the war transporting and firing bazooka rockets.
- The description of the dimensions and weight of both bazookas and M-1 Garand rifles is accurate.
- "Burp-up" exercises are described accurately.
- Lieutenant Colonel James Grier initiated training and boxing matches at Camp Butner to give the soldiers experience with hand-to-hand combat.

CHAPTER TEN:

- The phrase used in the second paragraph of this chapter, "I seen her a hunnert times," was actually said by a ten-year-old New Yorker who came to visit my family on the Eastern Shore of Maryland in the summer of 1956. While the phrase referred to the youth's mother and the fact that he didn't feel the need to go back home to New York to see her, I included it here because my dad thought it was so funny, it became one his favorite sayings for the rest of his life.
- The songs cited are real.
- The story recounted by Cecil Reese about the battle of Pearl Harbor is from his firsthand account, gained via my interview with him. As chilling as it is to read about, it was even more chilling to hear directly from the former soldier.
- The military point system was used to determine when soldiers went home.
- The 89th Infantry Division consisted primarily of replacement soldiers in 1945.
- The "Mission over men" doctrine was a necessary part of the military's strategy, but the soldiers themselves didn't like being considered expendable. My dad included.

CHAPTER ELEVEN:

- The descriptions of Camp Shanks, its buildings, celebrity visitors, different sections, and the fact that it was known as "Last Stop U.S.A." are all accurate.
- News from the front described in this chapter of battles on sea and land are accurate for the dates described.

CHAPTER TWELVE:

- The facilities, buildings, and areas at Buchenwald concentration camp are all described accurately.

CHAPTER THIRTEEN:

- It is true that additional children arrived in Buchenwald from the satellite camp at Ohrdruf.

CHAPTER FOURTEEN:

- The description of Sam's mother came, in large part, from my own grandmother, Maud Gibbons, whom I loved dearly. When she died, Reverend Purdue performed her service and one of her dear friends said the line to me about how my grandmother helped the community. She said, "It didn't matter what happened in the neighborhood, there was Maudie, with a right hot pie." I always loved that line and had to use it.
- Radio Flyer Wagons were the most coveted Christmas presents for young children, especially little boys, of that time period.
- The scents of both jasmine and roses, when there are none around, have long been touted as signaling the presence of angels. Whether we believe it or not, I loved the concept and decided to include it.
- The Christmas presents Betty purchased for Sam's sisters are accurate for what girls their ages would have received at that time, including the latest Nancy Drew book.

CHAPTER FIFTEEN:

- The journey down the Hudson River to Hoboken Harbor is described accurately.
- The description of the transformation of the *Queen Mary*, luxury ocean liner, is accurate, as is the description of her zigzag pattern and her speed across the ocean.
- The description of the reward Hitler offered his U-boat captains to destroy the *Queen Mary* is also accurate.
- Description of the lack of car lights and the fact that the Statue of Liberty's torch was dark as the soldiers sailed out to the Atlantic Ocean is accurate and was one of the things that broke my father's heart, as evident in his transcript.
- The description of full combat gear as well as everything about the soldier's lives during the trans-Atlantic journey are, unfortunately, totally accurate; much of the information came from the book, *The Bedford Boys*, by Alex Kershaw.
- The 89th Infantry Division did not travel to Europe aboard the *Queen Mary*, but my Dad, as a late replacement soldier, did. Dad didn't describe much of his voyage except to say he was seasick the entire time. As already noted, the description of conditions came from the book, *The Bedford Boys*.
- The description of the *Queen Mary* cutting the British Cruiser, *The Curacoa*, in half is taken from eye-witness accounts in the book, *The Bedford Boys*.

CHAPTER SIXTEEN:

- The 89th Infantry Division was hailed as "The Last Line of Defense."
- Descriptions of the "citizen soldiers," and the training they received are accurate.
- The *Man in the High Castle* is a television series and is

accurate as described.

CHAPTER SEVENTEEN:

- The description of the bombed out conditions in LeHavre in January 1945 is accurate.
- The description of Camp Lucky Strike, as well as storm damage, which led to the lack of space and the scarcity of rations during that time is accurate.
- My father really did make homemade rabbit stew when he got to Europe. He never said whether or not he shared it, but knowing how soft his heart was, I believe he did.
- General Patton's speech is quoted here verbatim and is known as his "Blood and Guts" speech. Part of it is reproduced in my story with the permission of CMG Worldwide, the licensing organization for his estate.
- During February 1945, General Patton was somewhere in France, but his showing up at Camp Lucky Strike came strictly from my imagination.

CHAPTER EIGHTEEN:

- The description of REIMAHG and the tunnels it occupied is accurate.
- The description of *Messerschmitts, ME262s,* is accurate; these planes were also described in the book *One Man's Journey,* written by Howard "Mike" Spencer; a *Messerschmitt* actually chased him.
- The series of tunnels close to Buchenwald's satellite camp, Ohrdruf, were designated as a "Western Office" for Hitler if he needed to escape Berlin in a hurry.

CHAPTER NINETEEN:

- While Block 66 did exist within the Buchenwald compound to protect children, my research never uncovered any escapes from there; that was a figment of my imagination.
- The names of the Resistance fighters are fictitious, but the treatment they would have received at being caught is described accurately.

CHAPTER TWENTY:

- The code in Sam's letter to Betty was used by my mother's cousin, Pearl Layton, whose husband, Jimmy, was a World War II soldier. Pearl is now 99.
- The scene of soldiers hanging their C-rations from truck manifolds was included in the transcript from my dad.
- "Forty-and-eights" are described accurately.
- The description of the *Volkssturm* and what it consisted of is accurate.
- The story of a German man being allowed to stay in his house when American soldiers occupied it came directly from a firsthand account in the book *Good Soldiers,* written by Richard P. Matthews, a comprehensive account of the 353rd Regiment of the 89th Infantry Division.
- The term "locked and loaded" is an accurate description of the readiness of the soldiers on March 10, 1945; source is the book *Good Soldiers.*

CHAPTER TWENTY-TWO:

- The description of a cyanide capsule (suicide pill) and how it works is accurate.
- The use of piano wire for gallows instead of regular rope in

many German prison camps was described accurately.

- The Nazis frequently used the torture method (known as "strappado") which included having the wrists tied behind backs and then roped up so victims' feet were dangling above a platform, causing shoulders and elbows to stretch beyond reason and finally pull out of sockets.

CHAPTER TWENTY-THREE:

- The battle described on March 12 was *not* a real, documented battle, but a composite of the accounts of battles from my research.
- The term "baptism by fire" is used in the military to denote a soldier's first live battle. The soldiers I interviewed all remembered when and where theirs took place.
- The description of crossing the Moselle River, considered the first real milestone for this group of soldiers, and the dates involved are all accurate and gleaned from several sources, including the interview with Erwin Davis and the transcript from my dad.
- The encounter with a German soldier on the other side of the Moselle River who asked Erwin Davis and his brother to capture him rather than kill him because he wanted to return to his wife and children, actually happened and was told to me by Mr. Erwin Davis the first time we talked.
- The battle that took place on March 18 at the *Marienburg* Tower actually happened as written, with German soldiers waving white flags and then shooting the Allies when they came forward. Unfortunately, this happened three times, as described in the book *Good Soldiers*.

CHAPTER TWENTY-FOUR:

- The names of towns listed at the beginning of this chapter are all real and were the locations of battles fought by one or more of the units in the 89th Infantry Division.

- The description of the men marching in "blackout conditions" with one soldier's hand on the shoulder of the soldier in front of him, including the part where the soldier in front disappeared, came directly from my dad's transcript.
- The description of Mike Spencer's plane crashing is partly accurate. Mike was a P-47 fighter pilot who supported Patton's troops from the air. The story he told about strafing a German train and then being surprised when they shot back really happened. The difference was, after the third try, he was able to get his fuel pump started again and he made it back to his base without crashing. A vivid account of what really happened is in his book, *One Man's Journey*. He allowed me, however, to take liberties with his story because I wanted him to meet my little band of soldiers.
- The description of Sam at a small farm where he asked a couple of young German girls to do laundry for him actually happened to my dad and came from his transcript.
- The description of chocolate the soldiers received is accurate. The Army made a deal with the Hershey company that the chocolate wouldn't taste any better than a boiled potato.

CHAPTER TWENTY-FIVE:

- The description of Sam shooting at a sniper is based on my dad's own experience. His story about that was one of the things that prompted me to write this book. It was that soldier about whom he said so many times, "He was probably just like me and would rather have been home having dinner with his wife and kids." While Sam is not exactly my dad, his philosophy about war is directly from my dad.

- The story about digging a foxhole is real and was one of the stories my dad used to tell us, except in Dad's true account, he didn't share the foxhole with anyone.
- The account of Eddie getting killed, with his legs being shot out from under him and then spiraling up in the air, is taken almost verbatim from my dad's transcript. He never said the name of his friend who died, but he did mention that the soldier was only eighteen and a scrawny kid and, according to Dad, "should never have been in the war in the first place."
- The story of Erwin being afraid that Ervin had been killed is real, as related to me by Erwin himself. The brothers had a pact that if one of them died, the other would take his high school ring back home to their mother. Thankfully, that didn't happen.

CHAPTER TWENTY-SIX:

- *Lebkuchen* is considered a German delicacy.
- *Birnen-Brand* pear brandy is manufactured in the Black Forest of Germany. The description of how the pear gets into the bottom of the bottle is accurate. I have a bottle of it in my kitchen and plan to open it when this story is released.

CHAPTER TWENTY-SEVEN:

- The description of how the Allies taking the Rhine River affected the outcome of the war is accurate.
- The description of river crossings as "on the jump" is accurate in military jargon.
- The story of Patton reaching down to clutch a clump of earth after he crossed the Rhine River ahead of his Army actually happened.
- From my dad's transcript, the fact that only one boat was

available to take them across the Rhine by the time his regiment was ready to cross is true.

- One of the lieutenants, at the time of the Rhine River crossing, removed the smoke bombs from his jeep so he could fill it with champagne, as described in the book *Good Soldiers*.
- The description of Sam and his friends floating a boat across the Rhine River came from my imagination.
- The description of the terraced hill the soldiers had to climb to take out a machine gunner's nest is accurate, as depicted in *Good Soldiers*. In my dad's transcript, he said, "I didn't think we'd ever get out of those damned mountains."
- The description in the last paragraph about the 89th Infantry Division being the easternmost infantry division and closest to the Russian Army by March 30 is accurate.

CHAPTER TWENTY-EIGHT:

- The descriptions of the countryside through the Thuringian Forest and of the Wartburg Castle are accurate.
- Martin Luther did translate the Bible at the Wartburg Castle and Goethe expanded on it.
- Hitler did work with the townspeople below the Wartburg Castle to fly a swastika from the tower, but contrary to my story, he was never able to make it happen.
- I took a huge liberty with facts here, when Hitler showed up unexpectedly for the meeting at the Wartburg Castle at the end of March 1945. By this time, he and most of his top officers were holed up in his underground bunker in Berlin and had been there since January 1945. I brought him to this meeting because I wanted Aldrik to feel pride and be appreciated.

CHAPTER TWENTY-NINE:

- The scene of the German officers being gunned down came directly from my dad's transcript and his stories to us over the years. When Dad's lieutenant ordered a soldier to kill the German officers, the soldier said, "I just can't do it, lieutenant." The lieutenant then actually uttered the words, "Well goddam it, I don't have any trouble doing it." It was the thing that shook Dad the most during the war and he never got over it. It was also the main reason he hated his lieutenant, although he never told us the lieutenant's name. I was able to locate a K Company roster and saw several lieutenants listed but refrained from using any of those names to protect their families should they ever read this book.

CHAPTER THIRTY:

- Carrier pigeons were occasionally used as a way to communicate when the senders worried their message might be intercepted.
- The descriptions of the activities taking place at Buchenwald, of prisoners being herded into the square and then marched out through the gate, along with bodies being burned are accurate.

CHAPTER THIRTY-ONE:

- The description of prisoners being executed in the square at Buchenwald is accurate, as told in survivor accounts.

CHAPTER THIRTY-THREE

- The description of the tunnels outside Ohrdruf has been enhanced by my imagination.

- The description of the *Raketenwerfer 43* is accurate, but I have no idea if they would actually have been found in those tunnels.
- The Davis twins were the actual soldiers who fired bazookas at the gates of Ohrdruf to open them, as told in Erwin Davis's war diary. Their shells landed perfectly, but didn't destroy the gates, so the soldiers cut wire and found other ways to get in.
- The description of what the soldiers found inside—piles of bodies sprinkled with lime, open graves sporting pine logs and pitch, the chamber containing a creosote pool where prisoners were dunked for de-lousing, along with the description of barbers shaving off all the prisoners' hair—is accurate, according to eyewitness and survivor accounts.
- The description of the death of the inmate known as a *kapo* is accurate from survivors' and soldiers' accounts.
- The description Rebekah gave of *appells* is accurate.

CHAPTER THIRTY-FOUR:

- General Dwight Eisenhower and General George Patton went to Ohrdruf to witness the devastation.
- The words spoken by General Eisenhower are taken verbatim from a portion of the speech he gave that day and is used here by permission of CMG Worldwide, the licensing organization for his estate.

CHAPTER THIRTY-FIVE:

- The 6th Armored Division fought at Hottelstedt, not far from Buchenwald concentration camp.
- Descriptions of the tunnels outside Buchenwald, as well as the description of the compound surrounding them, are accurate.

- The Bismarck Tower and palace of Anna Amelia are landmarks outside of Buchenwald and were, at the time, considered to be great places for picnics by the German people.
- The description of Captain Frederic Keffer being tossed up and caught by liberated prisoners of Buchenwald is accurate as well as the description of the inmates stockpiling stolen weapons and taking over the camp on the morning of the fighting at Hottelstedt.

CHAPTER THIRTY-SEVEN:

- The description of the facilities in Buchenwald, including the crematorium, the gallows, the whipping bench, and the pathology lab, that Sam encountered on his way to Block 66 are all accurate and taken from survivor and eyewitness accounts.
- Soldiers did give food to the prisoners prior to their release from the camp.

CHAPTER THIRTY-NINE:

- General Patton ordered the citizens of Weimer to tour the Buchenwald camp and to dig individual graves for the murdered prisoners. Photographs of the townspeople digging, with corpses all around them, can be found on the Internet.
- I did not find an account of exactly what the Weimar citizens' tours at Buchenwald consisted of, so that passage came from my imagination. I did, however, find documentation that when one German man laughed at the end of a tour, but within sight of the gates, the commanding soldier forced the entire group to repeat the tour.
- General Patton also ordered the townspeople of Ohrdruf to

tour that prison camp, but the burgomaster, Albert Schneider (real name) never showed up. When Patton sent soldiers to his home to drag him out for a tour they found Schneider and his wife dead, hanging in their living room.

CHAPTER FORTY:

- Harboring a Jewish person in a German home broke Nazi laws.
- Bombs fell on the outskirts of Zwickau on March 17, 1945.
- The description of families retreating to cellars during air raids is accurate.

CHAPTER FORTY-ONE:

- The descriptions of the towns encountered and the battles waged on the soldiers' march to Zwickau are all accurate.
- The description of Sam's lieutenant sending troops straight into the German army came from my dad's transcript. The difference is that the soldiers in Dad's unit were able to convince the lieutenant that it was an ambush and he rescinded the order. My version of the story came straight from my imagination.

CHAPTER FORTY-TWO:

- The description of the white flag at the top of the *Marienkirche* tower is documented in a diary from young people in a Zwickau church group at the time. The young people didn't know who put the white flag there, but they applauded it, nevertheless.

CHAPTER FORTY-THREE:

- The date of April 17 is actually a blown kiss to my middle granddaughter, Alyssa Lewis, whose birthday is on that day.
- Two British paratroopers led the march to the Zwick-Mulde River Bridge to disarm the explosives the Germans had set so the Americans couldn't come into town.
- When the American soldiers finally did march into Zwickau, they found white flags flying from everywhere, including the *Marienkirche,* the highest church tower, and saw children hanging out the windows, smiling and waving. The soldiers waved back. I don't, however, know if they really threw chocolate to the children.
- The story told here of Gerda's family being thrown out of her house is another one I heard from my father all my life. Dad's lieutenant insisted his unit take over a house where a German woman lived with her extended family and forced her to leave without so much as a blanket or food for her baby. With two small children of his own, my dad found this one of the greatest injustices of all. His lieutenant actually uttered the line, "I could kill that little son-of-a-bitch with my bare hands." When the woman's father came back the next day to try and get things for the baby, Dad happened to be on guard duty and he couldn't let the man in. It always sickened him that other human beings were treated that way and he hated his lieutenant even more.
- The word *arschloch* is the German word for "asshole."
- All of the dates and events related here, from the soldiers' learning that President Roosevelt had died in office, to Mussolini's being hung with his mistress on April 28, 1945, to Hitler's taking his own life on April 30, 1945, are true and accurate.
- The descriptions of Germany's surrender to the Allies in Reims, France, on May 7, 1945, at 2:41 PM German time, and the subsequent surrendering to the Russians the following day, with V-E Day officially occurring on May 9 are accurate.

CHAPTER FORTY-FOUR:

- I found, during my interviews with veterans, that what Sam said in this chapter about soldiers' remembering dates for significant events, regardless of the number of years that had passed, was true.

CHAPTER FORTY-FIVE:

- Writing this chapter was especially important to me. My dad was so traumatized by having to kick a mother and baby out of their home, he never got over it. When I decided to write this story, I knew my soldier would have the opportunity to return to the family and that he would do so. This is a nod to what my father wanted to do but wasn't in a position to do.
- Once the war ended, the 89th Infantry Division was transferred to the 8th Infantry Division.
- Envelopes of the time that bore the red-and-blue-striped border were actually air-mail envelopes and were made of very thin paper to lessen the cost of transporting them.
- My dad described the people walking from the prison camps back to whatever shreds of life they could find. The word he used to describe them was "pitiful."
- The name of the ship that returned Sam to the United States and the date of its journey are accurate, although none of the real soldiers I interviewed actually sailed on it.
- In his transcript, my dad talked about the fact that when he sailed back into America, he was thrilled to see car lights on and the torch lit on the Statue of Liberty.

CHAPTER FORTY-SEVEN:

- While celebrations and reunions from World War II do take place, I am not aware of a memorial like this occurring in Zwickau during 2015.
- The *Concert and Ballhaus Neue Welt*, built in 1903, does exist in Zwickau and is still open for events. I am not aware, however, of a World War II anniversary celebration ever held there and definitely not one in May 2015.
- In this chapter, Gloria Porter Bowie is one of the real-life veterans I interviewed, but I took liberties by moving her from her Navy job of repairing airplanes in Hawaii to repairing airplanes in Europe during the heaviest fighting.
- The speech given by the priest at the ceremony came from my imagination based on a number of articles I read about how Hitler was able to rise to power the way he did.
- The French awarded "Legion of Honor" medals to American soldiers who helped free them from German rule. Veteran Erwin Davis was presented with one.
- The woman on whom my character, Gerda, was based— Irina Sendler—was presented with the highest honor, the "Righteous Among Nations" award by the Chairman of *Yad Vashem's* Council from Israel's Holocaust Memorial Organization.

CHAPTER FORTY-EIGHT:

- The memory Suzanne described here of her dad welding wrought-iron porch supports and then pulling himself up parallel to the porch's floor using only his hands is true. I watched my dad do it. I'd give almost anything to actually have a picture of that.
- It is true that Auschwitz was the only prison/concentration camp that tattooed its inmates. A marvelous resource for this is *The Tattooist of Auschwitz*, written by Heather Morris about the life of Auschwitz Tattooist, Lale Sokolov.

Read on

FOR A SNEAK PEEK AT
THE NEXT BOOK

The Road of Regrets
(Working Title)

THE ROAD OF REGRETS
(WORKING TITLE)

SUZANNE

2015

The dad-shaped hole in my heart ached with the pain of his loss.

Only two weeks earlier I accompanied him on a bucket list trip during which he and his Army buddies from seventy years earlier reprised their trek across Europe during World War II.

For me, it was the trip of a lifetime.

For him, the *last* trip of his lifetime. He died less than a week after our return.

My father. Sam Ryan. Whom I had adored my whole life.

We held a service for him in Lock Haven, Pennsylvania, where we had lived for almost sixty-five years, then set off for his family farm in Prospect Park, Pennsylvania, close to four hours east, where he would spend eternity. Right next to my mother and surrounded by two of his brothers and *his* mother.

The route to the farm began as the same one Dad and I had taken earlier to Philadelphia International Airport for our flight overseas. But this time, my son, Steve, drove, leaving me free to observe the panorama of the Appalachian foothills.

Its canvas was breathtaking. White blooms dotted the deep green forest magnolias and shared their palette with yellow and purple-flowered vines entwined among them. Small blue clusters of wild violets burst from the grass below.

But the incredible beauty of the spring day failed to enthrall me as it usually did because my mind flitted from topic to topic, clutching at random thoughts. Anything to help me avoid the memory that Dad was gone.

A heavy sigh floated up from my toes and I sat back, aware that Steve merged onto Interstate 80 from Paul Mack Boulevard. The car swerved slightly during the merge and jolted my nineteen-year-old grandson, Sammy, from his nap in the back seat. He raised his head, looked around, then resettled his long legs to fit his space. Soft snores reached me again within seconds.

Something bumped my arm and nudged me fully back to the present.

"…ignoring me?"

"Huh? I'm sorry, honey. What did you say?"

"I said," Steve answered, "I see your body beside me, but your head is miles away. That's the third time I've asked you a question and you appeared to—"

"Oh yes, ignore you," I finished. "That's what you were saying."

"Are you okay, Mom?"

Tears filled my eyes and I struggled to control my voice before responding.

"Yes. I'm fine. But you're right. My mind floated back to the last time I traveled these roads. With your grandfather. The first day of our trip to Europe."

"I thought so," he said.

"We must have been at almost this exact spot when he tapped the window with his cane and told me these Appalachian foothills reminded him of the mountains he crossed in Germany." I stopped talking and shook my head. "I'll bet I had asked him about his experiences in the war a thousand times over the years. But he never wanted to talk about it. Until then." I swiped at a tear, then turned toward my son. "Oh Steve, I can't tell you what a special gift it was to visit that part of his life with him. To meet the people who were important to him then."

"And to find out your special connection with them, right?"

I knew he referred to the fact that the German woman Dad met seventy years earlier had saved almost twelve hundred children and babies from extinction in Nazi prison camps. Only a little more than a week ago, we were shocked to learn that I had been one of them. My dad even met me the night I was whisked out of Buchenwald Concentration Camp, an hour and a half outside Zwickau, Germany, along with twenty-nine other children, just before the American Army arrived.

The story was one we cherished. And once I told Steve and his family about it after Dad died, they cherished it too. Which really made me wish I had known it in time to share with my late husband, Steve, Sr., before a drunk driver snatched him from me five years earlier. My husband hadn't had a great relationship with his own father, so he adopted mine. He would have loved the part about Dad holding me the night I was smuggled out of Buchenwald. I knew Dad's siblings would love that story as well, since they were with him when I was adopted.

Steve and I filled our four-hour trip with memories of Dad, receiving sporadic input from Sammy between his naps, until at last we drove up the long lane to the Ryan farmhouse. My dad's youngest brother, Freddie, who still lived there with his wife, Sally, had the lane paved some years ago, so it no longer stirred up the dust I remembered from my childhood. We cleared the trees that bordered it, and the large yard surrounding the house came into view, the wrap-around porch wearing what appeared to be a new coat of paint. My heart soared to be back, then clenched as I remembered why.

The screen door slammed and Sally appeared, carrying a tray of glasses—iced tea with lemon, I figured, since I knew that was Uncle Freddie's favorite this time of year. Every seat on the huge porch, including the swing, was occupied and cars sporting colorful tags from several different states filled the yard.

At the bottom of the porch steps, I spotted my older grandson, Wally, holding baby Lizzie. His wife, Amanda, along with Steve's wife, Emily, stood with them and my heart filled with joy to see them. Wally had moved his family to Baltimore last year when he landed a residency at Johns Hopkins Hospital and I had only seen my great-granddaughter once since her birth.

We parked and got out of the car to be immediately surrounded by loved ones.

"Grammy," Wally said, reaching me first. His free arm encircled my waist and I didn't want to let him go. But I also wanted to hold little Lizzie, so I scooped her out of his arms and covered her with kisses, tickling her neck as I did. Her reaction was exactly what I needed. There's just something about a baby's laughter that delights your heart.

We hugged everyone else gathered around us in the yard, with Steve spending extra time hugging his wife. Amanda's maternity leave had ended, so Emily had been in Baltimore the past several weeks to help with Lizzie and would even return with the family for a couple more weeks after the funeral. Despite the fact that the reason for our reunion was a sad one, Steve had told me on our trip he looked forward to spending precious time with his wife.

I left them in their embrace and climbed the porch stairs to hug everyone there. My dad's sisters, Winnie—who had married Dr. Garrett's son, Paul—and Sarah—who married Dad's best friend, Billy Wainwright—had both built houses on the fifteen-acre family property so were already there, along with their children and grandchildren. Dad's oldest sister, Kathleen, had married Don Harrington, whose family owned the local department store, but they wouldn't arrive until the next day, Winnie told me, since they were on their way back from Florida where they lived for half the year. They'd get back in plenty of time, though, since Dad's funeral was scheduled for the Sunday before the observed Memorial Day Monday.

I settled into an upstairs bedroom in the big house, while Steve and Emily unpacked in one of the others. My grandsons had rooms at Dad's sisters' homes.

We visited with our large family and had a bite to eat before my Uncle Freddie came up to me and slipped his arm through mine. "Are you up for taking a stroll to the family cemetery to see the spot we picked out for Sam?"

My eyes filled immediately, but I nodded and leaned into him while he steered me through the yard and to the dirt path that ran beside the small patch of woods behind the house.

"Look there, Suzie." He pointed to our right. "You can see the strawberries just hanging, ripe for the picking. Sally's planning to make strawberry shortcake while everybody's here."

"I didn't remember your field being that big. Dad loved your strawberries, you know."

He squeezed my shoulder. "I do know that, Suze. And you're right —your cousin, Richie, and I have increased its size every year since Mr. Reynolds and his sons stopped renting the land—repurposed acreage from the cornfields, mostly. We actually have a fairly good commercial business for the berries now, with people coming from as far away as Philadelphia to pick them. We don't start that until next week, though."

We continued to walk and he filled me in on my Aunt Sarah's prize pumpkins and how he and Aunt Winnie kicked around the idea of building a chicken house but decided against it after she broke her hip the previous autumn.

We reached the cemetery and he leaned over to unlatch the gate of the wrought iron fence.

"Oh," I said. "This fence is new since last year when we buried Mother."

"Yeah, we did that after the deer kept eating the camellias Winnie planted on your grandmother's grave."

The grounds inside were immaculate with freshly cut grass, free from leaves despite the fact that one side of the fence was only inches from the first line of trees. The moss-free headstones formed a neat row with flowers peeping up beside most of them.

I knelt at my mother's grave and another bout of sadness overwhelmed me. "You know what hits me the hardest when I look at this?" I asked.

He shook his head and I pointed. "This line between her birth year and death year. That's such a measly little symbol to commemorate an entire life. It doesn't seem right to reduce all those wonderful memories to this small a space."

His hand squeezed my shoulder, then he helped me stand and pointed to several little orange flags on metal stakes. "We saved this spot for your dad, right next to your mom. His grave will butt up to the fence so it will be the last one in this line." He pointed in the other direction. "There's room at the other end, next to my grandparents, and Kathleen has chosen that for herself and Don. The rest of us will start a new row back here."

I blew a kiss to my mother's grave and we left the small cemetery. A few feet along the path toward the house we moved aside for the Carruthers Funeral Home truck and Uncle Freddie waved to the driver.

"That's Harvey Carruthers," he said. "His grandfather started the business. And was the one who took care of my brothers and mother when they passed."

"I love the continuity of life here," I told him. "Makes me homesick for a simpler time."

Uncle Freddie escorted me back to the wrap-around porch, then left me so he could check on some fencing. I entered the kitchen to find my aunts working around the big table. Their welcoming love for me was palpable.

"Oh good, Suzie," Aunt Winnie said. "I was hoping you'd join us. Most of the others car-pooled into town to visit the ice cream parlor."

She cubed baked chicken for salad while Aunt Sarah rolled out dough for biscuits. Sally, within months of my age, cut up strawberries and nodded to a large stack of what appeared to be photo albums on one end of the table. "I brought these for you, Suze. The girls," she said, nodding toward Aunt Sarah and Aunt Winnie, "aren't sure you've ever seen the oldest albums, with pictures of them as children when they were all on the farm together."

Aunt Winnie wiped her hands on her apron. "Look at this one first, Suzie. We figured out last night that it's a hundred years old and starts with our mother as a girl, then captures a few pictures of her wedding and early married life. It even chronicles all of our births, all the way through to Little Freddie."

Sally laughed. "I can't believe you still call him 'little,' Winnie. The man will be seventy-five in July and is six-foot-three."

Aunt Winnie winked at me. "Sally has to include that. Little Freddie never lets us forget his height, once he passed your father's by an inch."

I laughed too. Despite my unhappiness about Dad, the pain in my heart eased in the warmth of this kitchen surrounded by the love from these wonderful women. As my dad used to say about them, "They have hearts of gold and souls to match."

The album Aunt Winnie put on top did, indeed, show its age. The faded black cover peeled, with little bits of the padded cardboard breaking off every time I moved it. I positioned it flat on the table and carefully turned each page, enjoying the pictures of my grandmother, who died the same year my dad went into the service. There were even a couple of pictures of my grandfather, surprising to me, given the way Dad and his siblings had always felt about him. With my aunts' permission, I used my phone to snap copies of some of the oldest pictures, then turned the last page to find a bulge in the paper backing of the back cover. I tried smoothing it but it disintegrated under my fingers.

"Oh no," I said. "Look what I did. The paper just shredded when I tried to fix it."

My aunts crowded around me and I tried to re-stick the paper with my fingers, but that only made it worse. A large chunk peeled off and revealed a corner of red fabric. "Did you guys know this was here?" I asked. "It looks like some sort of book."

"Well, let's see it," Aunt Winnie said.

I picked at the edges and uncovered a slender book bound in red fabric.

"Open it," Aunt Sarah chimed in.

The pages inside, so thin they were almost translucent, exhibited spidery writing in ink that had faded to pale purple. I carefully turned to the first page and read, "Diary of Maud Irene Brewer." The word "Ryan" appeared under that first line in darker ink as if she had added that later. Which made sense.

"I didn't know Mom kept a diary," Winnie said. "Did you?" she asked, turning to Sarah.

"No. I wonder if Kathleen knew?"

"Oh my goodness," I said, "what I wouldn't give to read this."

"Go ahead, honey," Sarah said. "Neither of us has the eyes for it anymore. In fact, why don't you read it while you're here so you can tell us about it? I think it would be fun to find out things about Mom we didn't know."

"Unless we find out things we'd rather not know," Winnie said.

"Like what?" Sarah asked.

"Like what if she had sex with Mr. Reynolds when she rented him the farmland. I always did think his looks toward her were a little too frisky."

"Good heavens, woman," Sarah said, "you were only ten-years-old when she died. How would you even know what a 'frisky' look was back then?"

We all laughed. Great, deep belly laughs. Just what we needed.

"Well," Sally said when she could speak again. "If something like that did happen, I hope you'd be happy for her, when you consider the fact that her husband left her when my husband was born."

The knock on the screen door startled us and interrupted our easy laughter.

"Look, girls," Winnie said, "it's little Harvey Carruthers. How you doing, honey?"

Sally shook her head. "There she goes with that 'little' again. How old are you anyway, Harvey?"

"Close to fifty, ma'am. But I *was* little when I started working with my grandfather."

Uncle Freddie walked up the porch steps behind him and held the screen door open. "Yes, you were. I remember that, Harv. Did you find the flags I put out for my brother's grave?"

"Yes sir. And I'm awful sorry to bother you, but that's what I need to talk to you about."

"No problem," Uncle Freddie said. "Come on in." He pulled out a chair but Harvey continued to stand. "What's up?" my uncle asked.

Harvey cleared his throat and it was obvious he was very uncomfortable. "We found something, sir, and...well, we're not sure what..."

He stopped, lowered his head and fiddled with his cap before looking up again.

"Mr. Ryan—" He stopped speaking and his voice choked. He swallowed hard and began again. "Mr. Ryan," he said, "Please. You should...somebody...needs to come and look at what we found before we can continue."

CPSIA information can be obtained
at www.ICGtesting.com
Printed in the USA
LVHW021557261121
704514LV00007B/17/J

9 780578 864884